MAZES 1

Murder in Munich

Eric Sanders

Published by New Generation Publishing in 2017

Copyright © Eric Sanders 2017
Cover design by Dandy Sanders

First Edition

The author asserts the moral right under the Copyright, Designs and Patents Act 1988 to be identified as the author of this work.

All Rights reserved. No part of this publication may be reproduced, stored in a retrieval system or transmitted, in any form or by any means without the prior consent of the author, nor be otherwise circulated in any form of binding or cover other than that which it is published and without a similar condition being imposed on the subsequent purchaser.

www.newgeneration-publishing.com

New Generation Publishing

The Author

Eric Sanders was born in Vienna, Austria in 1919.

In March 1938 he stood on the roadside amongst the crowds watching Hitler enter Vienna after the annexation (Anschluss) of Austria by Germany. Later that year, he and his family fled Austria separately. Eric and his parents were allowed into Britain and his brother was smuggled into British held Palestine.

When war was declared, Eric joined the British Army, initially in a non-combatant unit (being an 'enemy' alien) and subsequently into the Special Operations Executive (SOE) – Churchill's 'Secret Army' as an operative trained to be dropped into occupied territories.

After the war he qualified as a teacher and taught until retirement in the 1980s.

Eric has written short stories for radio and published two autobiographies – one in Austria (Emigration ins Leben : Wien-London und nicht mehr retour) and one in the UK (Secret operations : from music to morse and beyond).

At 97, Mazes is his first novel to be published, but he has more in the pipeline.

Contents

PROLOGUE	1
CHAPTER 1 – THE DEFENCE OF THE REALM	5
CHAPTER 2 – THE CRANES OF IBYCUS	45
CHAPTER 3 – DRAMA IN THE STREETS OF MUNICH	89
CHAPTER 4 – THE NUREMBERG RALLY	129
CHAPTER 5 – AGENT RONALD BURNLEY	165
CHAPTER 6 – MAGYAR SINS	202
CHAPTER 7 THE VILLA IN HIETZING	238
CHAPTER 8 – THE LION'S CAGE	268
CHAPTER 9 – A MURDER IS PLANNED	302

Prologue

The gilded Angel of Peace, thirteen metres tall, was standing on a twenty-five metre high column, on the eastern bank of the River Isar in Munich. There were citizens in Munich who believed that the angel was more than a statue, that he saw everything that was going on below and let no evil deed go unpunished. They believed that although appearing to face east, the angel could turn north and south to overlook the woodland of the eastern bank of the River Isar, and turn around completely to see all that happened on the Maximilian Bridge and beyond it on the road leading to the centre of their beautiful city.

Usually there was quite a lot of traffic around the monument in the evenings but on this Thursday in October 1926, starting in the afternoon, black clouds roving across the sky were ominously joining into larger ones, and pavements as well as streets were speedily becoming less populated as the evening arrived. The eighteen-year-old girl standing at only a slight distance from the statue was feeling increasingly worried. She had a bad conscience because her mother was not aware that she was having a date with a man and, what was worse, as late as nine o'clock. It was almost half-past-nine and he had not arrived. But he had explained that he was sometimes working late. He had just turned twenty-one, reaching adulthood. She should have left and gone home at nine but he was so nice and so very handsome. Now she could not stop herself from feeling frightened. She looked up anxiously towards the angel.

The sky was getting darker. It was remarkably still around. The streetlamps had come on but their light was dull. The next moment a number of loud, raucous men's voices filled the air, approaching from the bridge: folk returning from the beer halls, obviously well loaded. She retreated anxiously off the footpath into a small open space inside the bushes. The drinkers passed by, singing the same melody again and again, each time more out of tune. A short distance behind them walked a single man, an Englishman, on the bridge, wearing glasses and a trilby. He, too, had been to one of Munich's famous beer halls, the famous *Hofbräuhaus* (Court Brewhouse). He had had only a half-litre of beer and took it slowly.

Prologue

The two Germans hadn't turned up. He wondered why but was glad. This was to be the last time, anyway. He did not like the two men. In his mind he called the smaller one the 'butcher', because of his looks. He, in particular, was a crude, unpleasant specimen. In fact, the Englishman did not like his task in Munich, had not liked it from the start. But he had accepted it because it safeguarded the arrangements he had made for his son's education.

The boy had the brains and the ability and this job's high payment guaranteed him the opportunity. Another week and Munich was done. He would resign from the firm altogether. He had quite enjoyed some of the work as a whole and it had raised the family's living standard beyond expectations. But it had not been fair on Alice, and their relationship had begun to lose its harmony. He would get an office job with easy hours and he would make it up to her. He reached the last section of the bridge when two men joined him, one on each side. It was the two Germans. He was surprised but not worried.

'I'm pleased to see you are well, gentlemen,' he said in perfect German.

The 'butcher' replied at the top of his voice. His speech sounded loud and aggressive throughout. His partner did not really take part in the conversation except for regularly adding gestures underlining his partner's statements.

'We won't waste yer time, mister. All we want is the notes you made of our answers.'

'I'm sorry, gents, but I can't do that.'

'Don't play games with me, man. Just bloody give us your notes and we'll leave you alone.'

The Englishman shook his head. 'They belong to my boss.'

'Yeah, and yer only told us last Thursday that you worked for the English and we've found out you're in touch with the English embassy.'

'So it was you who's been following me?'

They had left the bridge and were following the little road around the Angel's monument.

'Just give us your notes, man.'

'I'll tell you what I shall do. I'll pay you for tonight, gentlemen, although you didn't turn up and we call it quits.'

The 'butcher' broke into a curse.

Prologue

'*Verdammt nochmal*' (Damn you), 'I've enough of this. You still think this is a game. You don't know who you're dealing with.' He put his hand threateningly on the hunting knife in his belt.

His partner's imploring looks warned him of possible witnesses but at this moment there was nobody to be seen around them. Instead, although it was well past ten now, somewhere in the near streets a gramophone record, one of the latest inventions from America, was beginning to play out of the open window. It was a recording of *O Sole Mio* (Oh My Sunshine) sung by Beniamino Gigli. The girl in the bushes knew the song. She had spent the first ten years of her life in Naples. But the 'butcher's' curses had given the girl in the bushes another fright and she moved further back to a little open space. The Englishman had, despite the bad lighting, seen the bully's hand on his knife. He shook his head, now angry, himself.

'Don't be silly. Put this thing away. You're not frightening me. Anyway, I can't give you my notes.'

The 'butcher' shook his head, snarling.

'The notes, mister, or else!'

The Englishman shook his head decisively. The two exchanged a signal and taking the Englishman by surprise they crowded him in a well-practised manoeuvre off the road, half-way towards where the girl was standing. At the same time the 'butcher' put his hand into the Englishman's inside coat pocket. The latter automatically responded with a sailor's uppercut which surprised the bully. He tumbled backwards and fell to the ground, angrily cursing and shouting loudly and hurting in his solar plexus. That *solar* did not refer to Gigli's *'sole'*.

'You'll be sorry for this, you lousy Englander!'

The humiliation had bitten deep into his feelings as he scrambled upright. He pulled his hunting knife from his belt as his partner was pulling him up from the ground. At this moment he would have been foaming at the mouth, had he access to enough foam. He moved his partner out of the way and, holding the knife in attacking position, he moved forward, shouting threateningly.

'This is your last bloody chance, man, I'm warning you.'

The Englishman pushed his arms forward with the intention of moving both men out of his way and also raised his voice.

'Don't be stupid. I've enough of this. Get out of my way now and I shall not report you to the police!'

Prologue

He moved forward. The tall German actually stepped to the side, whereas the 'butcher's' uncontrolled rush forward ended in a collision. His knife hitting the other man's body the 'butcher' cried out angrily.

'Warned you!'

What took place in this moment was witnessed by four persons. The girl saw the glint of the knife. Shrinking back further into the bushes, she closed her eyes and covered her mouth, sobbing and scared of giving away her presence. The 'butcher', feeling his knife move into the Englishman's body, cried out triumphantly: 'I warned you!'

The 'butcher's' partner was shouting: 'Watch out! Don't, Kurt!'

The Englishman, falling into the arms of his killer, was crying out not so much a cry of pain as of unspeakable sadness:

'Arrghhhh!!! My son, my dear son. I'll never see you again.' His cry of pain, the long-drawn ah!!! was weakening as fast as he was breathing out his final breath. Seeing the angel up high above him, he added, in a deep long sigh sounding more like a father reprimanding his son than a victim his murderer, 'You silly man. The angel's seen your deed. The angel will punish my murder.' His voice broke with a short rattle. He was dead.

The 'butcher's' partner was crying out hysterically. 'What have you done! What have you done!'

Gigli's voice was booming: '*O Sole Mio*' into the night. The 'butcher', his bloody knife in his hand, turned on his partner snarling, 'Shut up! Just shut up, or else! All I've done is kill an enemy of the German people. D'you hear the noise from that record. That made sure no one could hear us. And you can see there's no blood outside his body. It all proves God's on our side, just as the Führer says. Now help me to clear up the mess. Don't forget you're in this as well and don't you dare try getting out of it.'

When the girl heard him say 'God is on our side,' it tipped the balance and she fainted. When she came to, she was on her own. Frightened and shaking, she cautiously looked around. There was no sign of anything having taken place there. A handful of stragglers were walking quietly on the road. They looked up astonished as the girl was running past them. She did not stop until she got home.

Chapter 1 – The Defence of the Realm

On this Tuesday, in October, 1926, the sun was shining through the upstairs window of a small bedroom in a small house in Reading, a small town north of London. Its glittering rays were conveying the warm wishes of the Indian summer. Ronald Burnley woke up with a start, urged by his unconscious conscience. A look at the clock confirmed his worst fears. He had forgotten to set the alarm last night. If he did not want to miss Professor Folloughman's Sociology lecture, or the company of Aimée, he'd have to forgo breakfast once again. He washed and dressed faster than was possible, hurried down the stairs and, crossing the kitchen with a hasty, 'Sorry, Mum. I'm late,' came to an abrupt halt in the doorway to the hall. His mother was not in the kitchen but, out of the corner of his eye, he had noticed the beige letter paper on the floor beside the breakfast table. For no obvious reason at all, it sent a rush of anxiety through his veins. He slowly retracted his steps and slowly picked it up. The letter heading confirmed it was from the Foreign Office, what was known as a letter telegram. His father often received those when he was home on leave, but he wasn't, it was addressed to his mother and it was black-edged. He knew he did not want to read it but he had to. He picked it up. He read very, very slowly, every word, including the letter head.

The Foreign Office European Section

4th Fl., Block B, 54 The Broadway, London SW1

Mrs. Alice Burnley,

58 Talfourd Avenue, Reading

October 11th, 1926

Dear Mrs. Burnley,

It is my sad duty to inform you that your husband, David Burnley, was the victim of a street killing in Munich on Thursday, 7th October. Mr. Burnley was one of our most

Chapter 1 – The Defence of the Realm

valued and capable representatives working in Europe and his contribution will be greatly missed. The Department's condolences go out to you and to your son.

Because of the special circumstances we have had to arrange immediate burial at the Royal Hospital Cemetery in East Greenwich. In the course of the next few days you will receive further mail, with details of your pension entitlements and other matters.

J.W.P.

Admin 7

Ronald stared at it, not wanting to believe what he read. His whole being was permeated by a twisting and deadening pain. Veiled by tears that forced themselves into his eyes, they ceased to see. He dropped the letter, which came to rest practically on the same spot from which he had picked it up and slowly walked back up the stairs. He heard his mother's and his grandmother's voices but at this moment he could not bear to see even them. Back in his little bedroom, still lit up by the glittering rays of the Indian Summer, he stretched out on his bed, no cheer in his heart and no longer carefree. He closed his eyes in an attempt to shut out reality, shut out the treacherous sun, shut out the world.

A few days later, Ronald's mother, Alice Burnley, and his grandmother, Mrs Constance Lloyd, were in the kitchen, washing up the breakfast things.

'You see,' Alice Burnley looked worriedly at her mother, 'He's not come downstairs again. He's still staying in, Mum. He comes down, has his breakfast, won't talk, not even to you, and each morning I think, *Today he'll go back to his studies*, but no, the only thing he goes back to, is his room. Goodness, that's two whole weeks already. It's not natural and it worries me, Mum.'

Mrs Lloyd's response was accompanying her words with commiserating nods. 'And him being so keen on his studies. He always says thank you, though, Alice. Yes, I've been telling them at the Whist Drive; "Our Ronald spends more of his free time there than he does at home", I've been saying.'

Alice tilted her head sideways.

Chapter 1 – The Defence of the Realm

'I know, it's hit him hard, Mum. I keep thinking I must do something. We may not be close but he is my son, my only child. But what?'

She started to move the dried dishes into the cupboard. Her mother attempted to reassure her.

'He'll snap out of it, love, I'm sure. Mind you, I wouldn't have expected it from your telling me always, that David never spent much time with you and Ronald, like. Of course, your David never did talk much to anybody. But I noticed, when he was home on his leave, he often had little chats with Ronald. And without your David I mightn't have been able to keep our little house. You've come to terms with it much faster, darling.'

Alice heard a meaning shining through her mother's words.

'Didn't I also always tell you, Mum, there's a special bond between father and son? Ronald not only looks like him, he acts like him, too. If ever there was a chip of the old block… except for the women. So, it's a good thing I didn't let Ronald bring any of his – er – friends home. It might have been a different one every week. And some o' them foreign. Me faster? I suppose, but that shouldn't surprise you, Mum. First, these two long years travelling around Europe with David, never settling down anywhere. He was always busy. Mind you, he always talked to a lot of the people we met. In their lingo, too. And they talked back. Then he sent us home for Ronnie's education. I was pleased. I mean, we hadn't – not for some time. Of course I've got this thing about big towns and we were always in the capitals. I hated it. In any case, he and I… You know, bit by bit, Mum – he was so absorbed in his job, so conscientious, he never had much time for anything else, not even for… You're right about the house. Mind you, he was always generous. It was the least he could do. I suppose that was his nature. I got to give him that. Not everyone gets to work for the Foreign Office. And the last two months, a special job, he wrote. Goodness, almost as if he was still in the Navy and going to sea. And now he's gone.'

'Going to sea? What are you talking about, Alice? David's never been to sea, since you married him, has he? I never quite understood how he came to be in the Navy.'

Alice tilted her head towards her right shoulder again.

'I only mean as if, Mum. You're right. He had this office job with the Navy, on land. Then they transferred him to the Foreign Office and everything changed. Something to do with the war. But he

7

didn't get called up. Suddenly he was learning foreign languages. David, learning foreign – I couldn't believe it. Special compressive courses he called them. D'you know he disappeared for six weeks at a time for each of them and I had no idea where he was. Three he did, or was it four. And he had no education. Still, he had this memory, my David had. Never forgot a thing. Frightening. Ronnie's got it, too. Like father... 'Don't tell anyone,' David said, 'So I didn't.' Of course, he got a good take-home, so I couldn't complain and...'

She stopped seeing her mother's expression.

'Sorry, Mum, you've heard it all before, I know. I've never told you this, though. When we travelled around together after the war, it wasn't too bad but – it was never really OK. Not like when we first met. Between us, I mean. And it got worse. Even when he was home on leave we didn't – you know what I mean. I think he put all his strength into his job and I mean all.'

She stopped, looking into the far distance, seeing nothing. Her mother knew she couldn't stop her when she was reminiscing about her disappointments in the past. She also knew that her daughter had contributed to the alienation. Alice changed to the present.

'When this letter arrived, it was a shock, all the same. So sudden. I'll miss him – on and off. But it doesn't really change anything in my personal life. Except the money, I suppose. I'm forty-two, Mother, and I'm not going to wither away on anything. I've still got my points.' Unconsciously, her hands moved as if demonstrating. She turned around and took the beige letter from the mantle-shelf. She had read it to her mother several times during the last two weeks. An inner need to punish herself? She began reading out loud once again.

'...my sad duty to inform you that your husband, David Burnley, was the victim...' she stopped there and her eyes moved to the last sentence: '...details of your pension entitlements, – Yours truly JWP, Admin 7. I wonder who this JWP Admin Seven is. I suppose he's a person.'

She looked up with tear-filled eyes. Her mother was about to put her arm around her when the doorbell rang. Instead, she went to the front door. It was the postman and it was another letter for her daughter. She handed it to her. Alice opened it and her eyes flew through it. Her face gradually developed anxiety lines, and then stretched into determination.

Chapter 1 – The Defence of the Realm

'I'm not going to London, Mother, and that's that. I don't like the town. I'll get one of my turns and I don't like having to do with officials and I haven't anything to wear.'

The last, luckily, was an exaggeration. She held the letter out to her mother who put her specs on and sat down. Letters with printed headings and from important places impressed her. She read it out loud – although not fluently.

The Foreign Office

European Section.

4th Floor Block B, 54, The Broadway, London SW1. Mrs. Alice Burnley, 58 Talfourd Avenue, Reading

October 25th, 1926

Dear Mrs. Burnley,

You are invited to call at the above office on Friday, 29th October, at 11.00 hrs. in order to meet one of the admin officers of the department in which your husband served. He will bring you up to date with all financial arrangements and also answer any questions you may have. You will be reimbursed for any expenses incurred in order to attend this appointment. Enclosed find details of how to find this address in London.

P. W. Cormody, Major.'

Mrs Lloyd put the letter down, admired the enclosed street plan and shook her head doubtfully, 'Don't you think you should go, Alice? It may be important.'

Seeing her daughter's tight-lipped expression, she suggested, 'If you won't, why don't you ask Ronald to go? It might be good for him, dear?'

'Ronald? Will he go?'

* * *

Chapter 1 – The Defence of the Realm

54, The Broadway was a large building, forming the corner of a small street, opposite St. James Park Underground Station, which led away from it towards Green Park. The street's name was Queen Anne's Gate. One of its famous residents was Rear-Admiral Sir Hugh 'Quex' Sinclair. Not many people knew he was the head of MI6, the foreign branch of Britain's Security Services. This morning, at his usual time, the admiral strolled through a lengthy underground passage to No. 54, Broadway. Real Secret Service stuff. By ten o'clock he was seated behind his large, ornate desk in his large, ornate office on the fourth floor, smoking an ornate, expensive cigar – well, expensive. He picked up the folder in front of him, which he had requested from Files that morning, in the hope it would help him in his decision. Not usually a problem for him. The label on the folder, in calligraphic handwriting, slanting slightly backwards, stated:

David Burnley

Personal details

Sinclair took a sheet of paper from it. He studied it for a while before starting to read. The sheet was a standardised, Gestetner-printed form with lines and columns, whose handwritten, neat but dry and lifeless entries were reflecting the steps and stops of a human life that had been everything else but dry.

Royal Navy

Personal File of: David Burnley.

Date of birth: 18 June 1875

Parentage: father master carpenter

Education: basic

1893:   Joined Navy, aged 18.

Sinclair read the notes of the man's early career in the Navy then picked up the next sheet. It was headed:

Chapter 1 – The Defence of the Realm

War Office
Intelligence Branch
Personal file of Lt. David Burnley
Salary Level Three.

This sheet contained individual comments by some of Burnley's superiors. After the first two entries, Sinclair's eyes flew through the notes, skilfully picking out relevant items, without bothering about dates and signatories:

'Excellent material. Unusually gifted –

'Low formal educational background obstacle to further promotion.'

The final entry, however, scribbled in almost illegible lettering, worse than a doctor's prescription and with lots of abbreviations, made him look again.

'Sat. 18 Aug. '17: Burnley total recall!

'Immed. Salary incr. to level 4 with prom. to captain authd.

To be enrolled in set of four SCLCs, ald for European field wk.

Personal file transferred to SIS secretariat.'

SCLCs stood for Special Concentrated Language Courses, ald for 'as laid down'. SIS, Secret Intelligence Service, was an alternative designation for MI6, sometimes including MI5 and other sections. Theoretically a minimum of four foreign languages was 'laid down' but exceptions had become more and more frequent, as the Service had grown. A 'concentrated course' meant six uninterrupted weeks of total immersion in the language. Sinclair knew that Burnley had, in fact, done a fifth one, adding Dutch to French, English, Italian and Hungarian.

The date of the entry caught Sinclair's attention. In 1917, he had been promoted Chief of Staff of the Royal Navy's Battle Cruiser Force and on the 18th August he had turned forty. Also on that day

Chapter 1 – The Defence of the Realm

the third battle of Ypres had begun, the one that turned the war in favour of the Allies. Thus this date was printed red in his memory. Then his eye fell on the signature. It consisted of one letter only, a capital C, written in green ink. Sinclair stole a look at the pot of green ink on his desk, inherited from his predecessor, Captain Sir George Mansfield Smith-Cumming, KCMG, CB. As his eyes lingered on it, a few high spots of that man's legendary career sprang into his mind.

Having dropped the Smith, Cumming was known as 'C', due to his initialling documents with a C, in green ink, not the only evidence of a quirky character. Sinclair continued the practice although his name did not begin with that letter. Some now interpreted it as meaning Commander. As the result of a road accident, Cumming had an artificial leg. When entertaining, he had a habit of startling his guests by knocking on it, asking whether he could enter. In 1923, pretending to be a wealthy German businessman, he travelled through Germany and the Balkans picking up valuable information, without speaking a word of German. It made the round within the Service. What made him unforgettable was an order that had gone out one day: 'All agents are to use the new type of invisible ink.'

The boffins had discovered that semen made a good invisible ink. Sinclair laughed to himself, recalling the motto adapted by the agents: 'Every man his own stylo'. The stylograph was the forerunner of the fountain pen. Sinclair's eyes fixed on the final entry:

'1/9/19: Burnley embkg on tour of European states, attd to embassies.

Survey of political & socio-economic trends/developments.

Programme Head: J. J. D.'

Sinclair put the paper back into the file. It did not help him with his problem. He had inherited and enjoyed the benefits of David Burnley's unique dispatches reaching him at regular intervals. Burnley, travelling through Western Europe, had resided in European capitals for approximately three months at the time, unobtrusively merging with the city's atmosphere and daily life, as if intending to settle there. This had worked particularly well when his

Chapter 1 – The Defence of the Realm

wife and son were with him. His command of the local language and his very ordinary appearance enabled him to make and nurture acquaintances with ordinary local people, the best sources of the information he wanted. By marrying the bits of openly available information to the bands of rumours that made up the conversation topics in markets, shops and coffee houses, he produced coherent pictures of the current situation.

Once the reliability of his accounts had been recognised, they became a major basis for the reports submitted by the Service to the Foreign Office and government ministers. Sometimes the copy of one of Burnley's dispatches was forwarded unchanged, except for spelling corrections and the Department invariably received high praises from its recipients. But three weeks ago David Burnley, only 51 years old, had died. His body had been found early in the morning, leaning against a house wall in one of Munich's streets. He had been knifed. His wallet was gone, which made it appear like an ordinary mugging.

Officially the Munich Police Crime Bureau was investigating but Sinclair was not holding his breath. He had no reason for suspicion, except that he was wondering vaguely why the mugger had taken the trouble to arrange Burnley's body into a sitting position against a wall. Could that be so that passers-by might not realise he was dead? As if the killer wanted his deed to be discovered as late as possible. Yet one thing did not make sense. Who would have had a reason for killing Burnley? He was not spying, nor was he the type to get involved with women or any nefarious business. Whatever the truth, Sinclair knew that on this occasion MI6 would and could not do any investigating.

He stepped to his tall, slim window, himself tall though not slim, feeling frustrated. If, as he was certain, the Munich law enforcement bodies had no knowledge of Burnley's affiliation with MI6, any investigative activity by MI6 agents might cause suspicion in retrospect. If that happened, the gentlemen of the British Foreign Office might receive diplomatic complaints and would come down heavily on the SIS. They would have to. No, the sad thing was that the Service had lost a man who was irreplaceable and the name and the existence of David Burnley were now a thing of the silent past. Except, of course, for Burnley's wife and his son. And the latter was due to call any moment now. For the head of MI6 to see non-Service

Chapter 1 – The Defence of the Realm

callers, was an exception. As if on cue, the door opened and Mrs. Bullock entered.

'Mr. Ronald Burnley to see you, sir.'

Sinclair was not ready. 'Ask him to wait a few minutes and...' he looked significantly in the direction of his chair.

She knew and picked up the mother-of-pearl pistol lying on the thick, coloured cloth in the middle of the small table beside his chair. She tucked it out of sight on the shelf above the fireplace and left. The pistol was Sinclair's prized possession but it would not do to be seen by visitors, who were unaware of his true position. Like all female employees in the Service, Mrs. Bullock was a product of the public schools. As a long-established first private secretary she emanated authority even when just saying, yes, sir. To Sinclair she was indispensable.

'Don't forget, sir, you're meeting Major Cormody for lunch,' she said and left. He looked at his golden pocket watch: eleven on the dot. The young Burnley was punctual. He was also the source of the problem with which the Admiral was grappling. To be exact, Ronald Burnley, himself, was the problem. Sinclair returned to the window, his favourite place when pondering.

In line with established practice, Mrs. Alice Burnley, the deceased's wife, had been invited to call, in order to be given information about her husband's work and the allowances she was due to receive. However, the reply received had not come from Alice Burnley but from her son, Ronald. It contained a sentence that had caused a minor blip in the department. The post secretary, scanning it, frowned, then passed the letter to one of the special screening officers who underlined the suspicious words: 'I have an additional reason for attending. I wish to apply for employment in your department, similar to that held by my father and hope you will give me the opportunity to put my request to you in person. Enclosed please find references from my tutor and teachers at the university.'

The wording had given rise to the suspicion that Ronald Burnley might know that his father had worked for the SIS and was the reason for Sinclair's decision to see the young man, himself. But the request, itself, was sufficiently unusual in many ways and had also roused his curiosity. Was this perhaps the occasion to experiment? He looked down at the section of London's busy traffic passing

Chapter 1 – The Defence of the Realm

below but, occupied with the traffic of his thoughts, he did not see any of it. It was rare for him to grapple with conflicting ideas.

The Service was always short of suitable men and, according to the references from the University, young Burnley was a highly capable and intelligent young man, an outstanding scholar in all his subjects. Like his father, he was possessed of total recall, speaking and writing several European languages fluently, with a working knowledge of a few more. He would very likely make a good agent. The defence of the realm needed men like him. Yet there were two other factors to be considered: tradition and class. People just did not apply to join the Secret Intelligence Service, if for no other reason than that it was secret. A small number of men, like David Burnley, entered it on recommendation from within the armed services. The established way was for SIS to recruit its agents from the universities. But Reading? There was nothing wrong with Reading as such. It had, indeed, just been awarded its Royal Charter, elevating it to a university in its own right. But it was neither Oxford nor Cambridge, the only institutions whose students belonged to the right class of Englishmen. True, before obtaining the charter, Reading had been loosely connected to Oxford. Not good enough. However worthy, the Burnleys did not belong to the class whose loyalty to the motherland was beyond question.

This was something that Sinclair really believed. On the other hand, not every agent working for the SIS had to be entrusted with the kind of job in which this kind of total and absolute loyalty was of the essence. Sinclair stopped himself. He was too much a man of action, to continue wasting time. He returned to his seat behind the desk and pressed the switch on his desk, which extinguished the green light over his door, a signal for the Secretary.

Ronald Burnley in the waiting room had also been standing by a tall, slim window, looking down into the same street and also not seeing the traffic. His thoughts were filled with what had brought him here. His mother appealing to him to attend the meeting in London had appealed to him immediately. It did more than that. It filled him with a purpose, which replaced his state of inaction and the purpose induced him to return to the university that very same Tuesday, as well as the following Wednesday and Thursday.

His mother was delighted, as were Aimée and her circle of friends and one or two other students at the university, all of them female. It has to be said that their delight was slightly premature

Chapter 1 – The Defence of the Realm

because he was too preoccupied to indulge in any course, be it study or inter. He replied to the letter, signed by P.W. Cormody, Major, and, on Friday, Ronald Burnley, aged twenty-two, tall, dark and handsome, arrived at St. James Park Underground Station in London. Emerging from the main exit, he turned right in order to walk down the street called Broadway, not realising that the station, itself, was No. 55, Broadway. It was a sunny day. He had never been in London on his own before and, momentarily forgetting what had brought him here, he had a smile on his face and buoyancy in his step. The appreciative looks from some of the female pedestrians he was passing caused him to walk on in the wrong direction. He looked at the little map. He had obviously gone too far, never a good thing to do.

He turned back and discovered No. 54 directly opposite the station. The shop fronts on both sides of the door to No. 54 did not indicate that the Foreign Office or any public authority was located in that building. But the letter said 4th floor. After a moment of indecision, he tried the main door and it opened. He climbed up to the 4th floor where a table barred his way. Behind it sat a man with a square face and bushy eyebrows, who held his hand out:

'Identity card or appointment letter.'

The voice was in harmony with the square and the bushy. Ronald handed him the letter. The man took it, his eyes scanning the text while, at the same time checking a list on the table before him.

'Ronald Burnley?'

Ronald nodded. As a boy, from the age of fifteen, for two years his mother and he had accompanied his father, moving from country to country in Europe and residing in major cities for varying periods. Wherever they stayed, Ronald attended school. He had effortlessly picked up knowledge and languages. His father, as far as wife and child knew, was employed by the Foreign Office, inspecting the British representative bodies abroad. This explained his being provided with office space in embassies, consulates, legations etc., as well as with typing services for the preparation of his reports and their despatch to London in the diplomatic mail.

Although this life meant that he did not have any lasting friendships with his peers during those two years, Ronald had found the life exciting and enjoyable. It also provided him with a more realistic view of the world than most teenagers. He could not fail to see the post-war misery that prevailed in some of the towns. And,

Chapter 1 – The Defence of the Realm

quite especially, it allowed him to be with his father. He recalled the early days after returning to Britain with his mother, his disappointment that they were not staying in London. Initially he also missed their gypsy life, although his widowed grandmother's little terrace house in the outskirts of Reading was a much better accommodation than the flats in big houses they had always occupied abroad.

Above all, Ronald had never ceased missing his father. Early in their wanderings abroad, he had become aware that his parents' relationship was not the best. He sensed resentment emanating from his mother and, without knowing why, sided with his father. Nevertheless, he had been quick in adjusting to his new surroundings, even that of the very traditional Reading Grammar School. Whereas his mother tried to make him appreciate the aspiring upper class atmosphere there, he found his grandmother's views more resonant in his own reactions. The day before he started school she said:

'They all think they're the cat's whiskers, Ronnie love, those posh grammar school boys. They'll not approve of you, you not playing cricket or rugger, like. You'll not make many friends there.'

He liked his grandmother, a matter-of-fact outspoken woman, although much of her personality was true Victorian. She had been wrong about the first prophecy but right about the second. As in the European schools the bullies found him too big and too strong to be of interest to them. Many of the other pupils found him interesting and he had to answer interminable questions about his experiences. Some of them even mixed up Austria with Australia and Vienna with Venice. He answered questions with patience and any irony contained in his answers passed unnoticed.

'No. They don't play cricket in Berlin, nor rugby.'

'Soccer and handball and courtball.'

'Courtball's played without goals and hands only, soccer with goals and feet only and handball with goals and hands only.'

'Everyone lives in flats in the towns on the continent. Except for the filthy rich.'

'The large front doors of the houses are always locked and my parents had to have keys. They were very big – no, not my parents.'

'Vienna's got only one canal and the Danube.'

'It's blue when the sky is blue and it flows very fast. From left to right when I saw it.'

Chapter 1 – The Defence of the Realm

'The Black Forest at one end and the Black Sea at the other end.'

Ronald had no difficulties passing the Higher School Certificate and the entrance exam for the university. The board had advised him to take Sociology and History plus a few subsidiary subjects, which happened to be available, such as Elements of British Law. He knew now that this was due to those subjects being short of students. He developed an interest in Sociology and in Law. He also enjoyed a fringe course on Logic. The truth was that he was attending university because his father had arranged it. He had no thought of connecting it to a future profession.

He came to like his studies because they fed an ever-hungry brain. And not only that. The university had female students, some of them from abroad. By and large, most of these girls behaved differently from the local girls, uplifting the atmosphere for him although, at first, he tended to keep to himself. His thoughts returned to the day when the mixture of shyness and vague fears was ended forever. He remembered every word and every moment. It happened after he had attended an evening lecture on 'The importance of marriage in British society,' a subject he found meaningless. As he walked from the room, one of the girls who had been in the audience, came to walk beside him on the way out, by coincidence, he believed.

'I am Aimée.'

'Ronald Burnley.'

She linked her arm in his, as if that was the natural thing to do. It was for her.

'What is what you think about the British marriage, Ronálde?'

Her French accent was strong and intoxicating and she used French words here and there. She pronounced his name emphasising the 'a' in Ronald. She was squeezing his arm closer and, when she turned to look up at him, he felt her breast caressing his arm, another natural action for her, but a new experience for him.

'I've never thought about it. I only went to the lecture because I take sociology.'

He was close to stammering.'

'Ah, *la sociologie,* 'ow interesting. You must tell me all about it. We go for a walk, yes?'

Looking into a pair of wide open unfathomable green eyes, he was lost. From that moment on she was in charge. They ended up, or rather down, in the near-by park, where Ronald lost his virginity and

Chapter 1 – The Defence of the Realm

a lot of his shyness. He had walked home in robot fashion and, inside, up the stairs, past his grandmother and his mother without saying a word. His grandmother, possessing great Victorian wisdom, knew exactly what had happened. She was not shocked, either. His mother was, when she eventually realised. He met Aimée two days later just inside the gates of the university. She was standing with a small group of girls, all of whose eyes turned in his direction. She walked up to him and said:

'You must meet my friends, Ronald.'

She again tucked her arms into his and led him to the friends, in order to introduce him to them and vice versa. Lamb to the shearing, a liberating experience. Ronald only heard the name of the first one, Danielle. His life had changed radically. A new subject had been added to his studies with Aimée as his chief tutor. He did not feel he was doing anything wrong. The girls certainly did not. For all the progress he made in the new subject, he retained a naiveness and an independence which added to his attraction. From his point, the girls with whom he had sex in the course of this first year at the university were friends and sexual intercourse was a natural part of that friendship. He was a good friend, often helping them with their studies and other problems. In turn, he learnt a lot from them in a subject called: *joie de vivre* (joy of living).

The news of his father's death, three weeks ago, had hit him deeply. He had never before experienced this kind of pain. He was lost, a leaf fluttering in the wind, feeling that there was no point in doing anything. Normal consciousness, however, had returned gradually and when his mother asked him to attend the interview in London in her place, it broke into his state of aimlessness. Quite suddenly, like an inspiration, he knew he wanted to continue his father's work. It would be a link. He had arrived in London early this morning and was wondering what the next hour would bring. The Secretary's voice interrupted his thoughts.

'Admiral Sir Hugh Sinclair is ready now.'

He had no time to deal with the momentary surprise at hearing who he was about to see. The secretary had opened the door and announced him. The next moment he was seated opposite the admiral. Another surprise: the admiral did not wear a uniform. And the admiral started to speak, giving him no time to ponder the fact.

'Good of you to come all the way from Reading to see me, Mr. Burnley. Accept my sincere condolences on your father's sudden

Chapter 1 – The Defence of the Realm

death, if you will. David Burnley was a valued employee of the Royal Navy and, at the time of his death, his position was equivalent to that of a commodore. The paymaster of the relevant department will write to your mother to let her know the precise amounts of an annual pension she will receive in monthly payments. It will enable her to maintain a comfortable living standard. I can also tell you, that a fixed proportion of your father's salary was paid regularly into a special fund from which your university studies have been paid. The balance still in the account is to be transferred to your name now, in accordance with your father's instructions.'

A little pause followed, during which Sinclair was scanning one of the papers in front of him. Ronald was grappling with the information he had just heard, when Sinclair continued:

'In the letter setting up this account, your father stated that he was deeply conscious of his own lack of a good education and his desire that you should have what he did not. These financial details will also be forwarded by the bursar, together with a closed letter left by your father. I had expected those details to reach me by today but, unfortunately, that has not happened, hmm. And that is really all I can relate to you.'

He considered standing up and concluding the interview. Watching Ronald's reactions had reassured him that he had no idea of his father's real job. But the young man's expressions also reflected his complete puzzlement at some of what he had been told. It was a moment of decision for Sinclair, or had he already made up his mind when he said:

'Have you any questions, Mr. Burnley?'

These new facts about his father and his financial arrangements had struck Ronald's thoughts like a series of exclamation marks, each ricocheting as a question mark as it entered his consciousness. So, yes, he had more questions. Only he was not quite sure what they were. Was that really all he was going to be told? Why should an admiral of the Royal Navy take the trouble to see him just for that? His father had said that he was working for the Foreign Office and he remembered once, inside a consulate, watching his father receiving a report someone had typed for him, signing it and inserting it in an envelope which was indeed addressed to the Foreign Office. There must be more things he had not been told. He was also battling with a feeling of awe.

Chapter 1 – The Defence of the Realm

Communicating with admirals was not a familiar experience for him. Indeed, he had never even seen one before. Not knowingly. Expecting an entirely different kind of interview, Ronald had filled himself with hope that he might get the chance of obtaining a job in the same Foreign Office department for which his father had worked. Somehow, that had all but collapsed now. Yet he was not willing to give his little dream up so quickly. And the admiral's last question re-opened a door. He did not reply immediately. Instead, he was looking at Sinclair, wondering what kind of a man he was. What he saw was a high forehead and flattened hair with a parting, topping a round face with a friendly, almost smiling expression. But the sharp self-assurance of an unaffected upper class voice oozed authority, a confident assumption of superiority.

The admiral had been observing and studying Ronald Burnley from the moment he set eyes on him. Was he, like his father, 'excellent material'? He certainly made an immediate impression on Sinclair, whose experience in the judgement of men was crucial to his Department's success. There was strength in the youthful face and the brown eyes, which, beneath a high forehead, were looking open and frank into the world. Burnley was about five foot ten, of average physique. He was clean-shaven. The little crows' feet radiating from the corners of his eyes suggested a sense of humour. Satirical? Amusing? The indefinable way in which the young man's features were assembled reflected a high intelligence and considerable self-confidence. Sinclair was left with an impression that there was even more to this young man than his looks betrayed. Ronald, at this moment, was not conscious of his own worth, but his need to know was great.

'Yes, I have, sir. Three, if I may. Did you know my father personally? Can you tell me more about his work? And – how must I go about applying for a post in whatever department he worked for, although I'm not at all clear at the moment what that was – in the Navy, you said?'

Sinclair nodded. He knew now what to do, admitting afterwards to himself that it was what he had intended to do all along.

'What is it about your father's work that attracts you so much?'

Ronald thought carefully before replying

'Europe, sir. When I was young, my mother and I accompanied him abroad and I enjoyed staying at different places and meeting different people - school kids, I suppose - in different countries. I

Chapter 1 – The Defence of the Realm

was too young to - to do things but I always knew that I'd like to go back and get to know the places and the people and the situation better.'

Once again a moment of silence took over, Sinclair's final moment of hesitation. Then he opened a drawer in his desk and extracted a sheet of thick paper. He put it in front of Ronald who stared at its heading: OFFICIAL SECRETS ACT.

'Mr. Burnley, I have decided that you are entitled to receive some of the information you have asked for but, in order for me to give it, I must ask you to first sign this paper. It is a legal document and your signature obliges you never to divulge anything of what I tell you to any other person whatsoever. Any. Please put today's date beneath your signature.'

Ronald signed and dated the document using his own fountain pen, without any comment and without even reading it. He handed it to Sinclair, who looked at his watch before speaking. The interview was lasting longer than he had anticipated. He picked up the sheet of paper with notes he had prepared for this eventuality and consulted it as he spoke.

'To answer your first question, Mr. Burnley, I did not know your father personally, although I knew of and about him. All about him, in fact, because I am in charge of the organisation that employed him. You may know that your father joined the Royal Navy in ninety-three, at the age of eighteen.'

Ronald nodded. Sinclair continued without stopping.

'Because of suffering from chronic sea sickness, he was transferred to administrative harbour duties three years later. His work was highly commended and, in nineteen hundred, he was moved to the Navy's London H.Q. where he became liaison officer to the Foreign Office. In that year he married your mother.' He looked at Ronald with what was almost a smile. 'You were born four years later but you probably know that. However, in that year your father lost his job, or to be exact, the job ceased to exist and your father was attached to the Naval Intelligence Branch. When the war ended the services that were in charge of the security of the realm, were re-organised and your father moved to the department that is concerned with potential threats and dangers from abroad.'

Ronald, who was absorbing every word, nodded slowly, speaking partly to himself.

Chapter 1 – The Defence of the Realm

'So my father was not employed by the Foreign Office as inspector of embassies? But the reports he kept sending to the Foreign Office? And he was always given an office and a typist to do his reports -' He interrupted himself, frowning. 'Are you saying, sir, that my father was a spy?' Ronald's voice carried only interest

Sinclair shook his head.

'No, Mr. Burnley, your father was most definitely not a spy. He was an agent of this department, yes. His rather unique task was to obtain facts and impressions about the post war situation in the different European countries. He did not seek out foreign state secrets, or any other kind. Your father was highly skilled in assessing events, currents and prevailing moods in his environment, which he put together in cohesive reports. Your father had an instinctive understanding of what was of the essence and his intelligence provided a valuable contribution towards our task of keeping this country secure. Some of his reports have directly influenced ministerial decisions.' He stopped for a moment before adding 'And that, I am afraid, is really all I can tell you, Mr. Burnley.' He rose.

Ronald followed suit. The information had been short but precise. Every word was safely stored in his mind.

'Thank you, sir. Neither my mother nor I knew what you have told me. I shall keep it to myself. I understand my father much better now.'

Sinclair nodded an acknowledgement, half expecting Ronald to depart. When the young man did not move, looking at him expectantly, he knew why.

'Your third question. You still wish to apply for employment with this Service?'

Ronald nodded firmly.

'I do, sir. If anything, more so.'

A long pause followed. Sinclair's reaction wavered between annoyance with himself and appreciation of the young man's determination. Then rational consideration took over and with it, his attitude changed.

'Very well. I shall arrange an interview for you with our recruiting officers. My recommendation will ensure you the chance of being put through the established, comprehensive chain of tests and interviews. Let me warn you. It may last up to seven days.'

Chapter 1 – The Defence of the Realm

He paused. He did not add that, without his recommendation, Burnley's background would ensure that he would not get beyond the first interview. But he had made up his mind. He wanted this young man in the SIS. Also he owed it to his father. He continued.

'I must make clear that whatever decision is ultimately arrived at by the Recruiting Board, will stand. I do not interfere in the Board's ruling. Nor, should you pass, can I offer you the task you are looking for. Things have changed and are changing fast. The Continent, today, is a breeding place for new threats and dangers and we have new enemies in the world. This Service has only one purpose, the protection of our country. However, if you join the Service, I may arrange for you to join the European Section. You need to understand clearly, Burnley, that this is a military outfit with military ranks and discipline. Once you are a member of the Service, your Section Head will decide your duties. Some of them may involve risks to your own person. So consider carefully.'

There were two distinct sides to the personality of Rear Admiral Sir Hugh 'Quex' Sinclair. His lavish lifestyle of expensive cigars, expensive wines and lavish dinner parties had brought him his nickname from Pinero's play, 'The Gay Lord Quex', described as the wickedest man in London. Sinclair was known as a bon viveur, a lover of good food and of parties. He was a well-known sight in upper class London, driving around in his large, ancient Lancia, dressed in elegant clothes, civilian most of the time, and wearing a bowler hat. He had to push the hat down hard on his head because it was too small, or maybe because his head was too big. The other side of him as the head of MI6 was a man devoted totally to his task, a man to whom the secrecy of his job and the organisation he led were the holy shrine.

He believed that Britain was the most civilised nation on earth and that the British way of life was far superior to that of the rest of the civilised world. He was resolved to do everything necessary to protect the existence of the British people and their way of life to the limit of the means available to him. To that end he would, if necessary, send his agents into life-threatening situations and to that end he might even go further. After Ronald had left, Sinclair returned to his favourite spot by the window. At his desk all his thoughts and actions were concentrated on the job. At the window, he would indulge in personal thoughts. If his judgement was right,

Chapter 1 – The Defence of the Realm

Ronald Burnley was going to be a useful addition to his team of agents.

When he had said that Europe was a breeding place for new threats and dangers he had stated the situation as reflected by the reports the European Section was receiving regularly. He had, however, directed an overload of his resources into the new, powerful Russian Communist society whose political ideology was a distinct threat to the capitalist freedom of competition that formed the backbone of the British economy and the British class society. Looking down at the peaceful street life below, the picture of the European scene rushed through his mind. Many idealistic people hoped and believed that the League of Nations, set up, following the Treaty of Versailles, would ensure peace for ever. Sinclair was one of many realists who had grave doubts. Passing resolutions was one thing; to get them executed was quite a different kettle of sardines. The governments of the League's democratic member states were likely to put their countries' interests first. As did Britain. That's what they were elected for, after all.

Threats to peace often began with political upheavals inside one country and the Charter of the League forbade interference in the internal affairs of a state, so the League could not interfere before such upheavals developed into threats to peace. The war had ended only eight years ago and already Europe was beginning to forget its lessons. In Italy, the Italian people had used their democratic votes to give Mussolini's Fascist Party a huge majority. Mussolini was a dictator and a murderer. It was common knowledge that he had ordered the assassination of Giacomo Matteotti, a Socialist. Of the five killers, the judges found two innocent and the other three guilty of unintentional murder and sent them to prison for six years. Hard on the heels of the judgment, Mussolini declared a general amnesty so they only had to serve three months.

Sinclair shrugged his shoulders. He did not see Italy, or Fascism, as a serious threat to Britain and the death of one foreign socialist did not trouble him. The contrary was the case. In Sinclair's judgment, of the European states, only Germany had the basic potential to cause trouble. He had been in Cologne when the seven year-long occupation of the Rhineland had ended, the British flag was hauled down and the last British regiment, the King's Shropshire Light Infantry, marched out. In the Kölner Dom, Cologne's impressive cathedral, a military band had played a medley of cheerful tunes. It included the Yankee Doodle and the Swanee River, which they considered to be the most suitable selection to be performed for British soldiers in a cathedral. It was the thirtieth of January and brilliant sunshine accompanied the outdoor proceedings. Sinclair had not left at the same time as the troops, being on observation duty, and he had not forgotten what he observed.

He, himself, spoke several foreign languages. A midnight ceremony on the steps of the cathedral, presided over by the city's Catholic mayor, Dr. Konrad Adenauer, ended with the congregation singing the German anthem, *'Deutschland, Deutschland über alles'*, 'Germany, Germany above all'. Oddly enough it was the anthem composed by Joseph Haydn for the Austrian Empire. The speeches were greeted by passionate applause and cries of support, especially when some of the speakers emphasised that the people had been innocent victims of the war and promised the restoration of Germany's glory and destiny as a leading nation. One of the most applauded and repeated statements claimed that the war had been lost not by Germany's brave soldiers but by the betrayal of her politicians, those representing the new democratic government.

The impression Sinclair took from this ceremony was that the Germans' arrogant belief in their own superiority had remained unshaken by their defeat. In his judgement, however, any feasible German threat was a long way away, far away. They had been beaten thoroughly. The new Communist Russia and the growth of Communist parties in all parts of Europe and even in Britain presented the only real threat to Great Britain. Therefore, his organisation's most important task was the surveillance of the European Communist parties and, above all, of the new Communist power, the Russian Socialist Federative Soviet Republic. He stepped to his table and, dialling a number, picked up the internal telephone.

'Cormody? Just to tell you I'm running late.'

'I'm in the same boat, Admiral. By the way, just received a third report from Germany, from Slater. He's in Nuremberg, now.'

'Anything new?'

'Rally by the new German National Socialist Workers' Party. Masses filling a huge square. Adulating the party leader, man called Adolf Hitler. According to the report he's a fanatic – top of the voice beer garden oratory – inflammatory – tirades against British –

Chapter 1 – The Defence of the Realm

rubbishes the democratic government in Weimar – hates the Commies, blames the Jews—'

Sinclair laughed.

'Is that all? He's got the Communists right at that. It might surprise the F.O., Chamberlain thinks the Germans love him now. Lunch at two, OK?'

Sinclair put the phone down. He stepped to the shelf to pick up the pearly pistol lovingly. He returned it to its customary abode and rang the bell for the indispensable Mrs. Bullock.

Ronald Burnley had left the office on the fourth floor, his mind filled with the admiral's revelations. His father's work had obviously been of great importance. It was equally obvious that his father's employers must be one of the official secret Intelligence Services. Why else did he have to sign the Official Secrets Act? Now he, too, would be serving the defence of his country. He had no doubt in his ability to pass the necessary tests. The thought of physical risks to his own person never entered his mind. If asked, Ronald would have rejected any suggestion that he was a brave man.

The truth was that he was not troubled by the kind of imagination that would cause him to worry about unknown dangers. He took things as they came and dealt with them as they came, often observing his own actions and reactions as if from the outside, with criticism as well as humour. Having been alone a lot during his youth he had been wondering often how others saw him. He became adept in interpreting people's reactions to him and in assessing their personality. Wanting to be liked, he was always working on his own personality. At the same time, he had built up his moral standards without any religious input. Of course he had had to attend the religious subject lessons in the different schools of the different countries but, with his father's full support, he did not participate in prayers and religious ceremonies. Thus the concept of having to pray to a supernatural being was not part of his personality. But he believed service in the protection of his country to be a moral action and was looking forward to this great change in his life. A naivety in his outlook on the real world was not obvious to others because of his wide knowledge.

Upon arriving back home, his mother was suffering from one of her traditional headaches so did not badger him for details of his interview. That she was going to receive a good pension was all that mattered to her. Ten days later, a Monday, he called again at 54

Chapter 1 – The Defence of the Realm

Broadway and commenced his recruitment interviews. Commuting to and from London he was passing daily through what Admiral Sinclair had called a chain of tests and interviews. They were aimed at catching him out in any inexact statements, exploring every aspect of his identity and views. They were meant to be intimidating as well as provocative. Ronald was fazed by none.

In the afternoon of the Friday he had to confront the whole of the Recruiting Board. It consisted of an array of Naval officers in splendid uniforms, each adorned by a long line of medals, plus a few corpulent civilians and one very tall, thin, bald one, whose dress codes and displays of medals ensured that they looked no less important. After answering a variety of final probing questions, the very tall, thin and bald personage informed him that he had passed and would be accepted into the Service. It was what Ronald had expected.

Returning to 54 Broadway on Monday, he spent the whole day in undergoing the registration routine. It required proceeding from room to room, each manned by a posh-speaking lady with a commanding voice, answering more questions, filling in forms and signing them. He dealt with it like a sprinter over low hurdles, exuding a light-hearted optimism of which some of the females did not seem to approve. He either did not notice or he did not care, mostly both, being carried on the wings of his enthusiasm. A zephyr of excitement was stirring his thoughts and foiled attempts to assess seriously this colossal change in his life. This was what he had always wanted.

He ended the process in a tiny room, occupied by a male clerk, well past his vigorous years, hunched and wearing glasses, who pointed him to a document on the desk. He was a former agent who, upon being shot in the shoulder, somewhere, sometime in the past, had retired from field work. Ronald found out later that this was normal practice – not being shot in the shoulder but being given office jobs in the 'Firm'. He sat down and studied the document.

Official Secrets Act 1920 *(1 & 2 Geo. 5 c. 28)*

Passed by an Act of the Parliament of the United Kingdom.

Replaces the Official Secrets Act 1911

Chapter 1 – The Defence of the Realm

The Act applies in the United Kingdom, the Isle of Man, the Channel Islands, and in overseas crown territories and colonies. It also applies to British subjects anywhere else in the world.

This document was much longer than the sheet he had signed in the admiral's office. He signed it, again without reading the text. When he looked up, his mind was clear. He knew that this signature initiated an entirely new direction to his existence.

Walking out of the building, he felt uplifted and energised. For the first time in his life he had taken an independent decision about what he was doing on this earth and it made him feel good, despite the fact that this was also the first time in his life that he had not heeded his father's advice: 'Never sign anything, Ronnie, without reading carefully what you are signing.'

Back in Reading, he informed his mother that he was leaving university, having accepted a job with the Foreign Office. He also told her that he was moving to London. She did not show a lot of emotion. The letter from the Bursar's Bureau, obviously of the Foreign Office, confirmed her comfortable income to the end of her life. As a result, she quickly decided that, still feeling young, she would have a go at enjoying it. She, too, was looking for a new direction and if her grown-up, somewhat alienated son was not around, it might be easier to succeed, a thought she would not have admitted, perhaps even to herself.

Another letter from the same Bursar's Bureau had already arrived at home on the day Ronald signed the Official Secrets Act. It gave him the details of the account which his father had set up for him. It was hugely more than adequate. Hitherto he had received a fixed amount of pocket money from his mother. He had not given a thought as to where it came from. He was not a big spender. Going out with Uni-girls was not expensive as they always went Dutch. But this letter changed his monetary status beyond any possible expectations. As soon as the bank had received two copies of his new signature, it would de facto be his private account. He looked at the figures with awe. He had never held a bank account before, nor had he been so rich before. His feeling of independence grew fast, which was strange since he had actually signed a contract that made him less independent than he had ever been before. He worked it out

Chapter 1 – The Defence of the Realm

for himself: a dependency, voluntary entered into, was part of independence.

As required, he returned to London on Wednesday and reported at the RB, the Registration Bureau. An hour later Ronald Burnley officially started his probationary period as a full-time agent of the SIS, aka MI6. Armed with a standard sum of money for which he had signed and a list of recommended addresses of one-room flats, provided by the SAB, the Service Accommodation Bureau, he embarked on the task of finding a small flat to rent. He had been informed that during his first year he would have to attend the coding school, as well as a variety of internal and external lectures, courses and other training programmes. He was also advised to learn typing. It made residing in London a necessity. All the places on the list were situated in the area south of the Kensington High Road. He decided to look at a few before making his mind up. That process stopped when he came to a small cottage at the southerly end of De Vere Gardens, the only complete house on the list. It was a terrace house and its location was ideal, close to Kensington Gardens, to the underground and to bus routes.

The house was empty and he had to collect the key from a shop around the corner. Apparently the owner was living abroad and Ronald was the first person to view it since it had gone on the register. The inside captivated his imagination. It was neat and clean and attractively furnished and it had electric lighting. He threw a glance into the two bedrooms upstairs. One had two beds the other just one. Unfortunately, renting one room was not on offer here. It was either the whole house or nothing. Although the rent was surprisingly low, it was still more than twice the average of the rents for the flats he had seen. They had landladies with a daily service of breakfast and an evening meal – not included in the rent. This one included the services of a cleaning lady an hour a day, also not included in the rent, but no other service. But eating out at restaurants was something he had got used to in his teens.

He forced himself to look at a couple of other addresses but the temptation was too great. 'I can resist everything but temptation.' With an inner smile, Ronald remembered Mr. Darlington, the English teacher at Reading. Because of his name his speech was interlaced with quotations from Lord Darlington's role in *Lady Windermere's Fan*. Some of the pupils, giggling and raising eyes significantly, had suggested that Darlington was also like Oscar

Chapter 1 – The Defence of the Realm

Wilde in other matters. Ronald did a quick calculation. His salary, the first one ever, would pay for his upkeep and, contrary to his initial resolution, he would draw from his new bank account to pay the rent. Holding on to the key, he returned to the SAB and signed the contract.

From there he went straight to Paddington Station, took the next train to Reading and went home to pack his things – one old and battered suitcase – and caught the last train back to London. At Paddington Station he had something to eat at a stand and then, feelings on a high, treated himself to a taxi. 'Number One, De Vere Court, Kensington,' he said to the bowler-hatted driver, leaning back in the seat as if this was his usual way of travelling. The taxi stopped outside the little front garden gate and Ronald paid the driver, including a 10% tip he had carefully got ready during the trip. He opened the front door and entered into his new home, the first one he had chosen, himself. He stepped into the hall, put his case down, switched the light on and heard a noise.

He looked up to where it came from and froze. At the top of the staircase stood a woman, wearing a long nightdress and holding a broom by the brush end above her head, which she seemed prepared to use as a weapon. It made a strange image. Her dark hair was loose, falling around her shoulders, her eyes looked frightened and her mouth was open as if she was about to scream. Ronald's mouth was stuck half open. She did not scream and they stared at each other for a long time, at least ten seconds. Then her features took on a determined look. She leaned slightly forward, sticking her chin out and clutching the broom with both her hands said:

'Oo are you?'

Her question broke the spell and her mouth also relaxed.

'I live here,' he said firmly. 'This house was supposed to be empty. So who are you?'

Her determined look changed to one of uncertainty.

'I am the cleaner. I come and clean the 'ouse every day. Today I think, nobody is 'ere, so I can sleep 'ere tonight. Why not? I do nothing bad...' One hand flew to cover her mouth. 'You – oh, *Mon Dieu!*' (My God). 'You are a tenant? I will lose my job. You will tell?' Uncertainty had turned into deep worry.

Ronald, however, was still staring. It made her aware of being in her night attire, but, holding on to the broom, she remained in her defensive posture, not sure of what might follow. She did not realise that despite the nightdress' thick material, the light behind her highlighted her outlines in every seductive detail. Ronald did. He also noticed that she was young and had long eyelashes, emphasising her olive-shaped dark eyes. Her French accent had immediately moved Ronald's thoughts to Aimée. Then he realised that he was staring. He relaxed and, appraising the situation, began to reassure her.

'I shall not tell. But I've nowhere else to go. I must sleep here tonight.' Then he added spontaneously, *'Vous êtes française?'* (You are French?)

In one moment she forgot all her fears.

'Vous parlez français, Monsieur.' The relief in her voice suggested that as he spoke French, he was alright. Everything was alright. *'Un moment, monsieur.'*

She turned around and rushed away. A minute later she reappeared without the broom, wearing a well-worn dressing gown and came walking downstairs.

'We shall talk, *oui*?'

She was taking command of the situation, the way Aimée always did. Ronald confessed to himself that he was sorry to have lost the image of the Amazonian silhouette at the top of the stairs. At the same time, it was obvious to him that she was not entirely truthful. She had come prepared with nightdress and dressing gown, so it could not have been an off-the-cuff decision. He followed her into the small living room, where she pointed to the small table and chairs. He sat down, whilst she drew the curtains.

'I make the coffee,' she said, 'you drink coffee? I 'ave no tea.'

'Coffee is fine.'

Ronald was beginning to wonder. This was London. Was he getting himself into trouble? He obviously could not send her out into the streets of the capital that late of night. He, himself, was tired and ready to turn in. She served the coffee in pretty little teacups and sat down opposite him. He said nothing, waiting for her to explain. She knew she had to and once she started, it all came out in a flow. Here and there he had difficulty in understanding because she spoke English. In an odd paradox, when she noticed he did not understand she repeated the bit in French.

Her name was Lisette, Lisette Bannister. She was fourteen when her mother married an English soldier in the last year of the war. They lived in the outskirts of Paris, but she only saw him when he

Chapter 1 – The Defence of the Realm

came on leave. After the war they had moved to England. Her stepfather was well-meaning but he and Lisette did not hit it off. Her mother was already ill, and had died two years ago. And last year he had got a new girlfriend who was jealous of his stepdaughter and things got unpleasant for Lisette. Then she met Guy, a very nice Englishman, *'un vrai galant'* (a true gentleman). Guy lived not far from here.

He was kind to her. But he had to go abroad and before he left he arranged for her to get this cleaning job with the lady who lived here with her young daughter. She was a good boss. And a few weeks ago, they, too, were going abroad for an unspecified time and the lady arranged that Lisette came to the house one hour every day, except on Sundays, to keep the house clean. Lisette received her wages from an agency. She went there every Friday for it. At this point she paused before producing the essence of her confession.

'My boyfriend Guy, he has let me stay in his flat, but a friend of him turn up. And he wants to – you know. He says he is a friend of Guy but I believe he is lying. Clarence Conker, that was his name.' She pronounced it Conkère. 'Like an English *marron, n'est-ce-pas*? But I am not like a book from the *librairie* you can borrow.' Her resentment was fierce. 'So I move out from the flat of Guy and – *voilà.*' (here I am)

An explanatory gesture, accompanied by a shrug of one shoulder, finished the sentence. Obviously he would understand. He spoke French after all. He said nothing.

'I do not know someone is coming to live here today.' She wrinkled her brow, thinking. 'Ah, it is the agence, *n'est-ce-pas*? They are renting you the house, hein?'

He nodded and made a quick decision.

'This is what we do, Lisette. I know there are two bedrooms upstairs. I'm tired and want to go to sleep. I must get up at eight and go to work. I take the room on the right and you take the one on the left. You know where everything is. Can you make the bed up for me?'

She nodded this time, pleased. Very pleased – happy. Luckily he had chosen the lady's bedroom for himself, not the daughter's which she was occupying, so she did not have to move. She looked him over with different eyes. Since Guy left she had had no friend, male or female, no one to talk to, let alone do things with. She missed all of that. Someone had heard her unspoken prayers and sent this handsome Englishman to her. There was something about his eyes. They were kind and – beautiful, there was no other word for it. Without another word she went upstairs to get his bed ready.

Ronald had the ability to fall asleep at a moment's notice. He did so now, although in a strange house, a strange room and a strange bed. Lisette went downstairs to clear the cups away. Then she went to bed. She took a long time to fall asleep, thoughts racing through her mind. She had never had anything like a real home. She had never known her real father. She was ten when the war started. She and her mother lived in one of the narrow back-streets of Boulogne-Billancourt, a western suburb of Paris and not far from the posh district of St. Cloud.

Her mother came to receive a variety of male callers in their home. She did what she had to, in order to survive. She would have fitted well into one of Émile Zola's novels. Lisette used to hide from these visitors – and with good reason. Despite this she could not avoid her first sexual experiences when only thirteen. It was the norm in her environment. With her mother's marriage to a British soldier, Private Alan Bannister, some sort of stability entered into their lives. When they moved to England, Lisette thought life was quite wonderful. She picked up the language very quickly. Despite that she did not get to know any Englishmen until she met the dashing and experienced Guy. It was her very first steady relationship. He was, however, a good deal older than she, which gave him a fatherly touch in her eyes and he was good company. He spoke French quite well, too. She missed that in particular when he left and the previous loneliness had returned with a vengeance. The looks, the voice, the expressions in the face of this Englishman who would probably throw her out in the morning, had stirred something in her that she had not experienced before – something intangible, a sensation pervading the whole of her being.

Lisette was far from being romantic. Life had made her a realist from early childhood. Now within the short space of an hour or so, her realism was dominated by this unusual longing drawing her, urging her. Perhaps he would allow her to stay? Her last thought was that she had not had sex for some time. Eventually she fell asleep…

She woke up early in the morning. It was still dark. She knew exactly what was drawing her, what she wanted, indeed, needed to do. In her bare feet she left the room and crossed over to the other bedroom. She opened the door softly. Ronald was fast asleep, lying on his right side as always and, as always, in the nude. She carefully lifted the sheet and two blankets up. There was sufficient light for her to see this wonderful male body. Suddenly he became sheer realism. This was the logical thing to do. Without a second's hesitation she discarded her nightdress and climbed into his bed to lie beside him. She snuggled close and fell happily asleep. He hardly stirred, although his body reacted in its natural manner.

At one moment, when dawn was colouring the London sky outside, both their bodies interrupted their sleep and what was meant to happen, took place, without words. Only short, expressive sounds, growing louder and faster were heard, until they breathlessly ended in the long-drawn notes of a harmony of joy and relief, after which they both fell immediately asleep again. Some things, some actions in life are unplanned, unavoidable and beautiful.

When she woke him up at eight, the way she used to wake up Guy, she had made breakfast. It was the kind he had been used to when living abroad, called continental breakfast in Britain: bread and butter and jam, fruit juice and coffee, and it was wonderful. They said little, only looked at each other from time to time. Out of the blue, Lisette said:

'I can cook, monsieur. I am a good cook.'

Ronald, trying to rationalise the situation, nodded as if he had received the answer to a question. He had just arrived in a new home to start a new life. He looked at her and nodded again. Lisette smiled a very happy smile. She, too, had just arrived home from a long, long journey. Were they both deceiving themselves? If so, they were not aware of it. Suffice it to say that when they had finished breakfast, Lisette was assured of a place to live and Ronald of enjoying daily meals *à la cuisine française* and both of each other's company as friends and lovers.

Within the space of seven days, Ronald's life had undergone a total revolution from a somewhat narrow, studious existence without any specific design to a life of interest, direction and with all necessary comforts. His interview with the Admiral had ended in a promise of action if not adventure. The encounter with the girl with the broom had provided him with a stable, uncomplicated relationship, replacing the casual sex with the Uni-girls by the regularity of a marriage without its bonds and responsibilities. Lisette, sophisticated far beyond her age, had been living in a world of low self-esteem, low expectations and, above all, total insecurity.

Chapter 1 – The Defence of the Realm

And one unexpected special night had converted it into a feeling of being safe and needed, of loving the world around her and looking forward each day to the next.

* * *

At 54 Broadway, in the morning, Rear Admiral Sir Hugh Sinclair entered his office by the usual route at the usual hour and sat down behind his desk. He was the one person in the building who did not pass the porter on the 4th floor to reach his office. A quick experienced glance through the stack of the morning's mail made him pick out two items to look at first. One was the expected set of reports on the latest entrant from the RIB, the Recruitment Interviewing Board. He looked carefully at the different results and the concluding summary. They all confirmed Burnley's judgement of Ronald Burnley. He was pleased, though not surprised. More than half of them added doubts about his background. He initialled the accompanying cover note and put the whole into the tray marked PERSONAL FILES ready for Miss Henrietta Alice Sherringham-Bingley, his exceedingly efficient private undersecretary. Her efficiency was known to all, as she, herself, reminded everyone at every opportunity and she would start a personal file for the new agent.

Sinclair opened the second item, a fat envelope carrying a post stamp, which denoted that it came from the Foreign Office postmaster. It had 'Section: Europe' written on it in capitals. He frowned, 'Europe'? It should have gone to Cormody. Inside was one open letter and another envelope which he scanned, puzzled. The handwriting on it looked familiar but surely that could not be? He picked up the open letter and looked at its brief content.

British Consulate, Munich

Consul-General Hugh William Gaisford

Consul Donald St. Clair Gainer

Pro-Consul A.G. Tyler

Handwritten: Moving to Prannerstrasse 11

The note was signed by Captain Craig Jameson, Security. MI5 and MI6 had both been installing agents in the passport offices of British embassies and consulates in Europe since the end of the war, a practice as yet undiscovered by the foreign governments. Captain Craig Jameson was an MI5 agent. Sinclair read on:

Enclosed package left with me by one of your bods, civilian, name David Burnley, posing as journalist (cover-name: Lloyd). Burnley requested forwarding package to you, in case something happened to him. He was killed in Munich back streets. Police assume mugging. Unable to pass suspicions to local authority. Any further info available will follow.

Craig Jameson,

Captain, Security

9/10/26

Sinclair picked up the contents of Burnley's package. It contained handwritten notes and a typed report with two blue carbon copies, the very report which Sinclair believed, had not been done because of Burnley's death. It was divided into four sections, more formal than Burnley's usual stuff, because it was a special report on a specified subject that had been requested. He looked at the heading.

Report No. 3

192 Munich

Sept. 24th, 1926

The Nationalsozialistische Deutsche Arbeiterpartei, abbr. NSDAP

(National Socialist German Workers' Party), generally called Nazis.

He hastily leafed through the pages, noting the paragraph headings and picking up stray phrases of significance.

1. 'Reactions to the Occupation'... German resentments of Allied occupation... High reparations punishing the innocent... Not impressed by League of Nations.

2. *'Mistake Government located in Weimar'... Over forty political parties in parliament... Stresemann's reforms insufficient... Many want Kaiser back... No confidence in Parliament...*

3. *'German Economy'... Much improvement... Upwards trend but too slow... Inflation still huge...*

Sinclair extracted the last three pages, headed: 4. 'Rise of the NSDAP' and began to read word for word. He had agreed to Cormody requesting David Burnley to investigate this new party, because several of his agents in Germany had warned about it in their reports, referring to the new leader as a dangerous man. He leaned back, to read the final section carefully:

Although an Austrian, Adolf Hitler was elected head of the NSDAP in 1921. He is called: Führer (=leader) of the NSDAP, an unusual title for the head of a political party. It signifies his absolute control over the membership, which has grown fast and is still growing, due to Hitler's oratorical skills. He shouts, rather than speaks, aggressively threatening the authorities and powers in charge, and promises that his party will change things.

He condemns the terms of the Versailles Treaty, claims that it was not the German soldiers who lost the war, but the politicians who stabbed them in the back. Hitler rails against the English and the French, against the 'inefficient Weimar Government,' but also against monarchists, against the very rich, against Marxists and Jews. He's hugely successful with mass audiences. His passion hits a strong note in the mood of the country and people from all classes are joining this party.

Thousands attend his open air rallies, applauding and shouting their support. Herr Ernst Röhm, a leading member of the NSDAP has organised a military unit of toughs, called Sturmabteilung, abbr. SA (= Storm Division). Its men wear brown shirts, jackboots and martial leather cross-straps and belts. At public meetings they chant stock phrases in rousing unison. Their official purpose is to protect their speakers but appearance and behaviour are threatening and, on occasions SA men physically victimise critics in the crowd. NSDAP propaganda stokes anti-Semitic feelings and behaviour.

In 1923 Hitler attempted to take over the provincial government of Bavaria in the Capital, Munich, with the help of his Sturmabteilung by force, supported by General Ludendorff. The attempt failed. The police killed some S.A. members and arrested others. Hitler, himself, was sentenced to 5 years' imprisonment in April 1924, but released in December 1924. In prison he wrote a book, 'Mein Kampf' (My Struggle). It details his ideas and plans for 'saving Germany from its enemies'. The book is selling in the thousands. The attempted putsch increased Hitler's following. He is seen as a man of action, which is underlined by the Weimar Government's helplessness in dealing with him. One NSDAP member, G. Strasser, has been elected into parliament. Membership of this party is moving towards the 10,000 mark and encompasses all classes.

One of Hitler's close supporters is Dr. Paul Joseph Goebbels, Ph.D. Heidelberg, a Prussian who has attended several universities. He has risen fast in the party ranks and is a brilliant orator. It is strange that such a cultured and highly educated man supports a man like Adolf Hitler. I have listened to speech by A.H. in a large beer cellar hall.

Summarising, in my opinion, Herr Adolf Hitler is a dangerous man. He believes in what he is preaching and successfully cashes in on widespread suffering and dissatisfaction in Germany. He appeals to a large spectrum of the population. He creates enthusiasm as well as fear, a dangerous mixture. Critics claim he will say and do anything to reach the top and many believe he will succeed. He is seen by his opponents as a ruthless man of action and politically untrustworthy.

D.B.'

Beneath the initials a scribble had been added:

Chapter 1 – The Defence of the Realm

'Have been followed in streets this week, since interviewing two young Nazis at Hofbräuhaus. Am trying to identify follower'

There was another note: *Hilda Strasser's father is the brother of Gregor Strasser, both prominent leaders in the Nazi movement.* It puzzled Sinclair but seemed of no importance. Important was that Burnley believed he was in danger. Sinclair had no doubts left. David Burnley had been murdered and very probably by Nazis, because he had been making enquiries about their party. And he, Sinclair, had approved his task. It was not the first time that his orders had put agents in danger and he knew it would not be the last time. But this time, for diplomatic reasons, he could not even set an investigation in process. Unless this Captain Jameson, the sender of the package, was doing so of his own accord, nothing could be done. He gave it a lot of thought. He had to hurry as the efficient Henrietta was due to collect his internal outgoing post within the next half hour. He slipped the report into an envelope, addressed it to 'P. Cormody, Eu. S.', marked it 'By Hand' and 'Re David Burnley'. He put the envelope into the Out tray, ready for the efficient Henrietta's arrival and turned his attention to other matters.

In the late afternoon he received a telephone call from the SAB, the Service Accommodation Bureau. He listened, raised his eyebrows and put the phone down. A few moments later he picked it up again.

'Cormody.'

'Yes, Admiral.'

'Perry, old chap, your latest addition should have been reporting to you by now. New man, Ronald Burnley.'

He rarely used Cormody's first name. It indicated a state of satisfaction, no more.

'He has,' Cormody said, 'waited here for me mid-day, when I returned from a meeting. Not much of a talker. Shy type?'

Sinclair smiled. He was always amused by the mixture of Cormody's brevity of speech, the touch of suaveness in his voice and the sense of humour behind some of his actions and dispositions, although he disagreed with him strongly on political issues.

Chapter 1 – The Defence of the Realm

'You were on the final interviewing board. I'm convinced now Burnley's murder was connected with what he was doing. You've got the report. There's nothing shy about his son. He moved into Sandra's house last night and today her French daily has moved in with him.'

Cormody whistled quite unsuavely.

'La belle Lisette? What will Guy say? Surprised you recommended him. Reading University! Opening new doors?'

Sinclair said, 'And I was surprised at your low-grading his contract. Probably wise. Listen, old boy, the lad's not top drawer but he's top knowledge on Europe. I'd like you to arrange his probation year to be absolved abroad.'

'Because of the father?'

Cormody was a little doubtful about this newcomer's probation to be absolved abroad.

'Ye-es. I think so.' Sinclair was drawing the words out. 'David Burnley's done what you requested. It seems that Crane and Guy were right about this Herr Hitler, and Slater's report, just recently. I suppose that's why you asked for Burnley's investigation. I dare say it's worth keeping an eye on the new troublemaker, but no more than one. Opposed to the Commies – useful. I know you agree with Foch. You'll find out he was wrong. Our real danger comes from the Russians, take my word. They've got ready-made secret agents in our communist party and the trade unions. Well, it's your playing field, Perry. It was your commission that cost Burnley his life.'

He put the receiver down, pensively. Should he send a copy of David Burnley's report to the Foreign Office? In October of the previous year, Austen Chamberlain, the Foreign Secretary, had taken a leading role in concluding the Locarno Treaty whose agreements eased the conditions under which the war debts were being paid by Germany and Austria and made other concessions, such as the recognition of Germany as a great power and her acceptance into the League of Nations. Chamberlain and his team were totally convinced that this was all that was needed to calm German resentments. They would take no notice of this report. He decided against forwarding it. Politicians came and went. The Service remained and had the responsibility for Britain's security. Cormody read David Burnley's full report before the day was out.

He had a strong personal dislike and mistrust of what he considered to be the German mentality. He believed that every

German attempt to disobey the Versailles Treaty obligations should be dealt with swiftly and effectively. That man Hitler had been railing against the Versailles Treaties from the word go. His party was growing too fast for comfort. Cormody believed that a democratic Germany was essential for peace in Europe. This new party, in Cormody's opinion, should be stopped now when it was within their powers to do it. He felt that the German people were much more the stuff of future danger to peace in Europe, than Russian Communism, as much as he was opposed to the latter. As a Section Head he had considerable authority and he would not yield to Sinclair on this issue but he had no say in the overall MI6 policies. David Burnley's report fully underlined his judgement. What he did not know at his moment was that someone else in his Section had read the report before him and been impressed by it even more deeply than he.

* * *

The European Section's latest addition, agent Ronald Burnley, had arrived early that morning for his first day and spent a couple of hours going through a seemingly disconnected protocol. More details were registered. He met men in other offices, without knowing the who, the what or the wherefore. They fed him 'vital' information, each of them implying that his was the most important. He also encountered a couple more upper upper-class feminine personnel and even a few genuine bodies back from the 'field' for a few days and working there that day. Just before being allowed his lunch break, he was sent to report to Major Perry Cormody, the European Section Head. On the stairs he literally bumped into a woman in a hurry. She was the super-efficient Henrietta Alice Sherringham-Bingley, the Admiral's private under-secretary. Apologising, he picked up the envelope she had dropped. Colliding with a man on the stairs was not unusual for Henrietta. She was quite adept in it and it gave her an excuse to talk to them. For the collider to apologise was a new experience for her.

'Not at all, I'm always in a hurry, you know,' she replied. 'In my position, I don't usually run errands. You're the new chappie, aren't you?'

He nodded. Being called chappie was a new experience for him.

Chapter 1 – The Defence of the Realm

'I say, you're going to see Major Cormody. Would you mind awfully?' She pointed at the envelope. 'Just leave it on his table.'

When he arrived at Cormody's office, the major was not in and Ronald sat down to wait in a minuscule ante-room for a few moments. Glancing at the envelope in his hand, he could not fail to notice his father's name on the envelope. For one moment shock was his only reaction. In the next moment he noticed that the envelope was not stuck down, so he reacted the way that any conscientious MI6 agent would have done, he inspected its contents. It meant spending another moment reading it. It became the longest moment he'd ever experienced up to date. He read every word with intensity and a growing sore heart. He, too, was puzzled by the note about Hilda Strasser and, like Sinclair, he did not consider it of any importance.

There had not been the slightest doubt in his mind, that his father had been the victim of a street mugging. Now, reading the security man's, Craig Jameson's covering letter and his father's scribbled last lines, he came to the same conclusion as the admiral: his father had been murdered by those Nazis he'd written about. Together with his father's judgement of this new German party, the word Nazi immediately assumed an ugly image in his mind. It was Friday, the 19th November 1926, a date he would never forget. Being blessed with total recall is not always a total blessing. Every word of the report was etched forever in his mind. And he was now the member of an organisation that might enable him to visit Germany in the foreseeable future. He did not know what his tasks were going to be in his new job, but there was one that he set for himself as a personal and primary duty.

Ronald thoroughly enjoyed his training in London. The bulk of his emotions were involved in his new task of becoming a skilled agent in MI6, a vista whose backcloth included recurring thoughts about his father. There was, as yet, little room for much else. He had always enjoyed being naturally fit. He now gloried in the growing standard of fitness he enjoyed at his daily morning sessions at the gym whenever he was in London. The programme was controlled by a Greek, called Patroclos.

It contained a system of exercises and unarmed combat, fine-tuning Ronald's body to a high level. The body's enjoyment was enhanced by an effortlessly pleasant home life: a tasty meal in the evening, the company of a beautiful and interesting woman and a warm body beside him at night with its natural physical delights. At university he had enjoyed French lessons in developing those natural

Chapter 1 – The Defence of the Realm

skills. They helped to produce an attractive existence to which he had no problem getting accustomed quickly. An outside observer might have branded Ronald as just another macho exploiter of his female partner. It was factually correct but not a true picture. Soon after the start of their relationship, he had given Lisette equal access to his current bank account, without restricting its use to household expenses. Yet, if asked, he would have had to admit that it was a situation of convenience which he took for granted. Lisette, herself, had no feeling of being exploited. She was aware of a powerful, inner surge.

As far as she was concerned she had fallen on her feet at last. She had also fallen in love with Ronald, love in the purest sense. A feeling she had never experienced before. But as far as she was concerned, this was forbidden fruit for her. In contrast to this emotional surge, she was suffering from a new, harsh, perspective of her past, an understanding of how her mother's and her own early life appeared, when seen through the eyes of what society called respectability. As a result she lacked self-esteem. Whereas she would never think ill of her mother, she was developing a desire for being respectable, herself. Or so she thought at this stage: wanting to be respected. She did not realise that Ronald had never given a critical thought to her past and did respect her, but he did not feel a commitment to being faithful to her. A significant part of Ronald was still the little boy who, naively, accepted and enjoyed presents as they came.

At the end of the basic training, Ronald had to fulfil half a dozen special commissions. Each was made up of two months' work in the passport office of a British consulate in Europe followed by one month back in London. During that month he had to attend at 54 Broadway, submitting reports, giving talks to newcomers and doing administrative jobs. He liked doing his European stints in places where he had been with his father. Yet, not only had conditions in those capitals changed a lot, but so had he, himself. He consciously had not attempted to reconnect with anyone he had known then. On the other hand, he fully took advantage of encounters of the sexual kind.

When, at last, Germany was next on the list, he sent a letter to Major Cormody, requesting to do this particular mission in Munich, instead of Berlin. His attempt of giving a cogent reason for the request was exceptionally weak and so was his expectation for his request to be granted. But he had to try.

Chapter 2 – The Cranes of Ibycus

During the last week of June 1928, the staff bulletin at the British Consulate in Munich displayed the information that the staff of the passport division was to be increased by an additional body, name of Captain Ronald Burnley. Captain Craig Jameson, the consulate's Security Officer, found this unusual, knowing that one more person on the staff would be supernumerary to the establishment. Jameson was a tall and lean man, with a square face and a high forehead. A permanent frown above a gently curved eagle's nose separated a pair of narrow grey eyes which could make the person facing them feel very uncomfortable. He rarely relaxed but an experienced physiognomist might detect hidden lines of humour in his face.

When Jameson read a follow-up memo with details regarding the posting, his frown deepened. On the other hand, one of the details, namely that Captain Ronald Burnley was going to remain with the consulate for a limited period, made more sense, as it did not make him a supernumerary. The man's name seemed familiar.

Ronald had been pleasantly surprised to have his request for Munich approved without any hassle. He even received an accommodation address in advance. Lisette realised that he was going to the place where his father had been murdered. On the morning of his departure, she said:

'Ronnee,' she always accentuated the second syllable. 'You will be careful, *n'est-ce-pas?*'

He looked at her, startled, and was hit by something in her beautiful eyes he had not noticed before – a sense of understanding, of caring, and a sadness. Quite suddenly, in one split moment, Lisette had established a new relationship with him. They were living together, they had sex together, but he had not met who she really was. During the fateful next two months abroad, the thought worked itself into his consciousness. He arrived in Munich on the first Sunday of July 1928 and went straight to the little flat whose address he had been given. The caretaker handed him the key and a brief note with an undecipherable signature. He reported to the consulate for work on Monday morning, showing the note, and was

Chapter 2 – The Cranes of Ibycus

directed to an office on whose door a small plaque read SECURITY. He knocked. A voice sounded the customary reply: 'Enter.'

He entered. The man, sitting on the edge of his desk, rose.

'Captain Burnley? I'm Craig Jameson. Take a seat.'

'Thank you, Mr. Jameson.' He sat down.

Jameson was not a man of formalities.

'Mr. Gaisford, the consul, is away and has asked me to receive you. As far as your job's concerned, it's straightforward. You have your own office; you'll be pleased to know. We don't touch political matters here; they're dealt with in Berlin. The consulate mostly deals with problems concerning British citizens in Southern Germany, with commercial issues arising and with applications by Germans wanting to visit Britain of which there are many – yeah?'

'Sorry, I was surprised about the last item, Captain Jameson.'

'Yeah. There's a few British organisations that work at rebuilding harmonious relations with the German people. It involves a lot of paperwork. Initially, our admin staff simply filed it the usual way. Now the FO's decided it needs re-organising to be separate and easily accessible, in case any of these visitors need re-checking. It's up to you to evolve a filing system. That's basically what your job is, here. But you're also required to do a routine check on each application, including the past ones, in case something's in the slightest way suspicious. You'll be your own boss and able to communicate with London if you have problems. It's hoped that during your time here, you'll catch up on the backlog and leave behind an up-to-date system that can be used by whoever takes on the job after you. In turn, I'll give you an insight into security issues. That's it, really. Feel free to come to me in all matters concerning your stay here. I hope you find your accommodation adequate. Any questions?'

Ronald detected a slight American twang in the captain's speech but that wasn't of any importance to him.

'The flat's fine, Captain Jameson – I'm glad to find you're still here.'

Still? Jameson was puzzled. He had never met this man before although he vaguely reminded him of someone. Ronald came straight to the point.

'Two years ago you sent a report to the Foreign Office about the murder of David Burnley.'

Chapter 2 – The Cranes of Ibycus

It took Jameson seconds to remember and the resemblance, too, jumped into place.

'You're in Sinclair's lot?'

Ronald nodded. Jameson looked carefully at him.

'You're his son?'

Ronald grinned.

'If I am, then the Admiral's never admitted it.' He nodded, 'David Burnley was my father.'

Jameson was not used to facetious humour. Taking it for granted that Ronald had seen his report, he added, 'I did acquire more information subsequently but it was of no practical use. I knew nothing of your existence. We'll have lunch at my restaurant, buddy, and I'll tell you about it.'

Ronald had long and often been telling himself that there was no chance of his ever finding out the truth about his father's murder, especially so late after the event, but to try had, for two years now, remained a compulsive emotion inside him. He knew that the SIS employed special agents for the execution of extreme, secret, often unlawful tasks, but he was not one of those. He knew that even if, against every expectation, he could trace the murderer, he would almost certainly not be able to do anything about it. Worse, his probation period was not ending until after the next stint, for which he expected to be sent to Austria. However, Jameson's words raised a tiny spark of hope. The man actually had more information?

At mid-day they walked together to the Security Captain's regular restaurant. When they entered, Jameson, with an elegant movement, flicked his hat in the direction of the line of deer horn shaped hat-hooks on the wall. Later Ronald found out they were deer horns which explained their shapes. Jameson missed and, without batting an eyelid, picked up his hat and hung it up. They sat down at his regular table and waited for two large glasses of beer to land in front of them before he started.

'One of our social contacts in the town is a pro-British Jewish family: *Justizrat*, that's the equivalent of a King's Counsel, Dr. Elias Strauss, and his wife, a G.P. and surgeon Dr. Rachel Strauss. They were introduced to us at an event at the English Library. Both are known for charitable and social works. She, for instance, regularly treats patients who can't afford to pay. A couple of days after I sent off the report about your father's murder, I was guest at one of their receptions. In a conversation about the new Nazi party, I heard Dr.

Chapter 2 – The Cranes of Ibycus

Strauss (med), mention that one of her patients had claimed to have seen a murder being committed by two Nazis. The date caught my attention.'

Ronald had difficulties controlling himself, while Jameson stopped to take a swig from his glass. Ronald automatically followed suit. Jameson continued.

'I enquired. She made plain from the start she couldn't pass on details about her patient but she did tell me that the patient was a young woman. She had told her that she had been in the Maximilian Park, that's by the river, late at night, waiting for a man friend who didn't turn up. She heard loud voices, thought they were drunks and hid in the bushes. She witnessed two men knifing a third and heard one of them gloat about having dealt with an enemy of their Führer. When she eventually came out from hiding, frightened and expecting to see a body, there was none.'

Seeing Ronald's narrowed eyes, his tight lips and clenched fists, Jameson stopped.

'I'm sorry, Burnley. I didn't—'

Ronald shook his head.

'I must know.'

'That's about it,' Jameson said. 'The doctor had suggested to her patient, she should go to the police, but the girl and her mother were adamant. Dr. Strauss's husband, the lawyer, was certain the girl's story would not be acceptable evidence. Convinced me, too. That's why I didn't send another report.'

Their meals were served and for a while they ate in silence. But Ronald could not leave it there.

'I need to speak to this woman. Do you think the doctor...?'

Jameson thought for a moment.

'I'm sure she'll be willing to meet you. Coming from you, the request will have more weight.'

Ronald was content.

'Thanks.' He began to relax.

'How do you like this place?' Jameson asked.

'Interesting name, Kühbogen, cows-bend or cows-bow? The beef tastes good.'

Jameson agreed. 'Can't fault the food. How was your first morning? Boring?'

'On the contrary. I've come across interesting applications. Some of the applicants even have family in Britain, from before the war.

Chapter 2 – The Cranes of Ibycus

One was visiting his brother who'd been a prisoner-of-war on the Isle-of Man and was allowed to stay. In Manchester. Amazing.'

'Yeah, amazes me, too. Shows up the stupidity of the war.'

The food and the beer were doing their bit to soften the atmosphere. Although Craig was almost ten years older than Ronald, that indefinable yet clear and immediate sense of immediate liking that happens sometimes, was building its bridge and by the time the dessert took its turn a bond had taken roots. Craig hadn't let his hair down like this for some time. An innate sense of humour had been suppressed for a long time. Apropos nothing, he said:

'It's only a few minutes' walk and, as you say, the food's OK. Why not use it yourself, whilst you're here? Join me?'

Ronald was visibly pleased.

'I'll be glad to. What do you do for entertainment?'

'Ah, there's one place you mustn't miss, buddy, when in Munich – the *Hofbräuhaus*' (court brewery). How about Wednesday night? Have you heard of it?'

Ronald laughed.

'Heard's the appropriate word, Captain Jameson. I was fifteen I think, no, sixteen, when I first heard it. In Vienna, at a wine-garden my father took us to. Amazing. The Viennese were starving but the wine gardens were full.'

To Jameson's surprise, he broke into song with a line of a famous drinking song: *'In München steht ein Hofbräuhaus, oans, zwoa, gsuffa!'* (In Munich stands a court brewery, one, two, down-the-hatch!) and toasted the world to each of the last three words, totally out of character but luckily not out of tune. Although he had kept his voice down, some of the other guests were looking in his direction. Normally, they did not hear anyone break into a drinking song in the middle of the day, at least not in this restaurant and never before an Englishman. 'The English aren't used to our beer' their glances were saying. Craig burst into silent, though visible laughter.

'After only one glass.'

Ronnie was in full swing:

'Glass? Don't insult it. This is a stein, a one-litre tankard. When you've half emptied it, it encourages you. So, naturally…'

Craig chuckled.

'One-and-three quarters pints, in English. But let's get one thing straight – for my drinking companions I'm Craig, OK?'

Chapter 2 – The Cranes of Ibycus

He did not add that he had not had any such for a very long time. Ronald was more honest.

'You're the first one I've ever had, Craig. Your German's pretty good, I noticed.'

'Guilty,' Craig said. 'I spent a year at Heidelberg. Didn't like it. German students are a peculiar race. Duelling code of honour. Scars in faces essential. They didn't like me either. But it was useful, learning the language, I mean. Matter of fact, I don't spread it around. It's useful, sometimes, if folk don't know. Everybody speaks English, so why bother?'

'I'll bear it in mind. You're right, I'm not used to that much beer and it's misled me.'

He did not add that what he heard from Jameson on his very first working day in Munich, had acted as a stimulating factor. Craig took another sip.

'So how about Wednesday? Do you know that a waiter there can carry six full tankards in each hand without spilling a drop? That's twelve litres.'

'I didn't. Are they empty? Sure I'll come but you've heard me sing, so don't say you haven't been warned.'

'No hustle. I'll raid our first-aid cupboard for cotton wool.'

At this point, conversation subsided into even more trivial topics. After the dessert Craig looked at his watch and waved to the waiter. There was no word lost about the bill. Each paid his own.

'Time to get back, Ronald. I got to see someone at the *Rathaus'* (Town Hall).

'In Vienna, my mother insisted, its name has historically to do with the Pied Piper.'

* * *

During the afternoon his mind was filled with speculation about what he might find out about his father's death. He also gave a frowning thought to his reaction to the beer. Never again! Just before he left, a clerk delivered a note from Craig.

'Change of Wednesday's plans. Instead of Hofbräuhaus, the Cafe Luitpold, Brienner Strasse 11. Consul and colleagues invited to drinks by Doctors Strauss. You've been promoted to colleagues. Opportunity to meet the doctors. From 9 p.m. Wear your best, place palatial. Pick you up 7.30. Craig.'

Chapter 2 – The Cranes of Ibycus

Whereas this 'Drinks' occasion turned out not to be the kind of social gathering Ronald enjoyed, it did bring him an invitation from Dr. Strauss (med), for tea the next day. He had prepared a mild cover story of being posted to Munich by coincidence so, naturally, being here, he wanted to find out as much as possible about what had happened to his father. A maid took Ronald's hat when he arrived. She showed him into a sitting room, which she called the '*Salon*', adjoining the surgery and announced him. To his surprise, he found her husband there, also. Their welcome was cordial and in good though not accent-free English. He guessed rightly that they had reservations about his enquiries. In his mind he thought of them as 'jus' and 'med' respectively. It was Strauss 'jus' who initiated the conversation.

'I understand that you have only just arrived in our city, Mr. Burnley? What are your first impressions?'

Ronald replied, 'Much better than I expected. No rows of empty shops. Not as much inflation as some of the European cities I've seen this year.'

The lawyer nodded.

'Since the devaluation in twenty-five, things have been getting better slowly. We have a good man at the top now.'

'Yes, Mr. Burnley,' Dr. Strauss (med) finished pouring the tea. 'Herr Stresemann has the right policies. Had you been here three years ago you would have had to carry a briefcase full of banknotes to buy one loaf of bread – if there was one in the shops for sale. Today they're talking about a golden age. Golden? Hah!' The last word was a strong ironic sound.

'It has at least begun to reduce the mob's support for Herr Adolf Hitler, I'm glad to note,' her husband said. 'Do they know about that man and his party in your country?'

'I do,' Ronald replied. After a short pause, he added, looking at the doctor med, 'According to what you've told my colleague, my father may have been murdered by Nazis.'

Dr. Strauss (med) nodded slowly in compassion.

'It must have been terrible for you and your mother, Mr. Burnley. The Nazis are ruthless people. They worry me. I'm less optimistic than my husband.'

Consulting his watch, the lawyer was rising, 'I'm afraid, I must leave. My wife is right about the violent element in that party, Mr. Burnley. I hope she can persuade the young woman to talk to you

Chapter 2 – The Cranes of Ibycus

but do not let your hopes rise. Whatever she claims she has seen and heard, she is not a good witness, quite apart from that it happened two years ago. Any counsel for the defence, cross-examining her, would be able to discredit her story. Another thing also, I regret to have to tell you: it might not be safe for her to appear in court. The lawless element in Munich is strong. On the other hand, should you find out something that is a fact and would be acceptable as such by the police, come and see me. I am in regular touch with a few decent *Kripos*, criminal police that is, who will look into the matter if they believe they might unearth evidence. They would also check out information at my request.' He prevented Ronald from rising. 'Do not trouble yourself, please, Mr. Burnley. It is a pleasure that I have made your acquaintance and I hope we shall meet again. My wife and I feel with you on your loss. We like the English and were strongly opposed to the Emperor's war policies. Now he is enjoying a comfortable retirement in Holland and look what he has done to his people.'

He emptied his cup, consulted his watch, and strode out. Dr. Strauss (med) refilled their cups.

'My husband trusts your discretion and is in favour of giving you our support. But he is right about the girl. She has been a patient since three years ago, suffering from hysteria. She is not a born German. Her mother was married to an Italian man. I cannot give you more details but I can tell you they are not well off. A little gift of money would be a strong inducement for the mother to let the daughter talk to you – if I can promise them that you will not involve them with the police. But what about language? I do not think they speak English and I am not—'

'Kein Problem, Doktor Strauss,' Ronald interrupted her and assured her, in fluent German, of his complete discretion in either language. She reacted in utter surprise, laughing at herself.

'You must forgive my words as well as my reaction, Mr. Burnley, your countrymen are not known for speaking German and speaking it as well as you. It was rude of me. Oh dear, one faux pas after another.'

He smiled reassuringly and did not mention his fluent Italian.

'How much do you suggest, Dr. Strauss, 10 Mark? More?'

'My goodness, no. That's too much. It might be interpreted as bribery. Five Mark is generous. I will speak to the mother. I suspect you will have to go to their place. I cannot offer you our house and I

Chapter 2 – The Cranes of Ibycus

do not think a public place would be wise. I shall send you a message.'

That evening Ronald gave serious thought to what he was doing. He must avoid making waves. He did not want either the German authorities or his own bosses to learn about his enquiries. Was interviewing the girl really a good idea? It did not sound as if, even if she had been witness to the deed, she was likely to provide any substantial information that might help exposing the murderers. His chances of finding them by himself were minimal. But he had to try. Then he had an idea. At lunch the next day he was at the Kühbogen before Craig and watched his entry routine, namely, his hat elegantly missing the deer horns. As soon as he had sat down, Ronald came straight out with it.

'I need to make a confession, Craig.'

Craig raised his eyebrows.

'Before we've ordered? Sounds serious.'

'Well... The report you sent to London two years ago, about my father's death. I read it.'

'I know that alr...' Craig, stopping himself, looked thoughtfully at Ronald. 'I see. You weren't supposed to. Then, how?'

'By accident. I happened to be delivering the envelope that contained it. The envelope was not stuck down so I read it.'

Craig, still puzzled, asked, 'Why tell me? You want me to do something connected with it.'

'You're a mind-reader. Yes, a follow-up.'

Craig, after giving it some thought, nodded. 'The answer's yes. I've a professional responsibility in this. What exactly?'

Ronald told him about his conversation with the Strausses.

'Would you interview this young woman for me, Craig? You know place and people, the whole situation in fact, better—'

Craig interrupted him, 'It'll be a pleasure. You don't look frightening enough, anyway. Let me have the details. Can I order now? I'm hungry.'

On Saturday Dr. Strauss's card was delivered to Ronald, simply quoting the girl's name, 'Rina Lenzio', and her address. He passed it to Jameson who confirmed what Dr. Strauss had said.

'Haidhausen. The poor quarter. Ah, it's adjoining the park where she said she was. OK, Ronald, leave it with me.'

At their Monday lunch, Jameson handed Ronald an envelope.

'I've made it an official report to the Foreign Office. Even if they suspect you've had something to do with it they can't blame you.'

Ronald saw the common sense in that. Whilst ladling the liver-dumplings soup, one of his favourites, he read through the report, typed on the Consulate's headed paper. There was nothing new, except for one small item, a musical one.

Confidential Report

9 July, 1928

Re: Murder of David Burnley, British FO, Oct. 1926

This statement follows my report of 8 October 1926. I've ascertained that David Burnley was murdered late on the night of Thursday, 7 October, 1926, in Maximilian Park, a park stretching along the east bank of the River Isar. Against my promise of complete secrecy, I was able to interview a young woman, an Italian by birth, who was in the park late that night and, from a distance, watched the murder taking place.

In my judgement her statement is correct as far as it goes, but according to reliable legal advice, given her state of fright, the relative darkness at the time and the distance from which she observed, she would not be a reliable witness in a Court of law. The girl who is now twenty years old, stated that she was waiting for a male friend near an open space in which the column and sculpture of the 'Angel of Peace' is located. Her friend did not turn up. She heard the sounds of loud men's voices approaching, reflecting protests and anger. She was frightened and hid behind bushes, about ten yards away. She saw men arriving, two of them holding the arms of a third who was wearing glasses and a hat. She thought he was only half-heartedly protesting, which suggests that he did not think he was in any serious danger. The men appeared to be demanding something from him, which he refused to give them.

This might possibly have been Mr. Burnley's report which he had left with me and which I forwarded to you two years ago. Next, shouting, struggling and scuffling broke out between one of the men, who she thinks was the thickset, smaller of the two, and the man with the hat. The first had a knife in his hand. She

Chapter 2 – The Cranes of Ibycus

saw its glint, and heard the other man cry out. She closed her eyes and covered her mouth, sobbing and scared of giving away her presence. Next she heard the killer telling his companion that the man's death was a just punishment for an enemy of Hitler. At this point the witness thinks she fainted, perhaps out of fear.

In telling her story, the woman displayed signs of extreme nervousness and anxiety, even two years after the event. She had left her hiding place only when she felt sure that the men had gone and found no sign of the victim. David Burnley's body was found the next day in a street not far from the park but there is no evidence to prove a connection.

The girl further mentioned that throughout the time that she was in the park, before and while she was hiding, the sound of a record at full blast was heard coming from an open window in a street near-by. She knows the song from her childhood in Naples. It is called 'O sole mio'. I have learned that the Italian tenor Beniamino Gigli's recording of it was on sale in Munich at that time. The girl also stated that she heard the killer say something to the effect that the record helped covering up the sound of their victim's shouts and this proved that God was on their side.

Should any other information on this matter emerge, I shall forward it.

Signed: Craig Jameson, Captain, i/c Security

Countersigned by: Hugh William Gaisford, Consul-General

Ronald could not read the document without experiencing moments of stark pain and anger. He suppressed it, but Jameson saw the signs. Over the years he had developed an immunity to emotions. The fresh, likeable personality of this young MI6 man was having an influence on his own feelings. He pondered over it. Was there a place in this business for emotions? Ronald, meanwhile, had come to his own conclusions.

'Thanks, Craig. So, two of them, both supporters of Hitler. But nix to take to the Justizrat.'

Chapter 2 – The Cranes of Ibycus

'You could tell him about the record, Ronald. The girl's account sounded lucid. If Strauss can get his police contacts to confirm it. Perhaps people sent complaints in and in my experience they would have done here in Munich, then we know at least that the girl was talking reality.'

Ronald shook his head.

'Still a dead end. No names, no descriptions. For two years I've been carrying this idea with me that, if I could be posted here, I might... With your help, Craig, I've come to know a lot more of what happened within an incredibly short time. But ahead – no light, not even a tunnel. What I see clearly is that there's no more to see. I'm here till October and I've got a job to do.'

His usually cheerful voice betrayed stabs of gloom. Craig switched subjects.

'There are also things here to enjoy, Ronnie. You haven't forgotten the lure of the excellent brew served in the steins of the illustrious *Hofbräuhaus*? I haven't had an excuse for a visit for a long time. It might cheer us up.'

'I'm game, as the partridge said to the hunter,' Ronald swallowed the last spoonful of his favourite soup. 'Just say when.'

'In that case,' Craig said, 'this Wednesday will not be too soon.'

And that spontaneous decision changed Ronald's stay in Munich in a way that neither of the two could possibly have foreseen. The zig-zags of the path followed by coincidence once again left their marks on Ronald's progress in life.

On Wednesday night they sat in a restaurant hall with typical Bavarian décor on the first floor of the *Hofbräuhaus*. Its chairs and benches on both sides of the rows of wooden tables were crowded, although not totally full. The air was filled with beer and cigarette haze and clashing sound waves, some of which were provided by a brass orchestra performing at the entrance end of the hall. Craig had ordered beer with Wurst and Kraut and a large pretzel for each from a passing waiter, as soon as they had sat down at one of the few empty wooden tables. Ronald was looking around.

'It's not unlike the Heurigen, the wine gardens in Vienna where they serve new wine which tastes light and feels heavy, my father's words. I wasn't allowed to taste it, so I didn't feel it. He said he wasn't strong enough to carry me home. The music's different. Only beer here? Where are the waiters carrying a dozen steins?'

Chapter 2 – The Cranes of Ibycus

'I don't suppose they carry them just to make an impression,' Craig explained, 'but let me warn you, don't ask for any other kind of drink. The Hofbräuhaus only serves beer and only its own make. I almost put my foot in it the first time I set my foot in here at the invitation of a local contact. He told me an anecdote. It was probably true because he quoted the exact date, a day back in 1908. A foreign visitor asked for a glass of lemon juice. None of the waitresses was willing to serve him but they bombarded him with invective and abuse. The guest refused to budge and insisted on his right to get what he ordered. He probably didn't understand their swearwords. In the end the manager, himself, had to come and serve him his lemon juice.'

'Had to?'

'This place is owned by the Bavarian government, I believe, so he probably had to. Anyway, you've been warned about the militant waitresses here, so be careful because I think one's just bee-lining us from behind you with our beer and pretzels. My host told me that they know swearwords that the average Münchener has not heard of.'

The next moment a waitress appeared from behind Ronald and put her tray down beside him. As she straightened up and they saw each other face to face, both reacted similarly, with a puzzled frown followed by a searching look which changed into the amazed astonishment of recognition settling in their faces. Hers was the first to thaw, as she said, wonderingly, 'Ronald?' which he followed, in the same fashion, but an octave lower, give or take a few semitones, with, 'Gerda?' For another few seconds they continued to peer disbelievingly at each other, then she stepped back giving him room to stand up and close his arms around her, a gesture which she returned in equal measure. When they let go, he exclaimed, *'Wie kommst du hierher?'* (How do you come to be here?) and she echoed with *'Wie kommst du hierher?'* followed by a repeat of the embracing performance, this time making Ronald pleasurably aware of her outstanding features. Craig, who had been watching this enactment of a cliché stage scene, and forever concerned with what was really important, had quickly put his arms protectively around the two steins, the litre tankards of golden brew she had deposited on the table. Worried that they might continue the act, he took a turn, albeit only the oral one and in English.

Chapter 2 – The Cranes of Ibycus

'Something tells me you two have met before. How about sitting down, Fräulein? There's an empty chair here. Then you can continue to relate how you come to be here in comfort and at less danger to the drinks.'

This included a typical English understatement, proof of Craig's anglification, as there was considerably more than one empty chair available at their table. The two let go of each other. The waitress smiled. A very attractive, if not seductive, smile, Craig thought.

'Thank you, sir. I cannot do this but I have a break in a half hour and then I can sit with you, if this is all right for you, Ronald?'

'Is it. I'll not leave this spot until you're back,' Ronald replied, somewhat sheepishly. Then he added brightly, 'You've grown, Gerda.' He did mean upwards.

'You, too. You can rely on that I return. I have so many questions. I am not a thin little girl anymore.'

To Craig, this sounded like an understatement, but he kept his opinion to himself. She turned to go then turned back again, 'This is very strange, Ronald. Two years ago I was seeing a man sitting in our bar over there who looks like your father, I think. Twice I have seen him but he does not recognise me. Of course, Vienna was a long time ago and I was a young girl then. Also he was sitting with two other men, young fellows. And I decide to myself that when this man comes back the next time I shall ask him if he is your father or not. But he has never come back again. Not even once. And now when I see you, for one moment I think it is him. You look a lot like your father now, Ronald. Oh, there is one of our *Oberkellners'* (headwaiters). 'I must go and work but I come back in half an hour.'

She turned and hurried away. Ronald sat down, about to issue an apology to Craig. But the words did not escape his lips because, suddenly, his awareness of her last words had hit him. Craig broke the silence.

'If it isn't a military secret? Who is this Hebe, this Bavarian cupbearer? And are you thinking what I'm thinking? Your father did refer to interviewing two Nazis at this place.'

Ronald's face had gone taut.

'He did. It's a colossal coincidence. Her name's Gerda Flenk and she's not Bavarian. I met her in Vienna, when my mother and I were there with my father. I was an immature 16 and she was a very mature 17.' He broke into a grin, 'She was never thin. I can't imagine how she's come to be a waitress here in Munich.'

Chapter 2 – The Cranes of Ibycus

His grin rapidly yielded to the returning thoughts of his father. When, half an hour later, Gerda rejoined them, Craig displayed an unsuspected sense of discretion and took himself to the bar for another beer. Gerda, herself, did not suffer from a similar sense. She sat down close to Ronald, speaking German with a Viennese accent, rapidly and uninhibitedly the way he remembered her.

'Do you remember, Ronald, I was very hot for you. You were the first boy with whom I kissed like that, you know. But you did not – so, after you left, I was going with the brother of a boy in my class. He was not so shy and I seduced him – instead of you. And I became pregnant. So my mother insisted I get rid of the baby and, after the operation, which is illegal in Vienna, I come to Munich, very unhappy. My father has an old friend here. You know what Austria is like. Full of Catholic strictness and hypocrisy. It isn't really different here, of course. My papa was a rebel and I've always been one. But he is a Communist and, at that time, I wasn't anything really. But what are you doing here? You're not a tourist, are you? Oh, I'm so happy to see you again, Ronald.'

Her cheek leaned against his, which he did not find unpleasant at all.

'So am I. To see you, I mean. It's some coincidence,' he replied, 'to see you again – here in Munich of all places. Gerda, what did you say about seeing my father?'

'I think I recognised him but how could he have recognised me? He's never spoken with me when you were in Vienna. Your mother I remember better. She did not like you go out with me, do you remember? Yes, the man who looked like your father. Well, he was sitting with these two characters – twice, I think, on the same weekday, but I'm not sure. You know, Ronald, they weren't your father's kind of people and for this reason I was not sure that it was him. Do you think it can have been your father?'

He had to swallow several times before he was able to speak, almost in a whisper.

'It was my father, Gerda. You didn't know those two fellows, by any chance?'

She could not fail to detect the excitement in his voice and, changing to English, asked with concern, 'What is it, Ronald? No, I do not know them personally. What is troubling you? Tell me.'

He hesitated. Then he could not help himself:

'My father was murdered in this town about that time, Gerda.'

Chapter 2 – The Cranes of Ibycus

She put her hand to her mouth, *'Oh nein! Dos is schrecklich.'* (Oh no! That is terrible.) 'Murdered?' Eyes wide, she looked at him, searchingly. 'You think these two fellows can have had something to do with it?' Forehead wrinkled, she nodded slowly, 'Yes, they can. In the Nazi SA. It would not surprise me. This is why you are in München?'

'No, not exactly, but—'

She broke in with suppressed excitement.

'Ronald! These two fellows, the same ones, you know, they still come here often. Always on a Thursday evening. They always sit in the bar. You see, that crazy man, Herr Hitler, has his first big meeting here, upstairs in the grand hall, when he has become the new leader of that party. I was still in Vienna then, but they have told me. Because of this, often Nazis come here, like a pilgrimage, and they brag about it to everybody and about what he will do when he is in power. Like these two men. They drink a lot, they shout a lot and make a challenge to other guests to drink prost to their Führer. Sometimes a guest does but not many. Sometimes there is almost a fight but we have some waiters who are very big and strong.'

She pointed in the direction of one of them on the other side of the hall.

'That's Michel. He's one of the headwaiters, but no one would start a fight with him.'

From what Ronald could see of the man he could well believe it, but his mind was concentrating on what she had said about these two men, hardly believing his ears.

'They still come here? The two men with whom my father was talking?'

She nodded.

'Yes, exactly. The same two. Most Thursdays. You cannot make a mistake about them.' She stopped, leaning forward anxiously. 'No, Ronald, do not try... Surely you will not...? They are violent, dangerous, these people, believe me. They call themselves socialists but they're not socialists, that is sure. They are more like the Italian fascists, with Mussolini, you know. And they have their private army, the SA, in uniform, brown shirts and big belts and jackboots. They make people frightened, you know. And these two men are in this army because often they sit here wearing the brown shirts and belts and leather boots.'

'I must find out their names and addresses?'

Chapter 2 – The Cranes of Ibycus

Gerda sat up, collecting her thoughts. This was no longer the boy she had known and she was no longer the teenage girl she had been. An undeniable fact. She looked at him long and steadily.

'You are determined, *net wahr?'* (Aren't you?) 'I can see that you are. OK, Ronald, the answer is yes. I can do this for you.'

'Do what? You mean, find out?'

She moved her face close to his.

'Ronald, my English boyfriend. Do you ever think of me? I've thought of you a lot. You were so shy and innocent. I have often wondered whether I will ever see you again and I dream when – are you married? Please, tell me, Ronald. Yes, I can find out about them, I believe.'

Craig was approaching, feeling he'd given them enough time, when he saw her cheek close to Ronnie's. He promptly turned back to the bar, ordering another beer. *I hope he appreciates the things I do for him*, he thought, feeling very virtuous. He stifled other, more private thoughts threatening to rise up inside him. He had done with all that years ago.

Ronald wasn't sure about his reply. It was true that he had been very innocent, but his rejection to her physical advances had been due to wafting fears and ignorance. He had often regretted it when thinking back. Aimée had freed him of both. Aimée had also taught him to see sex as a natural pleasure the way she saw it. Commitment or even faithfulness was not part of it. Successive experiences had reinforced this view. He knew by now, that this was in total contradiction to the professed standards of private behaviour in the wider environment he inhabited. He did not foster the occasional thoughts about eternal love and marriage. His parents' relationship was at least partly the cause of that. His thoughts strayed to Lisette. Due to the nature of events, the relationship with her was lasting much longer than any previous ones. He felt a high degree of responsibility for her and, when at home, enjoyed her presence as much as their lovemaking. He had always assumed that it was the same for her. Now, Gerda's question caused him to question his assumption.

'If you do not want to tell me, Ronald, it does not matter.' Gerda responded to Ronald's silence.

'No, it's all right, Gerda. I do have a girlfriend living with me when I am at home in London and I'm fond of her.'

Chapter 2 – The Cranes of Ibycus

'Just like me, Ronald,' she said, taking his hand. 'I've a boyfriend, Steffel. Steffel Holzer is a nice fellow and we live together in a friendship. It is a good friendship with no promises. He's working in Hamburg till the end of October.'

She was caressing his hand and, unconsciously, pressing it to her cheeks and her body. The deep-rooted feelings of her teenage first great love had returned with a vengeance. A long-felt unfulfilled expectation had taken over.

'You will come home with me tonight, Ronnie, yes? I want you to.'

The request was accompanied by such enticing looks from a pair of beautiful brown eyes that many men would have found difficult to resist. Ronald could not think of a reason to, especially as he did not want to. He stood up.

'I'll tell Craig.'

He made his way towards the bar. Craig saw him approach and met him half-way.

'I know, Ronald. You're not coming back with me. How do you do it?'

Ronald, slightly embarrassed, shrugged his shoulders. He hadn't done anything. Nobody had. It just happened, like sunshine or rain. In this case, more like sunshine.

From that night on he did not sleep in the small flat in Munich, provided by the consulate, but only used it during the day. Gerda's home, even smaller, was in the *Pfisterstrasse* (Pfister Street), within walking distance of the Hofbräuhaus. He had a key and, although on most days their respective working times were practically reversed, the relationship turned out wholly satisfactory. They both knew that there was a strict time limit to it. It could be said that this arrangement was a fringe benefit to Ronald's search for his father's murderers, especially as the two suspect Nazi Stormtroopers had turned up promptly the very next night. Gerda pointed them out. If asked, he would have been unable to describe what he felt looking at the two men who might be his father's murderers. The truth was that he felt nothing. His mind refused to focus on that point. Instead, following his MI6 training, he concentrated on their physical personalities. Both men were blond and, not wearing their Stormtrooper's get-up on that occasion, were dressed in the traditional Bavarian gear of open-necked shirt and colourful braces holding up their lederhosen (leather shorts). One of them was only about 1.75m tall, but stocky and muscular. His hair was combed backwards, without a parting and flattened by lots of Brilliantine. Within only a few days Gerda had established their names.

'The little one with the bulldog face is called Rudi Steger, Ronald.'

'One of his ears looks smaller,' he had noticed.

'Yes. I've seen it close. It looks almost as if someone has bitten a piece off.'

'Mahlzeit.'

It was a typical, spontaneous reply for him, with no intention of making a joke. She giggled. *Mahlzeit* was the equivalent of 'Enjoy your meal'. Neither of them realised that she was right. During his teens, Steger had belonged to a boxing club. It had rewarded him with a pair of cauliflower ears and, in one particularly vicious bout, Steger's opponent had bitten off the end of his right ear, perhaps mistaking it for real cauliflower. It is not known whether he swallowed it or whether he had bitten off more than he could chew. Steger's friend was five centimetres taller with an effeminately good-looking face.

'The one with the pretty face is called Horst Lünecke, Ronald. I think he's 'warm'.' (warm = homosexual)

Ronald recalled the word from his school days in Vienna. The boys had used it to describe homo-sexual tendencies. Ronald grimly memorised everything about the two men, names, looks and voices. As Gerda had said, they were loud-mouthed. Whatever they said seemed aimed at impressing or challenging the people around them. Steger's voice was raucous and his language coarse. Lünecke's thin falsetto sounded more educated but his remarks were regularly re-echoing those of his friend. They made an odd pair. As unpleasant as they appeared, they behaved as if they hadn't a care in the world, certainly not like men with a bad conscience. But Ronald had nothing to go on, and yet developed a growing conviction that they were the guilty men.

Only two small facts underlined this feeling. One was the quite powerful circumstance of the two being seen with his father during the last days of his life. The other was the description by the less than reliable witness, that the murder had been committed by two men, one small and stocky. Various impossible ideas were floating through Ronald's mind, such as that of confronting the pair and asking them straight out whether they knew anything about his father's death. It kept returning but only because nothing else occurred to him, but he knew it was not a realistic idea. When he asked Gerda how she had been able to find out the names of the two Nazis, she told him that she was the member of a group that was strongly opposed to the new Nazi party.

She did not tell him that they were radical socialists who called themselves SAG, Socialist Action Group. Remaining anonymous, they indulged in direct, sometimes illegal and even daring actions in support of their views. Gerda's request for support in investigating two Nazis who were suspected of having committed a murder was agreed unanimously. It was the kind of action that appealed to the group. Gerda's views and her political maturity were valued by the members and so was her judgment.

Ronald told Jameson that he had obtained the men's names and addresses, hinting at Gerda's involvement with an anti-Nazi group. Jameson warned him.

'Be careful, Ronald. Don't get involved with any local political group unless it's part of a job you've been given. You'll be booted from your outfit faster than lightning and that mightn't be all, especially if it's a left-wing lot and from what you've mentioned about your Gerda, that's most likely. You'd get some rough treatment even from the Consul.'

Ronald realised the truth of this. He had followed Craig's initial suggestion and recently had called on Dr. Strauss (jus), with a typed excerpt from Craig's report of his interview with Rina Lenzio, which detailed her hearing the 'Sole Mio' record being played on the night of the murder. Dr. Strauss (jus) had had to go out and Dr. Strauss (med) prevailed upon Ronald to have tea with her. In the conversation, deriving from the suspected two Nazis, the subject of the growing anti-Semitism in Munich and in Germany generally came up. Rachel Strauss was very concerned.

'Personally, Mr. Burnley, I fear it is growing. The incidences are multiplying and I believe Jews will be unsafe here very soon. I am especially worried about it affecting my children's education. In some schools, Jewish pupils are already victimised, and not only by other pupils it is known. This is not a good place for my children to grow up. I am trying to get my husband to agree for the family to emigrate to Tel Aviv, a Jewish town in Palestine.'

The subject widened into a discussion about the German and English education systems. Having been taught in so many different schools, Ronald had made valid points. Anti-Semitism was an issue with which he had hitherto not concerned himself but thinking back he remembered incidents, particularly in Vienna. Her fears and her willingness to give up the high standing and the high level of comfort she and her husband were enjoying in Munich, surprised him. So did her idea of moving to what he imagined must be an uncivilised region in the world. Above all, it was new to him that the couple had children, no less than five, three boys and two girls, ages ranging from five to nineteen.

Within a matter of two days he received a note from the Justizrat with a copy of his police contact's reply: 'On the night of the 6 October, 1926, the Isartal police station received several complaints from residents living in the streets near the Maximilian Park about the nuisance caused by the loud playing of gramophone records after 2200 hrs. By the time the local patrol car reached the area this noise was no longer heard. In consequence, no official action was taken.'

Yet, it did nothing to further Ronald's hopes. On the face of it he seemed to have made a lot of progress in a very short time. He had the names and addresses of the two men he suspected and he knew that Rina Lenzio's story was likely to be correct. But it did not bring him a single step closer to his aim and, whichever way he looked at the situation, he saw no avenue of progress ahead. He told himself he must put the whole thing out of his mind, but attempting to do so was wholly unsuccessful. The image of his father's murder in the park would not leave his mind and the very thought of giving up made him feel guilty. On Monday morning he received another note from the same address, delivered by hand. This one came from Dr. Strauss (med). Referring to their conversation about schools, she invited him to join her in attending the annual end of school year show of the Wilhelmsgymnasium (Wilhelms Grammar School). It actually took place two days later, the first Wednesday after the end of term. Her son Frederic, in the top stream of the fifth year, was going to recite a ballad in it. Her husband was unable to attend so she happened to have a spare invitation.

Ronald was no lover of poetry recitals but could not refuse and so, on the Wednesday night, found himself seated beside Dr. Strauss (med), in the assembly hall of the school. She introduced her sixteen-year-old daughter, Hannah, as well as Hannah's friend, Naomi Kiss, to him. The two girls were both pretty in their own way. Hannah looked a lot like her mother – slim, dark hair, dark eyes, and a face that displayed a serious intelligence. In contrast to her looks, she was bubbly, full of the joie de vivre and still very much the school girl. Naomi, although only one year older, was two centimetres taller. Her youthful figure already displayed the beginnings of a mature outline. Her gently curved nose in a slim, well-shaped face might have been its most outstanding feature, were it not for two large, unusually beautiful, deep, grey-blue eyes which looked out into the world seeming to ask a question. And those eyes kept looking in Ronald's direction throughout the evening. With the girls sitting on the other side of Dr. Strauss, he did not notice it. But Dr. Strauss did, feeling slightly worried. She felt responsible, having brought about this meeting. Unconsciously aware of being in the company of three attractive females, Ronald's anticipation of boredom faded and he yielded to the theatre-like atmosphere of anticipation in the hall. He was rewarded, finding the evening interesting and uplifting.

He was surprised by the quality of performances, and it peaked when it was Frederic's turn. The dramatic manner in which he declaimed a ballad by Schiller: *Die Kraniche des Ibykus* (The Cranes of Ibycus), heightened by a group of pupils miming the story on stage in sync with Frederic's recital, gripped the audience's attention. Ronald knew relatively much about plays by Friedrich von Schiller but had not come across this ballad. Frederic's clear voice, betraying only the bare beginnings of change, was telling the tale of the lyrical singer Ibycus, on his way to the Games in Corinth:

When crossing through a silent grove of spruces, he is attacked by two robbers, who end up killing him. At the moment of dying, Ibycus sees a flight of cranes passing overhead and calls out to them:

'Bear witness, cranes, as you fly further.

As there's no human eye about,

I call on you to 'venge my murder!

And with these words his life ebbs out.'

The crowds in Corinth are upset to hear the announcement of the murder of one of their best-loved performers. In the arena, the fearful song of the Erinnyes, the avenging spirits, is sending shudders through the multitudinous listeners. Suddenly the sky is darkened by the arrival of a flight of cranes and from the highest steps of the stadium a voice is calling out: 'Look up, look up, Timotheus, up there, the cranes of Ibycus!' The cry gives the two robbers away. They are dragged before the judge and confess their

Chapter 2 – The Cranes of Ibycus

deed. When Frederic's recital ended, the audience sat still for a few seconds before breaking into applause.

Dr. Strauss, visibly proud of her son, whispered, 'Frederic is very good in Greek. He has chosen this ballad, because it is based on an old Greek legend, which he read in his study book. The Drama teacher is a brilliant producer.'

At the end of the evening Frederic joined them and his mother introduced Ronald as 'Our English friend.' When they stood outside she said, 'You must come and meet the other children. We're not going away this summer.' Then she added, 'I forgot to ask you, Mr. Burnley, how is your investigation going?'

He told her that he was convinced now that the murderers were not ordinary robbers. He used the word unconsciously, still under the spell of the ballad. The three youngsters, who had lagged behind, talking to school friends, were catching up with them and now he noticed Naomi's eyes being fixed upon him. He could not help being impressed by their beauty.

When saying good night, shaking hands with them, Frederic said, in surprisingly good English, 'You will come and visit to us, Mr. Burnley, yes, please?'

The sincerity in the boy's voice remained in Ronald's busy thoughts as he left them. On his way to Gerda's flat, his thoughts were chewing and digesting the story of Frederic's ballad. Its tale of two murderers was reminding him of his father's murder and all kinds of ideas swirled through his head. In between, Naomi's eyes took fleeting turns in attracting his attention. Instead of going straight home, he went for a stroll through the streets, trying to straighten his mind into thinking rationally. A number of people in Munich had, within a short time, become connected to his personal issue, starting with Craig Jameson, MI5, whose involvement had begun two years ago. There was the young Rina Lenzio, whose statements had convinced him that his father had been murdered by two members of the National Socialist Party.

There was the Strauss couple. She had led him to the witness. Her husband, the lawyer, was prepared to take the matter up if Ronald could provide useful evidence. And there was Gerda Flenk, warm and passionate, who had offered warmth and sex and practical help from a militant group of radical young socialists, whatever that meant. And finally there were the two suspects, themselves – Rudi Steger and Horst Lünecke, Nazi Stormtroopers, complete strangers.

Chapter 2 – The Cranes of Ibycus

What kind of political party attracted men of that type? He needed to find proof of their guilt, but his fenced-in position proscribed any action that could bring him into trouble with his bosses and the local law.

He arrived late in the flat. Gerda was still up. Her welcome was dressed up as teasing. 'I was beginning to think that you were not coming tonight, Ronald. Gone home with this married woman you were meeting.'

He nodded. 'A very experienced woman, too, although she has only five children.'

She gave him a cuddle.

'You look preoccupied, *Liebling*' (darling). 'What is the matter? Why do you look so strained?' She dropped into German as always when getting emotional. 'Has something happened? You have only been visiting a school this evening, or…?'

'Yes,' he also changed to German, 'and no.'

'So tell me. What was going on there?' she insisted.

'A school show by the pupils, Gerda. Recitals, music, historical stuff.'

She did not say anything, but maintained her questioning look. Reluctantly he added, 'The son of Dr. Strauss recited a ballad by Friedrich Schiller. His name's Frederic, also.'

The way he said it, made her ask, 'Come on, Ronald – what ballad?'

'The Cranes of Ibycus.'

She thought for a moment, brows folded. Then she saw it: two murderers.

'Oh, Ronald, *Liebling*. You have not spoken about it the last few days. I have told you we want to help you.'

'Gerda, I work for the British Foreign Office. I must have no political connections or contacts in foreign countries. It's my probation year, Gerda, and it's hopeless, anyway. Real life is not a ballad. Your friends weren't flying above him when father was killed, Gerda. The two men won't fall on their knees and confess they are murderers. No, there's damn all I can do.'

It was a release from his inner tension as he spat it out in a challenging tone. Gerda had stepped back and now folded her arms. As she was wearing a nightgown only, it made her look less determined than she was.

Chapter 2 – The Cranes of Ibycus

'I understand your position but it makes me not very glad, Ronald. I cannot bear letting these murderers escape. And the way that these two men behave. I do not think that they are very intelligent. Just like the two who murdered Ibycus. But I am glad you have told me, Ronald. Come, *Liebling*, drink and bed. You must get up in the morning.'

Gerda did not relax him with the warmth in her voice, but his body was weaker than his spirit and, in a strange way, Ronald resented it. After he had left for work, she thought hard about the situation. She wanted so much to help him and not only for his sake. An idea was making waves in her mind. It did not occur to her that it was quite hopeless and unrealistic, but…

* * *

After the SAG's committee meetings which usually took place on Sundays, some of the members always had a glass of beer together in one of the town's Bierkellers where they often were joined by friends. One of those was Hannes Bohlmann, a man in his mid-thirties. He was more than someone's friend, he was a political sympathiser and supporter. Bohlmann managed one of Munich's fringe theatres. He also arranged itinerant play performances at venues throughout Bavaria, wrote plays and sketches and, when the occasion arose, even took a part on the boards. He sometimes assisted in productions for the local comedian Karl Valentin and for Bertolt Brecht, both men whose fame was in the rising. It was the last Sunday in July when Gerda spoke to Bohlmann.

'You told me once, Hannes, that you studied psychology before you switched to the theatre. Do you think it's possible to frighten or shock a person who's committed a crime in the past, into confessing it?'

The unusual question grabbed his interest. She told him about the murder of Ronald's father two years ago and about the son trying to find the guilty parties. She explained Ronald's position without giving away personal details. She described the two suspects and, finally, mentioned the Schiller ballad's relevance. Hannes guessed more than she let on and gave serious thought to the idea.

'I cannot be certain, Gerda, but I should imagine it is. There are parallels here with Ibycus but where do we find a catalyst, like the

Chapter 2 – The Cranes of Ibycus

cranes? Was there anything that took place during the murder? Something the murderers would remember?'

'I don't think – except a loud record played in the night. I'm sure, SAG would help.'

Bohlmann nodded doubtfully.

'It's within the realm of. My dear girl, I'd really love to do something positive against these Fascist Pharisees. But I can't see, how. Do you know, they've uttered threats against our work, even against Brecht. That rabble, criticising a man like him, a creative genius! Last week his Dreigroschenoper' (Threepenny Opera) 'opened in Berlin and the reviews – stupendous! He's an inspired man, a great satirist. Yes, I'd really – I'm beginning to get the germ of an idea, perhaps even an inspiration. Give me a day or two to think about it, Gerda. You really think they'd help?'

He looked in the direction of the other SAG members along the table. She nodded an affirmative and smiled. She knew him well and hoped he might come through.

* * *

At work, Ronald had established a filing system for documenting the details of past visiting permits to Britain. He had started to file them, a process that was slow and threatened to become boring. Occasionally he came across an interesting case, like the ones he had mentioned to Craig. But they were rare and, as the days passed by, he experienced moments of frustration beating against his equilibrium. Then came a weekend which became a memorable one for him. On Saturday in the morning he had found a note on his desk: 'I'll be at the Kühbogen tomorrow. Hope, you'll be free for the afternoon. Let me know by tonight if no can do. Important. C.J.'

And at night, Gerda, already half-asleep when he joined her, suddenly began to talk, unwittingly swallowing some of her words:

'*Liebling*, sorry, you asleep? Forgotten tell you, free tomorrow evening... must talk to you. Too tired now. Imp... import...' A deep yawn swallowed the '...ant', and was followed by a mighty last effort. 'Too sleepy. Come home early, Ronald, six o'clock, early, we talk before dinner, introduce friend long ago. Nothing anymore between, Liebling, just friends now...'

He replied, 'I'm meeting a colleague in the afternoon, Gerda dear, but should make it by six.'

Chapter 2 – The Cranes of Ibycus

He wondered whether she heard him but found out immediately.

'Colleague? Only colleague, Ronnie?'

'Definitely, *Liebling*. We're just good friends now.'

'Now? Ronnie, tell the truth. What was she before?' She sounded fully awake.

'Before, I did not know him, Gerda dear.'

'Him. Oh.'

He heard her drawing a long deep breath of satisfaction. The next moment she was asleep.

* * *

Ronald usually spent his Sundays in his flat doing a variety of things: writing brief letters to Lisette and to his mother and grandmother, repairing items of clothing, preparing his weekly washing bag for collection by the Consulate's cleaning lady and making notes for the reports he would have to produce for London and having lunch with Craig at the Kühbogen. The last couple of weekends Craig had not turned up. He did this time. Ronald was already sipping his beer at their regular table, when he arrived, wearing his old felt hat. As usual he flung it at the horns, missed, picked it up, hung it up, sat down and ordered his drink without a second's break and started to talk.

'First, duty. On Tuesday afternoon two French consular representatives will be conferring with two British consular representatives at the Market Hall from two to four p.m. Topic: Assessment of the new National Socialist Workers' Party of Germany. My French counterpart and I shall partake in the assessment. Each of us will bring a security officer for general security. You're the one I have chosen.'

'I thought you're the only security officer, Craig?'

'Exactly. You'll meet your counterpart before the start of the round table meeting and check out the premises with him. You'll both also attend the meeting.'

An afternoon away from the office. Ronald was pleased. Craig continued.

'Now to the reason for my note. When your father died, Ronald, I was not, myself, in direct contact with the police about it. His landlady had registered him with the police as a private foreign visitor. Don't forget he called himself Lloyd. He did get the temporary passport from us and had his reports typed here, that's true but I only exchanged a few words with him, when he entrusted me with his notes. The Consul, of course, received the official communication about a British citizen's murder from *Sektion Fünf* (Five), 'the local *Kripo*' (short for *Kriminalpolizei* = Crime Police). 'Last week I approved a request for a visit to England from a young German – Reinhard Schmidt.'

'Reinhard Schmidt,' Ronald interjected, 'You can't get a more German name than that.'

Jameson nodded and continued:

'He had an invitation and his father, Police Sergeant Christian Schmidt, came to collect the papers. We got to talking and I learned that he works in the Kartei Zentrale, the Documentation Centre. He was eager to show his thankfulness and I asked whether he could find out where your father had resided when staying here.'

Ronald put his hand on Craig's arm in an emotional gesture of appreciation. Normally his mother and he would have known the address from his father's mail but he had not yet sent any from Munich by the time he was killed. Craig went on.

'Sergeant Schmidt has come up trumps. He's even found an official letter about your father's belongings that had never been sent off. The house is in the *Einsteinstrasse*. Your father's landlady still lives there and expects us this afternoon, that's you and me. You're a friend of the family.'

They took the tram to the Max-Weber-Platz, from where it was only a few steps to walk. The house in the Einsteinstrasse was a substantial four-storey tenement building with a projecting yellow-painted central block topped by an attic flat beneath the gable roof. Jameson rang the bell of No.3 on the ground floor. He held his identity card in front of the spy hole in the door, whereupon the door was opened by a small, slim-faced woman in her early fifties. Her hair was grey and drawn together in a knot at the back of her head. Everything about her reflected the start of early ageing but her ocean-blue eyes with laughter-wrinkles were the dominant impression she made on Ronald. Later, when looking closer, he discovered also a few deep hardship-lines in her face. Whatever hardships she had experienced, they had not dampened her loquacity nor her hearty laughter which accompanied it, often without any obvious reason.

Chapter 2 – The Cranes of Ibycus

'One must be careful these days,' she explained. 'Please come in. I did not quite get your name on the telephone, Herr – ?'

Jameson had taken his felt hat off and held his slim, long hand out to be shaken by her small podgy one.

'Jameson, Craig Jameson. Yes, it is always best. This is Mr. Burnley of whom I told you on the telephone.' He was speaking German. Ronald was surprised by her firm grip.

'My name is Annemarie Weber, widowed. Please step in and make yourselves comfortable. My husband always assured our guests that he was not related to the Max-Weber-Platz.' Her laughter resounded through the rooms. 'He made everybody laugh, my Ludwig. Of course, that was before this terrible war. Can you imagine, he survived all the battles for three years and then he was killed in 1918, on the Marne, just when he was promoted to *Obergefreiter'* (senior lance corporal) 'and had been home on leave and our son was just called up. Here they are together in this photograph.'

They had followed her into the sitting room. She pointed at a framed photograph on a shelf. It showed the husband and the son, both in uniform and about the same height, but otherwise not resembling each other.

'We already knew the emperor was losing this war,' she was saying, 'and I was thinking they would both come back to me. At least, my Josef survived. He was taken prisoner on the day after he arrived at the front. Our dear God heard some of my prayers. But here I am, talking. Please, sit down, the coffee is ready in two minutes and I have made an Apfelstrudel. I know it pleases to the Englishmen as much as to us and you do not get it in England. Pardon me that I speak Deutsch only but you have told me, Mr. Tschemissen, that you both speak German. That is lucky, because my English is not very good.'

She broke into her hearty laughter. Already on the move whilst talking, the last words were said from the kitchen door. They settled on the chairs at the small oblong table, which was covered with a flowery tablecloth and laid for four persons. In the centre a long, uncut piece of apple strudel rested like a lazy caterpillar on an oval plate. When Frau Weber returned with a tray, holding four cups of coffee, a jug of milk and a small pot with sugar cubes, she was followed by a tall young man, whom they easily recognised as her son Josef. He explained he lived upstairs in the attic and a bell system was connecting him with his mother. He had, of course, known of their impending visit and his mother had pressed the bell, always a request for him to join her.

'Josef has done all the wiring. He is an electrical engineer, you see. And it was a good thing because only two days after poor Mr. Lloyd was murdered – such a terrible happening – and I was quite sad because he was such a nice man. You cannot imagine how shocked I was when the policeman knocked on the door in the afternoon and told me that he was found dead. You see, early on that morning I have gone to the police because he has not come back from his evening meal. That is your duty if you let rooms. Mr. Lloyd was always eating out. I could have cooked for him and much better than any restaurants, I am sure, without praising myself, but he was a journalist and interviewing people he told me. He was an important man but you know this,' she looked at Ronald, 'you are a friend of the family, Mr. Tschemissen has told me—'

Her son interrupted her, 'Mother, you go on too long. The gentlemen have come to—'

'Yes, you are right Josef,' she counter-interrupted, 'but I must finish this.'

She turned to Craig and Ronald who, after having begun to suffer politely, were becoming very attentive to what she was saying.

'Because the next day a man rings and he says he is from the police. So, naturally, I open the door. But he was not in uniform. He demanded to go into Mr. Lloyd's room to find out whether anything was missing. I'm not an educated woman, but I'm not stupid, you see, and how could he tell what was missing if he did not know what things Mr. Lloyd had to start with? So I ask whether he has a police identity card with a photograph. He says he is a detective and detectives do not need cards. So I say I cannot let him go into the room without an identity card. You see, I have always heard that a detective shows his identity card with a photograph of himself. Not all, just his face. So he looks very angry and threatens I better obey him or I will get in trouble.

So you can imagine I was anxious and behind my back I ring the bell to Josef, which is just beside the front door. Three times. I was not sure, whether he was in, but he was and he ran down the stairs because that was unusual, you see, three times. Of course, he has his own key and arrived just when this man has pushed me to the side and has closed the door behind him. You should have seen my Josef.

He is much taller than this man and he bent over him and told him to get out or he will throw him out. The man, I could see, was frightened of him. I assured him that we will hand everything over from the room to the police in the morning right away and he can look at all the things there. He curses and shouts he is a police detective and will come back with handcuffs, but when Joseph raised his fist he walked out. And he has never come back. I want to tell you this so that you know we have been looking after the things of Mr. Lloyd.'

What he had just heard excited Ronald.

'You and your son have acted very bravely. Please tell me one thing, Frau Weber, and Herr Weber, would you recognise that man if you saw him again?'

She looked worried.

'I do not know, Mr. Burnley. It is two years now, you see. He was blond, that I remember and he was at least four centimetres smaller than Josef. But his shoulders were wider, no, Josef?'

Josef nodded.

'Yes, you're right, Mother. I'm sure he was not police, but I'm not sure whether I would recognise him.' He unexpectedly dropped into English. 'But I could identify him, Mr. Burnley.

Ronald looked at him and Craig said, 'Are you sure of that, Herr Weber? How? Your English is very good. And would you be prepared to make a statement to the police about this?' Josef Weber smiled broadly which emphasised the resemblance to his mother.

'I was an English prisoner of war for a whole year and I had daily lessons at the camp. Your countrymen treated me very fair, Mr. Jameson. You see, that man had boxer's ears and the tip of his left ear was missing, as if someone had bitten it off. It can happen in boxing. I saw it quite close when he rushed past me to the door.' He laughed, 'I put my most threatening face on. I must confess also I wanted very much to sock him one, because he frightened my mother but I was not quite sure whether he was not perhaps really with the police as he claimed. I would certainly be happy to do anything to make him pay for his behaviour. A statement? Definitely.'

It was an enormous piece of news for Ronald. The general description fitted one of the two men his father had been interviewing, the one whose name, according to Gerda, was Rudi Steger. And he lacked a bit of his earlobe. There was a clear link between those men looking for something when they attacked his father and one of them trying to get into his father's room afterwards. Craig was probably right, suspecting it was the report he had written. If Josef Weber could identify Steger, it might well be enough for the Justizrat to initiate a police investigation. That would be a huge achievement. A new optimism arose inside him, complemented by his enjoyment of Frau Weber's Apfelstrudel. She broke into his thoughts as if aware of them.

'You must have another piece of my Apfelstrudel,' she said, whilst refilling the cups. Ronald forced himself back into being the appreciative guest, not a difficult task. He told her so.

'You were right about the Apfelstrudel and I have to say yours is particularly well done. I know it is quite difficult to make the dough so thin.'

The delighted Frau Weber rewarded him, by saying, 'I want to show you the room in which Mr. Lloyd was staying. I no longer have paying guests. I still have some of his belongings, Mr. Burnley. Do you think his family may want them? I've thrown a few things away, underwear and such. To tell the truth, I've given them away. The police promised me that they would write to his family and inquire whether they wanted things back but I think they did not have his address. You see, the address, which he had entered into my registration book, did not give a street and a number. Only Reading, England.'

'I have the address,' Ronald said, 'because I also come from Reading. Mrs. Lloyd has told me to use my judgement.'

'You see, Josef, Herr Burnley also pronounces it Redding, not the way you say it.'

Josef threw his arms up in mock surrender.

'You're right, Mother. But I learned to pronounce the word: reeding. So that was wrong, Mr. Burnley?'

Ronald shook his head. 'It is correct when it refers to books. But place names do not always follow rules.'

Honour was restored to mother and son. There was nothing special about the room. It looked comfortable enough. But when Frau Weber produced the suitcase, which was so familiar to him, Ronald had to make an effort to control himself. It contained two of his father's three suits, the maximum number he ever carried on his travels, two shirts and two ties, colour coded, to simplify his father's

Chapter 2 – The Cranes of Ibycus

choice of wear for the day. The shirts had obviously been washed and ironed. Ronald's decision took all of one minute.

'The family must owe you money, Frau Weber, and I insist that you let me put that right. I shall be glad to take these and deliver them to Mrs. Burnley when I return to England—'

Craig interrupted. 'We must do this the correct way, Frau Weber. I shall send a messenger to you tomorrow who will collect the case and give you a proper consular receipt for it. If you will be so kind to prepare an invoice for the rent and services owed to you, the British consul will pay your bill. We shall pass the clothes and case to Mr. Burnley, when he returns to England. If we had known your address this would have happened long ago, in accordance with regulations.'

Regulations? This was a new side of Craig. Frau Weber appreciated it.

'Naturally, Mr. Tschemissen. One must obey the regulations. But you owe me nothing, a few Pfennig, perhaps. Mr. Lloyd has paid enough in advance which is always my regulation.' She laughed heartily.

Ronald said, 'I thank you very much on behalf of Mrs. Lloyd, Frau Weber, for the way you looked after her husband and for the responsible way in which you dealt with the situation afterwards.'

Their hand-shaking good-bye was like that of old friends.

'You are always welcome Mr. Tschemissen and you must come and visit us before you leave München, Mr. Burnley.'

Ronald was going straight to Gerda's place from there, so they yielded to temptation in the form of a Wirtshaus, the nearest to an English pub, situated near the square, for a small beer before parting. It sported a large picture of Wilhelm II, the ex-emperor. The owner was obviously not a supporter of the new democracy. There weren't many people there, three old men in one corner playing cards, two well-cushioned, conventionally-dressed men, obviously discussing serious business, and one fleshy-faced man with a wooden leg who appeared to have already consumed more than was good for him. None of the guests took notice of the two Englishmen who hugged the most remote corner. They did not talk for a while, each of them thinking about the unexpected revelations provided by the Webers. Ronald was the first one to speak.

'I'd all but given up.'

Chapter 2 – The Cranes of Ibycus

Jameson agreed, 'Yes, it's beginning to look promising. But be careful, Ronald. Careful of your own position re your Gerda and her lot, and careful with Nazis. They're known to be a ruthless lot.'

Ronald grinned.

'I, too, can be without Ruth but have no fear, I'll be more careful than a tightrope walker above a den of starving lions. If I should step out of line, I promise, you'll not be connected with it.'

Jameson frowned.

'You can't absolve my responsibilities. Keep me informed of the steps you're taking. You're on the staff of the Consulate at present. It's my duty to look after your safety, too, even though you're like the arrow of a long bow, ready in the tautened string for release by the archer.'

Silence fell and Jameson ordered a second beer for both whilst Ronald thought about Jameson's words. The waiter, a mature man, better dressed than the average Wirtshaus waiter, served them. As he walked away, they heard him murmur, '*Engländer!*' The tone in which he said it was not one of admiration. They looked at each other. Ronald grinned, 'A brilliant observer and obviously one of Munich's dedicated anglophiles.'

Jameson shrugged his shoulders, 'At least he's not a member of the National Socialist Workers' Party. Which reminds me – you know the two fellows are members of Hitler's private army, the Sturmabteilung, SA for short, don't you? And I'm sure you also know that the SA was formed by Ernst Röhm, one of Hitler's personal friends. But did you know Röhm was openly known to be a homosexual?'

'No. It sounds unusual for an army-type organisation.'

'The regular German Army does not like it either. Personally, nor do I, Ronald. Something else. When Hitler and Röhm were sent to prison four years ago, Hitler was forbidden to keep a private army. So Röhm officially renamed it as an independent organisation, although everybody still calls it the SA and knows that it exists to protect Hitler.'

'Hitler didn't stay in prison long, did he?'

'Friends in high places. The Weimar government and democracy are unpopular, Ronald, though the present chancellor's not doing badly. For all that, four years ago Hitler ordered Röhm to leave. He's in South America now, reorganising another country's fighting forces. Hitler and Röhm were close and there've been rumours.'

'Are you saying that Hitler is a homosexual?'

'Some people do. Some say he has no sexual denomination whatsoever. According to my information, Lünecke, the one of your two suspects with the pretty face, was personally recruited by Röhm and was one of his favourites. I was sure you would be interested, Ronald.'

'Every little grain of sand… but is there enough to make a square yard of beach?'

'Whether the Weber's information is enough for the Justizrat to bring the police in? It's worth finding out, Ronald, if only because you're not likely to get any more. '

'You're right. Thanks to my father I'm sure I can afford the legal fees but—'

Jameson interrupted him, 'Hold your mustangs, buddy. You've got the wrong end of the stick here.'

Ronald looked up.

'Mixing your metaphors? I'd never beat a gee-gee. Never had one. How?'

'For a start, Ronald, you're not in a position. Say, you go to Strauss and give him what you've got and tell him to go ahead but without involving your name. How could that work? He has to be instructed by a real person or organisation which, theoretically, could be the police. That would be putting the cart before your two gee-gees, and add two more for your stable. His police contacts will need to know who he represents. Messy if he's not supposed to tell.'

'True enough, but I've no alternative.'

'Wrong, my impetuous young pal. You have but it's not the alternative, the "or". In this case the "either" is the correct way. Let me impress on you, Ronald, that it has to be done by the book. The murder of a British citizen is the legitimate concern of the Consul General, in his role as the official representative of His Majesty's Government and his task to protect British citizens abroad. Now that we have some evidence, it's precisely my job to put it to my boss. I'm convinced, Ronald, that Gaisford will take the next step and hire a lawyer to represent the Consulate in this matter. And I'm equally convinced he'll accept my recommendation that it should be the Herr Justizrat Strauss. All that's no more than my duty and has been over the years. I haven't become a Britisher for nothing.'

Ronald had listened, metaphorically open-mouthed. He had seen this issue as his private problem and it had not occurred to him that

Chapter 2 – The Cranes of Ibycus

there was an official side to it. He sat there, digesting what he had just heard and arraying the facts in his mind.

'You're suggesting, Craig, I put it to Strauss that we think there's enough evidence? No, the other way round. I ask for his professional opinion about the strength of the case we have.'

Jameson nodded.

'On the proverbial dot. Do exactly that and let me know what he thinks and I'll take it from there. Let's drink up and say good-bye to Willi, the last and past.'

Accordingly, they accompanied their final sip by a sarcastic 'Prost!' glasses held out in the direction of ex-Kaiser Wilhelm II on the wall, followed by more or less derogatory comments.

'Not a very wise man,' was Jameson's.

'He sacked Bismarck,' Ronald added.

'The black sheep of the queen's family was Kaiser Willi. The Dutch now have the pleasure of his company.'

Craig slowly and carefully gathered his felt hat from where he had hung it without even trying to have a fling, looking surprised that it was still there.

Ronald watched with interest and enquired, 'Would I be talking high treason, if I said, our side wasn't so wise either?'

Jameson looked concerned, 'Even higher.'

'Right. Then I won't say it. Not in the presence of your holy hat.'

Craig wrinkled his eyebrows. 'This beer was stronger than it looked, don't you think? There's only one hole in my hat, I'll have you know.'

'And large enough for cerebrating.' Ronald grinned.

Nevertheless, they were both walking straight as they left and once outside, parted. They successfully banished the attack of light-headedness, by willpower, despite its encouragement from the fresh air. That turned out to be particularly useful to Ronald who was unaware of things still to come on that Sunday.

* * *

Reaching the flat before Gerda, Ronald made himself a strong coffee in aid of counteracting any potential effects of the beer. She arrived minutes later and followed his example, though not for the same reason. They sat at the tiny table in the tiny kitchen space, sipping the strong brew in soundless harmony. When they had emptied their mugs, they moved the two metres into the bedsitting room and sat down beside each other on what could best be described as a large single-bed. After the usual long and enjoyable cuddle in which their clothes got into natural disarray and more, she made him sit up beside her again. Facing him, she took both his hands in hers. Ronald knew this meant she wanted something from him, something serious. She said nothing right away, only looked into his eyes, wondering how to start.

'By now you must have found out what colour they are, Gerda,' he said. 'I've not changed them since we first met. If you want me to confess my sins, sorry. I enjoy them too much.'

She laughed out loud.

'You make it difficult for me to be serious. All right, I tell you straight. It's about your father. Not really about him but about the two men who killed him.'

It was serious.

'I wish I knew that for sure, dear. What about them?'

'The last time we spoke, Ronald, you said you've given up doing something about them.'

'Actually, Gerda, that is no—' he began, but she cut him off.

'No, Ronnie, let me say my bit. Perhaps then you will change your mind.'

He tried again, 'Look, Gerda, there's no—' but she put a hand over his lips which he promptly kissed.

'No, Ronald, you must listen, I insist. When you told me this, I decided that I must try and do something on my own. I want that these fascists are punished.'

His eyes above her hand, widened in astonishment. She either did not notice or decided not to.

'And when you have told me about Ibycus, it has given me an idea and I have spoken to a friend who manages a theatre in Schwabing. His name is Hannes Bohlmann. Hannes is really good and he could easily get work in Berlin but he loves this town and prefers contentment to ambition. She took her hand off Ronald's mouth.

'That is kind of you, Gerda,' he said, 'I like breathing from time to time. I'm impressed by this friend of yours but...'

Seeing the signs of utter frustration in her eyes, he stopped with a resigned gesture. She continued quickly.

Chapter 2 – The Cranes of Ibycus

'He says the concept of the ballad is plausible and it may not be impossible to make these men confess by working on their fears and their imagination. He came to the Hofbräuhaus on Thursday and the two Nazis were there and I pointed them out to him. He knows of you but he does not know who you are. He is an enemy of this Nazi party because they are enemies of the modern theatre. Bohlmann has worked with Brecht, you know. He has studied Psychology, in Leipzig. He has worked out things I can do together with friends to make the two men perhaps betray themselves or even confess. I am going to do it, Ronnie, and you cannot stop me.'

She stopped, looking at him anxiously, awaiting his protests. But Ronald was struck into silence at that moment. This exceeded whatever he had expected and he had to think for a moment before replying. Encouraged by his silence she continued:

'Hannes also has said that if you would be willing to start the programme, it would help a lot. Only this one time, and nobody will know who you are.' She slipped her hands up to his shoulders. 'So this is what I wanted to say to you, Ronald. Can you not change your mind and help with this plan? Please say yes, Ronald. You see—'

'Yes,' Ronald said into her sentence.

'But why not? Is it not – What did you say?'

'I said yes! I tried to tell you, Gerda, but you wanted me to kiss the inside of your hand.'

She laughed out loud.

'You are hopeless. Why did you not stop me?'

He looked at her, amazed.

'This is good,' she said, 'we must hurry because we have dinner with Hannes at seven o'clock at the Donisl, that's where he always meets people to discuss theatre stuff.'

She got up and began to put her clothes in order. Watching her put her stockings straight kept Ronald sitting on the bed. She did not notice and continued talking.

'Hannes is very discreet, Ronald. He will not tell anybody about you. The Donisl is not far, just opposite the Rathaus. It is not as big as the Hofbräuhaus and not so famous but it is very old and a lot of the townspeople like it. Theatre people and artistic types go there. Why are you not getting yourself ready? I'll rinse the cups, whilst you do.'

* * *

Chapter 2 – The Cranes of Ibycus

When they arrived at the Donisl beer garden, a waitress showed them to one of the niches which contained only one table with only one guest, Hannes Bohlmann. He rose and embraced and kissed Gerda on the lips. For one moment Ronald feared he was going to get the same treatment when Gerda did the introductions. One could easily be overawed by Bohlmann's appearance. The man was an inch taller than Ronald. His grey eyes were attractively narrow and divided by a strong Roman nose. His dark wavy hair was not parted and almost reached his shoulders. The waves were undoubtedly natural and Ronald wondered whether they had influenced Bohlmann's choice of a theatrical career. The waitress took their orders and left, whereupon Bohlmann immediately broached the subject of the meeting in his mother tongue.

'Gerda has told me that you speak German, Mr. Burnley. Naturally, the script I have written for Gerda and her helpers is in German. Its aim is to drive the two Nazis into the arms of the law, if they're guilty, of which there seems little doubt from what Gerda's told me. As far as I'm concerned, these two are typical of the kind of their party, ruthless men of violence. I abhor everything these madmen stand for and I hope the gods will not allow them to get into the seats of authority. I want to persuade you to initiate the process. Gerda's told me that you look quite a lot like your father. She also told me that you have a connection with a lawyer. So, please tell me, Mr. Burnley, are you willing to take part, even if it means talking to those two criminals.'

Ronald did not have to think about it. What Bohlmann suggested sounded worth trying.

'Thank you, Herr Bohlmann. This is essentially my problem, my fight, but I accept help gratefully. Recent developments have reinforced my belief that these two men are guilty or at least one of them is. My father was very dear to me and I'm determined to do everything I can to make his killers pay. If I understand what you said, your idea is that I make them believe I'm my father. I suppose if they're superstitious… Perhaps that record that was played whilst the murder was committed could be used?'

Bohlmann's expression had increasingly reflected satisfaction.

'Mr. Burnley, your approach is the perfect approach. And your German is excellent. Yes, I intend to use the song as a psychological prop.'

Chapter 2 – The Cranes of Ibycus

'They saw it as divine blessing—'

Bohlmann cut in.

'Forgive me for interrupting you, Mr. Burnley, but I need to make something clear. After your scene with the two men, you're no longer part of the action. This is my play and the city of Munich is the stage. I've always wanted to produce a drama in the real environment. This is my opportunity and for a good cause. At the end of the seven days – I cannot make it last longer – I'll let you know what the position is. You understand it could amount to nothing?'

Now, belatedly, a voice inside him was warning, questioning Ronald: *Should I really do this?* But he had gone too far to back out.

'I do, Herr Bohlmann.'

With a satisfied smile, Bohlmann drew an envelope from the inner pocket of his colourful jacket.

'Great. I've not written a text for you to learn by heart, only key words. You must choose your own words, otherwise it will not sound natural. No, that's wrong. It will actually be better if you don't sound too natural. But you must not claim to be your father, only make them worry whether you could be. We must do or say nothing that is against the law.'

He handed Ronald a couple of sheets of paper, pinned together. Ronald's quick glance revealed a title: 'Campaign for Justice'. Beneath it was written: Play by Hannes Bohlmann. Another heading beneath that read: Act One. He could hardly believe it. Play?

'The two men will very likely come to the Keller' (cellar) 'this Thursday.' Bohlmann continued, 'Please turn up at eight o'clock. First floor. I'll be behind the bar. I've already—'

Ronald interrupted, 'Herr Bohlmann, will this not incur expenses? You must allow me to pay your costs.'

Bohlmann stopped, wrinkling his forehead.

'Yes, you're right, Mr. Burnley. Thank you. If you can do that, it makes you the de facto producer. When it is over I shall give you a proper invoice and also a receipt. Perfect.'

He held his hand out. Ronald gripped and shook it. Then Bohlmann remembered something else.

'Gerda said you've a connection to the police?'

Ronald was taken aback.

'Not directly. Why do you ask, Herr Bohlmann?'

Chapter 2 – The Cranes of Ibycus

'My best hope lies in wearing the two down, emotionally, to being willing to confess. If successful, then at this point it would be important to bring the police in as quickly as possible.'

'Yes, I have a contact to a lawyer and he has the necessary professional connections.'

Bohlmann had to be satisfied with that. The rest of the evening was taken up by a light meal and light conversation, mainly between Gerda and Bohlmann. The latter talked about some of his experiences connected with the theatre. His lively voice and amusing style of presentation were entertaining and Gerda responded with admiring comments. Ronald was torn between paying attention to the conversation and to his dumplings with Sauerkraut, another dish he had learned to love back in Vienna. At the same time, he was trying to digest a mêlée of thoughts. By the time they parted from Hannes Bohlmann, Ronald's mind was still spinning, like the eddy in a pond caused by the proverbial pebble.

In contrast, Gerda was talking animatedly all the way and her heightened mood lasted way beyond. It prevented her from noticing his silence, and once they were in bed, his reaction gave her no cause for complaints. At the beautiful moment of no return, two intuitive revelations entered the detached observer in Ronald's mind. The first was that Gerda and Bohlmann had obviously shared similar moments in the past. The second was that, whatever his own feelings for Gerda were, love was not one of them. Neither of the two truths affected him deeply. Like most of his experiences, he absorbed such observations as the way life worked, a river, widening or narrowing, sometimes running faster, sometimes slower, encountering whatever it encountered, yet forever continuing on its path.

He woke up at about two in the morning, disturbed by a dream of chasing fast images which he was unsuccessfully trying to catch or even identify. Slowly he relived the evening's event. The accumulated doubts about what had been agreed seemed to make it belong into the realm of the fantastic. Without disturbing Gerda's deep and contented sleep, he got up and made himself a cup of coffee. Relaxed, seated in the nude on the narrow chair in the kitchen, he embarked upon the attempt to make sense of his unease. How had he got into this situation? The Ibycus poem? It had given Gerda the idea. It was her initiative. So what was worrying him? Like Dante he found himself in a dense forest where the path ahead was lost, not visible.

Chapter 2 – The Cranes of Ibycus

Somehow his thoughts were spinning off into the past and to his father. It was a day in July '22. He was sitting opposite his father at one of the outdoor tables of a street café in Paris, just off the Champs-Elysées. A somewhat faded green awning was protecting them from the steady drizzle that was washing the pavement and the street, making them shine brightly and acting as a multiple mirror. His mother who did not speak a word of French had gone off on her own to do some last minute shopping. She and he were to return to Reading a few days later which was the reason why, sitting there, Ronald was struggling with a choking sensation in his throat. Leaving his father and their wonderful gypsy life was the last thing he wanted to do but it never occurred to him to dispute any decision made by his parents. His father was speaking to him and he knew it was his father's good-bye to him.

'You're not a little boy anymore, Ronnie, so I can talk to you, man to man. When I joined the Navy as a youngster, my boy, I didn't know what lay ahead and where it would take me. I had expectations of a great life of adventures on the sea – but it turned out differently. There's nothing so ridiculous, Ronnie, as a sailor who gets seasick every time a few waves are moving the ship's floor beneath his feet. But I'm complaining. I took that step and here I am.' He lowered his voice, leaning forward, 'See that man over there, Ronnie? The one just now sitting down, with the wide-brimmed hat. See the waiter rushing over to him? That's the famous Stravinsky, Igor Stravinsky, a Russian, a great, revolutionary composer. People can't understand his music. He's a good ten years younger than I. Being able to sit so close to a man like that in the flesh, makes my nomadic existence worthwhile.'

Ronald had seen the famous man. He wore glasses like his father and had a small moustache like his father. He also had a high forehead, in fact, Stravinsky astonishingly looked quite a bit like his father, who had not stopped with his exposition.

'I always missed not knowing anything about music but it's like wanting to be a sailor and being seasick all the time. I haven't got an ear for music. I would have liked for you to learn playing a musical instrument, Ronnie. But I know you'll make your own way. You're clever. You've picked up all these languages so effortlessly. You've inherited my unusual memory. Sometimes it's a great gift and sometimes a great nuisance, if not a burden. Use it well. And be rational, my boy. Emotions are OK when you're dealing with encounters that create them, more often than not in relation to the opposite sex. Remember also, they're not the weaker sex. That's something they've invented to get their way.' He actually smiled. Ronald had never before heard his father talk like that, or even as much as that, and only rarely seen that smile which contained the glint of love in it, love for him.

He had heard the rest of his father's words with an obstruction in his throat. 'Ronnie, if you ever find yourself in a situation that seems to be out of control, sit back and get methodical. Put all the known facts together on one side, and the unknown on the other. Decide what you're aiming for and make your decision. Consider alternatives in case something goes wrong. Like a chess player. Listen to advice, but don't let others talk you into doing something you don't want to do, no matter how persuasive they are. And, most important, Ronnie, do the right thing. Don't ask, my boy. You'll always know what that is.' At this point his father had stopped. If he now followed his father's advice should he really proceed with Bohlmann's irrational plan? But that was the point. He did not really think it was so irrational.

He had read and heard of people, even aggressive people, who were influenced by all kinds of beliefs, irrational and even mystical influences. If the two Nazis were amongst them then Bohlmann's 'Campaign' might well be successful. As far as Ronald could work out, he had nothing to lose by co-operating with it, nor had he a better alternative, in fact any alternative. He must. The very process of remembering his father had already clarified the main point for him. He would try every possible legal method of finding out who had committed the murder. He must therefore give Bohlmann's live drama production his best shot and damn the consequences. Returning to bed, more relaxed than when he had got up, moonlight stealing through the window lit up Gerda's peaceful face. Bending over, he whispered, 'But I'm very fond of you, *Liebling*.' Perhaps she heard it. Her lips seemed to shape themselves into a smile. But why did Lisette's words suddenly join his consciousness: 'Ronnee, you will be careful, *n'est-ce-pas*?'

Ronald did not inform Jameson of this latest development. At lunch on Monday, he told him he needed a little time before making a final decision. Jameson nodded and said nothing, although he guessed a lot. Ronald spent the next three days preparing himself for the scene in which he was going to play the leading role. He understood the psychology behind it and, following Bohlmann's advice, only memorised the major points he would express. A few practical questions still lingered in his mind. How could Bohlmann be so certain that the two would turn up this coming Thursday? Ronald could also not imagine how his own appearance was to take place. And what of the two men's reactions? Might they not turn violent? Ronald was not worried about his personal safety. He felt supremely fit. But fisticuffs weren't his style and, more importantly, he had to avoid being involved in a public row.

Before the performance of this reality play was due to start, he had to attend the mini Anglo-French conference at the Market Hall. Ronald's French counterpart was a man in his mid-thirties, tall, strong-bodied and a strong face. His name was Vincent Barbier and he was a member of the Deuxième Bureau, the French external military intelligence agency. They sat side by side, forming the point of contact between the two teams on one side of the oval table. Barbier's English was as good as Ronald's French, with the result that they were changing and mixing the two languages in their conversation.

Conversation was an exaggeration as it amounted to whispered comments about the proceedings and the participants. Barbier was a serious man of few words and not given to a lot of laughter, if any. Nevertheless, he was unable to remain serious when hearing Ronald's uninhibited and irreverent comments about the occasionally pompous speakers of both sides and he joined in with one or two sarcastic by-words and occasional smiles in his eyes and even around his lips. Under normal circumstances this might have led to a new Anglo-French amicable personal relationship, but for security men the luxury was not available and they parted without exchanging anything else but adieus. The conference itself did, however, produce a positive resolution, recommending their respective services a) to maintain proper surveillance of the new German party's progress and b) to collaborate closely in this task.

The text of the resolution was actually typed out in both languages by their respective teams of interpreters and secretaries and signed not only by the four representatives, as well as by their leading security officers.

Chapter 3 – Drama in the Streets of Munich

On Thursday, dressed in one of his father's suits and wearing his glasses, although not a moustache, Ronald made his way to the Hofbräuhaus. He had underrated the German thoroughness which was one of Bohlmann's qualities. On Wednesday evening Rudi Steger and Horst Lünecke each had received a card, delivered by hand, with a note, framed decoratively by interweaving misty-blue lines. The message on each of them, unsigned, was written in neat separate lettering:

'I shall meet you tomorrow evening at 9 o'clock in the evening at the Hofbräuhaus. I am sure you have not forgotten what happened two years ago.'

It practically ensured that they would turn up, even if, as was possible, they had buried the murder in their minds' recycle bins. When Ronald arrived on the first floor, Bohlmann was there already, standing behind the bar, dressed like one of the barmen, and drew him inside to stand on the side – in the wings – unseen by the clientele. He handed Ronald a half-litre glass of beer. 'They're on their way and will be seated side by side at their regular table, the one by the pillar, opposite. At the right moment, a third chair will be placed opposite them by Michel, one of the waiters who is assisting me. That's the one for you to occupy. When I give the sign, walk to it with your beer, around the pillar on the left, so that you arrive from behind their backs. Be careful because just before you reach your chair, the lights will go out in that section. They'll not know from where you've appeared. When you decide to finish talking to them – I leave that to you – call Michel for another glass of beer. If it works well, the lights will go out again whilst you make your way back here, again around the pillar. Michel will stay close all the time, so they cannot start anything. Just in case, you understand. He does not like them, either.'

Ronald was impressed. 'Michel?' He remembered Gerda's reference to him as headwaiter and tough guy. How did Bohlmann know they were on their way? His respect for the man grew. Guests had begun to fill other tables. He did not have to wait long when he saw the two men enter together at the other end of the hall, following a waiter whose height and wide shoulders suggested that he was Michel, which he was. When they reached their table and just before they sat down, Ronald could distinguish their faces. It was only the second time he was setting eyes on them, but this time he felt justified in believing them to be guilty. As he stared at them, a sensation of deep, deep anger mixed with an unconscious desire for retribution, gripped him. These two men had killed his father. For a brief moment he was standing there without his detached self-control. Every fibre of his being, every nerve-end joined into a determination to bring the murderers to justice. Bohlmann was observing him the way he observed his actors before they went on stage.

To a large degree seeing the whole of this project from a director's perspective, he had been wondering whether Ronald would be affected by stage fever. He was familiar with the tell-tales, having never been entirely immune, himself. But he saw no sign of it in Ronald's features. He saw the young man's face tightening up. He noticed his eyes narrowing in determination and something else, an emotion which he could not identify. It was the unspoken promise to his dead father. In that moment, Bohlmann, for the first time in his experiences, understood the difference between acting and raw reality and he knew he would never again undertake a similar task. At the table, Steger demanded that Michel rearrange the chairs the way they always had them. Michel replied he could not do that as they had booked for a third guest and, before they could say anything, left to get their beers.

When he put the steins in front of them, suddenly the lights went out in that section of the bar. Although the other lights in the hall, subdued for atmosphere as usual, remained switched on, for a few seconds vision in the bar area was blurred. When the full illumination returned, Ronald was sitting opposite the two men and immediately started to talk. He spoke in German, in a monotone, thinly sharpened by what was almost a threatening edge.

'Ah, Herr Steger and Herr Lünecke. Here we are again. You have not changed much in the last two years. A little uglier, perhaps.'

He took a swig of his beer. They stared at him. Steger, the thickset butcher type, was the first to respond.

'Who the devil are you? We don't bloody know you.' He spoke more loudly than usual.

Chapter 3 – Drama in the Streets of Munich

'I suppose it is all that beer. You think it can help you to forget things?' Ronald replied.

Lünecke was more polite. 'You may not realise, mister, but this seat is taken. We're expecting an old acquaintance.'

Ronald nodded, 'I've changed a bit. No moustache. Perhaps I looked older two years ago.'

Steger was getting agitated. 'You're off your rocker, man. You talk a lot of nonsense and it is beginning to annoy me.'

Ronald broke into song, softly, with little concern about the text keeping his voice monotonous:

'*O sole mio sta 'n fronte a te! Ma n'atu sole* – a lovely song, no? You must remember it.'

Both men reacted simultaneously, eyes widening, the first signs of real concern. They recalled the tune. Lünecke, still polite, but voice rising, raised his hands in a defensive gesture.

'You're mixing us up with someone else, mister. You must be at the wrong table.'

Ronald leaned forward, almost whispering, 'You thought this song was helping you, didn't you? But sound waves are eternal witnesses. And above his bronze wings an angel can see all around him. Angels can see in the dark. For an angel can use the night's senses, its eyes and ears.'

Momentarily the two men's faces froze into taut masques. Did it dawn on them that this stranger talked about something real? Was that something returning into their consciousness? Ronald was sitting up straight again, staring ahead.

'All murderers think they will not be found out. But that is not permitted. If necessary, their victim is sent back to make sure of their punishment.'

Steger pushed his chair back violently and stood up, raising his voice.

'Shut up you, you – you – arsehole! You can't frighten us? If you don't shut up, you'll—'

Michel stepped forward from behind the pillar.

'Did you call me, sir?'

Lünecke was tugging Steger's arm.

'Rudi, no. Sit down, Rudi. Remember last time.'

Steger sat down slowly. They both stared at Ronald, who had not moved. Lünecke tried again.

'You are molesting, mister. Leave this table, or we shall complain to the management.'

His high-pitched voice betrayed his bravado. Ronald slowly moved his head to look at him.

'The mills are grinding slowly but they never stop, Horst Lünecke. A murder is never forgotten.' He pointed his finger at him. 'Does Herr Röhm know what you have done? You were one of his favourites, weren't you?' Steger looked surprised. Ronald turned to him. 'And you, Rudi Steger, have you confessed it to your Führer? He will get to know, I promise it.'

Both men were glowering at him, uncertainty reflected in flickering eyes. Ronald, himself, had been taken over by his role at this moment and his action and speech had become slow and deliberate and containing a threatening undertone. He emptied his glass, looking at Lünecke again.

'And so will Herr Röhm in Bolivia.'

Lünecke's eyes widened in fear. Steger's face was looking uncertain. Ronald was rising slowly as he continued talking, making his final words weighty and deliberate whilst at the same time softening his voice into a fricative sibilance. He towered threateningly over them.

'One of you is a murderer. One hand guided the killing knife.' His words returned to normal as he said slowly. 'One of you may escape punishment if he confesses. He has this one chance. Think carefully.'

He rose to his full height and, turning his back on them, called out, 'Michel, another beer, please!'

'At once, sir,' Michel called back, re-emerging from behind the pillar.

The next moment the lights went out again, greeted by sounds of annoyance from guests at the other end of the bar. Taking his glass with him, Ronald slipped around the pillar, whilst Michel simultaneously picked up the empty chair and deftly deposited it at the table behind. It could not have been done more slickly if they had practised the manoeuvre for weeks. Ronald had disappeared into his hiding place in the bar, when the lights came on again. Steger and Lünecke turned from facing each other to stare at the empty space opposite them, when Michel appeared.

'Yes, sir? You called?'

Chapter 3 – Drama in the Streets of Munich

Steger, in a state of helpless rage, shouted at him, 'We did not. It was this bloody madman.' He looked around. 'Curse it to hell and damnation, where has he gone?'

Michel looked around searchingly.

'Madman, sir?'

Steger raised his voice again:

'The bloody bloke who sat in the extra chair you brought.' He pointed to where Ronald had sat. 'You said it was booked!'

Michel looked at the empty space, then shrugged his shoulders and said, in a propitiatory tone, 'Of course, sir.' He walked away.

Steger banged his fists on the table, shouting, 'I've had enough. I'm not standing for this. Waiter! Waiter! At once!'

Gerda's voice replied, *'Jawohl, mein Herr. Komme sofort.'* (Yes, sir, coming right away!)

The woman's voice made Steger fall silent. Gerda appeared, humming '*O sole mio*'.

Lünecke shot up. 'What's that you're singing, Fräulein?'

She stopped dead.

'My goodness, you've given me a fright, sir. I was just humming to myself. An old Italian tune, I think. '*O sole mio*'. Yes. It's Italian and means *Oh, meine Sonne*' (Oh, my Sun). 'Do you know it?'

Lünecke's agitation did not abate. 'Why are you singing it? Somebody sent you, tell the truth.'

'Sent me, sir? You called me, sir. I thought it came from this table. I'm permitted to hum, while the orchestra has a break. My friend has a record of it – Gigli, you know, Beniamino Gigli, the Italian tenor. A great voice. And a lovely tune, isn't it? If you want, I'll stop singing it. Tastes differ; like gorgonzola and goulash, my mamma used to say. What can I get you, sir?'

'Another litre for each of—' Steger started but Lünecke, on edge, interrupted him.

'Rudi, I'm not stopping another minute. Bring us the bill, Fräulein. Right away.'

She reached for her pad and pencil and wrote out the bill. She handed them the chit. Their eyes were staring emptily at her. Lünecke paid. The two men got up and left without uttering another word, accompanied by the sound of Gerda's humming '*O sole mio*' again, as she picked up their steins and wiped the table. Thoughts were bubbling to the top of Lünecke's frightened mind and before they reached the door, he spontaneously spat out aloud what he was thinking at that moment.

'Why should I suffer for something I didn't do?'

He had not meant to say it out loud. The malignant look in Steger's eyes and the movement of his hand to the grip of the double-edged hunting knife hanging from his belt was enough to shut Lünecke up. Neither of them was aware of Michel's proximity who, walking along the parallel aisle between the rows of tables, kept a close watch on them. He told Gerda what he had heard.

Ronald had left already and was on his way to Gerda's place, plagued by mixed feelings. His attack of anger had collapsed and the scene he had played out had drained him of emotion. Now his brain took over. Could his play-acting really have achieved anything? The two fellows had seemed affected. He thought he had detected specs of fear in the eyes of Lünecke. If Rina Lenzio's report could be trusted, he was not the one who had done the killing although it still left him an accomplice. Ronald did not wait for Gerda's return but went to bed, glad his part in Bohlmann's 'Campaign' was over.

* * *

Steger and Lünecke were walking through the streets, without uttering a word. Steger did not know how to interpret the strange man's talk. That he referred to the stabbing of the Englishman, two years ago was obvious. Yet, while wondering how he had got to know about it, Steger had no sense of the man being a ghost. He was wholly devoid of imagination. Horst Lünecke was the nearest to a friend he had ever had. What the stranger had revealed about Lünecke was new to him. Their companionship did not fall into any of the conventional pigeonholes. Their sexuality played no part in it. Sex played no part at all in Steger's life. That had something to do with his upbringing, something he could not or would not remember. The things the two had in common were a strong, submissive loyalty to their Führer, Herr Adolf Hitler, and a hatred of the human environment in which they had grown up.

Both had been shaped by similarities in their childhood experiences. They both hated their parents, but each in a different way. The hatred had widened to include all who were better off than they. It acted as justification for the method by which they replenished their pockets, carefully selective muggings. They always

Chapter 3 – Drama in the Streets of Munich

took place in the dark so that none of their victims ever set eyes on their faces. Occasionally their hatred of the human race was expressed by just beating people up who, they decided, had insulted them or were enemies of the party. In those cases, they did not hide their faces. Their victims' fears were sufficient protection. They enjoyed the feeling of power over other human beings. However, it was Rudi Steger who was always the ruthless and often mindless executor. Horst Lünecke, although mentally superior, was wholly under his influence. Essentially only abetting, he always made the decisions about what to do after the deed. So far, his decisions had ensured that they had never been caught, nor even suspected.

The killing of David Lloyd had not been planned. They were, at first, flattered to be interviewed by a newspaperman. All his questions had been about their wonderful party, the National Socialist Workers' Party. He was making notes about what they told him. Towards the end of the second meeting, he told them in answer to a question, that he was working for an English newspaper. It had been Lünecke who, whilst Lloyd had gone to the gents, expressed the worry to Steger, that their interlocutor might be an English spy. Otherwise why did he speak German so well? If the party discovered that they had given information about the party to an English spy, they would be in trouble. They decided to follow him that night and find out where he was staying.

They continued trailing him during the week. Their suspicions were confirmed when they saw him enter the English Consul's premises no less than three times. They decided they must not be seen with him again in public and they must get his notes of the interviews. In the evening of their next planned meeting, they waited outside his place for him and followed him on his way to the beer cellar. They returned crossing the bridge to the entrance of the Maximilian Park, hiding one on each side. When he arrived they grabbed hold of him in their established routine. He was surprised but displayed no fear. They demanded the notes he had written. Both men were used to their victims being frightened and freely handing over whatever they wanted once they had been softened up. But Lloyd continued to refuse handing over his notes. He was not expecting violence from these two, whom he had been treating to meals and beers. He did not even bother to tell them that he did not carry his notes on him. And when Steger attempted to take things from his pockets, Lloyd defended himself successfully and Steger hit the ground. He got to his feet and, in a fit of uncontrolled rage at this humiliation, drew and stuck his knife into Lloyd, killing him on the spot. When they emptied the dead man's pockets, they realised he did not carry his notes on him. Lünecke, scared of Steger and scared of what had happened, suggested moving the body in a street, nearer to the Hofbräuhaus, so it would look as if Burnley had been the victim of a mugging, a ploy they had used successfully before. That was indeed what the police report stated.

Now, two years later, on their way from the Bierkeller, each of them was struggling with a variety of anxieties. Steger suspected that Lünecke might be tempted to tell the truth, in order to save his skin. He was also angry at his own inability to deal with the situation. Lünecke wondered whether Steger might accuse him of the killing, which might be believed because the police was prejudiced against homosexuals. Mingling with that anxiety was a psychological one. Although more intelligent and better educated than Steger, he was emotionally much more unstable. The malleable structure of his mind contained more than average areas of uncertainty and vulnerability that were easily occupied by irrational fears and superstition.

Of course this could not be the man Rudi had killed, there were no such things as ghosts returning from the grave, but supposing there were? How could anyone else possibly know where the murder took place and about the record played in the night? And the Angel of Peace? Perhaps, after all, there were things beyond the human reality, supernatural forces? The two men separated at the usual place, without having exchanged a single word since leaving the Hofbräuhaus. Their respective one-bedroom flats were in the same street, not far from each other. That evening, haunted by their experience, both took a long time before falling asleep. When they did at last, both were hoping that when waking up in the morning, the light of day would somehow restore their normal world to them.

Waking up on Friday, Day Two of Bohlmann's 'Campaign', their hopes seemed to have materialised. The sun was shining, the street life was like every day and there was no sign of anything supernatural. Although neither of them was employed in regular work, their daily lives ran in a groove, which they followed: getting up late and doing nothing during the morning. As usual they met for lunch at the Au, a small tavern in Haidhausen, not far from the river. Both were gluttons, spending money freely on food and beer. For

Chapter 3 – Drama in the Streets of Munich

both of them the best food was represented by the traditional Bavarian fare. It meant that they consumed a lot of *Knödel* (dumplings) and drank a lot of beer. In mid-afternoon, as on most days and certainly on Fridays, they attended lectures and drill at their 'SA Gruppe 19' venue, as part of their military training. Together with a few others, they spent the rest of the evening at one of the beer cellars. By the time they went to sleep, the night before was no more than a bad dream.

Normally, their Saturday, an ordinary working day in Europe in those days, was a repeat of the Friday routine. They got up late, the sun was shining, the street life was like every day and there was no sign of anything untoward. They met at the Au for lunch as usual. Their Saturday menu started with a Semolina dumplings soup. The waiter served it without having to receive their order. Franz, familiarly called Franzl, was a big, heavy man in his forties, with a slight stoop and a slight limp, the result of a French bullet in the war. Like all good waiters, he had a good memory. That Steger enjoyed the *Knödelsuppe* (dumplings soup) could be heard distinctly. He and Lünecke were feeling totally relaxed, assisted by the long, enjoyable sips of their first half-litre beers. Steger quaffed his beer just as unmusically as he ate his soup. Their conversation began with the customary small talk about nothing. When the roast pork with *Semmelknödel* (bread dumplings) and cabbage salad arrived, relaxation reached its usual high point. After the unreal encounter on Thursday night, life was restored to its customary intellectual below zero level.

'Isn't the food here tasty, Rudi?'

'Yeah, yeah. I sure love the dumplings.'

'And, Rudi, have you seen, *Milchrahmstrudel* is on the dessert today?'

'I'm not bloody blind, am I? Of course I've seen it.'

Milchrahmstrudel, a warm curd cheese strudel with vanilla sprinkled over it, was a special favourite. After a moment's silence, except for Steger's chewing noises, Lünecke gave vent to his relief, raising the subject for the first time since Thursday.

'Someone was playing a practical joke on us, Rudi, no?'

'Of course, that's all it bloody was. I knew it from the start,' Steger asserted.

'But how did that man know so much? That I cannot understand.'

Chapter 3 – Drama in the Streets of Munich

'A few lucky guesses, Horst. But the bugger couldn't frighten me,' Steger replied.

Lünecke's doubts were not totally gone. 'I suppose you're right.'

'Of course, I am. No suppose about it.' He slapped Lünecke on the shoulder. 'Drink to that!'

They drank and clinked glasses, emptying them in one long swig. Steger felt on top of the world. 'The beer tastes frigging good today. Two more, Franz, and don't piss about!' he called out.

The waiter replied and complied, arriving with two half-litres on a tray. There was also an envelope on the tray. As he deposited the beers in front of each, he picked up the envelope.

'This has just been delivered. It's addressed to Table Seven, that's you, gentlemen.'

He deposited the envelope on the table and turned away, appearing not to notice their startled reactions. They had stopped eating, eyes fixed on the envelope which was not stuck down. Then Lünecke gingerly drew out a card from it. It looked familiar, the writing on it being framed by interweaving misty blue lines. He slowly read the brief message on it out to Steger:

'Enjoy your pork and your *Knödel* whilst you still can. The food at Landsberg will taste less good, as at least one of you will find out. You have not forgotten our conversation of Thursday night? My time here is limited and it is running out for both of you.'

Landsberg was the prison outside Munich, the one in which Hitler and Röhm had occupied cells after their failed Putsch. Steger's reaction was primitive. After sitting still as if frozen and staring at the card, he shot up and banged his fist on the table, knocking both beer glasses over and spilling their precious contents.

'Franzl!' he roared, 'You better come here, man! At once!'

The other guests stopped eating and watched the spectacle as the waiter reached Steger. The latter had risen from his chair and was holding his fist in front of Franzl's face, as he continued shouting in a voice vibrating with anger.

'Who gave you this letter?'

Franz stepped away from the fist without displaying any emotion. 'It was lying on the bar top,' he answered calmly.

'You're lying, you bastard – you're in league with them!' Steger shouted.

He tried to get hold of the waiter's shirtfront. Franz gripped his wrists effortlessly.

'Calm yourself, sir. Your behaviour is not acceptable at this restaurant. Eat up and leave. You'll not be welcome here again.'

From the bar at the end of the room a woman's voice was heard.

'I'm calling the police, Franzl.'

'Don't bother, Irma, I can handle him,' the waiter replied, forcing Steger back on his seat.

Once again helpless, Steger sank back into his chair, his vicious little eyes almost closed. Lünecke had remained seated, searching around the room. How could the sender of the card know what they were eating? How could he even know that they were here? He was obviously not inside the place and they were not visible from any of the windows. Lünecke's state of mind reduced his powers of reasoning to zero. He was re-visited by the fears that had been stoked on Thursday night. His respected, middle class, church-going parents had turned him out when he was eighteen and they discovered he was homosexual. It was against God's laws!

Much of what he had been doing, ever since, had been his way of repaying his parents, these honourable citizens. He had become callous but he was deeply insecure. Röhm would have protected him but Röhm had also left him. Now, staring at this card, his mind again took refuge to the only defensive thought it could muster: *Why should he be punished for a murder that he had not committed?* But he was afraid of Steger, just as in his childhood he had been afraid physically of his righteous father who frequently gave him a righteous beating with a broad, iron-buckled belt. For a while they both sat there silently, continuing to eat in robotic fashion. Franz had returned to serving the other guests who, perhaps disappointed, had returned to ingesting, the purpose which had brought them there. Steger and Lünecke did not order the *Milchrahmstrudel*. Steger had retreated into a state of grim numbness, so Lünecke, once again, paid the bill and they left the Wirtshaus hurriedly. Once outside, instead of walking the common part of their route together they separated immediately.

In fact, Steger's accusation had been correct. Franz was in league with 'them'. 'Them' was Hans Hollander, a member of Gerda's team, the oldest amongst them. When they had established that their quarries were lunching daily at the Au, Hollander took on this role in 'Campaign', because he knew Franzl well. They had been in the same company during the last year of the war and Franzl was more than willing to co-operate. The latter had factually not lied because

Chapter 3 – Drama in the Streets of Munich

Hollander really put the card on the bar counter. He'd enjoyed a quiet meal in a corner of the room throughout. Paying his bill, he added an envelope with the standard payment from Bohlmann's company.

'You played your part to perfection,' he said, 'and you've lost two customers.'

'A pleasure, old friend,' Franz replied. 'I'd have done it for free. Steger's a nasty piece of work, always rude and unpleasant. The behaviour he's displayed here today would chase my other clients away. Sometimes they've been wearing that odious brown shirt, the Nazi uniform. The right colour for the shit they are. These SA men think they're soldiers. Four blood-sodden years, I've had, wearing the Emperor's uniform and pipsqueaks like those two don't impress me.'

'I can add one thing,' Hollander said, 'We believe that Steger's committed some nasty crime. He's by far the worse of those two – which is no excuse for the other one.'

'That's what Irma thinks, too.'

Hollander left and went straight to the Hofbräuhaus to report the progress of Day 3 to Gerda. She would pass it on to Bohlmann when he called on her during the evening break. In the light of the day's information, he might give her additional directives for the next day's 'performance' which she conveyed to the cast when she met them behind the Hofbräuhaus early in the morning. It was a simple and effective chain of communication. Ronald, without receiving details of the action, was not part of it, but he remained as close to it as possible. He was saying to Gerda: 'So according to Michel, Steger, the one with the reduced earlobe, is the actual murderer.'

'That doesn't mean Lünecke's innocent, does it? Caught together, hung together, we say, Ronald. If he was innocent, he had to go to the police, don't you agree?'

'But there's a difference. And if Herr Bohlmann's scheme works, he could still do so.'

'It will, I'm sure of it, Ronnie.'

'You can tell him, that if the consulate's legal adviser decides that there's a chance of success, the Consul will immediately get in touch with the police.'

Bohlmann received the message with satisfaction.

Chapter 3 – Drama in the Streets of Munich

'That's important, Gerda. What we're doing – it's not unknown for a stage play to try and influence justice but everyone on the stage is known to be acting. This is different, you know.'

'Because we have no audience?'

He gave a short laugh.

'Huh, that sometimes happens in the theatre, also. But the two main members of the cast are press-ganged, so to say, and their real lives are affected. So if they're brought to trial then it'll have been morally justified. You see the difference, don't you?'

She understood that he was beginning to have qualms. 'I've put you into this position, Hannes.'

'I'm responsible for my decisions. I'm a fully-grown man. You may have found out.' He looked at her sideways. Gerda did not blush, nor did she reply. 'In any case,' he added, 'the performance ends on Thursday, happy ending or not.'

Using the real town, streets and houses as stage scenery, Bohlmann drew on public advertising as a useful prop and he was able to draw on the skills of a famous Jewish artist, Bruno Paul, who had in the past designed evocative placards for his productions. Paul had moved to Berlin but still did occasional work in Munich. On every Sunday, the brown-shirted SA marched through the town to the *Teresienwiese,* (Teresien Meadow) the large common on which the Octoberfest, the famous annual beer festival, took place. There they did 'keep fit' exercises. They used to be called 'Street fighting Skills'. Now Hitler, in pursuance of wanting to be seen as a democrat, had forbidden it but anyone watching would find that the exercises looked remarkably like street battle training. En route to the meadow, the marchers shouted slogans in rhythm with their marching step. The aim was to instil fears in their opponents and to recruit members. Both aims were increasingly successful. A lot of people always filled the pavements to watch them, many cheering them on but a few were secretly shouting hostile remarks.

Most of the marchers were proud to be the focal point of attention and also relished the crowd's reactions, even the hostile ones. Steger and Lünecke belonged to the latter category. But not on Bohlmann's Day Four of his 'Campaign'. As they proceeded, they began to realise that the same little rhyme, recited in loud, menacing tones by voices from the rear of the onlookers, was directed at them: *'Die Mörder sind feige, doch der Engel war Zeuge.'* (The murderers are cowardly, but the angel was witness.) They heard it again and again,

Chapter 3 – Drama in the Streets of Munich

even during the drill on the common. By the end of that Sunday, they were caught in a grip of tension. They separated silently, this time without the hope that in the morning it would all have disappeared. Instead, each of them was dreading what the next day would bring. They were not disappointed. Monday's communal rain made for a dismal atmosphere outdoors. For the same indoors, the postman delivered cards to both of them, each framed by the familiar interweaving misty-blue lines. Steger's said:

'You are not a true friend, Rudi Steger. You are prepared to let your innocent friend be hanged with you. You will not get away with it.'

Lünecke's said:

'Rudi Steger is a false friend. He is prepared to let you hang with him. Are you willing to suffer for a murder, he has committed?'

The two did not meet for lunch. Yet, using the same route at the usual time they found themselves walking within a few yards of each other to their SA drill. And suddenly stopping dead in front of a new poster on one of the tall round advertisement pillars, they found themselves side by side, staring at the picture of the Angel of Peace in the Maximilian Park. A golden halo, formed by two curved lines of small lettering stated: 'The Angel of Peace sees everything. No misdeed goes unpunished.' Although it seemed impossible that a public poster was specifically addressed to them, they both took it for granted that it was. It heightened the pressure inside them but they reacted differently. In Steger's more limited thought processes, the helpless anger was growing into rage. Staring at the placard, he began to swear loudly, threatening to make that nebulous accuser suffer, when he met him again. Pedestrians approaching crossed over to the other side of the road. In Lünecke the poster stoked the flickering flames of fear and superstition. When Steger had stopped cursing, one passer-by was heard saying to his companion that the placard was a fine example of Jugendstil.

* * *

On that Monday afternoon, Ronald was once again making his way to the home of the Strauss family, this time not for tea but for an appointment with the Justizrat. The lawyer's substantial office was on the ground floor. This time, Ronald was received by his secretary, an efficient looking woman of about thirty, with severe

Chapter 3 – Drama in the Streets of Munich

features and a reserved, dignified politeness. She took his hat, raincoat and umbrella. Dr. Strauss rose behind his desk.

'I am pleased to see you again, Mr. Burnley. Please take a seat.'

They both sat down. Strauss said, 'You're here to speak about your father's murder, right? Have you been able to find out more? When Kriminalkommissar Hirsch confirmed the loud music heard on that night, I began to think you had perhaps made some progress.'

'I hadn't then, Dr. Strauss, but I'm hopeful that what I have now, may be sufficient for bringing the police in. I'm here to ask your professional opinion about that.'

Strauss leaned forward, politely.

'Really. That sounds encouraging. Please let me have the details.'

Ronald detected a hint of doubt mixed with a hint of worry in the lawyer's expression.

'Before I do, Dr. Strauss, I should like to explain something personal. As I am an employee of the Foreign Office and only here in Munich as part of my probationary year, I must not be connected with any public action of this kind.'

The lawyer's worried expression deepened. Ronald continued.

'As it happens, I do not need to be. My colleague, Captain Jameson, whom you have met, is in charge of security at the Consulate and it is part of his job to deal with any action to be taken in respect of my father's murder. Therefore, if you decide that there is enough evidence to take this case to the courts, the Consul will request you officially to act on behalf of the British Foreign Office in this matter. I, personally, should be very grateful if my name were not mentioned at all.'

Surprised, Strauss leaned back, concern visibly turning into relief and restoring genuine interest.

'That sounds most acceptable, Mr. Burnley.'

Ronald wasted no time.

'The girl who was a witness to the murder will sign a statement with the details of what she has witnessed. You said, Dr. Strauss, that she would not make a good witness. Nor does she want to be one, but the statement may be useful. In it she claims that of the two men, the smaller, stocky one did the killing. She's the one who provided the information of the song *O Sole Mio* being heard throughout the time she was there. As this has been confirmed by the police it may give her statement more validity. My father's last

Chapter 3 – Drama in the Streets of Munich

report to the Foreign Office states that he had been interviewing two members of the National Socialist Workers' Party at the Hofbräuhaus and he was aware that he had been followed by someone during the week. For that reason, he passed his report about the interviews to Captain Jameson at the Consulate for safekeeping.

'After his death, Captain Jameson sent it, with his own report of the murder, to the Foreign Office in London. It was also the reason why Captain Jameson commented in his official report that he had reason to suspect that my father was not killed by muggers, as assumed by the police. He recently found out where my father was boarding at the time. My father's landlady has stated that on the day after the murder, a small, stocky man came to her place, claiming to be a detective and demanding to search the room which my father had occupied. His attempt to make a forceful entry was prevented by the landlady's son. The son observed that the man had cauliflower ears and the tip of one ear missing. Both, mother and son are prepared to appear as witnesses. By a totally lucky coincidence, an Austrian waitress at the Hofbräuhaus who had known my father in Vienna, had seen him at the Hofbräuhaus with two men on two evenings. Throughout the two years since then, these men, members of the National Socialist Workers' Party and of the SA, have continued to frequent the Hofbräuhaus regularly. The smaller one has cauliflower ears and the top of one ear missing—'

An amazed 'No!' from Strauss momentarily interrupted Ronald. Ronald merely nodded and continued.

'Captain Jameson has the names and addresses of the two men. We think it is not impossible that the other one might be willing to act as witness, perhaps in exchange for a lesser sentence, but we don't know this for certain, or whether it is legally possible. That's all I have at this moment, Dr. Strauss.'

For a long moment both sat in silence. Then Strauss stood up and gripped Ronald's hand across his desk.

'I am impressed, Mr. Burnley, hugely impressed. I'm in no doubt, we have a case and I think the quicker we get these two arrested the better. So tell Captain Jameson that I shall be happy to act on behalf of the British Foreign Office in this matter.'

He sat down again, slightly agitated and visibly pleased. Ronald took a deep breath. It looked as if he had come close to having achieved what at one time had seemed impossible.

Chapter 3 – Drama in the Streets of Munich

'I'm very glad, Dr. Strauss. Now there seems to be a real chance for justice to be obtained. You don't know what this means to me. I'm extremely grateful to your wife and you. Captain Jameson had the details I have just given you, typed out.' He put a closed envelope on the desk in front of Strauss. 'It's not an official document. That, with the necessary additional facts, like names and addresses etc. will be forwarded to you with the Consulate's official request for your legal services in the matter of my father's murder.'

He rose, forcefully controlling his feelings and aware that other clients might be due or already waiting, turned to leave. Strauss raised his hands.

'Please, Mr. Burnley. If I let you leave like this my wife will not speak to me again. You're held as a friend in my family. My son, Frederic, keeps mentioning you since your attendance at his school show. He is talking about going to England to study and has looked up information about your country, books and every available material. I have had to write to a relative of mine in England. Frederic now counts as the family expert on all matters English. So, Mr. Burnley, my wife and I would very much like you to visit us on the next but one Sunday, that's the 1st October. At any time from four o'clock, we have open house and friends drop in informally. And we'd be pleased if Captain Jameson would come as well.'

Ronald promised to come and to pass the invitation to Jameson. He did this at lunch the next day, another rainy one, when he also told him, 'Dr. Strauss agrees we have a case and will act on behalf of the Consulate, Craig.'

'OK. I'll get going.'

'Please hold it until Thursday afternoon, Craig. I might have more for you.'

Craig looked at him.

'Sure, buddy. I won't ask questions but I hope you've been careful.'

* * *

For Steger and Lünecke, the rainy Tuesday was also similar to Monday. Again they did not meet for lunch. Again they received a card each with the familiar misty-blue framing, this time containing the same brief message: 'Two more days!' There was one difference to Monday on their way to the drill. As they were walking on, they caught up with a sandwich-man who was walking slowly in the same direction. He was carrying two large placards on his shoulders, connected at the top, one in front, and the other behind. The rear placard stated: 'Behold the word of the Lord. Ye who have sinned will be punished.' Passing him, a vague feeling of apprehension made both of them turn their heads to see the front. The placard stated: 'Repent now, for the Angel of Peace is amongst us to witness our sins.'

Each of them jumped to the conclusion that the messages were directed at them. Correctly. Neither of them said anything, as they walked on, tense, until about a couple of hundred metres further on, they passed a second sandwich-man, carrying exactly the same messages. After a moment of rigid inability to move, Steger, fists balled, turned around and stepped into the man's path. The man was tall, with a paunch and a small head. The large boards covering front and back, made him look like a giant tortoise, standing on its hind legs. Manhandling him would not have been possible for Steger who, voice trembling in fury, shouted:

'I demand, you tell me who's paid you to carry these boards on this route and at this time, mister. And don't try to lie to me.'

'It's not a secret, sir,' the man said good-heartedly. 'The Dean of the Maximilian Church, a good man, sir, has ordered them.'

And as far as he knew that was the truth. He just did not know far enough. Steger could not think of anything to say. Inwardly fuming, he rejoined Lünecke who had remained rooted to the spot. Joining him, Steger saw an odd expression in his eyes which he could not interpret. It was Lünecke's attempt to hide his thoughts. For the second time within the space of three days, he had now seen Steger reflecting a position of helplessness, of humiliation, unable to frighten the man he addressed. Suddenly he saw him in a new light, no longer a strong man to be admired, although still to be feared. Steger, needing a scapegoat for his frustration, began to suspect that Lünecke might betray him. It was a turning point in Bohlmann's 'Campaign' who, however, was unaware of it.

Before they separated, Steger said in a menacing tone, 'I know I can rely on you, Horst. Anyone betraying me will be sorry, you know that.'

'Of course you can, Rudi. Of course.'

On Wednesday, each of the two men was woken up late morning by the grinding, cacophonous, effusive sounds of a barrel organ

Chapter 3 – Drama in the Streets of Munich

playing '*O Sole Mio*' again and again on the pavement below their windows. Lünecke tried unsuccessfully to shut out the sound by putting the pillow over his head and pressing his hands over his ears. Instead of rays of warmth, the melody was sending stabs of fear into his worn-down mind. Steger, however, once fully woken up, struggled to dress in a hurry. He was going to make the organ grinder tell him who was behind this harassment. By the time he rushed out of the house door, the street organ was gone. Both organ grinders had strict instructions not to stay longer than twenty minutes. Hardly had this version of the song disappeared, when the Gigli record of the song was heard coming from an open window near-by and, as soon as it finished, the same record was heard from another window and then a third. Both men spent the morning indoors, on edge. When they met in the afternoon, they were still on edge, both expecting to hear the melody again or something else to happen. But there was no more music and nothing else happened until they returned home in the evening, where another familiar looking card awaited each of them. Steger's read:

'I expect to see you tomorrow at the Hofbräuhaus at the usual time to hear that you will confess the crime you have committed. This is your last opportunity and my last communication. The truth is known and the truth can be proved. I have completed the task for which I came here. You know who I am.

Steger tore it in little pieces, and then started to throw things about in his room, shouting himself hoarse with curses and raving threats against the unknown enemy. He was not going to follow that invitation and nor would Horst Lünecke, he was certain. The content of Lünecke's card was different:

'I expect to see you tomorrow at the usual time at the Hofbräuhaus, to learn that you will bear true witness of the murder that took place at the Maximilian Park two years ago. If you do not come, it will mean that you are willing to share the guilt with your friend Rudi Steger. It is your choice. You know who I am.'

The differences were the result of Bohlmann's reasoned and hopeful assumption, that Steger had done the actual killing. From the reports he had received, he also judged that Lünecke was far more affected and frightened by the campaign and likely to talk. For all that, it was still only supposition. Ronald had been kept in the dark about the detailed progress of the campaign and was not asked take part in the final scene at the Hofbräuhaus. At Bohlmann's

Chapter 3 – Drama in the Streets of Munich

suggestion, Ronald had, indeed, not moved around outdoors very much during that week, a precautionary measure. On Thursday evening Bohlmann was at his place behind the bar, in truth doubtful whether either of the two would turn up. He turned out to be wrong when he saw Lünecke arrive. The man's face was drawn and he remained silent, when shown by Michel to the reserved table.

He sat down, looking around with anxious, unsteady eyes and the deep frown of blatant fear. He did not hear Michel's enquiry as to what he wanted to order. Michel did not insist and withdrew. Lünecke continued his waiting, his eyes turning, peering in all directions. He fully expected the being that had summoned him to suddenly be sitting opposite him. As nothing happened, he became restless and began to fidget. Suddenly the lights went out. When they came on again, his eyes were fixed on the chair on the other side of the table. It was still empty but behind it stood Gerda, with a tankard of beer, humming '*O Sole Mio*', as she set it down in front of him. He peered at her vapidly. His eyes fixed on the beer, then moved back to Gerda, with a look of fear that, for a fleeting moment, caused her to feel sorry for him. He had shrunk back into a moment of his childhood when he knew his father was about to strike him. Bohlmann, too, watching closely from the bar, experienced a moment of concern. Had he gone too far? He was aware of feeling a mental weariness.

After a couple of minutes, Lünecke began to take small sips of beer, slowly at first. They increased in size and frequency when nothing happened. He had sat there for a good half an hour, by which time his glass was approaching the emptiness that showed in his eyes. At that point a tiny hope had filtered into his mind, a hope that perhaps that vague, frightening threat did not really exist. He looked up when Gerda stopped opposite him again.

'You're Herr Lünecke, aren't you? Horst Lünecke? I've a message for you. I did not see who put the card on my tray, but I heard a man's voice saying "Herr Lünecke will know from whom it is." You look unwell, shall I read it to you?'

He nodded, his fears back again, unable to speak. She took the card from her tray and read:

'As you have come, Horst Lünecke, I am satisfied that you intend to keep your promise. You will be given the chance to tell the truth. If you waste it, I shall return. Go home, but keep away from your false friend. He has killed before!' She put the card down on the table. 'Your beer is on the house, Herr Lünecke, if you are not staying.'

He had been saved. His relief was overwhelming. His fears of punishment by some unknown, mystical authority had been lifted from him. He was taking long deep breaths like an exhausted runner at the end of his race. Looking up at Gerda, the expectant expression in her eyes reminded him of her last words. Nodding his agreement, he rose from his seat and, without uttering a word, left hastily, speed increasing, as if in fear of the decision being reversed if he lingered. Gerda looked after him. At this moment, relief was her reaction, also, and it was shared by Hannes Bohlmann who had left the bar to stand beside her. Gerda turned to him.

'I don't understand myself, Hannes. I've instigated this whole thing because I could not bear the thought that these murderers should get away with what they've done. This man's just as guilty as the other one. So how could I feel sorry for him, even for one second? Can you explain that, Hannes?'

Bohlmann shook his head and it was not the playwright who answered but the psychologist.

'Not really, Gerda. Except – he's still a human being. Not everything that we think and do can be explained to suit us. We have to live with who and how we are. I did not foresee my own reactions. I've been producing a play on the stage of reality, an experiment I've been thinking of for a long time: the ultimate naturalist drama. I'm glad it's over because some of the thoughts that have passed through my mind during the last few days were the last thing a sophisticated old stage-treader like me would have expected.'

She was surprised.

'You, too?'

He put an arm around her shoulders.

'Yes, ironic, isn't it? I've been playing god and I don't even believe in one. Look at it this way, *Liebchen*' (sweetheart). 'We undertook this for a reasonably moral purpose and we may have been successful. There are plenty of murderers about and if what we've done brings one of them to justice, it was worth it. Everything has a price and we're paying our share. I'm not sorry for either of the two Nazis, nor should you be. But to watch suffering is always painful. I've nothing else on this evening, Gerda. Let's have dinner together, the way we used to.'

Chapter 3 – Drama in the Streets of Munich

Gerda recognised that tone of voice, but she said yes. They sat in a corner at the Donisl.

'Thank your gang for their work, Gerda. They were superb. And, if you don't mind, keep my identity concealed.'

'They've praised your scripts, Hannes, and your efficiency. They were enthusiastic in what they were doing. They even roped in a few outsiders, personal friends who're probably still wondering why they were requested to do what they were doing. I share their appreciation, Hannes, and I'm grateful. No one else could have done it. Ronald asked me to make sure you let me have your invoice.' After a brief pause she added, 'I wonder how he's feeling now.'

Bohlmann put his hand over hers.

'Good, I hope. You'll get a professional bill. I must keep my secret enemy, the taxman, happy. Please, thank Michel and give him my best.'

'If it hadn't been for him, I'd have had a lot of stick from some of the staff for my fringe activities during the day. Not to forget your calls every evening, Hannes. About Michel. I know you've got many contacts in the town – but one of our headwaiters? How did you get him to help? I didn't even know you were acquainted. Although, Michel is different from the other waiters.'

She withdrew her hand. He pretended not to have noticed.

'Yes, he is. Let me tell you. It's not a secret.' He leaned back, adopting a reminiscing pose. 'At the end of the war, Gerda, there was an office in the Rathaus, occupied by a French major from the occupation. Courcy – yes, Armand de Courcy, his name. I'd just returned from Leipzig and got a job in his office as liaison officer. He arrived with a junior officer, Georges – I never knew his surname. Soon after I started, an English officer arrived. Now what was his name? Simon? Simmons? Yes – no, it was Simmonds with a "d". Major Jason H. Simmonds. Don't ask me what the H stood for but he always included it when he introduced himself. They shared the office, the French and the English. He, too, was a major. He, too, brought a junior officer with him as interpreter. That was Michel Heller, a German, like me. De Courcy did not speak English and the English officer did not speak any French. The French major kept sending his man – the one whose name I don't remember – away on all sorts of confidential tasks and errands. There were other German employees, a cleaner, a couple of typists and Ingrid, the office secretary. Ingrid was very pretty. Yes, she certainly…'

He stopped, seeing Gerda's smile. 'Anyway,' he continued, 'we were quite a sociable bunch. Ingrid, Michel and I were really running the office. Ingrid spoke neither English nor French. So Michel and I were kept busy, interpreting for everyone. The two majors, although they were Allies, had little communication with each other.' He stopped again. 'Gerda, that gives me an idea for a sketch. Tower of Babel scenario in an office – it could be funny. Anyway, the job lasted about a year. Then the office was closed and Georges and the two majors went back to their companies. But Michel stayed here in Munich. I've always suspected a case of *Cherchez la femme*, or, in this case, *die Frau* but, if so, he kept it well hidden. And when we met again, he was a headwaiter at the Hofbräuhaus, a bit of a surprise because he seemed to be too well educated for the job. And now you know everything.'

She gave a short laugh.

'I don't think anyone will ever know everything about you, Hannes.'

He raised his eyebrows quizzically and leaned forward.

'I meant to ask you to come home with me after the meal but I've the impression that—'

She interrupted him.

'Look, Hannes, when I came to Munich I was lonely and you were kind and – I was grateful. But – anyway, Ronald is waiting for me, I'm sure you understand.' She smiled sweetly.

'I do, Gerda. Now it's your turn. How come you know him? How does a girl from Vienna, working in Munich, come to know an Englishman so well who's only been here a few weeks? '

'Ronald was my first real boyfriend ever, Hannes. He was in Vienna with his parents when I was just seventeen.'

He looked at her, searchingly.

'Are you telling me he's the one who—'

'Certainly not,' she interrupted him. 'Ronald was much too shy. The truth is I was head-over-heels in love with this polite English boy, really in love… It's old hat now, Hannes, but I don't want to get into any more casual situations any more, ever. Sorry.'

Again he put his hand over hers, but this time in an avuncular way.

'No fret, Gerda. But I don't have the impression that he'll—'

'You're right, Hannes, he won't. I know that. All the same, to me it's a serious relationship.'

He nodded.

'Sure. Let's wind up the performance. In my judgement it was a good fifty per cent successful. I think there's a real chance that this fellow Lünecke will talk, so it's important that your Ronald gets on to his law contacts fast. You'll tell him that, won't you?'

Gerda squeezed Bohlmann's hand thankfully.

'You can rely on that, Hannes.' She rose. 'I must go. You're a good friend.'

She kissed him on the cheek and left. He looked after her with a wry expression of affection and regret, then called the waiter.

'I'll have another beer, Schani, to drown my conscience.'

Neither Gerda nor he was aware that in the afternoon, a Consulate messenger had delivered a letter to Justizrat, Dr. Elias Strauss. It requested him formally to represent the British Foreign Office, via the British Consulate in Munich, in the legal prosecution of the below-named German citizens for the murder, two years ago, of David Lloyd, a British journalist.

* * *

When Lünecke entered the house where he lived on the first floor, the caretaker, a thin little man with owlish eyes and a permanent expression of surprise in them, stepped from his ground floor flat. He had been looking out for him and broke into a deluge of words.

'Herr Lünecke, your friend, Herr Steger, came to call on you earlier on. He was hammering at your door and when it was not opened he started to shout and curse. Such language. So, Herr Krommel from number twelve, he came to fetch me. Your friend was shouting louder and louder. He shouted that you have gone to betray him and he will kill you. So I tell him I must fetch the police if he does not stop. Of course I say it politely and quietly because that is my way, as everybody knows. So, when other neighbours come out from their doors, he slowly controls himself. And now I tell you, Herr Lünecke, politely, because that is my way, that such a behaviour is not very nice. It is my responsibility to keep order in the house. I may even have to take an action, do something radical. Yes, I am seriously thinking about it. So, I hope you tell your friend. Some of the tenants have complained before about him and even both of you making a lot of noise outside the house door when you are coming back from – er – somewhere. Yes, they have, believe

Chapter 3 – Drama in the Streets of Munich

me. But it is understandable that young people are sometimes noisy. I understand this, because that is my way.

Also when you wear that smart brown uniform one must make allowances, I think. So, I've always said, your politics and private life is not my business. But you should talk to your friend. It is my duty to ask you this. Perhaps you can arrange that he does not call here. You understand that the landlord employs me to look after the house and if I tell him about the complaints, who knows what he will do. He might order me to ask you to vacate. Or even inform the police? One thing I should tell you, personally. I think your friend is perhaps serious. About killing you. Do you know he has a big knife in his belt? Perhaps you should go to the police, Herr Lünecke. I'm thinking of your safety so I hope you're not angry. It isn't your fault, of course, but he really ought not to behave like this.'

With those words he turned and hurried back to the safety of his flat, where his wife, a woman much larger than he, in all directions, stood in the open door. She closed it behind them, saying, 'You told him, Hildebrand. I didn't hear what you said but he was frightened, I could tell.'

Her husband stared at her, astonished. He could not imagine anyone ever being frightened by him. Yet her observation was correct.

On his way home, Lünecke had begun to recover his equilibrium. His fears of the unknown were receding because the mysterious person representing it had not turned up. By the time he had reached his house he had decided that perhaps he need not do anything. Now, within the space of a few minutes, the words of the anxious little caretaker who was always polite, because that was his way, had reproduced a large portion of very realistic fear. He went to bed, but sleep shunned him for most of the night. Only emotional exhaustion caused him to fall asleep in the early morning. The sound of fists hammering at his door woke him up and drove his fears to terror. Until he heard the words:

'Open the door! Police!'

Shouting almost cheerfully, 'I'm coming!' He dressed with alacrity and opened the door, feeling that he had been saved from a great danger. Again tenants issued from their flats to watch the spectacle of two policemen leading a happily smiling Horst Lünecke, in handcuffs, down the stairs. They had never believed that their caretaker would ever take any action, whatsoever, but they changed their mind that morning. His wife, too, was impressed. In contrast, Herr Hildebrand was more amazed than they, more amazed than he had ever been in his life. In coming years, he told the tale often. How he had decided that things had got too far and demanded that the police do their job, because, as everybody knew, he was the kind of man who did whatever was necessary to fulfil his duty one hundred per cent. The tenants of another house, not far away, enjoyed a similar experience that morning.

Theirs was much more exciting, however, because Rudi Steger's reaction to the arrival of two police officers was the opposite of his friend's. He refused to open the door and they got the caretaker to do so. When they entered the flat, Steger, wearing a pink nightshirt, was waving his knife threateningly in front of him. Whilst one of them entered and drew his revolver, the other one's truncheon knocked the knife out of Steger's hands, breaking a couple of his fingers in the process. He cried out and continued to struggle, shouting and cursing, whilst being handcuffed. The officer, who had drawn his revolver, saw Steger's brown shirt gracing the only chair in the room. It inspired him to a dramatic decision.

'Your pink shirt, Herr Steger, makes you look real smart and we'll do you the honour of letting you wear it whilst we transport you to your cell. After all,' with a sneering glance towards the brown shirt, 'you're trained to be tough and will not feel the cold. It's only September.'

The two policemen knew they were breaking the law although it did not specifically mention pink night shirts, but they assumed correctly that no one would make a complaint. Steger was led down the three storeys and into the police car outside, holding his broken fingers and cursing all the time. His store of swearwords and curses seemed to be inexhaustible. He was not an alluring sight. The officers had, however, also taken a complete set of his outer clothes and threw them after him when he entered his cell. Sheer police brutality. Steger, by then, had lost his fury and bluster and had sunk on to the bench in the cell, staring dully at the cell's dirty-grey walls.

Upon receiving the official instruction from the British consul, Strauss had not wasted a single minute. He immediately telephoned Department Five of the *Polizeidirektion* (Police HQ) in the Ettstrasse. There, Kriminalkommissar Hirsch, who had been waiting for the call, promptly issued the order for the two potentially dangerous men to be arrested early the next morning, instructing his

Chapter 3 – Drama in the Streets of Munich

officers to keep the two men well apart. Ronald and Craig received the information of the arrest on Saturday and celebrated at their midday meal.

'You've done well, buddy, though it may be best I don't know all the details,' was Jameson's comment as they clinked their steins.

'A major part of it was due to you, Craig, and I happily keep you ignorant of the fascinating rest. I'm lucky to have had your support. And it's due to you that London won't know about my part in it.'

Jameson shook his head slowly.

'I wouldn't be overly sure of that, Ronald, my pal.'

Ronald looked up.

'What do you mean? Must you report it, or do you think that Gaisford...?'

'I certainly don't. We're in different services, Ronald. The Consul will prepare a report on your work only. He's not interested in anything else. But I've heard that MI6 is always keeping watch on its new recruits. Why worry? You haven't done anything improper, have you?'

Ronald relaxed. He did not believe that MI6 would bother to keep watch on every newcomer, nor was there any way in which he could have been watched. For the rest of the lunch their conversation turned around the compilation of the case material Craig had to submit to Strauss. It needed to be formal, detailed and reliable. It had to be signed by the Consul and copies had to be sent to the Foreign Office. Everything had to be done by the book.

'I must mention you in my report, Ronald,' Jameson said, 'Your lot would never believe that you had nothing to do with it. Something to the effect that your calling on your father's landlady, gave an impetus to the ongoing enquiry, will do.'

Ronald nodded appreciatively.

'Long live all landladies, even those in the towns. Your law studies have come in useful, didn't they? What stopped you from completing them, Craig, if I may be nosy?'

'You're asking whether you may, as part of already doing it? The law I studied in Heidelberg was Roman law, not practised in Britain. I'd have had to start at rock bottom again in England. Instead, I studied Philosophy at Oxford. And when His Majesty was looking for men with some knowledge of Germany and the Germans, I left the university to follow my nose. Does that satisfy your ears?'

Ronald looked rueful.

Chapter 3 – Drama in the Streets of Munich

'I know; I shouldn't have asked. I'm sorry.'

'You only got what isn't censored. Please let me have a statement of all the facts you have and how you see the situation so I can check my notes before typing out the statement for the Consul, Strauss and whoever else.'

'I'll start right away, Craig.'

'That's good, because that's when I need it. The consul will also have to send information to your mother. In that, we don't need to mention you at all.'

* * *

Sunday was the Strauss's open day. As Gerda was free in the afternoon, Ronald asked her to come with him, but she declined. When leaving, he was startled to see what looked like the glint of a tear in her eyes but she closed the door on him before he could say anything. He decided he would return early. He reached the iron gate of the path to the front door of Kobell Strasse 13 at the same moment as Naomi Kiss coming from the opposite direction. Her smile, enhanced by those eyes, was bewitching and he had to remind himself that she was seventeen, legally still a child for another four years. They walked up the stairs together and, as he was about to push the bell on the door, heard the voice of Elias Strauss from behind them:

'No need, Mr. Burnley, I have the key. How good of you to come.'

The Justizrat and Jameson just caught up with them. Strauss opened the door, saying, 'How nice to see you again.'

Jameson stared at Naomi for a brief moment. Had she and Ronald come together. Surely not? Whilst Ronald was hanging up his coat, Strauss explained to him:

'Your colleague and I have just done a spot of work together. You may be interested to know that I've succeeded for the prosecution to begin on Monday the eighth October.'

Ronald required no explanation.

'The date of my father's murder.'

'It may have a psychological effect. I can confirm, Mr. Burnley, that you will not be called as a witness but, if you wish, you could attend the first open court hearing.'

Chapter 3 – Drama in the Streets of Munich

Ronald did not hide his satisfaction as they were walking towards the drawing room and replied.

'I don't know the exact day as yet, but I shall probably leave Munich before the first hearing.'

'Nein!'

It was Naomi's protesting little outcry, heard by everybody. Strauss decided he must talk to his wife about it. Jameson thought he must have a word with Ronald. Ronald was busy absorbing Dr. Strauss's news. They had ignited a jumble of images, which appeared dramatically in his mind: his father's face against the background of rain, Lisette's sadness when he departed, Gerda's glinting tear, the truculent face of Steger, passing like images on a ticker tape. He was standing beside the Justizrat in the drawing room, still without conscious awareness of his environment, feeling as if wafting on air. An emotional burden had dropped from his mind. He had come down to earth, newly-born and embracing a new life when, a moment later, Rachel Strauss began to introduce him to her guests. His smiling responses and good looks were captivating everybody. Jameson, as so often the observer, realised that on this afternoon his young friend was what the Germans called the *Hahn im Korb* (cockerel in the basket), the main centre of interest.

The Strauss family had taken a collective shine to Ronald. With this kind of personality, Ronald Burnley could probably reach the heights of his profession. But Jameson wondered. Somehow, Ronald did not seem to fit the sophisticated secret agent's role. Jameson was aware that his brief friendship with Burnley had drilled a few holes into the shell he had developed since losing his wife. His thoughts went back in time: the whirlwind marriage to a British girl, who was visiting a German pen friend in Heidelberg, the death of mother and baby in the first year of their marriage followed by a long period of a vacuum in his life. Emerging from the flashback stirred a dislike of the noisy, social atmosphere and he left, unnoticed, after half an hour, with a quick, formal 'good-bye' to the Justizrat. Dr. Strauss, Med, was just completing her introductions:

'Let me introduce Mr. Charlton-Haig to you, Mr. Burnley, a compatriot of yours who is running the English Library in Munich.'

Ronald responded politely. He did not really want to make any new acquaintances. However, he found the man interesting and pleasant company and promised to visit the library before leaving Munich, if time permitted it. Charlton Haig, too, enjoyed their conversation, deciding at the end, that this young man was not as guileless as he appeared to be. Ronald, moving from one member of the family to the next and other guests, was increasingly enjoying his visit. Hannah and Frederic barely moved from his side, like security personnel guarding an important personality. Ronald wondered whether Frederic would ever find out how hugely his school recital had influenced the course of events and why he was not called Fred.

During his conversations, he became conscious of Naomi's beautiful eyes following him. He suddenly realised that he had forgotten his intention of returning early to Gerda. It was time to leave. Looking around, he saw that Jameson was missing. At this moment he heard Dr. Strauss say, 'It is getting dark, Naomi, your parents might worry. Ira will see you home.'

Ira was the eldest son, aged nineteen, quiet if not reticent. He had just started university. Looking across, Ronald saw Naomi's eyes fixed on him questioning, urging. He was strongly aware of the attraction but he knew he must not offer to see her home. He excused himself and went into the ante-room for his coat in order to depart quickly. As he was putting it on, Ira and Naomi were passing behind him. Suddenly Naomi rushed back, put her arms around Ronald's neck and her lips found his. He unconsciously put his arms around her and, for one brief second, held her close. Her kiss was inexperienced, lips squeezed together, hard and long. Then she whispered, '*Ich werde Sie nie vergessen*' (I shall never forget you) – using the German formal word for 'you', child to adult, and rushed out after Ira.

And Ronald knew he, too, would not forget her. Upset and reproaching himself for this moment of weakness, he returned to the drawing room in order to make his good-byes. He made the round, receiving good wishes for his return to England from everyone – not quite everyone. Frederic complained bitterly for not having had the opportunity of hearing about life in England which, he claimed, Ronald had promised. He was joined by both Doctors Strauss, the medical one, who kissed him on both cheeks and the legal one who shook his right hand. Both asked him to call again before leaving Munich.

'Just drop in any time, Mr. Burnley, after work, no formalities, join us for supper. We eat at seven. Like one of the family, Mr. Burnley.'

Chapter 3 – Drama in the Streets of Munich

'Cook doesn't mind, she's the best,' Frederic chirped, 'Please say yes.'

Ronald did, but doubted he would and conscience-plagued left, suddenly in a hurry. Gerda was still up and flatly rejected any suggestion that something was wrong. He did not press her verbally. She was more loving in the night and more demanding than usual, waking him up several times with kisses and caresses. This also happened the following two nights. As always he accepted the gifts of the gods –of one of them, Aphrodite, to be more precise – but felt the lack of sleep, the absence of Hypnos, to be consistent, during the day. On both days he spent a lot of extra time, checking and listing all the work he had done and drafting a comprehensive report for the Consul, textually a basis for the report he had to submit in London. It resulted in his coming home later than Gerda who worked an early shift that week. Despite the tender nights, in the evenings Ronald sensed an atmosphere of tension which made no sense to him.

He was not the only one to be concerned. On Wednesday during her break, Gerda was cornered by Michel.

'You don't look happy, Gerda,' he said, 'Something is wrong. And don't say there's nothing. I've known you too long. Is it your English boyfriend? I should have warned you, he's not—'

She turned on him.

'My English – Ronald? What do you mean, you should have warned me? What's wrong with him?'

He raised his hand.

'Nothing at all, Gerda. In my opinion he's an admirable specimen of British males. But you're definitely not happy. Because he's leaving Munich? Tell me. You know I'm your friend.'

He had never spoken to her in this vein before and hit the right moment. She looked at him, eyes filling with tears. Then, spontaneously leaning her head against his fatherly chest, she lamented:

'It's Steffel.'

He patted her shoulder gently.

'What about your Steffel? I thought you two must have split when he left.'

'No.' She stepped back. 'I can't talk to you from that angle,' she explained. 'We had agreed, Steffel and I: each of us remains independent. We were just keeping company, you know.'

Chapter 3 – Drama in the Streets of Munich

'Of course,' he said, feeling old-fashioned. 'I should have realised. I always thought that Hannes was a bit too old. So, what is the problem?'

How did he know about Hannes? entered her mind briefly but she was too preoccupied with the current situation.

'Why I'm not happy? He's written he wants to marry me, that's why.'

That did surprise Michel. He gave it some thought whilst she was drying her tears with her dirndl apron. Perhaps he was not so old-fashioned after all.

'I see,' he replied. 'He's proving the old saying about absence making the heart grow fonder. But you don't want to marry him. Of course, in your case—'

She shook her head at his lack of understanding.

'That's the problem, Michel. I thought I would marry him when he comes back. He's got a good career ahead of him. And I couldn't marry a nicer fellow, don't you agree?'

'I do.'

'So now do you see?'

He shook his head.

'Let me get this straight, Gerda. Your regular boyfriend wants to marry you and you want to marry him. And your temporary filling, your English flame, is due to leave in two weeks' time. It seems to me, you haven't a problem in the world. It's Roman mosaics except for the nationality.' He glanced at her reaction. 'I see. You really want your Englishman?'

She nodded silently.

'That's the warning I should have given you, Gerda. He'll never marry you.'

Gerda nodded, dry-eyed.

'I know that, Michel. Hannes said the same. I've known it from the first day. Even as a young girl when I first met him, I knew that he would never marry me. Ronald isn't the type.'

'I agree with you there. The women will never let him, either. But I'm back to where I started. Your Ronald, whom you can't have, is leaving and your Steffel, whom you will have, is arriving. I'm not skilled in dialectics, like your father, but I can see no problem.'

She stared at him. Then it came forth in plaintive tones:

Chapter 3 – Drama in the Streets of Munich

'But, instead of not coming back for another month, Steffel has decided to come back this Sunday. A whole week before Ronald is going back to England.'

Michel found himself on the edge of disaster, i.e. a heavy temptation to break into uninhibited laughter. But he resisted manfully. She was deeply unhappy for losing a whole week of being with the man she loved deeply. And that was no cause for laughing. Instead he pulled her closer, looking soberly down into her eyes.

'Gerda, *meine Liebe*, you know exactly what you're going to do, don't you?'

She nodded slowly. She had known it from the moment the letter had arrived on Saturday. It was the reason why she refused to accompany Ronald to his friends, despite her curiosity about them.

'You're right, Michel. Thanks. But how did you know he's leaving? You've hardly exchanged a few words with him?'

'Oh, people tell me things. But I'm afraid, break is over. We have to return to work, young lady. We'll continue another time.'

She nodded cheerfully and set off. On Thursday morning, at the end of another affectionate night, whilst watching Ronald's methodical way of getting dressed and with a last possessive look at the disappearing muscular body, Gerda said haltingly, with little pauses for suppressing the tears that threatened her voice:

'I told you, *Liebling*, about my friend Steffel, didn't I? – When you came to stay with me, Ronald – who was staying here. – I, I've been saying good-bye to you – since last Saturday. – That's when his letter came.'

Although completely unexpected, it took Ronald only seconds to understand.

'I thought he wasn't due to return yet. Why didn't you say?'

'I didn't want to spoil our – our good-byes, Ronald. – He's coming this Sunday. – I must get the flat ready – you must move out. – This evening!'

She was unable to prevent a few heavy tears from filling her eyes. That was it. No trimmings. Ronald did not say anything. He felt something but could not translate it into words. Hurt? Disappointment? But he had no right. Gerda had made the prosecution of his father's murderer possible. She had given him an affectionate home life. Her tears proved the affection. She had been a good and very close friend. It had been like finishing an unfinished chapter, started a few years ago. He had happened to drop into this situation by coincidence. Was that wrong? There had been a surfeit of emotion in his life since he had come to Munich. The chapter was definitely ended, so why did he experience a feeling of loss? Gerda watched the changing expressions of his face. She intuitively understood him better than he did himself. Having said what had to be said, she recovered her equilibrium.

'My papa often quoted, "Freedom is the realisation of necessity." Karl Marx. I understand it now. I had to make a decision, Ronald. It was difficult but it was easy because I had no alternative. I cannot wait another eight years. Papa also quoted a funny rhyme: *"Die Hälfte seines Lebens wartet der Mensch vergebens."'* (Half of man's life is spent waiting in vain.)

Ronald knew the saying. But it was not really humorous. Gerda had been waiting for him? For eight years? Was that what she was saying? She looked at the little clock on her bedside cabinet.

'You must hurry, Ronald, or you'll be late. Please come for your things right after work. I don't want you to be here when I come home. It would be too difficult. You see that, don't you?' She turned away so as not to show the tears re-emerging.

* * *

Ronald spent a lonely weekend, filled with a sadness which turned beyond his understanding, when he suddenly discovered that he was somehow interchanging Gerda with Lisette. But he felt certain that Lisette would never reject him. But could he really be certain? And somewhere in the images drifting around in his mind, that of Naomi kept turning up also. In the end he took refuge in the fatalistic streak of his character, recalling his father's words, 'Don't argue with facts, Ronnie. They always win.'

After having been invisible during the weekend, Jameson turned up for lunch at the Kühbogen on Monday, elegantly flicking his hat towards the usual antler hook on the wall and, as usual, elegantly missing it, thus maintaining his one hundred per cent record since Ronald had known him. Ronald was pleased to see him. Carefully fitting his hat over the antler horn, Jameson sat down and spoke.

'I went to see Strauss just after he returned from the interrogation. Lünecke has agreed to bear witness against Steger. They promised him protection. They're sure that, even if Steger escapes the death penalty, he'll not leave the prison for a long time. Oddly enough it's

Chapter 3 – Drama in the Streets of Munich

Lünecke's testimony that provides Steger with an ameliorating circumstance. According to him, your father's success in repelling Steger and throwing him to the ground, led to Steger's furious reaction. Steger had only meant to frighten his victim with the knife. Steger's defence is that it was not he but Lünecke who did the deed. He does not know that we have concrete evidence against him. Strauss believes that Steger's not bright enough to hold out in cross-examination.'

Ronald took a deep breath, looking out of the window for a few drawn-out moments before saying slowly and with conviction, 'I'm so very, very grateful, Craig.'

He added no explanation. Jameson looked at him, 'I expected you'd at least break into yodelling. You can relax now, buddy. By the way, when I left Strauss, I thought I'd tell you right away and went round to your love-nest. I rang and knocked but no one answered.'

'I can tell you why. Gerda doesn't return before midnight and I wasn't there.'

'My conclusion, exactly. But it was the time you'd be back from the office.' A sudden thought entered his mind. 'You didn't have a date? With the glamorous young Naomi? You wouldn't.'

Ronald's voice was even.

'No, I would not. I moved out last night. By the time you knocked I was gone.'

Jameson could hear the resentment in Ronald's voice.

'I'm sorry, pal.'

It was meant for both, the unjustified suspicion and Ronald's news. Ronald disregarded it.

'I expect my travel warrants before the week is over, anyway.' Then he explained, 'The boyfriend's returned, yesterday, I think.'

Jameson changed the subject.

'I mustn't forget a message from the younger Strauss, Frederic. He came rushing into the office whilst I was there. In English, too. His speech, not the rush: "Please say to Mr. Burnley, he has us promised to visit us." And Strauss senior confirmed it. "We expect him for dinner," he said.' He added, trying to sound tongue-in-cheek, 'I hope you'll go, Ronald, otherwise they'll think I've not given you the message.'

Ronald shrugged his shoulders, still feeling irritated. Jameson handed him an envelope.

Chapter 3 – Drama in the Streets of Munich

'And I've got something else for you.'

He handed it to Ronald who withdrew its content and took a quick look at it, eyes flying across the first few lines. It was a carbon copy of Jameson's most recent epistle to the Foreign Office.

'Confidential Report, 23 August, 1928. Re: Murder of David Burnley. This statement follows my recent report. It is to inform you that, as the result of information obtained with the assistance of local citizens…'

Ronald stopped there.

'Thanks, Craig. I'm going to read this at home, if you don't mind.'

But before tucking it away, he glanced at the end: '…my final report on the murder of Mr. Burnley. As it has now gone to court, any further statements will be contained in the official consular reports. Craig Jameson, Security Officer.' Ronald thought ruefully: Jameson's final report. From the start, Jameson had been the safe rock supporting him. He should not be peeved by a friend's concern.

They walked back to the consulate together and before they parted he said, 'Sorry, Craig and thanks.'

Jameson responded with a little smile of acknowledgment. At work, Ronald sent his last test message to the Coding School and his last report on the Weimar Republic to Cormody, this one with extra emphasis on the growth of the German National Socialist German Workers' Party, briefly mentioning the Hitler rallies. He also commented critically on the system of proportional voting system in the Weimar Republic. He returned to his flat and was aware that he had nothing to do and nowhere to go. At this moment he did not feel one bit like a tough MI6 agent. And he owed Jameson and the Family Strauss. He changed and made his way to their home. His mind was heavy. He was feeling drained and vaguely resentful of something and nothing when he rang the bell at Kobell Strasse 13.

The following day, Craig Jameson entered the Kühbogen at lunchtime. Ronald was there already. Jameson, about to flick his hat, stopped, seeing Ronald's grin in anticipation of the established failure and switched to the manual safe method, for the first time ever. He did not realise how disappointed that made a number of the regular guests. Sitting down he peered at Ronald's cheerful expression.

'You look cheerful, buddy. Something's gone right.'

'I've got to give you the greetings of the ostriches, Craig.'

Chapter 3 – Drama in the Streets of Munich

'Ostr–? Strauss? So you did visit them. I'm glad. What brought about this change of atmosphere in your physiognomy?'

'It's a fair question, Craig, only I can't put my fingers on it. I went there miserable as hell and came back as happy as the laughing policeman.'

'What did they do? Tickle you?'

'That's just it. As far as I can remember they did nothing. Frederic asked whether it was true that in the City of London all the male workers are wearing top hats and trousers that are too short and told me I was ignorant because I don't know that Marble Arch holds the smallest police station in London.'

'You don't know such a world-famous fact?'

'Never heard of it. Have you?'

'Just as often as you.'

'Then Gabriele and Ernstl challenged me to a few games of Dominoes. They explained it to me and I'm proud to tell you that I won a game. Ernstl, who's seven and Gabriele who's thirteen won the other three between them. Well, it wasn't part of my Service training.'

'A grave omission, Ronald.'

'My grave. It was the same with Rummy. They play it with seven cards and with knocking, which I'm not used to, so it isn't surprising…'

'Of course not, Ronald. I'm sure if you had learnt to knock…'

'I managed to hold my own against Ira, though. A long discussion about Heidegger.'

'No manipulating of the real world? I'm glad you didn't let the side down, Ronald.'

'I agreed with Ira, actually, on Heidegger being an anti-Semite.'

'You've not mentioned the bubbly Hannah.'

'She's the most impressive of them, Craig. My father wanted me to become a musician but our gypsy life prevented him from getting me started, he once told me. I was pleased at the time, but last night, Craig, listening to Hannah, I was wondering. I'm no expert but she sounded great.'

'It seems to me they made sure you were being entertained, Ronald.'

'Perhaps, Craig, but it didn't feel like that. What got to me was that they treated me not like a guest but, genuinely, like part of the family. Nothing organised or artificial. I've not known this kind of

Chapter 3 – Drama in the Streets of Munich

family life and it felt pretty good, Craig. I'm popping there again tonight.'

'The food must have been tasty.'

'Vegetable soup. "It's not wise to have a big meal in the evening" – the Frau Doktor. I was so relaxed by then; a slice of toast would have delighted me. Of course, toast's not known in Germany. I promised to teach them "My Bonnie lies over the Ocean". Hannah can play the melody so I've no excuse. You'll never guess where I first heard that song.'

'It's Sunday, the day of rest for my brain.'

'At school in Vienna, as guest in the English lesson. The teacher, Herr Kögel, played the guitar and sang it to us.'

'You're no Caruso but you can sing almost as loud, I remember.'

They were silent for a moment. Then Ronald said:

'It was really the Frau Doktor, Craig. When I arrived, she welcomed me so heartily, and at the same time so matter of fact – as if I belonged. I was feeling guilty and said I wasn't going to be good company. She said an emotional hangover was a normal reaction. "Don't do anything," she said, "it will disappear by itself." It did. By the time I sat and listened to Hannah – Clair de Lune, one of few pieces of music I actually recognise – my hangover was gone and forgotten.'

* * *

In London, at 54, Broadway, in the morning of that same Tuesday, Admiral Sir Hugh Sinclair had entered his office at the usual hour. His quick glance through the stack of the morning's mail made him pick out an 'Inter-Service Telegram' from a 'good man' in Munich, already decoded:

'RB, assisted professionally by CJ, MI5, investigated father's murder with local v/p assistance. Kept out of limelight. Main suspect, almost certainly guilty, about to be tried. No rules broken. Top marks. M.H.'

Sinclair nodded to himself, his eyes expressing satisfaction, except for a tiny questioning raising of the eyebrows at the v/p – very personal. He pinned the telegram to the report from Jameson which he had received the day before and rang Cormody.

'Burnley's done it. Found his father's murderers. He's due back, isn't he?'

Chapter 3 – Drama in the Streets of Munich

'Yes, Admiral. Austria's next. And last.'
'It'll all go directly to you from now on, old chap.'
'Will you want to see him?'
'No, Perry. My personal interest's done.'

Sinclair was very satisfied with himself. At eleven, Miss Henrietta Alice Sherringham-Bingley, the exceedingly efficient private under-secretary, would collect and deliver all documents concerning Ronald Burnley he had kept. She had played her part exceedingly well. He no longer worried whether he had made a mistake in hiring from outside Oxford and Cambridge. He had successfully dealt with the murder of one of his men without the Service being involved in any way and he had added a good man to his team. Perhaps there were a few more like Burnley out there? Best not to overdo it. Burnley still had his final stint in Vienna, a place where many things happened. As in Munich, there was another good man there to keep an eye on him, except that he would be in the open from the start.

* * *

The next morning Ronald received his movement orders and travel documents for the first Thursday in September. Craig and he walked together to the Kühbogen. Approaching one of the tall advertisement pillars, they saw a young fellow hurrying away from it. They stopped and scanned the sticker he had stuck into the middle of one of the placards. It gave details of a special Nazi rally to take place in Nuremberg on the 14th September, at which Herr Hitler would speak, in person.

'Is there any other way?' Ronald asked.

'These adhesive stickers have become popular. Illegal,' Jameson said, 'but that doesn't deter them.'

'My father warned against Hitler two years ago. That's something I'd have liked to do.'

They reached the restaurant. Jameson upheld tradition by skilfully missing the antler hook. They sat down and the waiter appeared promptly. After they had ordered Craig said, 'What is it you would have liked to do?'

Ronald looked up, 'Continue my father's research into a political party that employs men like Steger and Lünecke and whose militia beats up political opponents.'

Jameson nodded.

'It must be part of most MI6 agents' job in Europe,' was meant jocularly.

'I suppose so. I enjoyed my Munich stint. A few unusual memories are going with me.'

'You're leaving some behind, Ronald. Unusual for a supernumerary.'

In the silence that followed, Ronald's eyes looked into the distance. Craig said, 'Who's the beautiful woman you're thinking of?'

Ronald turned to him, looking like a child caught in enjoying forbidden fruit, which was exactly what he was doing, seeing the image of two beautiful eyes and feeling two immature lips on his. He shook his head, relieved knowing that he never blushed, even when he felt as if he did.

'None that exists in reality as yet,' he said.

At this moment the waiter deposited a goulash with dumplings and the customary beer in front of each of them. Jameson raised his stein.

'Prost, buddy!'

'Prost, Craig Jameson!'

They clinked to the unknown future, fairly certain they were unlikely to meet again. Within two minutes of returning to their offices, Jameson rang Ronald.

'You best pop round right away.'

Ronald popped and received changed movement orders.

'Departure on Thursday 30 August cancelled. Proceed to Nuremberg on Thursday, 13th September. Meet Capitaine Vincent Barbier of the Deuxième Bureau at the Hotel Frankenhof, Nuremberg, where accommodation has been booked for you for three nights. Your task is to collaborate with Captain Barbier, Deuxième Bureau, in observing the rally of the German National Socialist Workers' Party on Friday, 14th September. Prepare an independent report on the rally. P. Cormody, Major.'

Chapter 4 – The Nuremberg Rally

The Nazi rally at Nuremberg was, as expected, a howling success, in the most basic sense of the word. The populist oratory of the speakers was driving a crowd of thousands into noisy acclamation and when Hitler stepped onto the podium the crowd response was ecstatic. He started in a measured tone in which he described how their enemies were not allowing the German people to recover from the betrayal by its false leaders. Gradually his voice was rising in emotional notes to a thundering level, as he promised that he would deal with all these injustices and restore the German master race to the position in the world to which they were entitled to.

It drove his audience into a hysterical ovation lasting several minutes, fired up by the disciplined, rhythmical chants of the Hitler Youth and the Stormtroopers. The rally left no doubt in their minds that it was only a matter of time before the Führer (leader) of this party would be the Führer of all Germans. Each of the speakers had made a point of including it in his repertoire, using the same text. 'We National Socialists respect the law and we shall achieve our goal by legal methods only!' The tenor in which the words were expressed, made them sound like a threat rather than a promise, yet the words contributed greatly to the unceasing growth of the party's membership and supporters.

'Do you think they mean it?' a woman standing arm in arm with her husband on the pavement, alongside the right flank of the Stormtroopers, asked her companion.

'No,' he replied, 'but the papers will publish it and that's good enough to dupe the masses.'

Two Stormtroopers standing in the ranks near-by, had heard him and stepped up to them.

'See you beat it fast, Mister, before the newspapers will publish that you had to be taken to hospital,' one of them rasped under his small moustache. The menace in his voice and the cold, ruthless expression in his eyes left no doubt that he meant what he said. In addition, his words were underlined by the other Stormtrooper's gesture in half pulling out the wooden baton from its leather sheath which was attached to his large military-type belt. The couple, not at

Chapter 4 – The Nuremberg Rally

all eager to enjoy this kind of public fame, hurried away, into the side street. The two SA men, aware of two tall men standing only a few metres away, did not try to stop them.

The two tall men had just met. One of them was a broad-shouldered man in his late thirties, square-faced, with brown hair and a moustache covering his upper lip. The other, younger man's strong face was clean-shaven, displaying humour crow's feet below brown eyes. They seemed to be fully immersed in listening to Hitler's oratory. Vincent Barbier and Ronald Burnley had successfully made contact the day before and enjoyed their evening meal together in the hotel restaurant. When Ronald had begun, in French, to express his pleasure at their reunion, Barbier interrupted him in German, keeping his voice low.

'Not French, Ronald, and not Vincent: Georg Barbier. I was born in Elsass.'

Elsass was the German name for Alsace, a territory situated between the Rhine and the French border. Its population was part French and part German. Bismarck had annexed Alsace at the end of the 1870 war in which Prussia defeated France. Alsace remained part of the German Empire until the Versailles Treaty returned it to France. Whereas this explained Barbier's perfect German, it was a surprise for Ronald to realise that Barbier was using a cover. The Deuxième Bureau obviously treated the German Nazis as enemies and as dangerous. That morning Ronald had started on the left flank of the SA ranks. When Hitler began to speak, Ronald had joined Barbier on the right flank of the SA ranks a few minutes before the Stormtroopers had stepped out of the ranks to threaten and intimidate the couple. Neither Ronald nor Barbier had missed a single word or gesture by the two SA men whilst, at the same time, Hitler's crescendo of threats and promises caused the acclamations of the crowd to reach a hysterical climax.

For one moment, it had looked as if the two SA men would actually proceed to manhandle the couple. Out of the corner of his eye Ronald had seen anger growing in Barbier's face and feared that if they did, Barbier would take a hand. If so, he would have to join him. The likely consequences were impossible to visualise and he felt they had escaped a great danger when the couple made off. The next step in their plan was to proceed towards the speakers' platform in order to have a close look at the Nazi orators before they left. This part of their plan, however, was not fulfilled.

Chapter 4 – The Nuremberg Rally

Ronald's eyes had followed the couple down the side turning. He nudged Barbier to look into the same direction. A limousine turned into the side street from the other end just as the couple disappeared around the corner. Ronald knew that up to now this turning had been kept free of vehicles by two policemen. This limousine, however, was not stopped by the policeman on duty at the far end, which had attracted Ronald's attention. It drove on and pulled up on the kerb beside the other policeman, about ten metres from the corner at which Ronald and Barbier were standing. The policeman actually saluted the driver. The car was a Mercedes-Benz and bore a shield depicting two trees. It obviously belonged to a VIP. Its driver, a tall, handsome man, wearing a chauffeur's cap, stepped out of the car, threw his cap inside and, with a wave of his hand, requested the policeman to guard it, who saluted again. The chauffeur, passing close by Ronald and Barbier, turned into the rally road.

'That's Count Winter's private chauffeur,' they heard one of the two Stormtroopers who had returned to their rank in the SA column, say to his neighbour.

'Count Winter? Now he's a true patriot, the count is, even though he's one of those bloated aristocrats, rich, I mean. I'm sure he's not bloated. He's different.'

'Yeah. He gives large donations to the party. One thing though. I've heard the count never leaves his castle. I don't know anyone who's ever seen him face to face and I live near the castle.'

The chauffeur was now walking along the side of the SA column and, as if casually, stopped beside an SA sergeant at the end of one of the ranks. Barbier's anger had gone, as he murmured, 'Why has this man come to the rally now that it's practically over?'

They saw the chauffeur exchanging significant glances with the sergeant.

'Perhaps that's his son and he's telling him at what time dinner will be ready at home,' Ronald replied. 'I'm amazed to hear that a bloated aristocrat is funding the Nazis.'

At this moment the crowd broke into thunderous applause and cries of adulation when, on the rostrum, Herr Adolf Hitler was shaking the hand of Dr. Goebbels. The SA ranks began to obey various orders by their officers whilst the crowd was swarming all over the place in different directions. Not only did Ronald and Barbier lose sight of the chauffeur but by the time they had worked their way to the front, Hitler and Co. had gone. Beside the platform

Chapter 4 – The Nuremberg Rally

on which they had spoken, a bald-headed, stocky man, busily putting the microphone equipment into his van, was surrounded by a small group of eager listeners. He had all the answers and willingly passed his knowledge to his questioners.

'After their rallies here in Nuremberg, they always proceed to the castle, Schloss Wintereschen, oh yes. Guests of Count Wintereschen, you must have heard of him. He only calls himself Count Winter, of course. He always sends a column of cars – cars? – limousines, oh yes, to pick the speakers up. And their personal staff, and Herr Hitler's bodyguard. They all spend the night at the castle, top luxury, oh yes. And tomorrow morning the count has them chauffeured to Neumarkt Station from where they return to Munich by rail. The organisation is perfect, I can tell you, gentlemen, oh yes.'

'But I've heard that nobody ever sees the count,' a fat little man with rosy cheeks and a green hunter's hat, threw in.

'Ah,' said the bald-headed stocky man who knew everything, raising his index finger importantly, 'there you're wrong. Herr Adolf Hitler has seen him, oh yes. Perhaps the only man who ever has. The count's suffering from a facial disfigurement, a war wound, so he doesn't show himself to the outside world. The thing is, the castle is a safe place for Herr Hitler and the others to relax. Believe me, nobody can scale those walls. And the moat's filled with sludge, a dangerous swamp, I can tell you. And there are only three bridges that lead into the castle and one of them's a footbridge. Not to mention the men guarding the three gates, and the dogs. Oh yes, no one can get into the castle. It's one place where none of Hitler's enemies, even English or French spies, or some of them traitorous Communists can get in.'

'Have you been inside the castle?' a thin-faced man with thick glasses enquired.

'Ah, that would be telling.' The bald-headed stocky man who knew everything was locking the door of the van. 'Anyway, gentlemen, I've done loading and duty calls, oh yes, sorry.'

He slipped into the driver's seat and drove off noisily, leaving a lot of exhaust to get up the men's noses.

'He says oh yes a lot, doesn't he?' the fat little rosy-cheeked man with the green hat, laughing and coughing, said to the thin-faced man with thick glasses.

'I wish my wife did it more often. Good meeting, wasn't it?'

Chapter 4 – The Nuremberg Rally

'No doubt about it. Hitler's the man, oh yes.' He put his hand to his cheek. 'Damn it, now I'm saying it – I'm having a beer before going back home, how about…'

Their voices faded as they walked away, side by side. Neither Ronald nor Barbier had heard of Count Winter before that day but it contributed to their overall impression that their governments were underrating the dangers represented by Herr Adolf Hitler. He was a man on the way up, a man who was cheered by the masses and supported by men of wealth. Count Winter was probably not the only bloated capitalist supporting the German National Socialist Workers' Party.

They left the square, walking in the direction of their hotel, without talking. Seeing a sign: Rudolfsbar, Barbier stopped and turned a questioning eye on Ronald who nodded affirmatively. They entered, their thoughts full with what they had seen and heard during the day. They sat back, enjoying a small cognac, when Count Winter's chauffeur, still capless, entered, followed by the SA sergeant, with whom he had exchanged glances. The two men sat down not far from Ronald's and Barbier's table. It was the chauffeur who ordered the drinks and it was the chauffeur who passed a bundle of banknotes to the sergeant. Ronald and Barbier looked at each other and shrugged their shoulders. Obviously the two men had some business together, nefarious maybe or worse, but it surely had nothing to do with the task of the two agents. The chauffeur was the first to leave. Passing the two agents, he threw a sharp, searching glance at them. His hooded eyes were the one feature in the man's handsome face that stood out. The SA sergeant left a couple of minutes later, after paying the waiter who thanked him effusively.

'*Recht schönen Dank, Herr Bergreiter. Hoffentlich sehn wir Sie bald wieder in Nürnberg.*' (Many thanks, Herr Bergreiter, we hope to see you again in Nuremberg soon.)

The SA man nodded briefly and left, frowning. The two agents at last settled down to talking about the day, in German, but keeping their voices down. Ronald said, 'I've a feeling you've found today's experience as depressing as I have, Georg.'

'You're right but though it's been the first Nazi rally I've ever attended; it was no surprise to me. What troubled me hugely, was the way those two Stormtroopers frightened that couple.'

'I noticed,' Ronald nodded, 'and was prepared for the worst.'

Barbier looked at him and smiled a rare smile.

Chapter 4 – The Nuremberg Rally

'It's true I should have liked to knock their heads together, Ronald, but you needn't fear I'd lose my self-control. My job is important to me and I would not have put you into danger. I hope you believe that because I think it's not impossible that we might work together again in the future. I've stressed to my section head how well I got on with you in Munich.'

It explained to Ronald why he had been given this job although he had not even passed his probation. He, too, enjoyed working with Barbier despite the man's taciturn nature. Ronald sensed that he was not a happy man. Even at their early dinner at the Frankenhof they did not converse a lot. They said good-bye at the end of the meal. Barbier had to leave early to catch his train. Back in his hotel room, he settled down to make notes for the report to his chef de section. He had no doubt that the German National Socialist Workers' Party was a fascist party on the march. Although he had not witnessed any actual violence, himself, his impression was that claims and rumours of the use of violence and threats of violence were true. The two Stormtroopers' intimidation of the elderly couple was a small piece of evidence pointing to that effect.

Barbier had spoken the truth when he assured Ronald that he would control his desire to interfere, but it was equally true that he might have been tempted to do so. He was a devoted patriot and, above all, that rare thing, a man without fear. He was also an unhappy man, having made a mess of his private life for some years. His reserved manner was the reason for his lack of friends. The freshness of Ronald's personality and his honest outspokenness had got through to him. His thoughts switched to his personal situation. He took an envelope from his coat pocket which had reached him just before he left Paris and sat down on his bed. The envelope had an English stamp and the letter was written in English. He had read the main paragraph several times already.

'I've held on to my pride for six years and I don't like myself for it. How often do I need to tell you that you were wrong, Vincent? After that one time, I did not arrange to meet Jonas again behind your back. But he turned up unexpectedly here and there. I was wrong not to tell you because I feared you might pick a fight with him. I never wanted to have anything to do with him. Why don't you believe me, Vincent, why? Janine is seven and Liliane is six. They are your daughters. I shall be thirty-two soon and I cannot bear this situation any longer. This is my final effort to restore our marriage. I

Chapter 4 – The Nuremberg Rally

shall come to Paris to see you. Tell me when is best to come but if you do not reply I shall come anyway to convince you that I love you and need you. Denise.'

For the first time since he had left her he was certain that he had been wrong. He had punished and tortured himself – and her – because of his suspicious nature. He had been unable to bear the image of her sleeping with that former school friend of hers. He had thrown two previous letters away, unopened. Now he, too, could no longer deny the pain of missing Denise and the children, his children. Like the gunpowder in a fuse that has been lit, is burning steadily, unseen, until it reaches the explosive charge, so had his pain and longing been burning inside him. He was close to exploding and suddenly there was clarity. He would meet Denise in Paris and if she would really have him back, he would leave the Bureau, leave Paris and France. That was the simple answer because that was what he wanted. And just as suddenly, still fully dressed, he was asleep, fully dressed.

At the same time that Barbier was reading his wife's letter, three other men were busy summing up their current situation. One of them was Armin, short for Arminius. Bergreiter, in the bedroom of a small boarding house in Nuremberg, who was getting ready for the next day. He was not returning to Munich as the waiter had suggested, but on leave, home to Hornberg, where his father was the assistant level crossing keeper. He patted his full wallet lovingly. It had been a successful seven days. He had proved his loyalty and his ability to Wotan and received his deserved reward. The Austrian professor, who had been in charge, was an odd character, a bossy man of few, mostly offensive, words. Armin had made all the logistic arrangements. The Professor had done the killing. Armin had watched. The professor's face was glowing unnaturally as he shot the Dutchman at close range with his Luger pistol which was equipped with a silencer. He had passed the weapon to Armin who looked after it until he was able to return it to the Professor back in Germany. The Führer, himself, would be pleased. Armin went to sleep, satisfied with himself. Like many of Wotan's private agents, he believed that Wotan was really Adolf Hitler, himself. That the chauffeur of Count Winter was the intermediary proved to him that Wotan must be a man of the highest level in the party.

Ronald in his hotel room, like Barbier, was writing down the basic points for his report to Cormody:

Chapter 4 – The Nuremberg Rally

'On platform: Röhm, leader of SA (Stormtroopers), Himmler, Goebbels, Hitler.

Razzmatazz: brightly coloured flags and banners, with large swastikas. Brass band – rousing martial tunes. Hitler youth collecting money from audience, faces demanding. Goebbels' oratory. Hitler stepping to microphone, dramatic: Band stopped. SA & Hitler Youth: rhythmical repetitive shouting: Heil Hitler. Hitler's voice rising loud evoking passion. Audience crazed faces: ecstatic, beyond reason. Promise to act lawfully. SA men threat of violence: elderly couple's criticism.'

Like Barbier's, Ronald's thoughts also began to wander touching on the people he had met in Munich. But his thoughts did not linger on Gerda. The image of Lisette occupied a lot of his thinking. Her concern for him expressed when they parted, had shaken him. He was taking her for granted but was he being fair to her? Disturbingly and worryingly, two beautiful eyes of a teenage girl also kept emerging for brief moments. His attempt at being rational about his relationships was not as successful as he had hoped. He did admit to himself that he was looking forward to seeing Lisette again, hoping to resume his uncomplicated lifestyle of pre-Munich. Yet, somewhere in a corner of his mind, a question mark had taken possession.

The third other man considering his situation was Count Wolfhart Hagen von Winter-Eschen, to give him his full title. He was seated at the large desk in his study in the castle, reading the report of one of his G-Agents. It had been sent to his secret partner and collaborator, code-named Loki, who had forwarded it to him and was addressed to Wotan. The G stood for *Gerechtigkeit* (justice), which required the death of the enemies of the German people. Arminius Bergreiter was not the only one of his agents who believed that Wotan was Hitler. No one suspected Count Winter who was using his tremendous wealth in order to run a large, secret organisation whose aim was to 'do away' with influential enemies of the German master race. Winter gave his support to Hitler because he believed that Hitler's aims coincided with his own and almost nobody who knew him, knew that he was Wotan. He was reading Bergreiter's brief report:

'I met the professor as arranged. We carried out our instructions successfully. No suspicion can fall on either of us. Justice has been done.'

Chapter 4 – The Nuremberg Rally

The Count nodded his satisfaction and picked up *Die Münchner Presse* (*The Munich Press*) which had arrived with the report and scanned the lines dealing with his act of justice:

'Murder in Amsterdam. Yesterday, early in the morning, the body of Ian van der Beck, the leading Dutch socialist, was found floating in the canal near the university. Foul play is suspected, but at present there is a complete absence of clues, according to the official statement by the police. Van der Beck was recently making the headlines in the Dutch press with his attacks on Adriaan Mussert, the ardent nationalist. Van der Beck accused him of being an admirer of Benito Mussolini and would introduce Fascism to the Netherlands. The Chief of the Dutch Criminal Police has issued a statement: A top investigator will be commissioned to investigate the death. The case will not be closed until we are satisfied that the death was accidental or that the murderer has been arrested.'

'Who will be just as successful as all the others,' Winter murmured.

The yellow light on the short wave radio on the desk came on for the special radio communication with Loki he had requested. He moved to the chair in front of it, put the earphones on and pressed the communication button. A red light lit up.

'Wotan to Loki, over.'

'Loki to Wotan, over.'

'Update.'

'The cells in Belgrade, Budapest, Rome, Bukarest and Warsaw are operational. In London, a few reliable contacts with active pro-Nazis have been established. In Paris, your infiltration plan is in progress. Loki, over.'

'*Prima*' (first class). 'Received Bergreiter's report and the Professor's phone call. Dealt with the remunerations, myself. Wotan over.'

'Bergreiter's one of the men you got from Röhm.'

'What's going on at the top?'

'Hard to say. There's a power struggle going on. Göring and Goebbels are opposed to Röhm. I'm not certain where Hitler stands. He and Röhm were in the war together. He's the only one with whom he's on first name terms. There's complete conviction in all quarters that the NSDAP will run the country within a couple of years. Loki over.'

Chapter 4 – The Nuremberg Rally

'Adolf Hitler's weaker than people realise. He's moving with the wind. Democratic means? The true German acknowledges strength and ruthlessness. People who stand in the way must be eliminated. For the time being we'll not let Hitler or any of his closest know what we're doing to smooth his path. Wotan over.'

'Except for Röhm?'

'Correct. A totally loyal man and a strong one. As long as Hitler is acting with smooth gloves, I have to yield the iron fist. Have you done the summary of our executions? Wotan over.'

'Effected. Locations of executions completed since 1927: Graz-Austria, Brünn-CSR, Debrecen and Eger-Hungary, Weimar-Germany, Belgrade-Serbia and now, Amsterdam-Holland. Total: eight. All executions are still unsolved cases. The Dutch killing will be seen as a political act but no suspicion can fall on our men. The list does not include the three men dealt with by the castle security. Accidental death by drowning in the swamp is entered in the local police records. Our anonymity is complete. Loki over.'

'Good. Next operation, Budapest.'

This time there was more than a trace of doubt in Loki's response. After a pause, he said:

'Another one in Hungary? Debrecen and Eger are still on their police files. You were going to do Perpignan next.'

'The priest can wait. Your information about the Englander's visit is reliable?'

'Totally, Wotan.'

'It'll teach them that no one is safe from Wotan's justice, not even an English lord.'

Loki never argued with his partner who was the real boss.

'Whom will you send?' he asked.

'Dietrich. Let him pick his own team of two. Briefing as usual.'

'Will comply, Loki over.'

'Good. End of schedule, Wotan over.'

'Loki switching off.'

He did. Wotan followed suit.

'Yes, I will teach them,' he said to the chiselled features of a perfect specimen of the master race in the mirror opposite. Loki did not know that the man known as Professor was an ardent, but wholly independent, Nazi, not subservient like their other G agents. Winter had handpicked and recruited him, personally. In turn, Loki, real name Count Odo von Brandtstein, was successfully keeping from

Chapter 4 – The Nuremberg Rally

Wotan that his own loyalty was not an unconditional facet. One major fact he withheld from Winter was that Himmler, who had taken command of the SS, had created a new branch whose major goal was the punishment of effective opponents and enemies of the Nazi Party. It was called The Brown Book but was supposed to be kept secret until it was capable of starting to function. More precisely, Brandtstein hid his resentment at being subservient because the count was the man with the money. He fell asleep toying with ideas of how to get rid of his dependency on the man who had chosen to call him Loki and himself Wotan. Count Winter knew that his money was at the root of his power over other men but he did not realise that it was also an Achilles heel. He went to sleep, self-satisfied as always.

The blanket of the neutral night fell democratically over Nuremberg, covering everything and everyone equally, young and old, good and bad, honest and crooked and weak and strong. It seemed as if the globe's inexorable spiralling was an eternal expression of irony.

* * *

Ronald's journey back to London was uneventful, almost approaching boredom. But it changed direction the closer he came to his destination and was replaced by his looking forward to seeing Lisette again. Her welcome more than justified his anticipation, at least to start with. Her arms around him, holding him tight, she whispered:

'I have missed you so much, Ronnee.'

He had always been thrilled by the way she said his name, putting the accent on the second syllable, as he had always been affected by the seductiveness of the French language. The touch of her body had always been magical. But he had never before been so clearly conscious of it. He noticed something else that was new. Lisette did not, as on previous occasions, ask 'Have you missed me also?' Instead, her arms around him and her head buried in his shoulder, she was eager to tell him her news.

'I am going to be very busy now, Ronnee, you know. I have become a student. Are you not surprised?'

'A student?'

Chapter 4 – The Nuremberg Rally

He said it softly into her soft hair, absorbed in the delight of feeling her.

'Yes. I should say, a double student, Ronnee. I go to the college and I go to the university.'

She had caught his attention, as they sank back onto the couch.

'My sweet, how can you go to university? You haven't passed any exams, have you?'

'That is true but it is not necessary, you know. I go to Clark's College two hours on three days. It is in Chancery Lane, have you heard of it, *chéri*? And I do a course in Philosophy, Ronnee, on one morning at the university. They all start the same week in October.'

Clark's College, a private commercial school, was not new to him. During his training, he had attended a concentrated course in typewriting there, a skill he had found highly useful. It was not, however, what his mind fastened on. Before he could ask, Lisette was already answering.

'It is you that has made it possible for me. The money I get from the bank every month. You have told me I can use it for important needs. I think my most important need is more education and I must also learn an ability to earn money. I do not want to spend all my life cleaning houses and it is wrong that I depend on you, *n'est-ce-pas chéri?*'

So she had lived on only the weekly cleaning wage from the LAB. He felt guilty. And she was planning on not staying with him, it seemed. For one brief moment during her explanations, he had experienced a resentment. Not about the money as such, but about her assuming, that she could spend it on something like this. The moment was cut short. It was the other way round. He was the one who had made the assumptions about her: the main one being, that her position was that of a housekeeper-cum-lover.

That she might not appreciate this situation had never occurred to him, especially the idea that she might want to pursue her own plans for the future, for being independent. This situation was a new one to him in more ways than one. In the past he had never given much thought to his relationships with women. He had taken it for granted that they would end sooner or later. And they always had done. But, unconsciously, he had not made this assumption with Lisette. It had never occurred to him that, sooner or later, she might say adieu, or that he might. But perhaps it had to her? For one other moment he resented being made to feel guilty. He did not notice that Lisette had

140

got up and left the room. His thoughts were interrupted by her returning with the laden tea tray, a duty she took for granted.

'Tea, Ronnee.'

He recalled their first tea together, the evening when he arrived and found her in occupation.

'Do you remember, Ronnee, the first time we have tea together? I have never forgotten it.'

He looked up.

'Nor have I, dear.'

Their eyes met. This was a new meeting. The old platonic sex relationship was in cinders. Was a new one arising from the ashes? Ronald asked, 'How did you come to enrol in these courses, Lisette?'

He was not prepared for her answer.

'Guy was in London again, Ronnee, and I have lunch with him. It was soon after you have gone to Vienna. I was feeling alone very much. I tell him I want to do something to make me better, to know more and to be more. I want to learn things. And he invites me to stay with him, you know.'

'Move back to him?'

A sudden pin-prick of pain had caught him but his voice did not betray it. Murdoch's lesson.

'Oh, no, Ronnee, only for the night. Guy, he was also in London before when you are in Munich and I go to him because he is an old friend. And I know you have an amour there. I- I read it in your letters, how you say, between the words. And when you go away again I think you will have others. Why not? You are free to do what you want. So I say yes.'

She stopped, looking to the floor. Ronald was struck into silence. Things to be said were crowding themselves to the fore but no further. He had no right to say them. Lisette's next words sounded as if from far away.

'And suddenly, Ronnee, I cannot do it. It is not fair to Guy, still I cannot. So I tell him. I have changed. I cannot help it. He has been my only friend, Ronnie, before I meet you. He is older and with his bushy eyebrows and Roman nose he looks like a big adventurer that is hunting tigers in Africa. He has big shoulders and muscles, you know, but he is really a gentle man, so kind. And a gentleman. He is not cross. He brings me home in a taxi and I promise to have lunch with him the next day at the Lyons Corner House.

Chapter 4 – The Nuremberg Rally

'They have music there, Ronnie, an orchestra, you know. And he brings *brochures* for education in London and he explains them and he helps me decide and then goes with me to the *université* and then to the Clark's *Collège*. I take *formulaires d'inscription* home, you know. Guy says he will pay but I cannot allow that. We say goodbye. He says it is better we do not meet again. I am sad a little, but I know he is right. Something, Guy has said is strange, Ronnee. He knows your name and he is your friend also, he says. How is that possible?'

Lisette had always spoken freely about everything and that included sex. He sensed that this flow of words was a relief for her own pent-up emotions. In him they produced stabs of pain and guilt, every time he heard her mention the name of Guy. In answer to her question he shook his head, meaning: no, he did not think that it was possible that the man knew him. She barely noticed it and continued with offloading her feelings. She stopped and she looked at him. Their glances met and fused. A chemical reaction? Whatever. They moved close and clasped each other tight. The bedroom upstairs was too far. They moved slowly to the couch and, without haste, undressed. They joined and began to move together. The sexuality was electric, the rhythm demanded acceleration, their movements grew faster and faster until their cries and sighs accompanied the beautiful fulfilment that their bodies demanded. It left no doubt in Ronald on whether he wanted their relationship to continue. In the process of falling asleep, quite suddenly, out of the blue, something became clear to him: Her Guy must be in the same outfit as he, himself. It was the only explanation for his claim that he knew of Ronald. It also explained how he had been able to find her the job with Sandy Heaven. The realisation ignited a thought process with a negative effect: Guy's assistance to Lisette, helping her to embark on with her new education, made Ronald feel small.

He should have been the one to helping her but all he had ever done was to receive, to take. 'You must always be sure you can look yourself in the eyes, my boy,' his father had written in one of his letters. With Lisette, Ronald had not lived up to it, he had not acted the way he should have done. Things had just happened. But he knew that that was an excuse. Munich had created changes inside him and whilst he was there, Lisette, too, had changed, but their relationship was continuing much the same way it had been before.

Chapter 4 – The Nuremberg Rally

Ronald's professional personality had not changed. His reporting stage in London followed the usual pattern: the early morning sessions at the gym under the guidance of Patroclos, the meetings with other agents at which he gave them an overview of his stint in Munich and the days when he was doing office work at 54 Broadway. The exception was a prolonged sitting with Major Cormody who questioned him on his experiences at the Nazi rally in Nuremberg. Ronald's collaboration with Barbier, a new procedure, had been approved by the Foreign Office's Special Services Committee. They had received a message from the Deuxième Bureau, praising the venture. Given that Ronald had not yet passed his probationary period, Cormody had been reluctant to send him, although the task, in itself, had not incurred any risks. Ronald had fulfilled it satisfactorily. His report presented a graphic picture of what was going on at the rally and described the Nazis Party's rapid progress as a possible danger to peace in Europe. Cormody was hugely impressed. He concluded that Sinclair's decision, for whatever reasons, to send Ronald Burnley to Europe on his probation, had born a fruit that Sinclair had not expected. Cormody gave a lot of thought to this result and started to plan ahead along new lines.

Ronald's next destination, his last probation stint in Europe, was Vienna. His departure date was the second Saturday in October. On Friday night Lisette prepared a special, two-course good-bye dinner by candlelight. Ronald, already seated, watched her carefully positioning the two solid brass Victorian candle holders into the middle of the small table. Then she went back into the kitchen for matches and returned to light the candles. Next she went into the kitchen and returned with the main course, her own version of a Hungarian goulash, on two plates. She realised they were out of turn and took them back into the kitchen. She returned with two bowls of liver-dumplings soup. When she sat down opposite him, she noticed something was missing. She went back into the kitchen, returned empty-handed. She stepped to the oak sideboard, pulled the top drawer open and returned to the table with two flowery serviettes, handing one to Ronald. She sat down again, meaning to look at him with a happy smile. She encountered a difficulty, stood up and moved the candles to the top of the sideboard, explaining.

'I cannot see your face.'

He started to laugh. She stared at him, then she joined in.

Chapter 4 – The Nuremberg Rally

'It is because I am excited. You have been back four weeks, Ronnee. You have gone to work so much but it was the best time we have had, Ronnee. You do not tell me about Munich. You have come back different. More alive. Something has happened. You only write about the food and the weather in Munich. I know you are busy and this is where your father – and... It is so good, when you are home. This I wanted to tell you.'

He still had not begun to eat. Her words were touching, stirring his recent attempts of clarifying their relationship. Before he could reply, she added, 'Ronnee, you will be careful in Vienna, *n'est-ce-pas*? I do not know what you do but I miss you very much when you are away. I have no right, I know, but I cannot help it.'

He experienced a stab of conscience. He tried to ignore it, but in vain.

'My work in Munich was not secret, dear. I worked in the office of the British Consul. It was humdrum office work. I wrote to you about it, Lisette. But you're right about something happening.' He spoke haltingly, searching for the best words. 'They found out that my father had been murdered and they arrested the suspect and he is coming to trial very soon.'

He stopped. Lisette looked at him searchingly.

'*Alors*, the weight on your mind, it has gone, no, Ronnee? That makes me happy. And I am hungry, Ronnee. If you do not start eating, I think you do not like my liver-dumpling soup. I have bought an Austrian cook book. I cannot make the exact dough, so it is a little different from what the book says. I use beef instead of liver and Charlie at the Kensington Market has told me that pepper is better than parsley.'

Both of them took their first bite into one of the dumplings. If Charlie at the Kensington market had seen their initial facial reaction he might have decided not to give the same advice ever again. However, that first bite reminded Lisette of something else. She rushed into the kitchen and returned with a tray upon which two glasses and a carafe of red wine had been waiting to be noticed. Their contribution not only added a touch of colour but also made a lot of difference to the taste of the meal, especially as they enriched it by a generous flow of sweet, intoxicating kisses. Their lovemaking that night had a new timbre to it which filled his thoughts during the coming days. The taxi arriving on time ensured his not missing the train for Dover.

Chapter 4 – The Nuremberg Rally

* * *

As he fell asleep in the train he realised why Lisette had been excited. She was starting her classes on Monday. If the ticket controller had not woken him up, he might have returned to Victoria Station in the same train. Obviously designed to keep him awake, the Channel crossing was unusually rough and, at Calais, he was pleased to step on solid ground and to find his train and his compartment. For the first time in his life, he was travelling on the Orient Express, albeit only second class. The lower of the two couchettes in his compartment was already made up and, after treating the luxurious meal in the restaurant car rather shabbily, he slept comfortably through the night. Unaware that it was the Firm's policy, he considered himself lucky for having the compartment to himself all the way from Calais to the Westbahnhof, Vienna's western rail terminus. By that time, he had more or less recovered in body and spirit, the internal kind. He gave the taxi driver, whose English was far from fluent, his destination. The driver was impressed.

'Wallnerstrasse 4, sir? This street is in the *Innere Stadt*, the Inner City – in the First District. You understand, every district in Vienna has a *Nummer*' (number) 'and a name. I know my Vienna. You must to the English consulate go surely, sir, no?'

'Yes.'

'You have just arrived from England, Sir, so you have probably an important position in the consulate, no?'

'Yes, I have. No, not important.'

Throughout the journey, the driver spoke almost without interruption about the sights they passed, his popularity amongst other drivers and his wife who talked a lot. Ronald's ears developed an immunity until they restored contact with the driver's frequency, hearing him say, 'Do you know, that your consulate is in the Palais Esterházy, sir? That is real class.'

'Palais?'

'One of our wonderful baroque buildings, sir. And the famous Esterházykeller, a restaurant. It was the Esterházy family's wine cellar. They had good taste, despite being Hungarian.'

They had entered a narrow street and he pulled up outside the entrance to an impressive two-storey building. It sported an iron balcony above the main door. The driver said, 'We are arrived, sir. If you want special prices for sightseeing in Vienna, in the *Innere Stadt* or even the outer skirts, for this am I the man, sir. You can rely on me; I know my Vienna. Or just a taxi ride. Here is my card. Just ring *Zentrale* and ask for me. Yes, just ask for Sonneker. It is easy to remember my name – Sonneker. We have had such an interesting conversation, haven't we, Sir?'

'Yes, indeed, highly interesting.'

Whilst getting out of the taxi and paying, Ronald's thoughts indulged in a linguistical excursion. He wondered whether the chauffeur's talkative wife might perchance be called Veronica: 'Veronica Sonnecker's bonnicker monicker.' He was not proud of it and gave the chauffeur a decent tip as behoved someone with an important position in a Viennese Hungarian palais.

As instructed, he reported to the Consulate's Passport Control officer, in this case: Major Alfred Murdoch, in Room 17. Ronald had been informed he was MI6. The major, not yet forty, tall, dark and athletically built, with velvety eyes and a small moustache, welcomed him affably.

'Bang on time, jolly good, Burnley. Keep it up. Your last probation assignment, I gather.'

'Yes, sir.'

'In case you don't know it, these premises only house the Passport Office. You'll be working for departments, as required. I'm instructed to keep an eye on you, did you know that?'

'No, sir.'

'Major will do. I've arranged that you'll spend one day a week, Thursday, assisting me. One of your tasks will be to keep my coded Z reports and accounts. The reports are from local informants; the accounts are my payments to them. I've also a small handful of field agents attached, pre-retirement older men, but you'll have nothing to do with them. Before you jump to conclusions, Burnley, we're not spying on the Austrian government. I'm keeping watch on the extreme left and, more recently, the extreme right also, vis-à-vis Britain's interests. We're on good terms with the *Geheimdienst*, the Austrian Secret Service. Questions?'

'Z reports?'

'Each of my local contacts is identified by a Z number.'

'You said coded, major.'

Chapter 4 – The Nuremberg Rally

'Simple play fair, using our illustrious head in London, sur- and nickname, you know both, eh? Anything else?'

'Are there are other MI6 members working here?'

'Alexandra Heaven. First class agent and charming woman, egad. Deals with visa applications, the department in which you'll be working. Only the Minister knows of our SIS identity. As far's the staff's concerned, we're security. The Consulate's just started employing a couple of Austrians in routine departments. Keeping a small eye on them is part of the job. Clear so far?'

'Yes, Major.'

'You're accommodated in one of our more luxurious rooms. A bit old-fashioned, but comfortable. You'll like it. The Ambassador's residence is located in the 3rd District. His grounds contain an accommodation building for non-VIP guests, looked after by our Hospitality Officer, Martin Shaver. He liaises with me on matters of security. Keeps an eye on guests. Very knowledgeable about many things and speaks languages.'

Ronald's room was by far the most comfortable and most old-fashioned he had occupied since starting on his European probation duties. The major had the looks of a Hollywood cloak and dagger star. He'd no opportunity for any dagger stuff here, but plenty for the cloak element. Ronald sensed that this situation was closer to what he had vaguely expected since joining MI6. It was the first time he was actually going to use a secret code for real. But why this concentration in so small a country, he wondered? When scanning the Z list, he found it interesting that one of the names was that of a woman whose husband was an active member of the Austrian Nazi party. This first meeting with Murdoch had provided a few little surprises for Ronald, but more were in the pipeline. A few days later he was checking passport replacement applications, when an attractive woman in her thirties interrupted him.

'You're Captain Burnley. I'm Alexandra Heaven. Major Murdoch will have mentioned my name. We must get to know each other.'

Before he thought of something to say, she added, 'This isn't the time and the place. We'll have tea together. Wednesday next week, four o'clock. My office, third on the right. Suit you? Fine, see you then, Ronald Burnley.'

She turned and was gone. He had barely managed to nod in answer to her question. Now he caught up with himself, allowing his

Chapter 4 – The Nuremberg Rally

astonishment to take over. Ronald Burnley. How do I address her? Dear Heaven? Are we having tea in her office? On Wednesday afternoon astonishment returned when he read a note on his desk: 'You'll need rainwear. A. H.' It was raining, typical October weather. On a scale from one to ten, astonishment rose rapidly to level five, when 'Dear Heaven' led him to the taxi waiting outside. It continued to rise. A ride of less than ten minutes took them to the *Kursalon* (Spa Salon) Hübner, an imposing Italian Renaissance edifice. It was situated at one end of a long narrow park, the *Stadtpark* (City Park), which ran between the narrow but deep bed of the River Wien and a section of the majestic Ring Strasse, a very wide road and avenue. The Kurhaus restaurant was large and resplendent in elegance as was the adjoining dance hall in which an orchestra was performing light music.

Their waiter welcomed Mrs. Heaven like an old friend and led them to her *Stammplatz*, verbatim a 'tribal place', meaning her regular table, in one corner of the hall. Without waiting for her order he left and returned five minutes later with a rose-flowered tray from which he unloaded two small rose-flowered pots of tea, two slim, small rose-flowered jugs of hot water, two similar jugs of cold milk and two slices of lemon on two rose-flowered porcelain saucers. The rosy-cheeked waitress following in his wake was also carrying a rose-flowered tray, from which she added two side plates and one large plate holding a half dozen tasty-looking open sandwiches to the collection on the table. Ronald noted that the sandwiches were not rose-flowered. Whilst the waiter poured the tea, the waitress deposited a slice of Sacher Torte on each of the side plates. The famous succulent chocolate gateau, whose patented ingredients had been invented by a chef working for the equally famous Hotel Sacher. It was taken for granted that Ronald liked Sacher Torte. Which he did. But he had not got to know this famous Viennese confectionery when he was in Vienna with his father, years ago. He suddenly noticed that the sugar bowl was not rose-flowered. A mistake? It contained cube-sugar and tongs.

When the waiters left, Mrs. Heaven remarked, 'I'm always impressed by their clockwork co-ordination.'

He nodded.

'Before you begin to think, captain, whether you're having tea with one of the Vanderbilts or the Rothschilds, let me disillusion you. I take taxis, even for short trips, for the sake of gaining time.

Chapter 4 – The Nuremberg Rally

We can afford the taxi and places like this only because the rate of exchange makes them ridiculously cheap for us.'

Ronald did not require the explanation. It had been the same, in some ways much more so, when he was here as a teenager. Whilst enjoying the tea and the Sacher Torte, he also enjoyed the accompanying conversation. It did not trouble him that Mrs. Heaven's questions and comments were transparently aimed at finding out more about him, but it did puzzle him. Why should one MI6 agent question another MI6 agent, notwithstanding that he was still a rookie. She must know that he would give nothing away that he shouldn't. Was he in for more surprises? They had reached Level Seven already. He was.

When refilling his cup, Mrs. Heaven said, 'This is a pleasant occasion. I feel we're getting on well, don't you agree?'

He smiled and nodded.

'Seeing that you're going to be with us for the next two months, I suggest you call me Sandy. All my friends do.'

Ronald's thoughts went into a somewhat light-headed spin. Surely he was not being propositioned? Sandy watched him as some of the weird thoughts going through his head were mirrored in his face, producing near-comical juxtapositions. Suppressing a mischievous desire to laugh, she reached out and, familiarly, put her hand on his arm, causing his confusion to reach an unfamiliar peak.

'Let me put you out of your misery. Martin Shaver, who keeps the staff register, noticed something interesting about your London address and passed it to me. You see, Ronald Burnley, my London address is exactly the same as yours.'

She watched the heavy frown of his trying to understand what she had said. It took her desire to laugh close to the edge. She succeeded in keeping it there as, after a dramatic pause, she said, 'To put it in another way, I'm your landlady.'

He openly exhaled the air of tension that had accumulated at the back of his throat.

'De Vere Court is…?'

'The very one.'

Was she punning? She continued, apologetically, 'When I brought you here I hadn't yet made up my mind whether to tell you.'

'I've passed?'

Chapter 4 – The Nuremberg Rally

He had recovered his equilibrium. She smiled sweetly. 'With distinction. If it's not against your religion to be on good terms with your landlady.'

'Will it affect my rent, Madam landlady?'

'Strictly speaking, I'm not. I've leased the house to the SAB until my job here is terminated. I understand, Lisette is still looking after it. She always kept it in good order and the girl needed the job badly. She's a nice person. You've met her, obviously?'

Ronald was fortunate in lacking the ability to blush, otherwise his cheeks would have lit up the Kursalon during the brief pause that followed. Finally, he looked her straight in the eye and said, 'I have. Lisette is keeping the house in good order. She's occupying your daughter's room.'

Sandy Heaven required no explanation. It was none of her business but it raised a first doubt in her about this seemingly nice young man. He was handsome enough and MI6 agents were known for that sort of thing. She had known one of them well. Too well. So Burnley was no different? He had been open about it. She decided to postpone judgement.

It was Sandy and Ronald, thereafter, but the house at De Vere Court was not mentioned again. Ronald's first thought upon her disclosure was that her daughter must be living in Vienna with her. He successfully suppressed a question to satisfy what was pure curiosity on his part. Tea at the Kursalon on Wednesday afternoons became a regular social routine. They were not entirely social because it was Sandy's task to bring Ronald up to date with the current social and political situation in Austria. Munich had lifted the worst of the pressure that his father's death had produced in Ronald. It enabled him to be back in Vienna and cope with memories of the time he had spent there, without feelings of bitterness. They had occupied a flat in Hietzing, a district in the western outskirts of the town, where Ronald had attended a *Realschule* (one of three types of grammar schools) for boys.

The foreign languages taught there, were French and English and Ronald had even found the English lessons useful as they helped him to improve his German. In turn the professor of English found his attendance useful. One boy, sitting next to him in the English class, declared himself his friend. His name was Heinrich Ullmann. He was round-faced and round-bodied and benefited from Ronald's help in English. But he was a bully towards other pupils, especially

Chapter 4 – The Nuremberg Rally

the only Jewish one. At the time, it had not been of significance to Ronald. Every class in every school he had attended possessed a few bullies. At a party in the Ullmann's flat, the only one he ever attended, he had made the acquaintance of Gerda who had taken possession of him. Ronald had accompanied her to her home and, just inside the house door, experienced kisses he had not experienced before.

On the last Wednesday of October, the weather was slowly but noticeably deteriorating. At the Kursalon the waiter made the kind of remark that any waiter in London might have made, as he put cup and saucer and the side plate with the Sacher Torte in front of Ronald.

'Hasn't the weather changed?'

Ronald seemed preoccupied, so Sandy agreed on his behalf. When the waiter had gone, she asked, Haven't you noticed the rain, Ronald? You look as if your head's in the clouds.'

Ronald looked up, then laughed.

'A view from heaven? But you're right. It's something I noticed this morning. We have a couple of Austrian lads working at the office, haven't we?'

'Yes. Why?'

'One is a small, brown-haired boy? Light-brown to be exact, looks quite young.'

She nodded. 'Eighteen. Herbert Sperling. He's had to repeat his Mathematics exam at the end of the summer. He passed it but can't start university till next September. His English is good.'

'I've not heard him say more than a few words. Can you tell me how he got the job, Sandy?'

'An agency called Nicholson's. What worries you, Ronald? In 1920 the occupation forces began to employ Austrian civilians in a variety of safe posts. Lt. Jim Nicholson was put in charge of finding them and sifting them. In due course, he employed Austrian staff, himself, in what had already effectively become an employment agency. When he was due for discharge, he married a member of his staff and stayed on in Vienna. He's got a link to the Austrian Security Service, which makes his sifting process pretty reliable. I do the final interviewing and hiring, Ronald.'

'And the other one?'

'Otto Nadler. Both are employed as runners, but Nadler, who's twenty-two and officially is called a messenger, receives an adult wage. He'll be able to apply for a step up at the end of his first year. He's a bit tight-lipped but has office experience and good references.'

Ronald wondered what step-up meant but did not ask.

'Thanks, Sandy.'

'Is there anything behind your questions, Ronald?'

'No-oh. Not really.'

She looked at him.

'Nothing tangible, Sandy, but – this morning, when Sperling brought my work file…' he paused.

'Part of his daily job, distributing the work files. What happened?' she asked.

'Nothing happened. When he put the file on my desk with his usual respectful "your folder, sir," I looked up and was surprised at the boy's expression – disturbed, unusually so. It couldn't have had anything to do with me, or the room. I told you it's nothing.'

'Are you sure that's all, Ronald?'

He thought for a moment.

'Hmm. A moment or two before Sperling entered, I heard raised voices from along the passage. One was his, I think. I didn't recognise the other one.'

'Question him, Ronald. As you say, it may be nothing, but let's make sure.'

* * *

On Friday morning, when the boy turned to leave, having delivered the work file, Ronald said, 'One moment, Sperling.'

The boy stopped.

'Sperling, when you brought my work file on Wednesday, you looked extremely unhappy. What was wrong?'

The unexpectedness of the question disconcerted Sperling.

'Wrong? There was nothing wrong. Really, nothing.' He was shaking his head, 'No, sir.'

The manner of his protest convinced Ronald that there was and Sandy's, 'Let's make sure', echoed in his mind. He said nothing for a couple of minutes, looking at Sperling whose discomfort was growing. Then Ronald dropped into German and not just German but into a touch of the Viennese accent. His tone was fatherly.

Chapter 4 – The Nuremberg Rally

'Look, Sperling, something was disturbing you very much, I've no doubt of that. If it was something private, then it's none of my business. Unless I can help you. But if it's connected with your work here, then you must tell me. I can promise you that, as far as my duty permits it, I'll keep what you tell me confidential.'

Being addressed in his familiar Viennese, added a further shock to Sperling's system. He hesitated, staring at Ronald. What he saw in Ronald's face was enough to trust him.

'Yes, I will tell you, sir. My father also says it is my duty. But I did not know to whom I can speak.' He was speaking in Viennese. 'You're right, Mr. Burnley, I was upset. It had to do with the other Viennese, who works here.'

'Otto Nadler,' Ronald said.

'Nadler, yes, Sir. After work, I usually walk to the Ringstrasse to get the tram. But the weather has cleared and on Friday, Mitzi, my girlfriend and I meet at Demel's. That's the—'

'The *Konditorei*' (pastry shop/cafe) 'at the Kohlmarkt.'

'Yes. With this job I can afford it, sir. We sit in a corner and I have just ordered, sir, gateau and apple juice, when I hear the voices of two men at the other end of the room. I look and one is Nadler. He is saying bad things about the English but a lot of people say these things and they don't mean anything. But when we get up and get our coats to go I see that the other man is wearing a big swastika on his chest. Still, it has nothing to do with me. Over the weekend I have forgotten. But on Wednesday morning, just when I come out from Mrs. Heaven's office, there is Nadler and he is walking beside me. He says I can have a rest and he will deliver the work files for me. I say, no, that is my job, and he says we are loyal Austrians and we must stick together against our enemies. I say nothing and he says other things like this and when we come near your office, Mr. Burnley, I say, "Leave me alone, Nadler." He stands in front of me and he says in a nasty voice, "If you're a traitor to our country then be careful. We know how to deal with traitors. And their families!" He is bigger than me, but I push him to the side and come into your office.' Sperling took a deep breath. 'That was all, sir. I'm not afraid of Nadler but when he said my family – I told my father in the evening and he has assured me he's not worried.'

'What did your father say?'

Chapter 4 – The Nuremberg Rally

'He has told me to do my job properly and to tell somebody here about Nadler. But I had no idea to whom I can speak so – I'm glad that you have asked me, sir. I feel better now.'

'Well done, Sperling. Are you certain that Nadler did not see you in the Konditorei?'

'Quite certain, sir. I only saw him through a gap. He could not possibly see me, sir.'

'Good. I must pass this on to one of my colleagues but if any action is taken I promise you that your name will not be connected with it. Now I better not hold you up any longer.'

Sperling's 'Thank you, sir,' was accompanied by a smile of great relief as he departed hurriedly, the remaining files clutched under his arm. Ronald typed out a confidential report on the spot and deposited it personally on Alexandra Heaven's desk. On Thursday morning when he entered Murdoch's office, the Major just finished a telephone call. He turned to Ronald.

'Re Otto Nadler. You've handled this well, Burnley. I've spoken to Nicholson and told him we have reasons for suspecting Nadler of being politically unreliable. He's promised to be discreet in his enquiries. I've also spoken to Colonel von Lebern.'

Ronald looked at him questioningly.

'Head of Austrian *Geheimdienst*' (Secret Service). 'Retained from the Imperial Services, true patriot and an enemy of the National Socialists. We'll have to await results.'

* * *

Ronald was happy in his job environment. Despite the improvement in the weather, he had felt no particular desire to visit places of his teenage memories. He knew it was his last probationary task and believed that both his superiors, Murdoch and Sandy Heaven seemed to be satisfied with his work. He had a good rapport with the staff and enjoyed the Thursday mornings in Murdoch's office almost as much as the talks with Sandy on Wednesday afternoons. By coincidence he even received answers to a question he had not asked her. He was standing in the door of her office, ready for the Kursalon tea, still by taxi, when she received a telephone call. She looked concerned when she came to the door.

Chapter 4 – The Nuremberg Rally

'It's Maria, my housekeeper, Ronald. Her mother's had a fall and she's taking her to the hospital. She'll not be back in time to collect Clare, my little girl, from the Kindergarten. I have to go. Sorry.'

'Of course,' he said.

'Actually, Ronald, if you don't mind coming along, we can still have our tea, after Maria returns. She won't be very long.'

'Of course,' he said.

They first went to the Montessori Kindergarten. Whilst Sandy was inside, Ronald had a pleasant conversation with the driver, a true Anglophile, who was one of two who regularly parked on the taxi stand by the consulate. Sandy returned with her little girl. Clare had Sandy's bright eyes and wore pigtails in the Austrian fashion. She took charge of Ronald from the word go, obviously convinced that he was there for her benefit. She must have learnt interviewing from her mother, he thought.

'My name is Clare. What's yours?'

'Ronald.'

'I'll be five years old in two weeks. How old are you, Ronald?'

'Twenty-six.'

'That's a lot more. Are you the new colleague with whom Mummy has tea on Wednesdays?'

'That's right.'

'Mummy says you like *Sachertorte*. I like *Apfelstrudel* best. Don't you like *Apfelstrudel*?'

'Oh yes, I like it quite a lot.'

'What about *Mohnstrudel?*' (poppy seed cake)'I like that best, also. Don't you?'

'Yes, I also like *Mohnstrudel*.'

'Mummy says, you make her laugh sometimes because you say funny things. Why do you do that?'

Ronald was stumped.

'I don't know. They just come out.'

He had no experience with children and did not feel entirely at ease. But the precocious Clare disarmed and won him over when, arrived at their house, she held his hand and they stood together, waiting, while Sandy opened the house door with a large key.

'We live here. On the first *Stock'* (floor). 'Isn't that a funny word? It's the same as a stick.'

Ronald laughed. The flat had as many rooms on just one floor as the house at De Vere Gardens had on two. And the ceilings were

Chapter 4 – The Nuremberg Rally

much higher. Ronald was aware that he did not feel at ease which had a lot to do with Clare who had taken possession of him, the way Frederic Strauss had done in Munich. There was a disturbing intensity about her conversation. She seemed to be competing with her mother for his attention. Luckily Maria, a large, plump comfortable woman, arrived soon to take over. After a spontaneous tight cuddle and kiss from Clare, he left with Sandy.

When they were at last relaxing at their usual table at the Kursalon, Ronald was still feeling the warmth of Clare's cheek against his cheek and her little arms around his neck and the touch of her child's kiss. Sandy had said very little, so far. She tried to explain.

'Clare's taken to you, Ronald. She doesn't meet many English-speaking people. She misses…'

She did not finish her sentence.

'I've taken to her, also,' he replied.

He had, but he felt he had intruded into Sandy's private life. But it had not been his doing. The waiter, coming by, this time asked, 'The usual, Mrs. Heaven?'

She was nodding, when Ronnie, spontaneously, said, 'I'd like an Apfelstrudel, instead of the Sacher Torte, waiter.'

'Of course, sir.'

The waiter looked questioningly at Sandy whose original nod of understanding turned into a yes to this new question.

For the rest of Ronald's stay in Vienna, Apfelstrudel had replaced the Sachertorte but he did not get an opportunity to meet Clare again. He thought of her often and when he did, his thoughts also regularly flashed back home to Lisette and to the Strauss family in Munich.

He met Sandy Heaven every Wednesday afternoon and Murdoch every Thursday. The most attractive feature of the weekly work day in Murdoch's office was the end of the day when they relaxed over a glass of beer. Murdoch used this occasion to prepare this junior MI6 man for his next stage. He had introduced the custom on Ronald's first Thursday.

'Pilsner, Burnley, my favourite brand. What's yours? You've been in Vienna before, I gather.'

'I was too young for alcohol, major. My father put his foot down with a strong hand. But I had beer at my last posting in Munich.'

Chapter 4 – The Nuremberg Rally

'You could hardly avoid it there. I suppose you came across the Hitler crowd there, Burnley.'

Ronald nodded, 'I couldn't avoid that, either, major.'

Murdoch noticed a slight change in Ronald's voice. 'The work there all right?'

'It was OK. I spent all of the time re-organising past applications.'

That didn't answer Murdoch's question, who now detected a question in Ronald's eyes and asked, What's on your mind?'

'This consulate's the only one I've worked in, that employs more than one SIS officer.'

'Coincidence, largely, but I'm doing my best to keep it that way. There are things going on here that may represent a serious threat to the peace and to the Austrian democracy and perhaps even to Britain. Vienna, in particular, is also an international spy junction for East and West.'

Ronald was astonished and that, too, showed in his expression.

'You're doubtful, Burnley, I see.'

'How can Austria be a threat? It's so small.'

'To be sure, Burnley. But Germany, next door, is big enough. Down at the moment, but they're an efficient lot, and arrogant to boot. The Kaiser claimed they're a master race, destined to rule Europe. He probably meant the World. Many of them believe it. It won't take long for them to recover. And our politicians are falling over themselves to regenerate Germany. What, if that fellow Hitler gets to the top? You've been in Munich. Formed an opinion about them?'

Ronald did not have to think.

'The Nazis? I think they're a dangerous and unscrupulous lot. But here in Austria?'

'Look at it, Burnley. History! Twenty years before the war, Austria already had a German National Workers' League. At the end of the war it became the *Deutsche Nationalsozialistische Arbeiterpartei*,' (German National Socialist Workers' Party). 'Look at the initials.'

'D-N-S-A-P!' Ronald was amazed. 'Practically the same as Hitler's party.'

Murdoch nodded.

'Indeed. It was exactly the same, initially, until Hitler moved the D into third place to show the difference. He's Austrian, too, as I'm

Chapter 4 – The Nuremberg Rally

sure you know. He's copied much of the Austrian party's programme in his own manifesto.'

'I've known none of this, major,' Ronald said slowly, 'but when I was here as a boy, I saw posters headed *Deutschösterreich*, Austrians who wanted to be joined with Germany.'

'Bull's eye, Burnley. You think the DNSAP doesn't exist anymore? Or the Austrian pan-Germanism? Mark my words, that's the focal point of the whole mess. The Austrian people, or at least a major section of them, see themselves as part of the German *Volk'* (race).

Another memory caught up with Ronald.

'When I went to school here in Vienna, boys swapped stamps, marked *Deutschösterreich.*'

'The Allies weren't allowing Austria to become part of Germany. But the push for it hasn't disappeared, Burnley. Any moment now, the Austrian DNSAP is about to declare itself a branch of the German NSDAP. There are Nazis in the upper echelons of the Austrian military and the civil service, as well as big businesses who're supporting Hitler. And here's the crunch: Von Lebern, head of the *Geheimdienst*,' (Secret Service) 'has knowledge of clandestine groups in touch with the German Nazis, who're organising and plotting a German take-over of Austria. They receive funds from Germany, too. Tell you something else, Burnley. It's not confined to Austria. There are pro-Hitler parties functioning in most if not all the European states. That's another thing about my work here. I have to keep an eye on the other half of the old Austrian Empire, Hungary. I visit there regularly.' He added facetiously, 'Not least because Budapest's a beautiful town. The stretch of the Danube that runs through Budapest, is even more beautiful than Vienna's. We've only got a legation there but Hungary's got several Nazi parties, would you believe. Most of them, if not all, receive funds from Hitler. Where does he get it from?'

Ronald was impressed. He had just received a sobering lesson in contemporary European politics. However, Murdoch's conclusions still seemed unlikely to him. After having lost the war so comprehensively surely even the Germans wouldn't dare to tackle the British Lion again. Murdoch raised his Pilsner, 'Prost!' emptying his glass. Ronald responded. Murdoch said, 'A bit of advice, captain. Watch your reactions – facial and vocal. We don't ask personal questions so I won't be asking you about Munich, despite a couple of give-aways.'

Chapter 4 – The Nuremberg Rally

Ronald did not reply. The only correct reaction was to heed the bit of advice.

On those Thursdays, Ronald came to know more about the currents behind the scenes of Austrian politics. He also began to get an idea of the nitty-gritty of Murdoch's clandestine organisation. Items of seemingly unconnected information from local informants and a handful of agents regularly landed on Ronald's desk, as well as receipts for payments signed on sheets of paper by initials, next to which the major had entered their Z codes. The few agents seemed to be doing duties at railway stations, reporting on persons arriving and departing and other miscellany. Keeping track of everything was laborious, but putting the bits of information together where they fitted was fascinating. The Thursday conversations over the Pilsner dealt with some of the situations that had arisen, often demonstrating Murdoch's skill and background knowledge. They also revealed the major's strong views on democracy.

'They say that Greece was the cradle of democracy but believe me, Burnley, it was not. That handle fits the British only,' he said on one occasion.

'I learned that the Greeks met regularly and that every man was free to state his opinion and they decided what to do by voting,' Ronald said.

'Every man, exactly. Women had no say and no vote, and all the necessary labour was done by slaves who had no rights whatsoever. That's not democracy in my book.'

'I couldn't walk into our parliament and speak and vote on what to do, major.'

'Our population's a bit larger than that of a Greek city-state. So we elect the people who do the debating and deciding on our behalf. We can get rid of them at the next election if we're not satisfied. Ours is the most democratic country in the world, Burnley. There are always people about who want to destroy our way of living and that's why we need a strong security service.'

'What puzzles me, major, is that the Nazis have supporters outside Germany.'

'It's a German disease, an infectious one. And diseases spread.'

'It amazes me even that so many Germans are willing to give up their right to choose their own government. I can't imagine that any Brit would ever support such ideas.'

Chapter 4 – The Nuremberg Rally

'There are crackpots everywhere, Burnley. Democracy has fault lines, weaknesses. Its opponents underline them. We've got to be on our guard and if we can't stop the disease spreading, by George, we'll make sure it doesn't gain the upper hand, Burnley.'

The conversation made Ronald recall his father's warnings against the Nazis. From there his thoughts roamed into the past. He decided to take a little peek at where, nine years ago, they had been staying in Vienna. Thus, on Sunday afternoon he took the Stadtbahn, Vienna's Metro railway, to the *Hietzinger Brücke* (Hietzing Bridge). It was a cold, crisp, yet sunny day, when he emerged into the open. Turning left, towards the Hietzing main road, he reached one familiar point, the Della Lucia Ice Cream Parlour, just past the bridge. Many of the boys from his class, including himself, used to frequent the place, enjoying the ice cream, the pastry and the company. It was open. He hesitated for a moment, then decided not to give way to temptation. He turned to walk on, when two men came towards him.

'Heiliger Bimbam!' (Holy Ding-Dong), the smaller one cried out, hurrying towards him, 'Ronald Burnley, my English pal!'

Ronald recognised him.

'Heini Ullmann.' They shook hands. 'How are you?'

'Fine. Couldn't be better, Ronald. What brings you to Vienna?' He turned to his companion. 'This man was my class mate in the sixth. He helped me with my English. Ronald, this is my friend Gernot Hederling. You must join us for a glass of wine and a *Torte*' (gateau).

The friend shook hands with Ronald but without any enthusiasm. Ronald was not overly happy, either, but could not refuse. It seemed he was unable to escape the Sacher Torte. They entered the crowded parlour and, hanging their overcoats on one of the coat stands, they sat down at the table nearest to it. A record was playing a popular hit: *Ich hab mein Herz in Heidelberg verloren.* (I lost my heart in Heidelberg). After Ullmann had ordered Torte and wine, he repeated his question. Ronald explained that he was working temporarily at the British Passport Office.

From that moment on, Ullmann's friend openly displayed resentment at Ronald's presence. He leaned back in his chair and whispered something under his breath to Ullmann. Ronald took a close look at them. Ullmann was still round-faced and round-bodied. His eyes were smaller than Ronald remembered. Then Ronald did a double take, seeing the small badge with a swastika on Ullmann's jacket. And there was one on Hederling's. Ronald's expression gave

160

Chapter 4 – The Nuremberg Rally

nothing away. He had to excuse himself and left the table, but only two steps in the direction of the uni-convenience, he realised that there was a long queue. Turning around to return to the table, he heard Hederling say: 'I can't on Thursday night. The villa meeting, Uli.' Ronald stopped, hidden by other customers. Ullmann's reply sounded envious. 'The *Geheimaktion!*' (secret action). Can't you get me in?' – 'Shut up, Heini! You're not supposed to know.'

At that moment, Ullmann exclaimed, 'Look who's just entered, Gernot. That dirty Jew, Blau.'– 'the one who was in your class? The one you gave your daily treatment? Is this a class reunion?'

Ronald's eyes flew to the man standing in the open door, looking around. He recognised him, too: the little Jewish boy who had been in the same class as Ullmann and he. But now he was tall, with slim shoulders and dark bushy eyebrows, wearing dark-rimmed glasses and a leather cap. Ronald had the impression that Blau had noticed Ullmann, although he walked straight to the other end of the room where he sat down. Ullmann and Hederling were continuing their conversation. Ullmann was saying, 'Yea, that's the one, Sigi Blau. He's doing well now, working in his father's jewellery shop, I've heard.' – 'Like all the stinking Jews, enriching themselves at our expense. Listen, Heini, get rid of your Englishman and we'll give the Jew boy a reminder of his school days, a taste of what'll come to all of his race soon. It'll make up for having made me shake hands with the Englander.'

Ronald made a quick decision. He would get involved. He turned and made his way to the table where Blau had sat down, still wearing cap and overcoat. Ronald tapped him on the shoulder, speaking German.

'Excuse my disturbing you, Blau. I don't know whether you remember me.'

Blau looked up, puzzled, and took his glasses off. He peered at Ronald for a few seconds, then recognition dawned.

'The English boy. I don't recall your name,' then he remembered something. 'You were friends with Ullmann.'

He was about to rise, politely. Ronald's hand held him down.

'He sat next to me. I helped him with his English. Please don't stand up. I'm not his friend. You saw him when you came in, didn't you?'

Blau nodded cautiously, still puzzled.

161

Chapter 4 – The Nuremberg Rally

'I've overheard them. They intend to beat you up when you leave here. May I suggest you leave now, before they have finished their Torte and wine?'

'I'm not afraid of the Nazis. I've an appointment here. But not for another twenty minutes.'

'Lady friend?'

Blau nodded, smiling.

'This is our favourite rendezvous place.'

'Then you surely want to avoid a brawl in the streets. I came in with them. Couldn't refuse and didn't know. Look, I'll leave right away. If you follow exactly five minutes later, I'll meet you outside and walk with you to meet your lady friend before she gets here. Is that not possible? They won't try anything against the two of us. And if they do, they haven't a chance.'

Despite his decision to get involved, he hoped that it would not happen. Blau only took a second.

'Ronald! That's your name, isn't it? You were popular. Fine. I'll see you outside.'

Ronald returned to his table but did not sit down. He grabbed his overcoat from the stand and, whilst putting it on, said, 'I'm sorry, Heini, must leave. Meeting someone. You'll have to finish my Torte and the wine. Thanks anyway. Bye.'

They looked surprised. And pleased. Ullmann neither rose, nor held his hand out, which suited Ronald. He disregarded the friend, Hederling, altogether and strode out. The sweet memory had turned sour very fast. He waited outside until Blau joined him. They belatedly shook hands.

'Let's wait for them here, if you don't mind, Sigi.'

'Good. That way I can't miss her. You've remembered my first name?'

'Sorry, no. Ullmann used it. We only used surnames in the class.'

'You were the exception. Everybody called you Ronald. I can't remember your surname.'

That was a topic, Ronald wanted to avoid.

'Yes, funny thing about names. Ullmann's friend is called Gernot. That's the name of one of the characters in the *Nibelungenlied*, (Song of the Nibelungs) one of Kriemhilde's brothers. Professor Neugebauer was a great fan of Middle High German, I recall.'

Chapter 4 – The Nuremberg Rally

'You do have a remarkable memory, considering German isn't your mother tongue.'

'Here they are, Sigi.'

Blau's sudden departure had caught Ullmann and Hederling by surprise. They finished and paid in a hurry and rushed out to catch up with him, finding him and Ronald, barring their progress. They were taken aback seeing him. Ullmann said plaintively, 'You said you were meeting someone.'

'I did. You remember Sigi Blau, don't you? When I saw those ugly swastikas, I couldn't possibly sit down with you. Anyone wearing them is not my kind of company.'

Unexpectedly, Gernot Hederling cut in, 'You talk big now, Engländer, but not for long. The next time you won't be so lucky.'

'Lucky? I've heard it before. It wasn't the brave German soldiers who lost the war. Blame the nasty Jews. Convenient lies, but typical.'

Hederling, fists clenched, said nothing. Sigi stepped closer.

'I'm not surprised you're a member of this political party, Ullmann. I remember, you were a nasty bully at school and always eager to let me feel it. You were bigger than me, then. Now you're only bigger horizontally but now's your opportunity.'

Blau was nearly as tall as Ronald. They topped both Nazis by a good five centimetres, each. After a long minute of facing each other, Hederling said, 'Come on, Heini. I'm not wasting my time on these nobody's.'

They turned and went. Ronald had lost the appetite for reminiscing. His thoughts were heavy and as soon as Blau's girlfriend came in view, he took his leave. He reported the main points of the incident to Murdoch who, surprisingly, was interested.

'Is that all he said, Burnley? The villa? No address?'

'No, major. I'd remember.'

'I know, secret action. A pity you didn't hear more. A great pity.'

'I'm sorry, major.'

'Von Lebern's looking for a plotting Nazi Geheimaktion' (secret action). 'I'll pass the name of this Gernot Hederling to him.'

* * *

The last week of November had arrived but the expected letter from 54 Broadway, informing him that his probation period was over, had not. As Shaver who dealt with the diplomatic mail, regretted

Chapter 4 – The Nuremberg Rally

regretfully. Ronald was impatient. He would ask Murdoch on Thursday to contact London on his behalf. Murdoch had left for Budapest on Tuesday. He returned on Thursday, in time for their social end-of-day Pilsner session, at the same time restoring Ronald's equilibrium which had been attacked by a rare touch of peevishness. It did more than that. Upon their first 'Prost!' before Ronald had even uttered the 'st', Murdoch handed him a letter, without its envelope. Putting his glass down, Ronald looked at it. He recognised Cormody's letter heading, then held it out to Murdoch.

'It's addressed to you, major.'

'I've also one addressed to you, but read mine first. The second para will do.'

Ronald read:

'The Service Council, considering your report, has accepted your recommendations. Your application for leave has also been approved. You will depart from Vienna on Sunday, 2 December, 1928 and report to this office on Tuesday, 4th December, 09.30, for a five days' term of home duty. Your leave will terminate on Saturday, 22nd December, as requested. Your request for Captain Burnley to stand in during your absence, has also been approved.'

Not sure whether to feel resentful or uplifted, Ronald returned the letter to Murdoch in exchange for the envelope addressed to himself. He opened it and his eyes flew hastily across the single page. He had completed his probationary year to full satisfaction and his army commission as captain was now substantive. His first assignment was to occupy Major Murdoch's office at the British Passport Office in Vienna, fulfilling duties as instructed. A handwritten note, signed by someone at the LAB, stated that the 'housekeeper' at No.1 De Vere Gardens had been informed of his additional absence. Ronald, decided to be positive and listened to Murdoch's instructions.

'As of today you're no longer required to do admin jobs. Officially, during my absence, Burnley, you're my replacement but, I'm afraid, without my level of authority. I want you to continue your usual tasks plus telephone calls and correspondence. Use your discretion. Matters that require immediate action, pass to Heaven. She'll be in charge of security during my absence. Even so, a lot of responsibility will be resting on your shoulders. I know, you'll do well.'

Chapter 5 – Agent Ronald Burnley

Ronald's new responsibility began with a sealed dispatch from Colonel von Lebern, of the Austrian Secret Services, delivered by hand. It stated: 'Otto Nadler is a paid-up member of the DNSAP. The information was not available at the time of Nicholson's routine enquiry. Thank you for detail re Geheimaktion. Von Lebern, Colonel.' The signature was hidden in the large round stamp of the Austrian Geheimdienst (Secret Service). The next day the post brought a letter from Nicholson's Confidential Agency. It contained the same information with apologies. His signature, too, was validated by a rubber stamp.

No official or business communication was considered valid without a rubber stamp's stamp. It was Ronald's first issue to deal with but clearly beyond his level of authority and he passed both communications to Alexandra Heaven. *What level could be higher*, he thought. Two days later he was sitting on her left behind the large table in Murdoch's reception room. On her right sat Captain Philip Hutchings, in uniform, a senior member of Murdoch's field team. This was not the Sandy Heaven of the Kurhaus afternoon tea. This was a woman with stern features, exuding authority. At one end of the table sat Rose Lavender whom he had met. She was one of the shorthand typists, there to take notes of the meeting. Upon Mrs. Heaven's request she called Otto Nadler in from the waiting room. He was carrying his overcoat over one arm and held his wool cap in his hand. The procedure was brief. Mrs. Heaven addressed him in English.

'You know why you're here, Herr Nadler. When I interviewed you for this post, you stated that you had no hostile feelings towards Great Britain. You also stated that you were not a member of a political party. Two days ago we received information that you are a member of the National Socialist Party. This, in itself, and your lying about it disqualifies you from employment with the British consulate.'

Rose Lavender handed her an envelope and put a cyclo-styled form on the table in front of Nadler.

Chapter 5 – Agent Ronald Burnley

Mrs. Heaven explained, 'The envelope contains your wages for this week, Herr Nadler, plus a payment representing a week's notice. Please read and sign the form in front of you which is a receipt as well as a statement to the effect that your services are no longer required.'

Nadler, looking sorry for himself, signed silently. She handed him the envelope, saying, 'Captain Hutchings will see you off the premises.'

Nadler put the envelope into his inner coat pocket and rose. As he turned to go, he said in German, forcing the words out between his teeth, 'I'd like to know who betrayed me. You'll probably not tell me. But I can guess.'

Ronald had prepared for the question, in fact hoped for it and answered, also in German.

'I doubt that. The traitor was you, Nadler. When you are sitting in a Konditorei, it is not advisable to raise your voice, especially when cursing the English. You were sitting at Demel's with another man who was wearing a swastika. I happened to enjoy a *grossen Braunen*' (large coffee with cream) 'and a Sacher Torte. Naturally, we had you investigated, Herr Nadler.'

Nadler was staring at him dumbfounded and open-mouthed, whereupon Ronald added, 'I wonder what your party leaders would say if they heard of this.'

It was the final blow. Nadler's shoulders were sagging visibly as he turned and walked out, followed by Captain Hutching who, looking over his shoulder, was blatantly grinning. Miss Lavender passed Ronald as she departed. A whiff of her perfume wafting past his nose made him realise that the saying 'nomen est omen' had much greater validity than he had hitherto believed. Alexandra Heaven turned to him with the hint of a smile on her lips and a question in her eyes. He nodded and said, 'I lied but I had to protect my source.'

'I was surprised at his collapse,' she said.

'Like a Doberman with a larynx infection,' he added.

She laughed out loud.

The rest of Ronald's locum days rolled on without any excitement. The work was not exactly mind-stretching. Due to Sandy's two days' absence there was also no Wednesday afternoon tea at the Kursalon as he decided not to go on his own. Except for the great improvement in the weather, nothing worthy of mention occurred. The regular Friday visits by the portly Martin Shaver provided welcome interruptions.

Shaver who, smiling more than the average smiler, was acting as postman for confidential documents between the Residence and the consulate, during the coincidental absence of his only assistant. Walking on foot from the Consul's residence where he was based, he ended his duty calls at the Passport Office in Ronald's office for half an hour's rest before walking back. Over a cup of coffee, Ronald enjoyed their conversation except for the part in which Shaver regularly described his manful efforts of stemming his midriff's expansionist efforts. Once that subject was out of the way, the talk would switch to current developments in Austria. Shaver had an expert grasp of the economic and political spectrum. Sipping his coffee, he offered his wisdom to an appreciative listener.

'It's not surprising that the Austrians are dissatisfied, Burnley. One not unreasonable reason is their fear that, having been reduced to so small a country, they're not going to be economically viable. Also they don't like their new political system.'

'But wasn't it the Austrians, themselves, that forced their Kaiser to abdicate?'

'They did, and a good thing it was, although he wasn't the worst, as Kaisers go. In fact, he was quite popular with many of his subjects. Now there's massive unemployment, many things have been going wrong and they blame the democratic government.'

'Why shouldn't they be viable, Shaver? They grow plenty of food and keep cattle and pigs and seem to have enough to feed themselves.'

It was naive but Shaver did not tell him that.

'Selling on the home market alone, is not enough to maintain the Austrian economy. And you can't grow a lot in the upper largely snow-capped regions of the Alps. Harsh winters, too. Almost all Austrian farms are smallholdings, their fields are on up and down land. It's good for skiing but makes ploughing tough. In the summer they keep their cattle on the Alpine meadows.'

Ronald grinned, remembering songs and relevant jokes, said, 'That's where there's no sin and they yodel to each other across the valley instead.'

Shaver laughed.

'The cowherds and the cowherdesses. The yodelling phrases are codes for rendezvous at night and if the cowherd makes a mistake and ends up on the wrong meadow, the girl there will have pity on him, or the other way round, I've heard. It's not that I've had the experience. But it must be a healthy outdoor life.'

'I've an idea, Shaver,' Ronald said, 'you take a course in yodelling and volunteer cow-herding on one of the mountain tops for a season. You'll end up experienced and fit and possibly even shotgun-married.'

'I'm against the death penalty, Burnley, but in your case I might make an exception.'

At the beginning of Ronald's last week, two items of interest landed on his desk. One was a personal letter, delivered to the Residence in the diplomatic bag, and brought over by Shaver who assured Ronald he would not tell. It was from Craig Jameson, forwarded via London:

'The trial went well. You may want to know that Steger has escaped hanging, due to intervention by an anonymous personage, Nazi-friendly, I guess. Dr. Strauss, jus, will keep an eye, in case there are attempts to get Steger out sooner. But Strauss appears to have health problems and I have heard that the family is seriously planning to leave Munich. Lünecke has continued his service with the Nazi Stormtroopers. According to Dr. Strauss' police contacts, he is still under observation, but has not indulged in any further criminal activities. Rumours have it that his patron, Herr Röhm is expected to return from South America soon, in order to resume the command of the SA, his creation, after all. Craig.'

The other item, a white envelope with Murdoch's name on it, had been delivered to the consulate by hand, the customary practice. It contained a sheet of lined paper, torn out from a notebook. 11 names were scribbled on it, under the heading of *'Heimliche Nazis in Wien'* (Secret Nazis in Vienna). The names came from informant Z-13 on Murdoch's list. All that Ronald was really required to do was to file it the usual way. But this was an opportunity to do something useful. As the names were not in alphabetical order, he assumed that they were in order of importance. Picking up the top three names he went out into the field, aka the streets of Vienna.

By Monday, he had collected a considerable amount of data about them, an Austrian army officer, Major Ferdinand von Hetzendorf, a civil servant, name of Otto Weinsteiger, and Dr. Adolf Mahr with a top degree in Archaeology. The latter had moved to Dublin to take charge of the Irish National Museum. During his

Chapter 5 – Agent Ronald Burnley

years at the University of Vienna he had been a member of the National Socialist Students Society. Ronald stuck the list and his information into a red envelope. He also received a hand-written note from Sandy, reminding him that she was back and would be at the Kursalon as usual. When he arrived there, he was surprised to see a man seated with Sandy, who, a glass of wine in his hand, rose when Ronald reached the table.

'Ronald, this is Mister Gedye, a British journalist. He's working for the *New York Times* at present, so be careful what you say.'

She said it smilingly. The two men shook hands, murmured their how-do-you-dos and sat down.

'We're old friends, Ronald,' Sandy said, 'Mr. Gedye rang yesterday because he wanted to meet you. You weren't in your office, so I asked him to join us today. I hope that's OK.'

Ronald nodded, although he was by no means certain. Thoughts were racing through his mind, trying to find a possible reason for this man wanting to meet him. Ronald had never had anything to do with American affairs. The only American he had ever known was Craig and he wasn't one anymore. But a Brit working for an American newspaper? Above all, Ronald wondered about Sandy's contact with a journalist and as good as forcing him to meet that journalist. He took a quick hidden look at him. He saw a slim man with a narrow face, intelligent eyes beneath a tall forehead and the lips of a pipe smoker. He mentally prepared himself for whatever unexpected matter might arise. Gedye put his glass down.

'I, too, hope you don't mind, Captain Burnley. I'm grateful to Mrs. Heaven for giving me this opportunity. She and I have an interest in common, about which we both feel very strongly: namely the political developments in Austria, one specific aspect of it. I've just spent a few days in Munich. A local journalist had sent me details of a murder trial in which the accused was a member of Hitler's Sturmabteilung. In my attempts at finding out more about it I came across your name a couple of times but was unable to obtain any information about you.'

It could hardly have been more unexpected. Ronald was thinking fast. He had to make sure that his name did not appear in any article anywhere about his father's murder. Sandy knew nothing about that event, of that he was certain. She obviously trusted Gedye. He was going to be very careful in what he said to the man.

Chapter 5 – Agent Ronald Burnley

'Mr. Gedye, when I was working in Munich, I made friends of a German lawyer and his family. He was going to prosecute the Nazi accused of the murder. But by the time the trial took place I had left Munich. I doubt I have any information that would be useful to you.'

Gedye raised his hand defensively.

'Captain Burnley, please let me explain something. I'm not looking for this information in order to write about it. My only interest in this trial is my overwhelming concern with the German Nationalist Socialist Party and, more directly, with its growth here in Austria. The American government as well as the British one, do not seem to take serious what is happening and what, in my opinion, is a fast growing danger to the new European democracies. I see it as my most important task to do everything I can in order to open their eyes. That is my sole concern. Any information that helps me, is important to me and I guarantee complete confidentiality. I shall neither publish nor pass on any names of my sources, I assure you. That is the reason why I did not approach you directly. Mrs. Heaven shares my concerns.'

Both of them looked towards Alexandra Heaven, who nodded and said, 'Ronald, I neither know nor wish to know what this is about, but if I hadn't full confidence in Mr. Gedye, he would not now be sitting here. He and I are fighting the same battle. If he says he will not print your name or anything personal about you, you can trust him. He's proved it to me many times. If you have any information that can help him in unveiling the threat the Nazis represent, you can safely entrust it to him. Not in my presence, if you prefer.'

Ronald relaxed. He believed her. He was impressed by Gedye but even so he was not persuaded to talk. Gedye had risen and, holding his glass in a toasting gesture towards Sandy, emptied it. He turned to Ronald.

'Tokaj, my favourite wine. Captain Burnley, I'm staying at the Imperial on the Ringstrasse tonight, room 317. I shall be back there by eight, after dinner. I would have liked to invite you to dine with me but I am aware that this could be misinterpreted. If you haven't arrived by nine o'clock I shall know that you've decided not to come. I shall understand it. But I hope you will. For now, I'm saying cheeri-o. I'm pleased to have made your acquaintance.'

Sandy and Ronald looked after him. Then Sandy sat back and waved to a passing waiter.

Chapter 5 – Agent Ronald Burnley

'Now we can relax to what we're really here for, Ronald. Your good-bye. We'll have Sacher Torte with Tokaj to prove that parting can really be sweet sorrow.'

'Coined by a romantic barber, no doubt,' he quipped, then added, 'but instead of Sacher Torte, a slice of Apfelstrudel, please.'

She nodded and the waiter left. She gave Ronald a searching look. His eyes met hers steadily.

'Your Clare, she's grown on me, Sandy. I keep remembering her. She's a love.'

She nodded. 'It's easier being an SIS agent than being a mother. She's asked after you several times. She never knew her father. I thought about inviting you again. It might have made things harder for her. I told her you had to go back to London. I hope you understand. Will she, one day? The job I'm doing is important and I need it as much for her as for her future.'

Ronald lacked life experience but his understanding grew as he listened. Then she smiled and the tension was gone. At this moment their drinks and strudels arrived and they relaxed. Sandy made not a single remark about Gedye and his quest. During the enjoyment of his sweet sorrow, Ronald made up his mind. The taxi that brought them back to the consulate, later took him to the Imperial. At eight in the evening he was knocking on the door to room 317 and was eagerly welcomed by Gedye.

'I appreciate this more than I can say, Captain Burnley, because I feel it was a difficult decision for you to make.'

317 was a suite and they sat down at a small table, on which two glasses of Tokaj and biscuits were waiting, evidence of Gedye's optimism or, perhaps, shrewd judgement. Ronald wanted to get this over with as quickly as possible although he found Gedye an interesting man.

'I decided to come but I doubt, Mr. Gedye, it will be helpful to you. The murdered man was my father. As part of a fact-finding mission about the National Socialist Party, a couple of years ago, he was interviewing two members of the Nazi *Sturmabteilung*' . 'Probably when they realised that he was a British journalist they demanded the notes he had made of the interviews. They killed my father because he refused to hand them over. He did not even carry them on his person at the time. Only one of the two men, the one who did the actual stabbing, was tried and found guilty.'

Chapter 5 – Agent Ronald Burnley

Gedye had listened attentively. He understood the emotion that was pulsating behind the dry words of Ronald's brief account as well as the stark drama that had taken place in Munich. After Ronald had finished, neither of them spoke for what seemed a long time. As if the air between them was filled by a melody in minor, whose slow fading out they dared not interrupt.

'Captain Burnley, I am so very sorry. This initially seemed to me to have been a political killing. But you're right. It does not tangibly assist my goal. I believe these Nazis to be utterly ruthless and ready but I need facts to substantiate my judgement. I suspect that certain killings in various parts of Europe whose victims were politically known as anti-Nazis, were arranged by the Nazi machine.' He paused for a moment. 'Mr. Burnley, if you ever do come across anything that you feel might help me in my quest, I should be very grateful to receive the information. Mrs. Heaven would probably know where I can be found.'

* * *

Ronald departed from Vienna a day before Major Murdoch returned to find his detailed additional report about three of the *heimlichen* Nazis in a dark-red envelope on his desk.

The tension inside Ronald, heightened by the meeting with Gedye, subsided gradually during the uneventful journey. What was left of it disappeared at the moment of Lisette's welcome. Her joy at seeing him again filled him with warmth. Lisette was happy that they were spending Christmas together. Neither of them, for different reasons, was used to a Christmas tree at home and they had no inclination to start the practice. But Lisette had prepared her own version of a Christmas dinner. She was talking animatedly whilst ladling food from the bowls in the centre of the table onto their plates.

'This is our second Christmas together, Ronnee. Do you remember the first? We are only ten days together and I think I shall make a good meal for you. But I do not know anything about Christmas in England. Then you come home and you say you are going to Reading to your mother and grandmother for the weekend. And I quickly say I have promised to visit my stepfather. Do you remember?'

Chapter 5 – Agent Ronald Burnley

He was holding knife and fork in his hands, about to attack the food on his plate and, remembering, for the moment, disliked himself.

'I remember,' he said.

'One moment, Ronnee. I get the sauce from the kitchen. I hurry.' She returned very fast, carrying a large jug. 'This is really a milk jug. We must buy one for meat sauce. In the book I read it should be cranberry sauce, Ronnee, cranberry is sweet. You cannot put sweet sauce on a meat dish, so I make beef sauce. I lied about visiting my stepfather but when you have gone I decide I shall visit him and I was surprised because Shirley, the girlfriend of my stepfather, is very pleasant and they invite me for Christmas Day also.'

He relaxed.

'Perhaps because you weren't living with them anymore, Lisette.'

He had not known any of this but remembered he had not been particularly interested at the time. He was about to sink his fork into the meat when she stopped him again.

'Sorry darling, I have forgotten the salt and pepper and the vinegar. I get them.'

She did, bringing the condiments on a small, round metal tray, which he had not seen before.

'It says in the book that I should make roast turkey. Do you mind, Ronnee, I have done chicken? I do not know turkey but chicken is an old friend. Why don't you eat, Ronnee? It will get cold. Your letters from Vienna, Ronnee, they make me very glad. They are short like always. I know you cannot write about your work but I know also you do not sleep with anybody there. It is how I feel, Ronnie. I do not demand from you. You are free, I am free. In one letter when you have had tea with a colleague, you write you miss me. You have never written this before...'

She smiled happily, a beautiful and touching picture. He knew when he had written that letter. It was after meeting Sandy Heaven's little girl.

'I did miss you, Lisette, very much.'

'I tell you one thing, Ronnee. I am very hungry. If you do not start eating, I think you do not like my cooking. It is true I have not made plum pudding as the book says. Charlie at the Kensington Market has been helping me with his advice and he say apple pie is just as good. He is out of plums. And I have made something very special.' She lifted an upside down large bowl from a large plate. This is called *bûche de Noel*.'

Ronald furrowed his brow, '*Bûche*? Firewood? It looks like a fat slug, only less repulsive... *de Noel*? Ah, a yule log.'

She took no notice, pointing first to a carafe-shaped container, then to a large beer bottle.

'You have a choice, monsieur. This glass bottle has cider and Charlie, he says, it is as strong as wine and if you do not like it so strong you can drink this.' She peered at the label. 'It is called lambswool.'

He looked at her, head cocked sideways.

'You are joking.'

She shrugged her shoulder.

'This is an old English drink, Charlie says. It is ale with spices in it. I do not know what spices. It is because you are not old that you do not know.'

After this fair comment, very little was said. They ate and they drank and they kissed and they drank a little more and they kissed a little more and they made a little love and then they made a little more love and so on – nothing new and yet always new. They both slept long into the next morning and when they woke up, they got dressed very slowly. They did not get very far before they stopped to make love again, also very slowly. Exhaustion then put them back to sleep, holding each other tightly. For her it was the great love with passion. For him it was the fulfilment of a need with much affection. He did not believe he could improve on the relationship.

* * *

Ronald reported to Cormody immediately after his Christmas leave. He no longer was beset by the feeling of awe which had predominated on the early occasions. Looking at Major Cormody with an independent air, he became aware of how round many things about him were, his head, his eyes, his body and even his mouth when he opened it. Incongruously, he looked like a small fat man when seated, but was five foot eleven tall. That and a certain persuasiveness in voice and diction enhanced the authority that his position gave him. He never was at rest. Whilst talking to Ronald, he was picking up letters and communications from his IN tray, added a

Chapter 5 – Agent Ronald Burnley

scribble on some of them and dropped them into one of two OUT baskets.

'Major Murdoch has recommended you to be given a new assignment I have just set up. It was designed by him when he was in London. You'll occupy the new Austrian desk at the Cypher School, code-named Blue Danube. For your information, the other desks there are the BaSca, the Baltic-Scandinavian and the EasCo, our Eastern Contacts. Organisationally you're part of the Western & Central European Group, referred to as WaC, but you'll be on your own.'

He stopped to re-read the paper he had just checked, before allocating it to its basket. Ronald was wondering whether the abbreviation for his Austrian desk was going to be BluDa, or BOYO for Be On your Own, but he did not express these profane thoughts. Cormody continued.

'You'll handle all the traffic with Austria, any material pertaining to Austria. Hungary, as part of the former Austria Hungary empire, will be included. You'll do your own coding. When applicable, add explanations, interpretation, as well as comment. You'll have the full assistance of the admin staff for typing and other services. Three copies of each report are required, one to be kept with the desk file, one for the head of WaC. The third for me. Questions?'

'The Code and Cypher School, where I received instruction during my training, sir?'

'Indeed. However, the school's major function is to ensure that encoded communications by Government departments are secure. That includes researching the cyphers used by foreign governments, which provides useful information about potential foreign threats.'

Ronald understood that 'researching' was a euphemism for spying on foreign communications. He had another question.

'Just Austria and Hungary, sir?'

Cormody's answer echoed Murdoch's explanations.

'It will enable us to get a fairly full picture of things happening there which, to a large degree, are a mirror image of what is happening in the whole of Europe, especially Germany. Vienna is a junction of foreign agents from East and West, North and South, second only to Switzerland but much less controlled by police and special services. A lot of significant information is being traded there. I share Murdoch's concern over the rise of this man Hitler and his party. I don't need to tell you that the Danube also flows through

Hungary. But you may not know that even in Hungary several pro-Nazi parties have come into being. We hope that by providing reports specifically concentrating on that region, His Majesty's Government may give the progress of the Nazis a little more attention, captain.'

Cormody put the last of the IN papers into its tray, then looked around, searching for something. Ronald picked up the sarcophagus-shaped paperweight with a removable mummy on top and Egyptian symbols on the side, hidden behind one of the baskets and held it out to Cormody. Cormody, surprised, deposited it on the paper stack in the tray and stood up, topping Ronald by a complete inch. For one split second he looked at Ronald, not as the Section Head would at one of his agents, but as an older man at a younger man, young enough to be his son. For one split second the younger man saw a world of past pain hidden in those round, amber eyes. Ronald had listened with mixed reactions. He was uncertain whether to be pleased with the new task.

The school was situated in Queen's Gate, a short walk from De Vere Court. Ronald was surprised to find that the operational staff of about thirty men, amounted to only half the size of the support staff. His Blue Danube work space, the size of a small office, faced one of the high safety windows. It contained a desk with telephone and typewriter, two chairs, a filing cabinet and a safe to which, except for the Admin Office, only he had a key. As far as the job was concerned, he started from scratch, designing and developing routine, filing system, priorities, everything. In addition, he could rely in all its aspects on the secretarial work of a highly experienced and efficient administrative staff whose advice helped him a lot. Any material relating to Austria obtained from intercepted telegrams, reports from agents in the field including Major Murdoch in Vienna, and even press cuttings, were delivered to his desk. His own reports, decoded, analysed, explained and interpreted, were typed and the copies distributed, as laid down by Cormody.

A secret agent Ronald might be, but to all intents and purposes he went out to the same work place each morning after a good breakfast, came home to the same home in the evening to a good meal and went to bed with the woman he had found in the house when he moved in. She, too, went out to a school on most days. He had signed up, willing to forgo a life of domestic stability, a share and share situation, but that was exactly what he now had. He accepted the gift without reservations. However, one aspect of the sharing was one-sided. When he came home from his school, he was unable to talk about what he had been doing and what had happened during the day. Lisette, on the other hand, brought home lively topics, especially on the days of her philosophy classes. Starting from a very small base, she was eager to learn and to understand, to relate and enrich her life and her experiences. Their evening conversations usually turned around her daily studies.

'Mr. Anstone said that Plato used the Socratic method in his *republique*. His republique?'

'Socrates was Plato's teacher, Lisette. *The Republic* is the name of Plato's book. He wrote it as a dialogue between Socrates and his students. Socrates asks them questions so cleverly that their answers prove his views to be right. That was his method.'

'They are not very clever, Ronnee, are they, if they fall for his trick always?'

'Not a trick. Just one method of finding the answers. Socrates was a great thinker.'

She looked at her notes.

'Plato advocated a just society. But Mr. Anstone says, the Greeks had not a just society.'

'My boss in Vienna said the same. Ideas of right and wrong were different then, but I suppose it's true.' He added, 'Plato taught Aristotle and Aristotle taught Alexander, the Great.'

'That is what he also tells us. So many names, Ronnie.'

'One of my teachers in Reading used rhymes as *aide-mémoires*, like: Plato was a hot potato who loved a good debate-oh.'

She laughed, 'This is not an English word, Ronnie.'

He grinned, 'This is.'

She thought for a moment before she got it and laughed. Their conversations became a regular institution. Machiavelli, Descartes, Rousseau, Hegel and Kant all played their parts in filling their evenings. They naturally led to other topics and sometimes to long discussions. Lisette was learning fast. They listened to the radio together and they went to the cinema, the new place of entertainment. On Sundays they explored London. Their love life was no longer the only tie between them. In a way it had been demoted to equal place with their other interests although it never failed to take precedence when challenged. From time to time Ronald visited his mother and grandmother, although the atmosphere there was always strained. At his first visit he had told them about living with Lisette. His mother's deluge of criticisms was not a total surprise.

'My God, Ronnie, how can you do such a thing. Shameful, I call it. Well, it's your life. But don't you bring her here. I don't want to meet her. Foreign, too. My goodness, are English girls not good enough? French, of course. Like those – er – easy-going university students you went around with. Oh yes, I knew what was going on. Well, it's your life.'

'You'd like her if you met her, Mother.'

'Don't you dare bring that...' She stopped, seeing the look in his eyes. 'I don't want to see her, that's all. When you find a nice English girl and marry her I'll be pleased to meet her. This woman I don't want to see, Ronald, and that's that.'

The initial anger rising in his eyes had changed to pain. He said no more because he had nothing to say. Conversation with his mother had shrunk to meaningless remarks. His grandmother always enquired about his well-being but he knew that, at heart, she felt the same as her daughter. Every time she saw him to the door at the end of his visit, she said, 'Please come again, Ronnie. I miss you, and I know your mother does. It's not easy to change the ideas which you grow up with.'

His cautious answers to Lisette's questions when he came home were sufficient for her to understand the situation. He thought that if his mother and grandmother would meet her, they would change their minds. Lisette, however, was as firm in declining as his mother.

'They will never make me welcome, Ronnie, I understand this. And you would not have wanted to meet my mother when she was alive, and I do not want you to meet my stepfather, and we are not married and English people think this is not nice, and...'

She would run out of words and of breath, coming close to losing her self-control. She recovered and succeeded in presenting a smile, combined with a shrug of her shoulders. He knew she was right, generally, although he believed he would have wanted to meet her mother. She had put no emphasis on her reference to marriage, but his mother's words had unwittingly inserted the thought into his mind. Perhaps knowing as a boy that his parents' relationship was not a good one was the reason why marriage had never figured as a goal. Now, eager to change the mood, he picked on something in Lisette's words that appealed to his facetious sense of humour.

Chapter 5 – Agent Ronald Burnley

'You're right, Lisette. One thing is certain, my darling: "and" is a great favourite of yours.'

'What is?'

'No, "and" is. You like the word "and", Lisette.'

'You tease me, Ronnie.'

'Not really, dear. You used the word more than half a dozen times in just two sentences.'

She gave it some thought.

'But it is a very useful word, *n'est-ce-pas*?'

'You've said it, Lisette. My English teacher in Reading liked to give us examples of unusual juxtapositions of words. Once he gave us a sentence in which the word "and" was used five times without any other words between.'

She looked at him suspiciously.

'What was the name of your English teacher?'

'French.'

'You tease me again, Ronnie. This is twice, so you must be punished.'

In a couple of seductive steps, she transferred to his lap and sank her lips on his for a long kiss. When she was about to let go, he didn't.

'You're right, my lady. My offence was terrible and I deserve a lot of punishment.'

He was lying because his English teacher's name had indeed been French. She obliged and one thing led to another and a detailed description would require too many ands.

* * *

Many of their Sunday mornings were spent walking in Kensington Gardens or Hyde Park ending with lunch out. Sometimes they listened to the outpourings of the demagogues at the Speakers' Corner, an area just inside the Marble Arch entrance to Hyde Park. The experience was as new to Ronald as it was to her. Every time they went there, Ronald recalled Frederic Strauss in Munich, who knew that there was a police station inside the arch. As they never went through it, he did not get to check the information. On their first visit to Speakers' Corner he said:

'Do you know that there is a police station inside one of the arch supports, Lisette?'

Chapter 5 – Agent Ronald Burnley

'No. Is this true? There is no sign there. How do you know this?'

'A German boy in Munich told me.'

She looked at him sideways.

'You think I believe everything, Ronnie. Tell me how can these people say some of the things, they say. That policeman over there can hear everything they say.'

'He's here to protect them. They can say what they want and criticise whom they want, as long as they don't preach violence,' Ronald explained.

'Criticise? But not the Government, *hein'* (eh), 'Ronnie?'

'Wrong. They can criticise the Government, the Lord Mayor and God – but not the King.'

'Re - al - ly?'

If Ronald had meant to impress Lisette with this show of free speech by the orators as well as the hecklers in the audiences, he had succeeded. She found the speakers interesting and some of the hecklers funny. Until one Sunday the show backfired on him. They reached the place a little earlier than usual to watch the first of the speakers, accompanied by a few helpers, set up his wooden platform. One of his companions attached a name-board in front. It said: Imperial Fascist League. Another fixed a flag on the structure. Its emblem was a Swastika joined to the Union flag with the letters IFL in the centre. Ronald stared, finding it hard to believe. 'I can't imagine that anyone in Britain would ever support such ideas,' he heard himself say to Murdoch. A trickle of folk, some young and seemingly rough types, was gathering around the platform. It got worse. A few yards to the left, another speaker was setting up his platform-cum-lectern of gleaming metal. His poster read: British Fascisti. The crowd assembled around the IFL platform in front of them was larger than that of the BF but there was no recognisable gap between them. Ronald and Lisette remained standing at the back. The IFL speaker was the first to get going.

'Ladies and Gentlemen, my name is Arnold Spencer Leese and I'm proud to tell you that I'm the founder of this frontline organisation. The frontline in the battle to preserve the Union and the British way of life. This wonderful country—'

'Hear, hear!' came shouts from the listeners.

'This wonderful country of ours,' he continued, 'is suffering from a festering disease which the IFL will cure. The disease is called the

Chapter 5 – Agent Ronald Burnley

Jews.' That was received with applause and supportive calls, except for a solitary man's high voice:

'Go home and cure a few cows, Mr Leese!' which raised a few laughs.

Leese was unperturbed.

'The gentleman is obviously aware that I'm a veterinary surgeon by profession which is why I know the Jews don't belong here. I abhor their inhuman method of slaughtering the cows.'

Ronald was disgusted. He disregarded Lisette's attempts to say something to him. Another voice cried out, 'You don't know what you're talking about. You're more wet than vet' which also got laughs. At this point the neighbouring speaker opened fire and Ronald, already deeply disturbed, moved slightly to hear him better. Lisette followed him.

'Ladies and gentlemen. I'm William Joyce and I'm not a vet. I'll start right away by confessing that we, the British Fascisti,' he pronounced it 'fassisti', 'agree with the IFL about the Jews. The Jews are hand-in-glove with the enemies of this country. In case you really don't know who I mean I'm referring to the Communists. They're running the Labour Party and the Trade Unions. Their aim is to turn this country into a Soviet state like Russia. And they'll succeed because our so-called democracy's too weak to resist. In Germany Herr Hitler will change things but at present there is only one government in Europe that stands up to communism, that of Benito Mussolini...'

Ronald had enough.

'Let's go, Lisette. I can't stomach anymore.'

Ignorant of the fact that Joyce was not an Englishman, he kept asking himself how an Englishman could support the German National Socialists and Mussolini's Fascists. He was not good company for the rest of the day. It did not improve when, in the evening, Lisette took a tabloid-size newspaper from her handbag and handed it to him.

'Somebody gave this to me when we listened to the speakers, Ronnie.'

He checked its name: *The Patriot*. Publisher: Duke of Northumberland. He read some of the articles, then threw it to the floor, something she had never seen him do before.

'You are very upset, Ronnie. All day. Such people are not important.'

Chapter 5 – Agent Ronald Burnley

'The Duke of Northumberland? A member of the House of Lords and he prints these fascist, these racist ideas? I've been ignorant.'

'He is only one man. He does not count.'

He picked up the paper and pointed at one of the headlines.

'Look at this, Lisette: Jews do not belong in this country. And here: Jews are plotting the destruction of Great Britain. He should not be allowed to print such lies.'

'You have said everybody can say what he likes, Ronnie.'

'Yes, democrats who uphold free speech. But people who want to abolish it? Like the fascists in Italy. The German Nazis aim to do the same. I learned all about them in Munich.'

'Why are you so upset, personally? This is not like you.'

He looked at her, then at *The Patriot* in his hand and then back at her.

'It's true. I'm disappointed and disenchanted. I've always believed that here in Britain such ideas don't exist. I've been living in a fool's paradise, Lisette.'

She was caressing his hand.

'Fool's…? Ah, *oui*. It hurts, *mon chéri*?' She put her arm around his shoulders.

'It does, Lisette. My boss in Vienna called Nazism a German disease. But these people, the Imperial Fascist League, the British Fascisti, the Duke of Northumberland, they're home-grown. That drills deep holes into my soul. I've lived here most of my life and I did not know about this?'

Suddenly he remembered.

'Lisette, were you trying to tell me something when we stood there?'

She looked at him with widened eyes.

'It is a little too late, Ronnee. I see somebody I know.'

'I'm sorry. Who was it?'

There was a touch of concern in her voice when she replied.

'I think I see Mr. Conker standing close to the second speaker, Ronnee, and cheering.'

'Conker? Clarence Conker? Your friend Guy's friend?'

'Oh no, Ronnee. Guy says, he is not his friend. Only they work in the same job.'

Ronald was shocked. If, as he thought, Guy worked for MI6, then this Clarence Conker was doing so, also. In that case, how could he applaud the British Fascisti? Under cover perhaps?

Chapter 5 – Agent Ronald Burnley

After that Sunday, Ronald began to visit the public library in Kensington on Thursdays after work, in order to find out more about the British fascist organisations. Following the librarian's advice, a middle-aged woman with a tiny nose and thick glasses covering her large fish-like eyes, he consulted *Whitaker's Almanack*. He found out that the Duke of Northumberland was the local Chief Magistrate in his town, as well as the owner of large tracts of land. He found more information in the *Statesman's Year Book* and other sources and absorbed a lot of facts about Britain's political parties.

When he arrived one Thursday, the librarian was talking to a slim man with a high forehead and a thick wavy forelock, whose book she was just die-stamping. When Ronald reached the desk she said to the man, 'This is Mr. Burnley, one of my regulars, Mr. Martin. He's studying the British political scene. Perhaps you can give him some advice?'

Martin raised his eyebrows, as Ronald acknowledged the introduction.

'Only too happy, but I warn you, Mr. Burnley, my advice is not neutral. If you wish to get a good understanding of what Democratic Socialism is about, I suggest you have a look at the *New Statesman*, a weekly publication. Thanks to the wonderful Miss Carp, there's usually a copy on the reading tables over there. It's published by the Fabian Society.' His smile was almost impish. 'I shall read it myself regularly from now on.' He looked up at the clock on the wall. 'Sorry but I'm late.'

He picked up his book and swinging his umbrella, left hurriedly. Ronald looked after him.

'Who is he? What did he mean?'

'I can tell you, Mr. Burnley. You've just met a very interesting man, and an important one. He's ever so nice, too. Mr. Kingsley Martin has just come down from Manchester. He was the leader writer for the *Manchester Guardian* up there. A Liberal paper, by the way, with a capital L. What he said to you, was a bit tongue-in-cheek, for he's the new editor of the *New Statesman*.'

Ronald nodded but she had not finished.

'And he's written two books. We've got them both here. *The Triumph of Lord Palmerston* is one. The other, *French Liberal Thought in the Eighteenth Century* has just come in. So you see, he's quite a celebrity.'

Ronald turned to go but stopped as she had not finished yet.

'Do you know that Mr. Kingsley was a conscientious objector during the war and did only non-combatant war work? That's what's so wonderful about this country, Mr. Burnley. Where else in the world could a man refuse to be a soldier during a war because of his convictions?'

Ronald agreed, a little bit of faith restored. His father also had quoted the fact as example when they had talked about tolerance. Thinking about it as he was walking home, led to his being hit by new arrows of doubt which had to do with his work place. The other operators at the Cypher School were not attached, like Ronald, but directly recruited employees with pension payments etc. He was also, by far, the youngest man in the hall in which they worked. Both factors were obstacles to fraternisation, although he spent his breaks in the same canteen, poshly called refectory. In their conversations he'd heard a lot of remarks about what should have been done with the 'conchies' which together with many other subjects created an image of great intolerance. The image was given colour and shape one Thursday in the Library when he briefly scanned the issue of the *New Statesman*. His eye got caught by a short article headed: 'How unbiased are our security services?' It described incidents concerning two trade union leaders and a Labour M.P. The incidents were similar and the article suggested that the three men were being harassed by the Secret Services, whose agents were eager to find evidence that these men had secret links to Soviet Russia. The article closed with:

'The Government has to rely upon the unbiased advice from the country's security services. Yet British foreign policy reflects only hostility to communism, although almost daily reports point to fascism growing at an alarming rate in all European countries. Are our security services more concerned with the threat to the profits of big business than that to our democratic institutions?'

The paragraph stirred an impression that had been sown in Ronald's thoughts in the recent past. Now it grew into a seed bag of doubts. Was the SIS really more concerned with protecting the wealthy upper classes than the population as a whole? He recalled overhearing the radio operators in the refectory talking about the workers' hunger march. They condemned the marchers, asserting that their action was organised by Russia. Ronald had been in London at the time between his European probationary stints. The event had received support from some of the newspapers. He had read of it in the news and had been perturbed to read that the police arrested women who knocked on miners' door to door to collect for the march. He could not work out what their offence was, especially as he believed that marching in the streets in protest was a democratic right. But one of the operators, he had a lot of light-brown curly hair and little chin, had stated with the voice of authority, 'In my considered opinion, such marches and strikes amount to high treason. If I were in charge, I'd have all participants shot. For a start, I'd ban the Communist Party – and the Labour Party, whilst I'm about it.' It was only talk but reflected the man's biased attitude and of the colleagues who agreed with him. Ronald's father had instilled strong democratic ideals in him and he believed in equal rights and free speech.

Had Sinclair been aware of Ronald's deliberations he would have decided that recruiting from outside Oxford and Cambridge had been a mistake after all. But Sinclair was not aware and Cormody's quarterly report on Ronald stated:

'Captain Ronald Burnley's work is wholly satisfactory. His reports and assessments of the political situation in Austria are mature. In my estimation, Captain Burnley, despite his youth, qualifies as an expert on Austrian affairs. P. Cormody, Head of European Section. April 1929.'

If Ronald had seen the review, he would reasonably have assumed that he was due to continue running his Blue Danube for a long time still. He might also have admitted to himself that he was getting a little bored with it. As it happened he would have been wrong on the first count, due to something he, himself, had done. It was the little research, on the three names of secret Nazis, he had undertaken during his last week in Vienna. When Murdoch read it, he tested its contents with Oberst von Lebern, head of the Austrian Security Service.

Ronald's analysis of the first two men on the list, especially that of Major Hermann von Hetzendorf, tallied in every detail with what Lebern let slip about the man, accidentally on purpose, to quote a common saying. Murdoch was puzzled about Ronald's information on Dr. A. Mahr. Why would an Austrian Nazi choose to reside in Ireland? The museum job did not seem an adequate explanation. He first tried to do it the proper way and telephoned Major Douglas Korrie, the head of the Irish Section, who was an old friend of his. Korrie was unable to help.

Chapter 5 – Agent Ronald Burnley

'I haven't an agent in Dublin, Murdoch, and no line to Doran. You remember him?'

Doran was the resident agent in Ireland and reported directly to Sinclair. Murdoch did remember him. The three, each of them a bit of a maverick, had served in the same intelligence branch in the last year of the war. Korrie's mentioning him was a hint to which Murdoch responded.

'Mine isn't really an official enquiry. Thanks Korrie.'

'If you get to obtain facts about this Doctor Mahr, I'd appreciate a copy, Murdoch.'

Murdoch did get in touch with Doran and sent him a coded request for information on Professor Alfred Mahr, Viennese Nazi, curator of the National Museum in Dublin.

As Murdoch's handful of British agents in Vienna was steadily decreasing in numbers, his group of Austrian informers was increasing in importance. When Murdoch was in London, Cormody asked him to take a trip around the British embassies in Europe, with the purpose of establishing a direct liaison between the various heads of security in the embassies, specifically in respect of the progress of fascism in Europe. Murdoch had agreed but was concerned with keeping his Viennese informers network to be kept running smoothly. There was only one person who could do this: Ronald Burnley. In his current monthly communiqué to London he wondered whether Captain Ronald Burnley could be sent to Vienna to run his office during his absence. At first, Cormody did not feel it justified interrupting Ronald's current work at the Cypher School. But a combination of circumstances induced him to change his mind. One was that an appraisal of the Blue Danube desk made clear that up to date it had not brought about any changes in the government's foreign affairs policies. The other was that one of Murdoch's British field agents, due for retirement, arrived in London and was available for a desk job. Out of the blue, Ronald was given the task of introducing him to the running of the Blue Danube desk as well as travel documents for Vienna together with orders to look after Murdoch's office during his absence. When Ronald informed Lisette, he was not surprised at her expressions of unhappiness, but this time she also displayed resentment.

'You are pleased, you go away, Ronnee, *n'est-ce-pas*?'

He felt guilty. 'Not in the way you think, darling.'

'In which way then, you tell me.'

Chapter 5 – Agent Ronald Burnley

'I have not enjoyed the work I have been doing and am pleased to leave it. It is true I look forward to more interesting action. You will be all right for money, sweetheart, and I shall not be away for very long. I have no choice, my darling. I've to go where they send me.'

Lisette knew that. She had begun to believe that theirs had become a stable relationship. Now she was suddenly unsure. The baggage of her past was still weighing her down. Ronald, in turn, resented being made to feel guilty. Thus, suddenly their relationship was out of tune. Lisette, in particular, had begun to enjoy the stability of a love affair, that beautiful experience that requires no questions, in which neither past nor future is of importance, only being together counts. But an affair of passion has a limited life and theirs had reached the point at which it had to be decided whether it had been a penny serenade or the overture to a more complex symphony. Lisette was scared deep inside her that she might lose him. It was a thought she could not bear. She accompanied him to Victoria Station but not as far as the train. Her eyes were closed when she kissed him outside the entrance to the platform. It was a long and deep kiss, which contained her fears and questions, her love and her desires, and weakening hope. When their lips separated she walked away quickly, yet Ronald could not miss the sadness in her eyes as she turned away.

* * *

When he arrived in Vienna he found that not only Murdoch was away but also Sandy Heaven. His responsibilities, should anything serious take place were awesome. But nothing did. Throughout the three eventless weeks in Vienna, the major part of his thinking was occupied with an enquiry into himself. Lisette's reaction, her sadness, had left an impression, he was unable to dismiss. The question of whether his attitude was fair to her took hold of his thoughts. He had always believed in what was referred to as free sex and he had assumed that she saw their relationship in the same way. But she had never been as independent as he was, and he began to understand that if he left her she would be left with nothing: no home, no economic security and no one to give her affection and love. His assumptions had been a kind of convenient rationalisation, the wrong kind. Strictly speaking, rationalisation was not even the correct word for it. What security she held seemed to depend entirely upon him. Ironically punning to himself, he remembered that his job was to maintain security. But his thoughts also made him aware of something else: He, himself, could not conceive his life without her. He knew what his father would say and he knew what he had to do.

Midway through his last week in Vienna an answer to Murdoch's request from Murdoch's old friend Doran arrived. Ronald, pleased to have something to do, decoded it. He found it more than interesting. It informed Murdoch that Mahr was using his position to obtain Irish support for the Nazis. He was a friend of De Valera, a prominent leader of Ireland's struggle for independence from the United Kingdom, and had founded a branch of Hitler Youth in Dublin whom he trained personally every weekend. Murdoch returned from a successful tour of selected British embassies before the third week was ended. He was alarmed at the information from Doran, especially as Doran hinted that Sinclair showed little interest in his reports. After an urgent telephone communication with Cormody he passed a personal request to Ronald.

'I want you to take the information about Mahr to Major Douglas Korrie, the head of the Irish Section, Burnley, by hand. Report to Cormody to receive the official order.'

Ronald had originally considered staying over the weekend which would have given him a chance of tea at the Kursalon with Sandy who was due back at the weekend. But by now he had discarded the idea. He was eager and looking forward to seeing Lisette again and left Vienna promptly.

He had not informed her of his return details and at Victoria Station took a taxi. Fifteen minutes later he opened the door to his house. He called out, 'Lisette!' but received no reply. The next moment a woman came out of the kitchen. She was sturdy, had short brown hair, a high forehead and intelligent, wide black eyes which were looking him over as if he were an exhibit. Their expression was less than friendly.

'Who are you?' he asked. 'Where is Lisette? What are you doing here?'

'You must be the wonderful Ronnie. If you're not, I want to know what you're doing here.'

He dumped his luggage on the floor and turned to the stairs. She put her arm across.

'Don't. You'll wake her up. She's asleep. She's all right but she needs the rest.'

'I have this odd idea that I live here,' he murmured, moving her arm aside.

He rushed up the stairs and opened the bedroom door softly. Lisette was in bed, asleep. She was wearing her underclothes. He stepped close, not knowing what to make of this. He heard a sound. The woman had followed him and stood in the doorway. She kept her voice low.

'If you come downstairs I'll make us a cup of tea and explain. I was about to make one for me when you turned up. Lisette was not expecting you, was she?'

He shook his head and followed her downstairs. She pointed to the living room. He sat down at the table. He was in his own home but a strange woman was in charge. It seemed to be his fate to meet strange women in this house. She came in with a tray holding exactly the same things that it would have, had Lisette brought it. She noticed his puzzled look.

'Yes, I've been here before. Lisette and I are friends. We're in the same course at the university and, after classes, we often have tea together, sometimes at my place, sometimes here. You're usually still at work.'

He began to see a little daylight.

'What happened? It seems I owe you thanks. I'm sorry if I was rude before.'

'That didn't surprise me from someone like you. Lisette fainted in class. She recovered quickly and I brought her home. You owe me two shillings and seven pence. That includes the thruppenny tip for the taxi driver.'

He disregarded the insult.

'What is wrong with her? I must get a doctor.'

'That's hardly necessary at this stage. Don't tell me you don't know what's wrong.'

It was time for him to take charge. 'It's none of your business but if you're implying that Lisette is pregnant, you're wrong.'

His words did surprise though not faze her.

'It is my business. I'm the only friend Lisette has in London. She's alone in the world and you're taking advantage of her. Of course, she thinks you're the greatest thing since paper was invented. It's easy for you to say she's not pregnant but how could you tell – a man?'

He looked at her searchingly and made a decision.

'You can call me Ronald. How about you? Are you usual enough to have a name?'

'Celeste.' She spat it out. 'Celeste Whiteman, if you're really interested.'

'You look an intelligent woman, Celeste, so perhaps you can work out how I know that Lisette is not pregnant, for, I assure you, I do know. You're also wrong with your other assumptions but if I tried to explain, you probably wouldn't believe me so I'll not bother. Nor do I care. I shall call the doctor tomorrow morning. I'm grateful to you for your help today and for your friendship with Lisette. She did and does need a friend. And, if you could call in during the day tomorrow I should be even more grateful because I am forced to go out. I'm happy to refund your cab fare coming and also for going back home. Peace now, Celeste Whiteman, at least whilst we're having tea. How about it?'

She nodded, thinking about what he had said, although he could see in her face that she was not letting go of her views. The rest of their conversation was kept neutral. She had come to London from Manchester a few years ago, with the intention of studying medicine. That was as much she would give away. He repaid her taxi. She refused to accept money for a taxi fare home. Judging by her clothes, simple blouse and skirt, but expensive material, she was not poor but she insisted on taking the bus back. He did not argue and was pleased when she left as soon as she had drunk her tea. He saw her to the door. In the doorway she said, 'Your doctor will probably call early. I'll come mid-morning to look after Lisette whilst you're away. I'll buy the wherewithals for a meal. You can pay me when you return.'

She walked away before he could say anything. Lisette was still sleeping when he went to bed but she woke up in the night and her arms found him. She snuggled close.

'Ronnee. You are back. This is not a dream.'

The next moment he heard her regular breathing. Feeling reassured he, too, fell asleep. He got up early and made breakfast. Celeste had said 'your doctor' but there was no such person. They had not needed a doctor since living together. He telephoned the Personnel Bureau at 54 Broadway and discovered that both, Lisette

Chapter 5 – Agent Ronald Burnley

and he, were covered by a Service Health Insurance Scheme. The keen-to-be-of-assistance lady offered to call the doctor for him. She rang back a few minutes later. A Doctor Rosen would be with him within the hour. Thankfully, he took the tray upstairs and, after depositing it on the hinged table board by the window, sat down on the edge of the bed. For a few moments he just looked at Lisette's features, the softly curved nose, cheeks, chin, mouth, her eyelids with naturally long lashes. Then he bent down and softly rested his lips on hers. They responded. When he let go, her long, dark eyelashes rose to almost reaching her eyebrows. Did she know how beautiful the complete assembly was?

'Ronnee.'

Her eyes were shining. They seemed to grow larger as she looked at him. He saw a tear rising in each of them and his eyes threatened to follow suit. He quickly put his cheek against hers. They remained like this for a long time, the time it took for her to come fully awake. She sat up.

'It was not a dream. When did you arrive, Ronnee?'

'Yesterday, late afternoon. You were asleep.'

She looked down on herself.

'I was asleep? I am in my *culottes cami*' (camiknickers). 'What…?'

'You fainted quite unphilosophically, during your Philosophy lesson, dear, and Celeste, your shining lady in armour, brought you home.'

'Celeste, yes, I remember. I've slept since…? I must have done. I've never fainted before. Perhaps it was something I have eaten? How do you know – oh, yes, you've met her. Shining lady? She's a good friend. I must get dressed.'

She started to push the blankets away. He held her hand.

'Please, darling, stay in bed until the doctor has been. I've brought breakfast up.' He pointed to the table.

'Doctor? I do not need a doctor.'

'Just to please me, darling, and to convince your thorny friend that you're not pregnant.'

She stared at him.

'This is silly. Of course I am not pregnant.'

'We're agreed on that, but you did faint and I am worried. To reassure me, darling.'

Chapter 5 – Agent Ronald Burnley

'But I do not have breakfast in bed and I need a good wash and change my underwear. I do not know you know a doctor, Ronnee.'

She had slipped out of bed and rushed about, exchanging camiknickers for panties and a nightshirt.

'I don't. His name is Rosen.'

She looked up.

'I know Dr. Rosen, Ronnee. I was here when he has come to see the little baby Clare, and Mrs. Heaven. That is the lady who owns this house, did you know that, Ronnee?'

He did not have to reply. She had hardly slipped back into bed when the doorbell rang. Ronald went downstairs to open the door. Dr. Rosen was a tall, thin man, with wide, slightly stooping shoulders, hair greying at the edges. He had the kindest eyes. Ronald led him upstairs.

'Thank you for coming so quickly, Doctor. I'm Ronald Burnley. My fiancée, Lisette Bannister, fainted yesterday whilst attending a class at the university. A friend brought her home and put her to bed. I arrived from abroad later in the day. Lisette has slept through until this morning. She seems to be all right now although I have the feeling she's a little fragile, Doctor.'

He followed Rosen upstairs and stood in the room during his check-up. It seemed to take an eternity. At last he followed him downstairs and they sat down at the table.

'Miss Bannister is well, Mr. Burnley, you can relax. She's getting up now but I have suggested she does not go to her classes this week and rests as much as possible.'

'And the fainting?'

'I can't diagnose a cause. It could have come from something she ate, as she suggests. She believes she had a feeling of nausea, which gives support to this possibility. On the other hand, it is extremely rare for that to create fainting. Miss Bannister does suffer from anaemia, a disorder of the blood, which is more likely to have caused her to faint, although it, too, is rare for someone of her age. I'm prescribing a course of iron pills which should improve the condition considerably. She must follow the instructions that will come with the pills and use them all up. I don't expect any repetition but you have my telephone number on the prescription.' He added, 'Your employers are dealing with my bill, Captain Burnley.'

Chapter 5 – Agent Ronald Burnley

Ronald handed him coat and hat in the hall and accompanied him to the door at the very moment that Lisette came down the stairs and Celeste was ringing the bell. He opened the door.

'Thank you, doctor. – Come in, Celeste. The patient is alive. – Sit down on the couch, darling. You have a visitor. We can all relax now. Dr. Rosen has come up roses – sorry.'

The 'sorry' was to the doctor for the pun, who gave a brief laugh as he hurried away. Ronald faced Lisette.

'Lisette, my darling, I've to rush out and report to my boss. I expect to be back before one.'

He was back sooner as Cormody turned out to be in a great hurry, himself.

'Major Korrie will see you on Saturday. His office is not in this building. My secretary will give you the exact address.' He handed him an envelope. 'Your current orders after Korrie.'

Ronald returned home to lunch with Lisette and Celeste. It ended in complete harmony with Lisette washing up, Celeste drying and Ronald putting away. As soon as they had finished, Celeste even proved that she had finer feelings by leaving. They were alone at last and sat side by side on the couch. His arm was around her shoulders, her head, eyes closed, rested against his shoulder and the only sound waves heard floating through the space emanated from the quiet, regular breathing of two people at peace. Such moments do not happen often enough in life and must be treasured. They were. Until the silence was broken by a male voice saying, 'Will you marry me, Lisette?'

There was no movement, except that Lisette's eyes opened slowly, looking upwards to see his eyes above hers. He read the answer in them and his lips reached out to kiss each of her eyelids as she closed her eyes in total relaxation. This could have been considered the happy ending of the story: 'and they lived happily thereafter.' Neither Lisette nor Ronald had been brought up on fairy tales and when their new reality had settled in their hearts and minds, the brains came into their own to discuss a few down-to-earth aspects.

'You do know, darling, that I shall continue to be sent away on jobs.'

'I know this, Ronnee, but you will always come back to me, *n'est-ce-pas?*'

'Toujours, mon amour.' (Always, my love.) He emphasised the rhyme.

'So you see, I shall not be lonely even if I am alone sometimes. I shall be Mrs. Burnley.'

He said, 'My experience in getting married is less than small. Is the town hall all right with you?'

'Ah, we marry *à la mairie*? You see? You are not the only one who can make puns. Yes, *naturellement* it is all right. I do not like *la grande cèrèmonie*.'

'I am free this week except for having to report on Saturday morning, so we can marry on Sunday. I must also find out what we have to do. Rings, I believe, are necessary, to denote that you've become Mrs. Burnley and we are each other's property.'

'Ronnee, I do not marry you for to becoming Mrs. Burnley. I become Mrs. Burnley because I marry you. I do not marry you for a ring on my finger, *chéri*. I wish that we belong to each other, not like property, but like true friends and you will be my love till the end of my life.'

He raised her hand to his lips in a spontaneous gesture. The next morning, he walked to the Registry Office at the Kensington Town Hall. When he came out, the wedding was fixed. His step was buoyant and his mind was content. In the afternoon bits and pieces of conversation concentrated on the wedding arrangements, e.g. Lisette undertaking to purchase two rings. And during the night it was celebrated by the kind of *grandes cèrèmonies* they both enjoyed.

When Ronald stepped out of Westminster underground station on Saturday, the sunny sky was reflecting his mood. He stopped for a moment looking round. To his left, guarded by the bronze statue of Boadicea, riding defiantly high in her chariot, Westminster Bridge was crossing the Thames. Facing him, on the other side of the road, Big Ben, London's famous clock, sat on the tower above the northern end of Westminster Hall. Its northern face, the only one never to be lit up fully by the sun, drew Ronald's eyes as if it had something to tell him. It did the next moment when the quarter bell struck the time: it was ten-forty-five, exactly. He waved a thank-you. There were, as always, a lot of people milling around the area. He turned right, passed the small ABC restaurant and turned right again into Whitehall. Actually the lower end of the great thoroughfare was not called Whitehall then. A terrace of twenty-two narrow houses,

Chapter 5 – Agent Ronald Burnley

starting at the corner, was called Parliament Street, proclaiming its importance as the original street leading north from Parliament Square.

Ronald stopped outside No 43, a narrow, one-storey, dark-grey building, and looked at his watch: too early. That would not do. He crossed the road, walked on into Whitehall and turned into Downing Street, where he stopped beside a sizeable group of Italian sightseers crowding the pavement. Their guide was a tall, slender English woman with a horsey face and intelligent eyes and a cultured voice, and obviously a pessimist as she was carrying an umbrella in her hand. When he reached them, she was just pointing to the building opposite, stating in a matter-of-fact voice that the door opposite, marked 10, was the entrance to the home of the British Prime Minister, Mr. Russell Macdonald. The group stood silent for a few seconds, staring at the door, then one of them, a fat little man, stepped forward. Facing his friends, he delivered a short, passionate oration in Italian, which Ronald had no difficulty in understanding.

'Look well, friends. Look well! The head of the most powerful nation on earth lives in this ordinary house. That is style. In Italia every *villano*' (peasant) 'thinks he must live in a *palazzo*.'

Ronald decided that the little man had to be the Italian version of Mr. Pickwick. 'Signor Pick-a-wicka,' he told himself. The guide continued her explanations, pointing to the neighbouring building, No. 11, the Finance Minister's residence, and other tidbits, after which she turned and the group followed her umbrella, held high like a flag in battle, into Whitehall. So perhaps she was a utilitarian, not a pessimist. He looked at his watch and he, too, left Downing Street, where he turned right. His brief visit to Reading the day before ran through his mind. His mother was her usual self, only more so.

'I'm glad, Ronald, you are not getting married here in Reading. It's not even a proper wedding. No bans, no preacher, no celebrations. An ordinary postcard, no wedding invitations. You ask me to travel all the way to London. Really.'

'I'm sorry, Mother, I realise that travelling to London might be a strain but I've had little time to arrange it and Lisette was not well. Neither of us wanted a church wedding.'

'Like father, like son. He didn't want a proper wedding, too. I soon changed his mind. Of course, Mum and Dad arranged everything. Your bride's the girl you told us about some time ago, the foreign girl, isn't she?'

'She hasn't got any parents, Mother. She's a lovely girl and you'll like her. Look, we'll come up for the day, next week. I promise, we'll come to see you both as often as possible.'

'She's lived with you all that time and she's not well and you're marrying in a hurry. You think I could ever like a woman like that?'

That hurt. His grandmother had been silent. Now she took charge of the conversation.

'I'm afraid, it'd really be difficult for us to travel, Ronnie. I've to use a stick now. But your room will always be ready for the both of you. Give your Lisette our apologies and our good wishes. You will tell her?'

When he left he kissed both of them fondly but he knew he would never bring Lisette here.

* * *

As he entered 43, Parliament Street, by far the narrowest house in the street, Big Ben's fourth strike of the hour rang out. Eleven more accompanied him up the steep staircase to the top and he knocked on the door to his right, just beating the eleventh strike. A sonorous low voice with a Scottish inflection bade him enter. The man seated on the office stool behind the small desk, was stocky, with a small well-formed face wearing glasses, dominated by a high forehead whose thinning hair showed a lot of grey. Without looking up from studying a large photograph through a magnifying glass, he pointed to the chair in front of the desk, 'On the dot. Take a pew, Burnley. Good of you to've come.'

Ronald acknowledged his host's welcome and sat down to face him on the only chair available, its back to the window. Waiting for Korrie to move, he turned his head around and was startled to look into Big Ben's face which filled the whole of the window frame. The clock seemed so close that he felt he could shake hands with it – if it had any.

'An amazing sight, don't you agree?' Korrie's voice made Ronald turn back.

Korrie was putting the photograph into a desk drawer and the magnifying glass into a pigeon hole of the shelving by his side.

Chapter 5 – Agent Ronald Burnley

'One of the reasons I held on to this address,' he explained, 'something the plebeians at 54 don't understand. I had negotiated the lease of the building, personally, with the Government's Commissioner of Works. I had to go and see Jowett, Frederick William Jowett, himself, that – he's a radical socialist and I'm a radical anti-socialist. But, ye ken, he surprised me. Pleasant man and we had a pleasant talk and when they wanted me to move to 54 Broadway, I dug my heels in. And here I am and here I stay. I've had a call from Vienna, so I know why you're here.'

Ronald thought it was quite natural for someone called Doug to have dug his heels in. He took the manila envelope that held Murdoch's letter from his inner pocket and handed it to Korrie. Korrie extracted its contents.

'Not stuck down. So you know what's inside, Captain?'

He began to read whilst Ronald was replying.

'I decoded it, Major Korrie.'

Nodding, Korrie murmured bits of what he was reading: 'Curator Irish National Museum… Austrian!… Raise support for Nazis?… Friends with De Valera?… One of the movers and plotters… Running a Hitler Youth organisation? – I can't believe it…What kind of organisation?'

He looked up, 'Do you know?

Ronald replied, 'When I was in Munich, Major, the Nazis were just forming one: military drill preparing teenagers for becoming Stormtroopers. I saw a battalion of Hitler Youth at a Hitler rally in Nuremberg – in brown uniform carrying standards and shouting pro Hitler slogans.'

Korrie looked at him steadily for a few seconds then, murmuring 'So you were there,' read the rest of the report silently. He then returned it into the manila envelope, which he put into the drawer, and took the large photograph and the magnifying glass from the drawer.

'I'll be thanking Murdoch directly, Captain. Odd, having to obtain it like this.'

Ronald realised he was being dismissed and got up. Not quite knowing what to do, he saluted and turned to leave. In the doorway, he heard Korrie say:

'Good job, Captain.'

It did not quite make sense to him but Big Ben chose that moment to strike the quarter hour again, one stroke, confirming that

Chapter 5 – Agent Ronald Burnley

the interview was ended. Ronald hesitated for one moment, then closed the door gently behind him.

Upon reaching the ABC restaurant he decided to have a cup of tea before going home. He needed to relax in neutral territory. He entered and sat down by the window. The waitress put the tray with tea and, as requested, a macaroon added to the two biscuits, in front of him. She pointedly pointed out that had he arrived ten minutes later she could have only served lunch. He got the point and paid his bill immediately. She was pleased and left him to his state of joyous expectation. He took his latest orders out of the envelope:

'Keep-fit, unarmed combat and small arms refresher course.' And the last paragraph under Field Work: 'Escort and individual tasks, Germany, Austria, Hungary.' So Cormody continued to employ him in that part of the world. 'Nothing exciting but better than a fork through my tongue,' he said to himself.

He liked travelling. His thoughts moved eagerly to his immediate future with his heart overflowing to such an extent that talking silently to himself was no longer adequate. He looked up at Big Ben whose voice was resting before the next strikes were due and willing to listen.

'I'll tell you something in confidence, big fellow. When you strike eleven tomorrow, I'll be starting on the greatest operation of my life, past, present and future. Code name Lisette. I don't know why it's taken me so long to get started. You're lucky. You always know what to do and when. By the time you'll strike twelve tomorrow, we'll have added the sealing wax, so don't forget to ring out your blessing from your superior height.'

Out of the corner of his eye, he noticed the waitress looking at him. Big Ben had obviously heard him and confirmed it by striking four times to announce the full hour then followed it up by ringing the twelve clangs to announce the end of the morning and telling Ronald, it was time to go. Ronald could take a hint. He finished his macaroon and emptied his cup. Lunch customers were entering. Soon this place would fill up. He got up and left, more relaxed than he had been when he entered. Outside he gave a last wave to the clock, whispering *'au revoir, mon ami'* and, as the twelfth strike clearly called out 'adieu', he entered the Westminster underground station.

* * *

Chapter 5 – Agent Ronald Burnley

The wedding ceremony on Sunday turned out to be a simple, straightforward affair. Ronald had put on his best summer suit and added an azure-blue tie. The doorbell rang at a quarter past ten, Celeste stood there beside a bespectacled, Mephisto-bearded man, who wore a white carnation in his buttonhole. Celeste, too, had a white carnation fixed in her hair. She made the introductions.

'Ronald Burnley, the bridegroom, Mr. Emmanuel Anstone, your second witness, Ronald.'

'Your philosophy teacher,' Ronald exclaimed. 'How do you do, Mr. Anstone, this is very kind. I've heard so much about you from one of your students.'

'It's a pleasure, Mr. Burnley. I've heard about you, too.'

They shook hands.

'Lisette is upstairs, getting ready,' she said.

Celeste produced a dark-red carnation and fixed it in Ronald's buttonhole. He was surprised and touched, remembering that his grandmother had told him once that a dark red carnation meant lasting love. He was genuinely sorry that she and his mother were not present and, at this moment, promised himself to do what he could to improve their relations. Lisette chose this same moment to appear at the top of the stairs. Ronald looked, stared and held his breath for that moment. She did not hold a broom above her head, nor did she wear a transparent nightshirt. She wore a simple blue dress and had a dark-red carnation in her hair. A single word filled Ronald's mind as his eyes followed her progress down the stairs: 'Lovely.' He murmured it to himself: 'Lovely.' He took her hand as she reached the bottom of the stairs and, once again, said, 'Lisette, my darling, you look lovely.'

She gave him a glorious smile and said, *'Naturellement, chéri. It is how I feel.'*

Then she saw the other two.

'Mister Anstone! Thank you for coming. Celeste, thank you for everything.'

She turned to Ronald, 'Ronnee, Celeste, she has done everything. She knows everything. She is so *capable.*'

Ronald had been convinced of that when he first met her. It was another sunny day, and it took them only ten minutes to walk to the Town Hall. On the way, in addition to the cheery sunrays, approving glances and smiles fixed on them, despatched in their direction by

Chapter 5 – Agent Ronald Burnley

passers-by who, seeing the carnations, guessed that their wearers were on the way to a wedding. Outside the town hall, on top of the steps, they passed a photographer with his camera and tripod. They had to wait in the registrar's waiting room for a few minutes. Ronald, studying the notices, learned that the same office also registered births and deaths which reassured him no end. He wondered whether they ever got mixed up.

The door opened and half a dozen people issued from it, three men wearing the conventional penguin suits and three women in evening dresses. They were all smiling equally happily which frustrated Ronald because he was unable to make out which of them were the pair that had just become wife and husband. He hoped, they knew. The rest of the event passed smoothly. The registrar led the proceedings in a manner which gave the impression to Ronald that he had done this before. The date was Sunday, 16th June, 1929. Questions were put and answers were given and written down in calligraphic writing. A legal document was signed by all of them. After Lisette's promise to love and obey and his to love and cherish, rings were slipped on fingers and finally, by the authority vested in the registrar, Lisette Bannister became Mrs. Lisette Marie Burnley, after which Ronald was permitted to kiss the bride. The 'Marie' was new to him, but, to make sure, he kissed both of them.

When they stepped onto the top of the stairs outside, Ronald discovered that the photographer was one of Celeste's capabilities who during the next three minutes took half a dozen mixed photographs. The speed told Ronald that Celeste had paid his lowest fee but he was touched by her doing it. They walked down the steps. The next moment, a few people dressed ornately, two of them more so than the others, rushed past them into the building. As they passed, Ronald murmured.

'I wonder, what they've come for.'

He reacted to Celeste's raised eyebrows with a sweet smile. They started to walk, when Ronald stopped short, cocking his head to listen with a smile. Lisette looked at him.

'What is it, Ronnee? I can only hear church bells striking.'

'That, Mrs. Burnley, is my friend, Big Ben, wishing us a happy life together. I told him all about our wedding yesterday. He's very reliable.'

Anstone, caressing his beard, smiled. 'You don't need to study the philosophers, Lisette, you've married one.'

Chapter 5 – Agent Ronald Burnley

They turned into De Vere Gardens. When they reached their house, Ronald, who had secretly feared that the capable Celeste had also arranged a party to celebrate, was almost shocked when she and Anstone would not come inside. Celeste, kissing both of them on their cheeks, was brief.

'I wish you a happy life together. I may see you some time, Ronald, when you're in London. I'll see you in class, Lisette.'

Anstone added, 'I, too, wish you both a happy and a long life. I'm pleased to have met you, Mr. Burnley, and to have taken a part in your happy event. I don't expect you in class this week, Lisette, but I'm going to change your name on the register as soon as I get back.'

They departed. Ronald felt positively guilty for being pleased. Lisette knew why.

'Celeste, she wants to arrange a great meal for us for celebrating, Ronnee, but I do not accept. I think we do not want a party. Was I wrong?'

They had entered the house and walked into the sitting room and sat down on the couch as if rehearsed. They sat side by side, cheek against cheek, the way they had done so often in the past. But this time was different. He had not answered her question. Now he turned towards her and his lips on her lips, gentle and tender, gave her his reply. After which he whispered:

'We'll do our best to make their wishes come true, Mrs. Burnley, a happy and a long life, together, *n'est-ce-pas*?'

She leaned back, closing her eyes. A long sigh of contentment escaped from her lips.

'Mrs. Burnley. *Enfin*' (At last). Celeste, she says I should keep my old name also but from the night when you have come to this house for the first time I have wanted to become Mrs. Burnley. It was my only wish in my life. And now I am Mrs. Burnley. I am so happy, Ronnee.'

'That makes three of us, Lisette.'

She shot up.

'Three? That is bigamy. It is not allowed. Who is this lady?'

'Her name is love, my love. I insist she stays with us, wherever we go and wherever we are, Lisette. And we'll share her and everything else in equal terms.'

These were beautiful words, words he really believed at this moment.

201

Chapter 6 – Magyar Sins

Whilst Ronald was still office-sitting for Murdoch in Vienna, an event took place in Budapest the Hungarian capital which had wide-ranging effects on him and others. It was a Sunday in early June, 1929, when Bela Gabor, a thirty-seven-year-old businessman from Szeged, was woken up by the melodious two-note trumpet signals of fire engines out in the streets. His head felt as if seven little men with big hammers were banging against it from inside. When consciousness slowly gained the upper hand over the moments of drowsing back into sleep, he realised that he was lying, fully dressed, on top of an unopened bed. Almost fully, for his jacket was slung over a chair, which stood beside the closed window, and his shoes on the floor were not neatly side by side, as was his custom.

It was day-time and he seemed to be in a hotel room. Of course! He was in his hotel in Budapest. Yet the room looked unfamiliar. Even the jacket looked unfamiliar. Sitting up, Gabor focused on the single window. Behind it, the sun was bathing a panorama of rooftops from whose chimneys thin columns of smoke were drawing grey vertical lines onto the canvas of an ocean-blue sky above, evidence of there being very little wind. The muffled noises of vehicles passing in the street below were hurting his ears. He began to remember – the party last night, a birthday party, yes, that's what it was, his birthday, with intoxicating gypsy music and even more intoxicating Tokaj. A lot of Tokaj, sweet and very strong. Gabor loved both, the music and the wine. But Ilona had not been there. Years ago it had been the passionate surge of gipsy violins that had brought them together at a birthday party, or rather at two birthday parties. The memory was a potent part of the headache that was pulsating inside his forehead. For Ilona was no more.

Last night there had been an almost beautiful woman with long eyelashes and very red lips there, wearing a mini silk-bodice, over-tight, emphasising the swell of the rolls of flesh bulging along the latitude of her bellybutton. The pathetic aim was to appear seductive as well as to hide the fact that she was no longer as slim or as young as she had been a good many years ago. Singing with passion about

Chapter 6 – Magyar Sins

yearning, love and desire, accompanied by the ever-fervent sounds of the gypsy orchestra, her undulating movements were designed to send her male audience into shivers of ecstasy. She probably still succeeded with some of them. Behind her, three similarly semi-clothed women were swaying in a rhythmical harmony whilst their voices were harmonising her tune. He shuddered at remembering them – and the fawning birthday toasts by his drinking companions, two of them, yes, Miklos, large and fat and Janos, small and fat. Or was it the other way round? Gabor was paying, of course.

It was his birthday, eve of birthday, to be exact. He had wanted company and an excuse for a brief relapse. Just this once – the last time, for he had definitely stopped drinking since recently. His depressing, inner loneliness had been in charge for too long. Three years was a long time. Today was not only his birthday, it would also have been hers, Ilona's. As he drifted once more back into semi-sleep, he was there, at that same restaurant. It was early June 1924. His friends had brought him to Budapest to celebrate his birthday with Gipsy music and Tokaj. And at the neighbouring table another birthday party was toasting the young woman, called Ilona, who was seated at the end of the long table. The birthday cheers and conversation and laughter at both tables ran in parallel but, from the very start Bela and Ilona had looked at each other again and again and more and more frequently. Quite suddenly, Bela, his glass of Tokaj in his hand, had got up and walked across to her table. He stopped in front of Ilona and the two were seeing no one else. Gradually both their friends were aware of it and both tables became silent, watching. Then Bela raised his glass.

'My name is Bela Gabor. It is my birthday today, also. I've been in a dream, since setting eyes on you. Will you please come into my dream?'

She stood up and, raising her glass, was smiling a happy smile:

'I am Ilona. Yes, I want to share your dream.'

Their collective friends broke into enthusiastic cries and cheers and even a few tears of emotion as he and Ilona linked arms and emptied their glasses and kissed each other on lips as sweet as the Tokaj. And within days they had turned the dream into beautiful reality until…

Gabor reluctantly returned to consciousness. This time he had come to Budapest to attend a trade conference. It was part of his new start. The two fellows who tagged on to him were also attending the conference. Full memory was returning. He cautiously moved his legs around to sit on the edge of the bed, holding his throbbing head firmly between his hands to prevent it from bursting. What he needed was strong coffee and aspirins. Or more Tokaj, the hair of the dog. Suddenly he heard voices from next door. Men were entering. What was happening? Who were they? He heard chairs being moved, then a man's thin, high voice.

'Not a bad meal. They're right about the Hungarian cuisine.'

It was spoken in German. All Hungarians, under Austrian rule, spoke German, generally with a clearly identifiable Hungarian accent. Bela, himself, spoke it like an educated Austrian. But this was German German. What were they doing in his suite? He looked around him. It began to dawn on him that this might not be his room at all. In that case what was he doing here? The next voice, unusually deep, rasping, and with a razor-sharp edge of a man used to giving orders, made him sit up, disregarding his headache.

'I've brought you up to my room to recapitulate quickly. Then you will proceed to your rooms, after which we shall not be seen together. Your luggage will be in your rooms by now. Mine is already here, as you can see.'

'Just as well,' it was a third man's nasal voice, 'The rail journey in third class was no fun. Wooden seats, brrr. You're right about the food, Dantzig. Damned fine.'

The rasper continued:

'I've booked my suite for three days and your rooms for seven, as planned. I'll repeat the details this last time, for there must be no failure: Tomorrow, Monday, you'll be out after breakfast, sightseeing the town. Make sure you are remembered at some of the sights, but not too ostentatiously. You will be at your places, keeping the hotel entrance in sight, by three thirty. When you see the car arrive, get ready. It will be the hotel's Rolls Royce. You cannot mistake it. You better not. At the exact moment that Lord Davidson steps out of the car, you, Dantzig, will detonate your explosive cassette. Cast it into the middle of the road. It isn't dangerous but will make the right kind of noise and is certain to draw attention and cause hysteria.'

Bela was startled. Explosive? Suddenly his mind was sharp and focused, as in the old days. A quick look confirmed to him that this room was not his hotel room. It had its own door to what must be the passage. Next door the rasper continued rasping:

Chapter 6 – Magyar Sins

'As soon as you hear Dantzig's explosion, you, Eisner, will follow suit with your cassette. It will increase the chaos. You will both immediately disappear amongst the crowds. Next, you will carry on with your sightseeing and return here in the evening, ignorant of what has happened. The second explosion will be my signal upon which I shall step out from inside the hotel to meet the Englishman who will be rushing up the hotel steps to get inside quickly. It will be my pleasure to welcome the English lord who does not like our Führer and shoot him at close range. He will no longer insult the German people. I'll make my escape in the commotion with the help of our Hungarian cell. That part is not your concern. You will do your tasks with precision, so that the detonations take place in quick succession. Questions?' He paused.

Gabor, realising he must get away, was hastily lacing up his shoes, whilst the speaker continued.

'None? Good. You stay in Budapest for the rest of the week, friends from Munich enjoying themselves. You will not get drunk! You may be interviewed by the police but you will not be suspected. Our local friends will lay trails to lead the police to left-wing revolutionary groups and the Russian consulate. A word of warning. Wotan's plans are always perfect. Should you make a mistake, you can be sure of punishment. Remember, there is nowhere for you to hide from him.'

The man paused again. Gabor heard the scraping on the floor of a chair. The speaker had risen.

'You will go now. I shall take a little relaxation, myself. Heil Hitler!'

Whilst two responding Heils sounded, Bela made it to the door as fast and as quietly as possible. The passage was empty. He was on the third floor. Lift and stairs were at the end of the short corridor. He took the stairs. Suddenly he realised he had left his jacket in the room. He decided it did not matter. Forever a man of caution, he had left his personal documents and the bulk of his money in the safe of his hotel, carrying only enough cash for the evening's outing, and most of that had been spent. He moved unhurriedly through the lounge. Outside he looked up at the hotel sign. It was the Hotel Merleg. He saw a connection. His hotel, the Starlight, was situated in Merleg Utca (Street). The headache had returned but he did not allow it to interfere with his concentration. He stopped for a moment to consider. Those Germans were certainly Nazis. And they had

Chapter 6 – Magyar Sins

Hungarian collaborators who were likely to keep the hotel under observation. It was also possible that someone in the hotel worked with them. Or both. He had to assume the worst scenario and decided it would not be wise to go straight back to his hotel. A great deal of insecurity still existed in Hungary and he had suddenly become one of its potential victims. After a few seconds of thinking, he had no doubt about what his priority must be.

Bela's presence in the hotel room had indeed been detected and he had been seen. Dietrich, he of the rasping voice, had found the jacket in his bedroom and the signs of someone having lain on the bed. He made enquiries and found out that the maid on night duty had opened the room for two men, assuming them to be hotel guests. One was a tall fat man, who had convinced her that this was the room of his friend who was very drunk. The hotel receptionist confirmed that he had seen a man walk out of the hotel around midday who, he thought, was not a guest. He described Gabor as well as he remembered which was not a lot but he had noticed that the man did not wear a jacket, unusual in this hotel. Dietrich, not wanting to draw attention to himself, did not pursue the matter.

He was convinced that, whoever the drunkard was, his having slept there was no danger to his plans. On checking the jacket, he only found a railway return ticket to Lillaförd in it. He would pass these details on to the Budapest cell's contact he had been given. He left the jacket in reception with the strict instruction to let him know if someone came to claim it. The jacket was not Bela's. Miklos had brought him to the room with the correct number but in the wrong hotel. At the last moment, in a hurry to get out, he had deliberately swapped jackets, in the hope of finding some money in Bela Gabor's. He did and rejoined Janos at the restaurant, both intent on delighting in some feminine delights. But he had left his railway return ticket in his jacket.

Captain Harry Nolan, a slim, sinewy man of middle height, his head crowned by unruly, flaxen hair, was the security officer on duty at the British Legation in Budapest that Sunday morning. As usual, it was a quiet day for him. He was on the telephone answering a call from an old friend of his, a British travel writer who was speaking from Vienna, Austria.

'No, we're a legation, not an embassy. His Majesty's ambassador here is only a minister.'

'What's the difference, Nolan?'

Chapter 6 – Magyar Sins

'The difference? Less of the mazuma, I suppose. You could make it a day-trip, old boy. We're in Táncsics Mihály Utca, in the Old Town.'

'Nolan, my friend, do you want me to rupture my tongue?'

'You're a travel writer, aren't you? It's a long name but a small narrow street – on the Várhegy, the Castle Hill, in Buda. Very picturesque to walk through, a nightmare for driving.'

'The other side of the Danube, Nolan, isn't it? Lovely gypsy restaurants, I remember.'

'You would. I've been here for almost a year and haven't set foot into one.'

'Knowing you, Nolan, I believe you. You were always a bit straight laced.'

Suddenly Nolan's security light on the internal telephone in front of him flashed.

'Hold it for a moment. 'He picked up the receiver and listened, surprised and suspicious, then said, 'Sorry. Got to attend to something, old boy. I hope to see you here before you leave Vienna.'

He put the receiver down and hurried to the legation's reception room to deal with an unusual caller, a Hungarian who was not wearing a jacket. Nolan had told his friend correctly that the British government was only represented by a minister in Hungary. He very correctly had not informed him that he, himself, was a member of the legation's security team, headed by Major Urban Pemmington. The major and his team occupied the corner house next to the legation, a fact that was not known to the local citizens. Its main door was in the side street. That a doorway connected both buildings, was not even known to the Hungarian authorities.

When Major Pemmington sat down at his desk early on Monday morning, he was not the happiest of men. He had just returned from London, where he had been questioned by one of the Foreign Ministry's parliamentary undersecretaries. He had found the man's know-all attitude frustrating, to say the least. The under-secretary was, all the time, twiddling his thumbs, alternatively one way then the other. He had listened to Pemmington with a supercilious smile, his frequent interruptions implying that, of course, the major had to make his answers sound very important. He gave Pemmington the impression that, desirous of impressing others with his knowledge, he was the type of man who did not know how little he knew.

Chapter 6 – Magyar Sins

'I think, Major, that your lot, like some of the civil service wallahs, look at things a little overcautiously, wouldn't you say?' the undersecretary had said at the end.

'I keep my reports close to the facts, sir. Admiral Horthy is an authoritarian. His government has difficulties coping with the country's economic problems. Poverty and shortages are mirrored in the political situation: extreme left wing parties and extremist right wing, pro-Hitler parties, are growing. Many Hungarians would like the emperor back. These are facts, sir.'

'Just as I said, Major. You see things blacker than they are, take my word for it. Hungarians wanting the Austrian emperor back and a handful supporting that insignificant little German megalomaniac? Really. It's your job to look for dangers and that's appreciated.' He stopped twiddling and rose. 'Thank you for having taken the trouble to see me, Major Bennington.'

He had not even got his name right, nor Hitler's nationality. Before leaving London, Pemmington had reported to his MI5 boss, Sir Vernon Kell. Kell had been one of the first 14 men in the newly-named Military Intelligence Section 5 (MI5) at the beginning of the war. The team had been successful in discovering practically all German spies in Britain and German military spies during the war. But Pemmington's considerable knowledge of the country and its people had got him posted to Budapest as British occupation representative during the occupation period. When the British Legation was established in Budapest he naturally moved in as security officer. Kell, too, was mainly concerned with the growth of the left in Hungary. Actually and strictly speaking, MI5 was concerned with internal security but the circumstances had created exceptions.

'Do keep your eye on the communists and fellow travellers, Major. They're the real danger. Supported by the Soviets, that's the problem, since they've murdered their czar.'

But Pemmington saw dangers at both extremes of the political spectrum and the report he found on his desk, when he was back early in the morning, was about to add evidence to this. Nolan, after interviewing Bela Gabor, had decided that the man's story had to be taken seriously and suggested he stay at the legation for the next few days. Gabor agreed, whereupon Nolan offered him the use of the second, somewhat tiny, bedroom in his own flat, above the Legation offices, a simple way of ensuring he could keep an eye on him, until

Chapter 6 – Magyar Sins

his story had been fully investigated. Nolan's immediate action had been to accompany his new house guest to the Starlight Hotel, where Gabor packed his case, collected his money and paid his bills, luckily unseen by either of his two drinking companions.

After returning to the legation, Nolan had typed his duty officer's report and had it delivered by hand to the major. Reading it with growing concern first thing in the morning, Pemmington propelled himself into action. He knew one part of the man's story to be a fact, one that even Nolan was not aware as yet. He, himself, had informed Commander György of Lord Davidson's campaign in Britain against the growing fascism in Europe. It had led to the forthcoming state visit by his lordship which had been kept secret. The Hungarian's reference to it suggested his story was true. The situation in Hungary was obviously even more dangerous than he had reported to the undersecretary in London. German assassins planning to murder a member of the House of Lords here in Budapest? And with local assistance? That was the most disquieting aspect of the situation. He embarked upon a sequence of four telephone calls in descending order of distance, London, the head of Six-Two, the third to the taxi stand and the fourth to Nolan, asking him to report at eleven. Then, grabbing hat and walking stick, he left. Giving the impression of a gentleman about town, he had only a couple of minutes' wait outside the bar at the corner, before the taxi drove up. And, like a gentleman about town, he gave the driver the address of a bar in one of Budapest's major streets. He was back in his office in good time, still troubled, but satisfied that the situation was under control.

The major's office was distinguished by a lack of surplus furniture. It contained only the basic necessities, including an old typewriter protected by a grey dust cover, which lived on the small table by the window. Pemmington typed all his confidential matters by himself, quite fast, despite using only the two index fingers. The typewriter, a Remington, was the most valuable item of all his equipment, not only because it was a souvenir. At the end of the war he had given hospitality in his home and considerable assistance outside it, to Sam Grenville, an American officer, who spent two weeks in London, researching incidents concerning American soldiers that had taken place during the war. When returning to London a year later as member of the American Embassy, Grenville had turned up at Pemmington's house and, carrying it in a rucksack, had put the typewriter on the large bureau in Pemmington's study.

'This, my Limey friend,' he expounded almost without taking breath, 'is one of the earliest Remington typewriters in the world. One of the first ever to include an upper and a lower case with a shift key, so you can shift – from one to the other. Natty, ain't it? My paw purchased it for his office in Ilion, state of New York if you asked, back in eighteen-eighty. It sports the famous QWERTY, designed by a friend of the family, fellah called Sholes. It's been sitting in a store-room back home. I can't type and I don't. You can't either but you do. Its maker meant it to be used and I mean it to be a memory of your Yankee pal. A Remington for a Pemmington. Sheer poetry. Hope, you'll find it useful.' When Pemmington opened his mouth to thank him, Grenville said, 'Sorry, Pemmington, can't stop. We'll have a drink some time,' and rushed out. The drink was still outstanding. The walls of Pemmington's office were bare, except for one small studio photograph of a young soldier with sad eyes. It, too, was a memory as was evidenced by a newspaper cutting below the photograph:

'In the evening of Saturday, 23 August 1916, Corporal Andrew Pemmington, on the last day of his leave at his parents' home in St. Leonard's Street, Bromley-by-Bow, East London, was seeing his girlfriend home. It was close to midnight when he returned home. We can imagine that his head and his heart were filled with joy and sadness, when, at that very moment, the bomb was dropped from the German airship, the Zeppelin. It was a direct hit. His sister and his mother were still out, visiting an aunt. It remained a direct hit in his family's hearts for the rest of their lives. His father received the news on the front.'

Pemmington lost his customary smile together with the inclination to laugh and, with rare exceptions, reduced his speech to brevity.

Nolan knocked on the major's office at eleven hours precisely and, hearing the brief 'Enter', followed its invitation. As always, he was struck by the bareness of the room. He wondered whether the young man in the picture might be Pemmington's son. There was no obvious likeness and one quite definitely did not ask Pemmington personal questions. The walls might be bare but Major Pemmington's personality filled the room. A sturdy, handsome man in his fifties, he was the kind who was not easily overlooked. Beneath a high forehead, wide, grey-blue eyes under heavy lids seemed to be looking permanently into a far distance. When fully

Chapter 6 – Magyar Sins

opened, they lit up his square, moustached and slightly wrinkled face. They did now.

'Read your report, Nolan, good job. Sit.' He pointed to one of the chairs in front of his desk.

Nolan sat down.

'Your impression of the man?' Pemmington asked.

'He's made a good impression on me, major. For a civilian, the way he's dealt with the situation was remarkably smart. He speaks English well, with barely an accent.'

'Normal thing for a Hungarian citizen should have been the police.'

Nolan agreed.

'Yes. It made me suspicious at first, sir. Also, his reference to a Lord Davidson. He insists the plotters are German Nazis. He has little confidence in the local police. Also, he says, he admires the British and one of his best friends has settled in England – which obviously can be checked. That, in itself, wasn't enough to allay my suspicions but I have to say I find it difficult not to trust him. He seems to be utterly straight. I suppose, you'll want to – ?'

Pemmington finished the sentence, 'Question him? Unnecessary.' After a short pause he added, 'Just returned from Dohany U' (U = *Utca*=street). 'Saw Commander György.'

Nolan's eyes opened wide. It was not Pemmington's meeting that surprised him, but the fact that he had informed him of it. He, himself, had only once been at the small bar in Dohany Utca, a regular location for clandestine meetings by or with members of Six-Two. His task at the time had been to deliver a communication to a Six-Two agent. Nolan had almost missed the building, with its brickwork painted a pale green, in harmony with the dark green wooden window frames. Looking like many in Budapest, it was easily overlooked, especially as it did not display a house number and the bar's name sign was small and grey. The severely handicapped barman, ex-sergeant in György's regiment during the war, led him to a small shed-like room in the back, beyond the toilet. There Nolan had met a man in uniform. After verifying each other's bona fides, Nolan had handed him the document and, as part of the cover, joined him for a beer in the bar before leaving. Picking up a dull-brown envelope from his desk, Pemmington went on:

'György took prompt action, immediate orders on the phone. Knows your man well. Had his record card translated for me, whilst I was there. Explains why you're impressed.'

He withdrew a grey sheet of thin paper from the envelope and handed it to Nolan who read it aloud:

'Bela Gabor, born Szeged 1st June, 1892 where he grew up. Youngest Imperial intelligence officer during war. Recruited by Department Six-Two in 1921. Top marks in physical fitness and unarmed combat. Main task, supervision of fast developing pro-Hitler groups in home town Szeged, executed with great efficiency. In '25 married Ilona Borovski, ex Russian. Resigned from Six-Two in line with Department's policy of using single men only. Within two years built up lucrative private business. 1927 wife Ilona died suddenly. Gabor sold business, withdrew into isolation. Occasional outbreaks into carousing and drinking.'

Pemmington said, 'Six-Two kept tabs on him. Gabor's attendance at trade conference in Budapest last week was significant of recent signs of recovery.'

'That explains a lot,' Nolan remarked, 'but does it actually prove he can be trusted? And if so, is he right about what he claims to have heard? The morning after a long evening's carousing?'

'György trusts Gabor one hundred per cent,' Pemmington said. 'Greatly concerned by reference to local cell. No knowledge of one.'

The shrill sound of the telephone interrupted him. He picked up the receiver.

'Pemmington.' – 'Yes, Commander.'

He pulled his note pad close and, scribbling on his pad, listened without interrupting. He hung up with a 'Thank you, Commander,' and turned to Nolan.

'Answers your question, Nolan. György confirms, 3 Germans booked in at Hotel Merleg yesterday morning. Two singles, one suite. One of them brought a jacket to reception, left in his suite by previous occupant. Demanded to be informed if claimed. Make sure, Nolan, your man does not go near the Merleg Hotel.'

'Will do, Major. So he's on the level. But this lord…?'

Pemmington nodded:

'State visit kept secret. Have rearranged Lord Davidson's itinerary. Hold on to Gabor till Wednesday, if possible. Can't detain him legally, though. György's request.' The Colonel leaned back in his chair 'That's all, Nolan.'

Chapter 6 – Magyar Sins

'Right-o, sir.' Nolan left.

After his meeting with Pemmington, Commander György had taken a quick look at the files of the known pro-Nazi parties, five of them:

Böszörmény: National Socialist Labour Society

Count Festetics: National Socialist Peoples Club

Sandor Jernitz: Nazi Workers' Association, Szeged (runs anti-Semitic paper)

Rajniss: National Defence League, Szeged. (obtains funds from Germany plus earnings as gigolo. Weekly: Magyar Futár)

Zoltan Mesko: smallholders and agricultural workers, Szeged.

He was puzzled. They all pursued representation in the parliament and they all knew they were kept under observation. It made no sense for any of them to be involved in illegal activities. Yet Gabor had referred to a local cell. György took a report from a drawer in his desk. It was headed: State Visit. It informed him that Lord Davidson, a member of the British House of Lords, had made international headlines with his speeches about the new German National Socialist party. He warned against trusting the Germans and his less than polite references to Herr Hitler were reported in the European media. György, charged with the visitor's protection, had kept the arrangements for the visit a top secret. The hotel management only knew that a guest of the government had to be collected from the main station. As he sat there, pondering, the agent he had sent to investigate at the hotel, entered and reported. When he had finished György had rung Pemmington with the request of keeping Gabor at the legation for a little longer.

On Tuesday György's men dealt with the plotters efficiently. They kept the two Germans Dantzig and Eisner under observation from the moment they left the hotel in the morning until they took up their positions in the early afternoon. There was no sun in the Budapest sky on that Tuesday, but it was humidly warm. It did not rain either despite a distant Homeric roll of thunder from time to time, sending a warning of impending doom.

At the moment at which the Rolls Royce pulled up in front of the hotel, Dantzig and Eisner promptly produced their sequential explosions as instructed. Seconds later they were in handcuffs. The bangs did startle passers-by but not into panic reactions. Upon hearing the detonations, the leader, Dietrich, meticulously true to his plan, stepped outside the hotel entrance. He had his hands casually

Chapter 6 – Magyar Sins

in the pockets of his long overcoat, which hid the large bulge his Luger pistol made in his right trouser pocket. At the moment of the car door being opened, his right hand began its stealthy movement towards the pocket. The moment it left the coat pocket, both his arms were grabbed, and twisted backwards, less than gently, by two agents in plain clothes who, appearing to be hotel guests like him, had followed him from inside the hotel. He was handcuffed, before he could utter 'Heil Hitler' and bundled into the back of the empty Rolls Royce whose door had been opened. Dietrich was unable to move between his two captors. Not that he tried. He was stunned into inaction. Captain Szilagyi Buda, one of György's officers who was supervising the operation, the one to whom Captain Nolan had delivered the MI6 document some time ago, popped his head into the car.

'Welcome to Budapest, Herr Dietrich. The British Lord Davidson sends his regrets. He would have loved to be shot by you. The Rolls Royce only came here to transport you to prison.'

Dietrich said nothing. Buda, who hated the Germans for personal reasons, was enjoying himself.

'You'll be pleased to know, I'm sure, that Lord Davidson arrived safely in Budapest early this morning. Did you really believe press details of his visit? Are you naïve, or just a German *Dummkopf'* (dumb cluck)? 'Don't strain yourself. You'll have plenty of time to contemplate the answer. We shall even feed you whilst you do that.'

Dietrich only stared at him, still in shock.

'I note, you're speechless at our generosity,' Buda went on, 'I can also tell you, that His Lordship who is not fond of your party, today addressed members of the government and of our parliament in special meetings. He will be on his way back to London tomorrow. So, if you can smuggle messages from your cell to your local comrades, tell them they must hurry if they want to do the job you failed to do. Whoever sent you will not be pleased with your performance. But you'll be safe from his disapproval in one of our old-fashioned prison cells.'

He laughed heartily as he withdrew his head and sat down beside the driver. Dietrich was unable to comprehend what had happened. Who had betrayed them? It had to be someone in the Hungarian cell? Not the man who had slept in his hotel room? That, he did not want to believe. Fear began to rise in him at Wotan's reaction who was known to punish failures harshly. Not until he was in the prison

Chapter 6 – Magyar Sins

and pushed less than gently into his cell, did he open his mouth in protest. To be precise, he was snarling, as was his wont, in German.

'You have no right to imprison me. I am a German citizen.'

Szilagyi Buda who had accompanied the guards, smiled an icy smile.

'Such arrogance – and ignorance. You should have studied the Hungarian laws, Herr Dietrich, before breaking them. If you commit a crime in Hungary, you are subject to those laws. I am delighted I had a lot of hand in catching you in the act. I sat with my men right next to you in the hotel lobby. I even smiled in your direction once. I must confess that in some matters we are not as efficient as the Germans. Our legal processes are very slow. You will enjoy our hospitality for much longer than you had planned. Much, much longer, Herr Dietrich.'

He turned to go then twisted his head back for a post script.

'You Germans are famous for your meticulous planning, as you've been telling the world. I suppose that explains your having lost the war, which has given us our independence. Your two fellow plotters have already admitted their part. They, unfortunately, cannot be charged with an attempt to murder, only with conspiracy. Thanks to your inefficiency, even you can only be accused of attempted murder, so you may get away with only fifteen years – if you're lucky.'

György, too, was satisfied but he now had a new problem. He telephoned Pemmington.

'Major, I must assume that members of a secret Hungarian Nazi cell were indeed there to assist Dietrich's getaway. They will know what has happened. I've gone through police records and I now suspect, that perhaps as many as three unsolved murders during the last couple of years, all of men who were politically active, may have been assassinations rather than civil crimes. I have plenty of problems with the known fascist organisations. An unknown one is a new and serious threat, major. If they identify Gabor, his life will be in danger and, as long as I do not know who they are, I cannot protect him. Could you look after him for a little longer?'

Nolan was willing.

'It's fine with me. He's not very talkative, which suits me,' he said.

* * *

Chapter 6 – Magyar Sins

Sandor Jernitz, founder and leader of the Hungarian National Socialist Workers' Association, was seated in his mother's kitchen in her flat at Szeged.

'This is the first time, Mamà, that Wotan has failed,' he said to his mother. She was the only person in the world from whom he had no secrets. 'György's men foiled the plan.'

'He shouldn't send outsiders to do jobs here.'

'His method protects our identity. His executions are never carried out by nationals of the same country. The man's a master planner. He's had three leading anti-Nazis executed here in Hungary and one in Romania that I know of. Not a single thing ever went wrong.'

'You must assert yourself. You're as good a man as this Wotan.'

'At the right moment, Mamà. The day this useless democracy collapses, I'll take over all the other fascist parties and Hitler *úr*' (Mr.) 'will have to deal with me. In the meantime, Wotan's generous funds are useful for running the Action Cell. Think about it, Mamà. I command these men of my cell and none of them knows that it is me. Nor does the powerful Six-Two.'

'So what is troubling you, Sandor?'

'Wotan may blame me for the fiasco. How did Six-Two get to know about the plot?'

* * *

Petrasovic, head of the Action Cell's Budapest branch, had been rung by Dietrich on Monday morning to report on the unknown intoxicated sleeper in his hotel room. He had agreed that it was of no importance. But watching the arrests on Tuesday from his car, parked opposite the hotel, he realised that the sleeper in Dietrich's room was the most likely explanation for the arrests. He spent a good few minutes uttering his favourite swearwords, '*a rosselo egye meg!*' (bloody hell), before taking any action. After watching Dietrich being driven away, he walked into the hotel. Showing his card as a journalist, which he was, he questioned the receptionist and the hotel manager. Both were keen enough to talk to the press and Petrasovic was even shown the jacket left behind by the unknown sleeper.

'The German guest they just arrested, brought it to the desk on Sunday,' the receptionist, a little man with a tiny moustache and a bald patch crowning his head, explained excitedly.

Petrasovic did not believe that the owner of the jacket would ever turn up but nevertheless said:

'If anybody comes for the jacket, gentlemen, do let me know. Here's my business card.' He was wrong again. When Bela had not turned up at the next evening's party, Miklos, broke and eager to recover his return rail ticket, called at the Merleg, the hotel where he still believed Bela was staying. The receptionist, the little man with the tiny moustache and the bald patch crowning his head, found no one called Bela Gabor in the guest register. Miklos insisted:

'I know he is staying at this hotel. I brought him here and he told me the number of his room, himself,' Miklos said. 'I had to take him there, myself.'

'May I enquire, why that was necessary, sir?' said the receptionist.

'Well, he – he was not well,' Miklos said reluctantly and meaningfully at the same time.

The receptionist suddenly saw daylight and removed his hand from his moustache.

'He was – er – a little tipsy, your friend? May I ask when this happened, sir?'

'On Sunday night,' Miklos said.

'And to which room did you – er – accompany your, friend, sir?' the receptionist enquired.

'I can't remember the number now, but it was on the third floor. Your chambermaid knew where the room was. She unlocked the door for us,' he said triumphantly.

'She's been reprimanded. Because, sir, it was not your – er – little tipsy friend's room. As I told you before, sir, your friend is not staying at this hotel, nor was he staying at this hotel on Sunday night. Well, he was but he was not – er – registered here.'

Miklos was defeated. He turned to go, when the receptionist's next words brought him to a halt.

'If you should find your friend, sir, would you tell him, that he left his jacket behind.'

'You do? You are? Holy Laszlo, that's marvellous. Let me have it, please,' Miklos urged. For the next few minutes the dialogue became even more involved than it had been at the start. In the end it was finding the ticket to Lillaförd that did the trick and Miklos received his jacket back. He was happy. The receptionist was not, having counted on a generous tip. Miklos could have done with a generous tip, himself. The receptionist recalled the reporter.

'One other thing, sir. A reporter from one of the major newspapers is interested in this matter. He would like to interview you. I could arrange it. He might even pay for it.'

Ever hopeful, he really meant 'pay me.' Miklos had no objection to a newspaper interview, as long as it took place before he left and he gave the receptionist his hotel details. Within the hour Petrasovic called on Miklos at his hotel in Szeged and invited him for lunch during which Miklos gave him Bela Gabor's name, which was all he could tell him. Petrasovic had no idea who this Bela Gabor was and saw no point in pursuing the matter further. He sent a brief but precise report, which reached Jernitz on Saturday. But Jernitz knew exactly who Gabor was; the Six-Two officer who had harassed him during the early twenties. And who now, undoubtedly, had interfered in his activities again, this time even more effectively. Jernitz had not the slightest idea how and where to find Gabor. He expressed his anger by uttering his favourite swearword. '*A kutyafáyát!*' which refers to a dog's chosen tree for pissing on. But before the day was ended, his mood improved. One of the handful of people whom he paid a small regular sum of money in exchange for passing unusual occurrences to him was the old caretaker of the building in which the British Legation had its offices. Jernitz rang the man in the evening as he did every Saturday. Novak had only one item for him, namely that a Hungarian had called at the Legation.

'On a Sunday and without a jacket, imagine, sir.'

'I suppose you don't know the man's name and his address, Novak?'

'I know his present address, sir, because he is still here, in the flat of the British security captain, would you believe? Something's going on, I think. The British! Can you imagine?'

* * *

For Jernitz, things now dovetailed neatly. He did not care about Dietrich's arrest. Nor did he know or even suspect that Gabor had heard a reference to his cell. But he jumped to the logical conclusion that Gabor was working for the British. Pleased that he had solved

Chapter 6 – Magyar Sins

the problem of how Six-Two had got to know of the plot, he quoted Gabor not as a suspicion but as a fact in his communication to Wotan. He felt a pride in his efficiency. He had proved that he was Wotan's equal and that none of the other Nazi leaders were his equals. He was the only man worthy of being the leader of all Hungarian Nazis. He was going to assert himself on this occasion and decided to start with the British. He, personally, produced a set of anonymous threats and sent them, together with detailed orders, to Petrasovic. They included a description of Bela Gabor.

Gabor had informed Nolan that he would go back home to Szeged before the end of the following week. Any potential danger was surely over by now. That was when an envelope in the Legation's mail, was addressed in capital letters to BELA GABOR. Bearing no stamp made it a suspicious item and Nolan had opened it. Written in large capital letters on a sheet of pale yellow paper was a message: *'EZÉRT MEG FOOSZ PIZETNI!'* (You will pay for this.) Gabor held the paper against the sunlit window to check the watermark.

'This writing paper comes from Szeged,' he said, staring at it, 'my home town, Captain Nolan. I must go and see Commander György. Please pass my request to him.'

A new idea had suddenly settled in his mind. Nolan, disturbed, nodded. They, whoever they were, had not only identified Gabor as the man who had foiled their plans, but even knew where he was. He typed a brief report, marked it urgent and, together with the threat, had it taken at once to Pemmington. Reading both, the latter picked up the phone. A few minutes later, he sent an intercom message to Nolan for Gabor who read it out loud.

'Commander György will arrange seeing you. He suggests you accept the legation's hospitality for a few more days to give him time. I, too, would prefer it. Returning to your hometown immediately could be dangerous.'

Pemmington realised that Gabor's presence would also be endangering the lives of the Legation's personnel. His call to the Foreign Office produced a flurry of calls between the Foreign Office, the Home Office, ministers and civil service officials, MI5, and even Sir Hugh Sinclair. None underrated the seriousness of the matter. The Under-Secretary who had belittled Pemmington's report, now recalled vociferously how impressed he had been by him. The next day, Kell rang Pemmington, after which the latter picked up the internal phone and spoke to Nolan.

'Need to see you and the Hungarian right away.'

Ten minutes later they entered his office. Pemmington shook Gabor's hand before they sat down.

'I'm Major Pemmington, in charge of the Legation's security. You speak English.'

Gabor replied.

'I studied in Oxford, English for one year, then two in European Law.'

Pemmington already knew this.

'Mr. Gabor, on behalf of His Majesty's Government, I express our thanks for your quick action which prevented a serious crime against a prominent British citizen. For security reasons, we cannot let the incident become public knowledge at present, I'm sure you'll understand.'

This, of course, suited Gabor also. He nodded. Pemmington continued, 'The threatening note, which arrived yesterday, indicates that you have become the target of a secret Hungarian cell with links to a German organisation. The threat has to be taken seriously. Commander György has informed me that such a cell is unknown to his department. He and I feel that it is not safe for you to return home to Szeged in the near future.'

After a short pause he went on:

'As a result, there is a sensitive matter I wish to raise with you, which I have discussed with Commander György.' He paused again. 'Before I do, I should like to put some personal questions to you. You're at liberty not to answer them but it will be very helpful if you do.'

Nolan was listening with fascination. He had never heard Pemmington speak other than in a clipped military fashion. This was a different man, one who spoke the smooth language of a diplomat. Gabor, features taut, brows knitted, was listening with great concentration. His half-closed eyes were scanning Pemmington's expressionless face. Then he made up his mind.

'I shall answer them, Major Pemmington, if I can.'

Nolan half rose from his chair, looking questioningly at Pemmington. The major shook his head.

'No, stay, Nolan. You're part of this.'

Nolan sat down again. Pemmington turned to Gabor.

Chapter 6 – Magyar Sins

'Mr. Gabor. How strong are your personal ties in Szeged?'

Gabor's mind was searching for what lay behind the question when he replied, 'Not very, Major Pemmington. For the last three years I've had no personal involvements.'

'Family? Yours? Your wife's?'

Gabor shook his head. He was beginning to fathom where this might be going and it troubled him. Nevertheless, his answer was comprehensive:

'There's no one. My parents died during the war. I have lost contact with distant relations, long ago. Ilona, my wife, came from Russia. She had no family here. No friends because of my job with Six-Two. No, I've no personal ties in Szeged any more. But, forgive me, Sir, before I say anymore, I urgently need to see the Commander. I believe I can be useful in this matter.'

Pemmington smiled without parting his lips.

'He, too, wishes to see you. I'm aware of your early connection with Six-Two.'

Gabor nodded. If he was right about what was coming, then the Englishman would, of course, have obtained all the available information about him. Pemmington continued.

'Mr. Gabor, Commander György is certain that your action has put you into a unique position of personal danger. I concur and my superiors in London agree that we have a responsibility.' He gave special emphasis to his next words. 'His Majesty's Government is offering you residence in Britain, under a different name, together with the necessary documents, initially for a period of four years. At the end of these four years you will have the opportunity of applying for English citizenship, or return to Hungary. You will also obtain an adequate living grant for an initial period of one year. You should discuss this with the Commander before making a final decision. Captain Nolan will arrange transport and accompany you to your meeting with Commander György as soon as time and place are fixed.' Pemmington stood up. 'Mr. Gabor, I look forward to your early decision.' He held his hand out, 'Until then.'

Gabor had risen also, a beehive of personal thoughts buzzing through his mind. He shook Pemmington's hand without uttering a word, and turned to leave. Nolan, too, had got up. Pemmington's voice stopped him.

'Mr. Gabor can make his own way, Captain. Need to have a word with you.'

Chapter 6 – Magyar Sins

Nolan sat down again. Pemmington waited until Gabor had left.

'Remarkable fellow. Self-controlled. Something bothering him about the offer.' He stood in front of his desk. 'If Gabor accepts, you'll accompany him to London, Nolan. György's truly worried about the German connection.'

Nolan said nothing in reply but plenty to himself. Since this posting he had only seen his ageing parents once a year. He missed them and knew how much they missed him. And Adrienne. Was she still free? They had come close to an understanding the last time he was in London, but his damnable shyness. But her last letter still – this time he would for certain. He got up.

'I'll start getting ready, Major.'

'One more thing,' Pemmington said, leaning backwards to open the drawer of his desk.

Nolan moved to sit down.

'Don't sit down, Captain.'

Nolan shot up again. Pemmington handed him an envelope.

'Confirmation. Agent DSS 9. Came through last night. By the way, want you to carry a pistol on your journey. Know you fancy the three-two. Authority to draw in envelope. Congrats, old boy. Well deserved.' He shook Nolan's hand. Nolan was barely conscious of the handshake and took hold of the envelope as if it contained a great treasure. It did. He had done it! He had come through the ranks, not like the others who were recruited from the universities and such. DSS. It stood for Diplomatic Security Service but, with the number, it made him a fully-fledged MI5 agent. A boyhood dream materialised. Harry Nolan was an insignificant man in many ways but he was also a rare man, a truly dedicated patriot. He had proved it on several occasions. Fear had taken second place. Duty had always dominated. At last he had found the recognition he deserved. Pemmington had sat down.

'That's all, Nolan.'

'Right-oh, sir.' Nolan walked out of the room, inches higher than when he had entered it.

A couple of days later, Commander György sent a car for Bela Gabor which made Nolan's escort unnecessary. The car took Gabor to one of György's less-known interview rooms in town. By comparison, that of Major Pemmington was luxurious. What the room lacked in luxury was made up by the warmth of reception of its occupant who embraced Bela like an old friend. Bela had not

Chapter 6 – Magyar Sins

seen him for five years, but György wasted no time with polite conversation.

'Are you going to accept the British offer, Gabor?'

Gabor had been less surprised by the effusive welcome than by this question. For the first time since knowing the Commander, he wondered what kind of a man he really was. He saw a round, fleshy face with lively eyes and laughter wrinkles. György's comfortable figure gave the impression of a bon-vivant and everyone's favourite uncle. Gabor knew both to be true as well as misleading. His father had told him that György was a high-level chess player in his youth. He did not know how his father had come by this information but he did know that his boss had a sharp, analytical mind. Gabor's thoughts returned to the moment.

'I've really come to ask whether I could re-join the Department, sir,' he said. 'That threat was written on letter paper sold in Szeged shops. There could be a connection with some of the men I used to keep under surveillance. I assure you, I've kept fit all the time, since resigning.'

György was aware of that.

'Indeed. You look good, Gabor.'

'I'm eager to return, Commander, if you let me.'

György shook his head.

'Strictly speaking you've not left, you're on reserve, but your usefulness in Szeged would be close to zero, I'm afraid. German money is somehow flowing into our fascist parties' cashboxes. They even receive amounts from the top layers of our so-called democracy. My agents need to be unknown to everybody, inside and outside. You're too well known.'

Gabor realised that this was final.

'You're advising me to leave Hungary, Commander?'

György's right hand was squeezing his lower lip, an old habit when he was unhappy about something. Ask a man to leave his country, especially this man? *Am I getting old?* he asked himself. He straightened up, a movement that caused his stomach to attain more prominence.

'As a student I was one of those campaigning for the republic. It landed me in prison twice. Now we have it as well as the rudiments of democracy. I'll do everything I can, to preserve it, Gabor. It means being ruthless at times. You were one of my very first recruits and you were also one of the best ones. The truth is that last Sunday

Chapter 6 – Magyar Sins

you added to my problems. If you hadn't, things would have been even worse. As head of Six-Two I prefer you to go. It's time to acquaint you with something you don't know. Jordàn, your father, and I, we served in the same company. We were more than comrades, we were friends, so I qualify. And as a friend I strongly advise you to go to England. They have real democracy there.'

Gabor nodded. It was fate. He had got used to the idea during the last forty-eight hours. György said.

'If I succeed in dealing with this new problem, I'll let you know. You're remaining on the reserve for another four years. Then you will have to decide. The legal existence of our pro-Hitler parties is the flipside of our democracy. A secret murder group is something different. Your father held strong views: against the Kaiser, the war, big business and more. Here, it's still risky to express such views in public. In England you'll find real freedom of speech, my friend. And I'll know, you're safe.'

Gabor, standing up, was overcome by what he saw in György's face who suddenly remembered something else. He opened the drawer to his left and took out an envelope covered with several notes and rubber stamps denoting its passage to different destinations. He handed it to Gabor who recognised the English postage stamp.

'It's addressed to your original address in Szeged, Gabor, delivered recently. A conscientious clerk there contacted us and tried to get it forwarded to your present address. You were not there and the same clerk forwarded it to Budapest. It landed on my tray a couple of days ago. As you can see, it has been opened at the Szeged main post office but was re-sealed. Gabor's eyes had remained fixed on the address on the envelope. He recognised the writing. György's look encouraged him. He tore the envelope open and read the few lines on the small sheet of writing paper. He stood aghast, unable to speak for a moment then said, 'This changes everything, Commander. I would have gone to England anyway.' Looking up, he added, 'My best friend from way back is dying, Commander György. I must go as quickly as possible. Can you help me?'

György shook his head.

'Your best chance is to accept Major Pemmington's offer. I'll ask whether he can speed it up. The alternative would take a year or longer, Gabor. This letter has been on its way for almost a month. If your friend…'

Chapter 6 – Magyar Sins

Gabor nodded. He knew what the Commander was saying.

'Yes, I understand. But there's his wife and the little boy. I attended their wedding.'

He could have said a lot more but did not and left a sadder man than when he had arrived. György rang Pemmington.

'He's agreed, major. For private reasons he now wants to get to England as fast as possible. Could it possibly be speeded up, Major Pemmington?'

* * *

On his way, Gabor felt unhappy. If he hadn't let himself go after Ilona's death, he might have got that letter much sooner. About three months ago, he had been on his way home one late night. Much the worse from too much Tokaj, he bumped into an old woman. She raised her stick.

'Look where you're going, young fellow!' Then she recognised him. '*Ishtenem!*' (My God) – 'Bela Gabor. You're drunk, boy.'

'I know,' he had mumbled.

She took his arm and led him to his home. On the way she talked about his parents whom she had known and about Ilona. She got him into his flat and helped him off with his outer clothes. He started to talk about his unhappiness but she was not impressed.

'Such a lovely big flat. You're sorry for yourself, Bela Gabor. A hero in the war and a coward in peace time. If you don't put a stop to it, you'll end up in the gutter. Your father, God rest his soul, would never have given way like this. And your Ilona, you think, she would appreciate what you're doing? Where's your self-respect? Get back to a life. You owe them that.'

During the ensuing days, 'You owe them that' was returning again and again into his mind and striking at his conscience. She was right. He owed them that, his parents and Ilona. He did not even recall the woman's name or where she lived but she had done the job. He stopped drinking and began to rethink his existence. He attended the trade conference in Budapest, his mind focused on returning to a rational way of life. He would go back to business. Perhaps he could even buy his own back. His thoughts went back further. Andras Kalman had been his best friend in the army. He had remained in his infantry regiment when Gabor was transferred to a security unit. Halfway through 1918, Kalman, wounded badly, was

Chapter 6 – Magyar Sins

first sent to a military hospital just behind the frontline. It was overcrowded and understaffed but soon after the armistice he was transferred to a hospital in Budapest.

They had doctors and nurses from abroad there. He was in the care of Irene, a young English nurse, Irene Stone. On Gabor's first visit it was obvious to him that his friend was in love with her. On his next visit they informed him that they would get married and move to England as soon as he had recovered. Andras was so happy and Gabor was happy for him. He was Kalman's best man at the wedding. The kept in touch by occasional letters but when Gabor married Ilona the correspondence fizzled out. Ilona was a wonderful wife. But she died. She died, still so young. He lost his bearings completely then. The Kalmans' little boy must be ten now, Gabor worked out – Daniel, yes that was his name. She had written for help and he had not even replied.

After speaking to Pemmington, György sent for Szilagyi Buda who reported:

'I'm pursuing two lines, Commander. The hotel manager told a newspaper man, Arpád Petrasovic, a free-lance hack, about the jacket. Petrasovic interviewed the jacket's owner, a man named Miklos, one of Gabor's drinking companions that night. Miklos would have given him Gabor's name. Did the secret cell obtain the name from Petrasovic? I've put him under supervision.'

'Well done, Captain. And the other line?'

'How did they find out that Gabor was staying with the British? There's only one possible source, the caretaker, don't you think, Commander?'

György nodded.

'Of course.'

That was an obvious clue. Pemmington had found out some time ago, that the porter at the legation was passing bits of information to newspapers. Pemmington had informed Six-Two at the time and György had agreed not to do anything about it. It enabled Pennington to occasionally feed the caretaker facts the Legation wanted to become known. György nodded.

'Yes, a Hungarian staying at the British Legation is something he might pass on. He wouldn't know Gabor's name, but he'd know when he arrived there which might be enough. Check it out but, if possible, do it so the major can continue to make use of him. Odd, it's another newspaper angle.'

Chapter 6 – Magyar Sins

Late that night, one of György's men rang the caretaker's bell at the British Legation, soon after the man's return from the local bar. The caretaker was in his fifties, small and corpulent. The Six-Two agent was tall, had wide shoulders, wore dark glasses and when he spoke his voice contained a threatening tone. He briefly held up his identity card.

'I have questions for you. If I don't like the answers I may have to take you back to H.Q. for a more persuasive interrogation, not an attractive experience, I can tell you.'

The little man was shaking.

'Only a bit of beer money, sir. I'm not doing no harm, sir. Here, see by yourself. The three papers I ring if I've got anything interesting, sir, and they're paying me a few pengő.'

He handed the Six-Two man a list of three newspapers, all three small local papers. The caretaker was too frightened to protest, as he saw this valuable source of his beer money disappear. He had never thought of making a copy and wondered whether he would remember the telephone numbers. The Six-Two man let him sweat a little before asking one other question.

'This is everything? I warn you. If I find out you've held out on me, I'll be back and you'll be sorry. Play straight and you might get the list back and can go on earning your drinks money.'

The caretaker grasped eagerly at the offer.

'Oh, thank you sir, thank you. There's one that's not on the list. Because they ring me, sir. It's not always the same voice. Usually on a Saturday, sir. A newspaper agency. Every week they send me a five-pengő note through the post. They're the best, sir.'

The Six-Two man clasped the porter's shoulder, squeezing hard.

'What did you tell him, when he rang last? The truth, man!'

'Only about a man knocking on the door on Sunday and staying at the Legation. In the same flat as the captain. The English! He wanted to know his name. But I didn't know it.'

'That was all?'

'He said it wasn't newsworthy but he'll pay anyway. And he did. – I know one thing, sir.'

He hoped this information would please his frightening circumlocator:

'One Saturday, when the man was speaking with me, I heard an operator say, "Szeged Exchange, what number do you want?" So this agency must be in Szeged, sir.'

Chapter 6 – Magyar Sins

It did please the man who said, 'OK, you've told the truth. Here you are.' He handed the porter his list back. 'One advice, old fellow.' His face came close to the caretaker's, 'You don't mention my visit to anyone or I shall get ver-ry cross.'

He turned and was gone leaving a shaken but greatly relieved man behind who almost shot out of his skin when hearing his wife's voice behind him.

'What for the sake of Maria in Heaven are you doing out here in the middle of the night, dear? Were you talking to someone?'

She stood in the doorway, wearing only her nightshirt, a small, plump woman, well past her thirties. She had switched on the sitting room light behind her and the nightshirt emphasised the circular circumferences of her body. In her husband's state of excitement, it roused sensational sensations that had not been in evidence for some time.

'Nothing, my heart. I thought I heard a noise. Come to bed, my dear.'

He put the list back to the telephone shelf and, his arm roaming over her considerable waist and buttocks rushed her back into the bedroom. The Six-Two man would have been surprised at the effect his visit had on them. Indeed, they, themselves were surprised, especially the wife who, after a squeaky little cry of '*Yoi, ishtenem,*' (oh my goodness!) and a more distinct shriek, 'Mária, Jószef!' was too busy to ask any more questions.

György spent the next morning producing his regulation report to his military Chief of Staff. He typed quite fast using only two fingers. Like Pemmington, he never allowed his secretary to type sensitive material but, unlike Pemmington, he never kept carbon copies. The facts were filed securely in his head. Before starting, resting his cheek and a portion of his two chins in his hand, he was arraying the essentials in his mind:

One: a reporter, called Arpád Petrasovic, had interviewed the manager of the hotel and Miklos, the owner of the jacket. Miklos must have given him Gabor's name, yet no article had appeared in the press relating to the incident. The reporter had to be considered a suspect who might lead them to the secret cell.

Two: the caretaker's information established his caller as residing in Szeged. The pert sylphs at the Szeged telephone exchange had now been instructed to assist the police by reporting the names of all

Chapter 6 – Magyar Sins

callers to the British Legation. Names could be false, but telephone numbers not.

Three: the letter paper on which the threat had been written was of a make sold in Szeged, evidenced by its watermark. It was delivered by hand; therefore, it had been forwarded to a Budapest collaborator. A secret cell stretching from Szeged to Budapest?

Four, Szeged. The town had a large, well-to-do Jewish community, whose existence had produced two pro-Hitler parties, feeding on anti-Semitism. Both parties were putting up candidates at elections. Would either of them risk their positions in order to assist German Nazis with an assassination? If obtaining the name of Bela Gabor indirectly or directly from Petrasovic, either of the leaders of the two Nazi parties in Szeged would have recognised it from their early experiences when he kept tight check on their activities. That might be the missing link for, if that same person was also the one receiving the porter's information, it would be obvious to him that Gabor was the man who had appeared at the British Legation. If it was not Rajniss or Jernitz, and if Szeged was the place from where the recent threat originated, then the existence of a third, hitherto unknown organisation, had to be assumed. That was the worst scenario.

Five: Bela Gabor had got into this by sheer accident but if one of the two established Szeged parties was involved they might assume he was still active with Six-Two. Given that Gabor had gone to the British Legation they could even assume a connection there. In that case, Gabor might be in even greater danger than György had first assumed. A secret group, perhaps even a secret German Nazi cell, prepared to participate in the assassination of a British politician, would think nothing of killing a Hungarian.

György did not realise how close he had come to the truth and he thought that running this secret lot to earth would take time. Once his friend Gabor's son had left Hungary he would feel easier. The sooner the better. Finally, there was the other question which had arisen: had some of the previous, as yet unsolved murders, been successful assassinations by German Nazis or even that local cell? It was another possibility he had to look into. György's report was addressed to General Imre Hadik von Czokas-Pogany but it did not include all these deliberations. The General had been titled with the 'von' which made him a dwindling member of the aristocracy, by the Austrian Emperor back in 1879. His unusually wide chest was

Chapter 6 – Magyar Sins

top-heavy with a kilo weight of decorations but kept in place by the terrace of an enormous stomach above small, thin legs. György suspected him of now being an admirer of Adolf Hitler. After having handed the report to his secretary for posting, he suddenly remembered something else. He took another look into the files of the Nazi parties. Yes, there it was: The mother of Sandor Jernitz was German. It might mean nothing or everything. He felt strained and tired and lonesome and decided he needed some long longed-for relaxation. Relaxation meant two things for him: good food and good company. He picked up the internal phone and called his driver.

'I want you to take me to the *Margitsziget'* (Margaret's Island), he looked at his watch, 'in thirty minutes exactly. Then you can take the rest of the day off.' He hesitated for a moment then picked up the other receiver and dialled the exchange.

'What number, sir?'

'If you're as pretty as you sound, I'd like a number with you.'

It was an oft-repeated semi-jocular opening, semi, just in case the reply was unexpected.

'Oh, I'm even prettier, sir, but I don't think my husband would approve.'

Which was an oft-repeated semi-jocular response although she was not married, semi because she kept her options open. He laughed.

'In that case make it the Fekete *Etterem'* (Restaurant). – 'Lajos György for Teréza.'

She did and a moment later he heard a familiarly coquettish voice.

'Lajos! I thought you had forgotten me.'

Her words sounded the way they did 15 years ago and in his mind she looked the way she had looked 15 years ago.

'Rizuska, love of my life. – You know I cannot forget you. You should have married me.'

'I might have, if you'd asked me.'

There was a serious note behind the banter.

'But I did ask you. Many times.'

'Only with your lips. I couldn't compete with your other, real love.'

This was a diversion from their usual raillery. He frowned, uncertain what or whom she meant.

'Real...? You knew the woman meant nothing,' he said.

'Igen' (yes), 'Lajos, I did. You mean women. You were handsome in your uniform and you were almost slim. I knew that Anuska and Juliska and Jolánka and Katinka were just samples of your wine tasting. I did some of that, myself, Lajos. No, I mean your real, real love – your job. So I followed your example and mine became the same, though not quite so important for the nation.'

'You have never said these things before, Rizuska. What has brought this on?'

'I've been wondering lately about how close I am to "too late", Lajos. Do you never ask yourself that? Don't try and answer that, let's take what's available, like me. Just now I take pity on you and tell you that we have gulyas and paprika dumplings and poppy seed strudel on the menu. When are you coming?'

His job? Six-Two? She had not said this before. But she was right. He had always been passionately dedicated to his job, twenty-four hours a day, sometimes.

'Rizuska, you're the queen of Margit Island and you're the queen in my heart which is still in the same place. I'll be there within the hour.'

'And when you have added five centimetres to your midriff you will rush off again.'

'Rush? With the extra weight of these five centimetres? Only if you throw me out, *drága*, my sweet. I've taken the rest of the day off, just to be with you and that, surely, deserves a reward.'

He held the receiver away from his ear as she broke into a passionate flood of words, some of them a few uncomplimentary, but probably well-deserved names.

'You would not be so cruel, Rizuska.'

Smiling, he listened to another flood, then put the receiver down gently. Teréza spoke faster than any other person he knew but she still was as attractive to him as when he had met her on his first leave back in 1915. He had come to the little restaurant with Jordàn Gabor. She was assisting her mother who owned it. Jordàn had left them when he saw what he saw in their eyes. Speaking to Jordàn's son had re-awakened memories. He should have married her. Perhaps it was not too late. But he could not give up his job. There was no one else who was driven as much as he to watch over the security of the new Hungary. The internal telephone rang.

'Sir, your car is here.'

Chapter 6 – Magyar Sins

Two days later, another unstamped letter addressed to Gabor was dropped into the Legation's letter box. This one said: 'YOU HAVE INTERFERED WITH MY PLANS. THE PENALTY IS DEATH. WOTAN'

Pemmington sent it immediately to György. Both were extremely perturbed by the name Wotan turning up. It meant that Gabor had heard correctly. Both sprang into the already agreed action. Within 48 hours, all the material and documentary evidence of Gabor's existence in Szeget disappeared. Personal items passed to him included a pair of binoculars. At the Legation, security was strengthened. It was quite possible that the secret enemy was watching, but there was little that could be done about that. Large-scale unemployment in Budapest meant that there were always a lot of young people hanging about in the streets. Gabor chose Bill Jordan for his new identity, the English spelling of his father's forename Jordàn. He received his British passport, officially the Legation's replacement of a lost one. Additional documents would reach him en route in Vienna and the rest upon his arrival in Britain.

The Legation was indeed under observation by two private detectives who were looking out for a man, described as about 1.80m tall, black hair, high forehead, strong nose, hazel brown eyes. At variance with the Bible, for six days the two private detectives sharing the task were, to all effects and purposes, resting. On the 23rd June, a Sunday, the one on duty almost missed his chance of labouring on the seventh. His eyes had followed a female in a flowery dress, similar to one that his current *barátnő* (girlfriend) often wore, walking on the opposite side. When she reached the door to the legation, two men emerged from it. Suddenly the watcher gave himself a jolt. One of them was about 1.80m tall, had black hair, a high forehead, a strong nose and hazel brown eyes.

The next moment a taxi pulled up in front of them. As the two men stepped inside, he clearly heard the word 'station' being said to the driver. He got on his bike, making for the bar just around the corner, to make his call to the newspaper agency whose telephone number he had been given. Five minutes later Petrasovic rang Jernitz's office number in Szeged, but was informed by the telephonist that there was no reply. He was stumped. This had never happened before. That morning Jernitz had received a telegram from *Die Flamme* (the flame), supposedly a German newspaper:

Chapter 6 – Magyar Sins

'RE HOTEL SLEEPER STOP MEET AND BRIEF EXECUTIVE REPORTER AXEL TODAY VIENNA TRAIN STOP BUDAPEST MAIN STATION STOP RED RUCKSACK STOP W STOP'

'Executive' meant that the man was sent to eliminate someone, in this case, obviously Bela Gabor. Jernitz resented receiving what was tantamount to an order. But resenting was all he did for the sender was the secret boss who held the purse strings. Swearing, as was his wont, Jernitz realised that this was something he must do himself.

He rushed out and caught the train to Budapest. He arrived there in time to reach the platform at which the Vienna train had just arrived and met Wotan's red-rucksack-carrying executive reporter, Axel, at the ticket barrier. The man, walking with a slight stoop, had light-brown hair and wore glasses over his sea-blue eyes. Despite the hot weather, Axel wore a dark-blue jacket over his white, open-necked shirt and dull-green loden trousers held up by Bavarian-type flowery braces. He looked more like an insignificant small-business type than an assassin. But assassins come in all shapes and colours. Jernitz, himself, did not appear particularly significant, either. The two insignificant-looking men had started to walk toward the station exit when, suddenly, Jernitz spied and recognised Bela Gabor, carrying a small suitcase striding towards Platform Two, where the Orient Express was standing. It had steamed in noisily a couple of minutes ago and it would stand there for another 28, before continuing to its next stop, Vienna.

Jernitz was one of only a tiny number of people in the whole of Budapest, indeed the whole of the world at this moment, who would know and recognise Gabor. For him to be in the station at that very moment was an acrimonious irony of fate. Jernitz understood at once what was happening. Gabor was about to leave Hungary – for London, of course. He must have been working for the British all the time! It was a highly convenient coincidence for it also enabled Jernitz to get rid of his unwelcome new guest. He put his hand on the man's shoulder to stop him and was taken aback by his snarl.

'Keep your hand to yourself!'

He removed it.

'You're too late for whatever you've come to do, Herr Axel,' he said. 'The man you're supposed to deal with is departing.'

He pointed towards Gabor who was just entering Platform Two. Axel grasped the situation in an instant.

Chapter 6 – Magyar Sins

'Find out which compartment whilst I get a ticket!'

It sounded like a command. It was a command. Jernitz hurried on to Platform Two, got a platform ticket and caught up with Gabor who was strolling slowly towards the front of the train. He was by himself, as Captain Nolan had gone to buy newspapers and chocolates. Thus, Jernitz took it for granted that Gabor was travelling alone. He kept a few metres behind him getting ample cover from the crowd, some seeing off family or friends, others just sightseers, peering at the famous train, looking for celebrities. Gabor clambered on to carriage Nr.4, one of the couchette carriages of the train.

Jernitz watched the windows until he saw Gabor's figure appear. He waited a few seconds, then cautiously entered the carriage and established that Gabor occupied the compartment with seats 37 and 38. Jernitz was not surprised to see that both were 'Reservé Reserved Reserviert' in three languages. The British would, of course, make sure that their man had the whole compartment to himself. He left hurriedly and, walking down the platform, unknowingly passed Captain Nolan who was on his way to compartment 38,39 in carriage Nr.4. Jernitz found Axel waiting outside Carriage 9, a non-sleeping carriage, which only went as far as Munich, and gave him the information:

'Carriage 4, reserved seats 37 and 38.'

Axel nodded patronisingly and said, 'You will inform W.'

Jernitz also nodded and rushed off, just managing to catch the train that had brought him, to return to Szeged. He was wondering at the man's German idiom. It had the tint of an educated person, daubed with an accent sounding slightly Austrian. Jernitz was pleased to have got rid of a man who was touchy about his shoulder being touched.

The engine of the Orient Express had begun to build up steam, which escaped in noisy thick swathes from underneath the front carriages, and ten minutes later the train was chugging out of the station, quickly gaining speed. The assassin did not enter carriage 9 to occupy his seat. Instead, he moved through the train to reach carriage 4. On the way he was volubly polite to other passengers and told a ticket inspector whom he passed that he was visiting a friend in Carriage 4. They would all remember him and the way he was dressed. When he reached Nr. 4, he noticed that the curtains of the door and the window of 37/38 were drawn. He rightly assumed that

Chapter 6 – Magyar Sins

the door was locked. He took position at the entrance to the carriage, about three metres from the compartment door, lit himself a cigarette and waited. Sooner or later his victim would step out into the corridor. Axel was a patient man.

At first, Nolan and Jordan were each busy with their own thoughts. Gradually, however, a conversation of sorts developed. Nolan was more talkative than was his custom. The exhilaration provided by his promotion, and looking ahead to the reunion with his parents and, hopefully, his future wife, required an outlet. He yielded to it by talking about London, a city he loved, and how much he was going to enjoy a few days there. Sensing Nolan's emotion, Jordan began to respond and gradually even warm to his English companion whose words up to date had not risen above the level of professional topics and polite remarks. Now the security man came over as a real person with a private life. Jordan's own mind began to raise images of happy moments with Ilona who had given him so much. Nolan looked at his watch. It was six o'clock.

'We're approaching Vienna,' he said. 'I expect a member of our Embassy there to call on us there, with papers for you and perhaps some for me. How about a drink before the bar closes?'

Jordan declined politely. No backtracking ever again! Nolan told him to lock the door and, stepping out into the corridor, closed it behind him. Bending forward to flick a speck of dust from his trousers, he was startled by an unknown, cold, threatening voice saying:

'*Guten Tag, Herr Gabor! Es ist Ihr letzter.*' (Good day, Mr. Gabor! It is your last!)

Nolan's reaction was fast. Simultaneously with turning in the direction of the voice his hand reached for the Colt in his shoulder holster but even as he touched it a bullet hit him in the chest. After a second's immobility and silence, during which his eyes opened wide, he uttered, 'No-o-o-o!' a weak, long-drawn cry fading into lasting silence. It was born not from the pain he felt but from the great, terrible disappointment that raced through his mind: no parents, no Susan, no special agent. He collapsed, blood spouting from the bullet hole and rapidly painting his shirt a dull red. Did he realise that he had fulfilled his duty of protecting Bela Gabor? For one split second, Axel imagined the compartment door was opening and raised his Luger again but, of course, there was no one else in there. He calmly pocketed the gun which had a silencer attached and walked into the neighbouring carriage. Seeing its toilet occupied he

Chapter 6 – Magyar Sins

continued to carriage 6, where he locked himself into the cubicle, a cool, experienced killer who enjoyed what he was doing.

Bill Jordan had just stepped to the door to lock it behind Nolan, when he heard a stranger's voice, followed by the shot and Nolan's cry. He knew the sound of a shot, even if muffled. Startled, he opened the door the tiniest fraction. Through the gap he caught a glimpse of a man's shoulder and arm and a hand clasping the distinctive butt of a German Luger. He was not going to quarrel with a gun and closed the door, locking it at the same time.

He peered through the edge of the curtain that covered the door's window and saw the upper part of a red rucksack moving away, then nothing. After a long minute he slowly and cautiously opened the door. The passage was empty except for the body on the floor. One look was enough. He had learned to recognise the eyes of death in the war. Gripped by a great sadness, he stepped back into his compartment to pull the emergency alarm, then sat down, the door ajar, to keep watch over the dead man who had come close to being a friend. The alarm was not only a signal to the engine driver but also to the little cubby hole that housed the train's security guard. Vienna's main station, the *Westbahnhof* (West Station), was less than three minutes away and the engine driver, assuming a health emergency rather than a murder, decided not to stop but to take the train into the station.

Meanwhile the security guard, a Frenchman, named Carron, was hurrying towards Carriage Four, the origin of the alarm. In Six, he passed a passenger walking the opposite way. The man, carrying an art folder under his arm, wore a large, wide-brimmed hat and a thin, white cotton jacket. He stood politely to the side to let the guard pass. The guard could not know that the man's jacket was dark-blue on the inside. He did notice in passing that the toilet's sign 'engagé' was displayed. He possessed a key but had no reason to embarrass whoever was inside. If he had, he would have found a red rucksack on the floor and a Luger pistol with a silencer inside the rucksack. He would have also discovered that the little window was stuck and could not be opened. The 'engagé' sign continued to deter other passengers from trying to enter.

Carron reached Carriage 4 and came to an abrupt halt in front of the dead body, lying twisted beside the part-open door to the compartment of seats 37 and 38. For a moment the Frenchman turned his eyes away from the sight, fighting with the oncoming

Chapter 6 – Magyar Sins

nausea. He had never seen a dead body before, nor had he come across a murder. The bullet hole and the blood around it made it gruesomely obvious that that's what it was. The dead man's jacket was open. His right hand was touching a pistol, which was half-lodged in its holster. Through the open door to the compartment he saw a passenger seated, whose eyes gave the impression of looking inward rather than seeing what was in front of them. Having heard the killer's words, Jordan knew that he had been the intended victim. He found this hard to take.

After his brief moment of weakness, the Frenchman acted with precision, as laid down in the rulebook. He locked both doors to the carriage, then hammered on the doors of each of the occupied compartments and shouted a brief instruction, not to leave their compartments and keeping their doors closed. Whether his words, in French, were heard against the noise of the train was doubtful but none of the doors opened. Passengers in this carriage were all going further than Vienna.

Bill Jordan, roused by the security guard's shouted request, locked his door. The train was already entering the *Westbahnhof,* Vienna's West Station, and noisily slowing down. The security guard had no way of preventing passengers from getting off other carriages and leaving the station. Axel could not have found his disappearance easier. He had reached Carriage 9 and sat down in the seat for which he had paid. Although this was the first time the other passengers set eyes on him, they seemed to take little notice of him, except for a little boy who was fascinated by his hat. As soon as the train stopped, Axel and one other passenger left the carriage and stepped off the train. Within seconds he had mingled with the crowd on the platform and, at the platform exit, handed his ticket to the controller. He went straight to the station cloakroom where, upon submitting a ticket, he obtained a small suitcase. Once again he paid a visit to the public toilet, where he changed into the clothes contained in the case. It was the final transition into his real persona, a suit and tie.

Outside the station he took a taxi to the State Opera and from there a tram to his home address. He was safe and felt good and fulfilled, and satisfied for having executed his task as efficiently as always. He was one of very few who knew Wotan's identity and communicated directly with him. His last action in respect of this operation was the telegram to Count Winter: TASK ACCOMPLISHED.

Chapter 7 – The Villa in Hietzing

The moment the train stopped, the French security guard called a railway official to the window who listened, horror-struck, and rushed to the station master's office. The station-master on duty reached for the telephone. Only 14 minutes later, Oberkommissar Alfons Zulka, based in Margareten, Vienna's 5th District, tieless, wearing dark trousers and a loose grey jacket, accompanied by two junior detectives, both in uniform, arrived and was directed to Carriage 4. Zulka, 1.83 m tall, could hardly be described as slim. He was a widower, 52 years old, but as fit as he had been at 30. He was known in the Force for his sense of humour and a better education than many. On the phone he had impressed on the stationmaster not to let the news of the murder leak out to the general public. After listening to the security guard's brief and concise report in heavily accented German, he took over. He took a notepad from his inside pocket and made a sketch of the body's position to which he added detailed notes, describing conditions, clothing and even the expression on the dead man's face. When he had done that, he took the pistol from the dead man's holster.

'American colt, nil comma thirty-two centimetres, not fired,' he said to the security guard, as he was writing it down, 'also used by the British, I believe. Joined the train at Budapest, you say? Interesting. Unusual, too.'

Next he emptied the dead man's pockets, listing everything on his pad. Except for Nolan's passport, which he put into his inner pocket, he passed each item on to his detectives who, following established routine, loaded them into the solid leather case, the type known as Gladstone bag. Zulka had the Frenchman date and sign the list. Next he got his men to put the body into one of the empty compartments and ordered them to unlock the doors to the carriage and man them to prevent passengers from entering or leaving.

Finally, asking the security man to accompany him as witness, he embarked upon the task of interviewing the carriage's occupants. Disregarding the dead man's compartment for the moment, he started with the passengers next door, two elderly German ladies

Chapter 7 – Conspiracy in Vienna

returning to Munich from a holiday in Istanbul. Zulka had to knock hard, accompanying it with shouts of *'Polizei!'* before one of them opened the door. His immediate impression persuaded him that he would not obtain a lot of useful information here. The one who had opened the door, answered his questions and ended each of her answers with a nonchalant wave of her hand, as if to say 'you know, what I mean'. The other one confirmed everything her friend said with the word, *'Genau'* (exactly) plus authoritative nods which forced her to hold on to her straw hat in order to prevent it from falling off her head.

'I did hear a man… Herr Kommissar, but the noise of the train, you know, I couldn't – I'm…'

'Are you sure, madam, you did not hear some word? I consider you a reliable witness.'

She smiled a superior smile.

'You are right, Herr Kommissar, but – no, wait, I do – *Guten Tag*, yes, it might have been Guten Tag, definitely, *Guten Tag*, I'm sure, but I couldn't…' Realising something serious must have happened, she produced a complete sentence. 'You've got to be careful, Herr Kommissar, not to say things if you're not sure, my dear Papa always said, and he was a supervisor.'

She did not explain what he supervised and Zulka wondered how being a supervisor made her father's words more important than if he had been one of those supervised by him. *Guten Tag* (good day) suggested that the murderer was either Swiss, German, or Austrian. Neither of the ladies had heard the report of the shot, which he found just a little puzzling. The nodding lady took the initiative on that question.

'You've no idea of the noise, Herr Kommissar. This is the Orient Express, after all.'

'Is it noisier than other trains?' he enquired politely.

She threw him a searching look.

'We always keep our door locked on this train. No chance of some international conman to get into our compartment. *Nein, mein Herr*, we're too experienced for these crooks.'

'Thank you very much, ladies,' said Zulka, beating a retreat.

An even older man, a priest from Bucharest, on his way to Strasbourg, was the sole occupant of 33/34. He spoke German but had heard nothing at all. It did not surprise the Oberkommissar when

Chapter 7 – Conspiracy in Vienna

he realised when he had to raise his voice in order for his questions to be heard.

'I was concentrating on the words of the Apostles,' the priest explained, holding up a little volume, 'My soul was immersed.'

The detective shouted into his ear that he wanted to have his *Name* (name), and the priest retorted that he did not have a *Dame*, (lady). Zulka shouted even louder, whereupon the Priest replied, 'Of course, I give you my name. There's no need to raise your voice, *domnule'* (mister, sir).

He took a large wallet out of one of his deep pockets from which he extracted a card with his name which he handed to Zulka who thanked him and left him to re-immerse his soul. The couple in 31/32 had heard less than nothing. They were travelling to Paris on a delayed honeymoon. When the man opened the door, his shirt buttons were in the wrong holes, his shirt collar was skew-whiff and his partner's hair, blonde above mousy-coloured roots, was in a mess, despite her continual attempts at smoothing it. From their reactions, the loving glances and significant smiles they kept exchanging, Zulka concluded that their souls had also been immersed, albeit not in the Apostles. The Swiss businessman in the end compartment was returning to Zürich from Athens. He, too, had heard nothing, having been absorbed in studying the details of a deal he had concluded.

'It is a very important deal, Herr Kommissar. It will make my company a lot of money.'

He seemed to have difficulties in concentrating which, Zulka concluded, had to do with the distinct odour of Schnaps emanating from him. When he asked the Swiss whether he was selling wooden horses to the Greeks, the man replied:

'No, Herr Kommissar, we only deal in wooden cuckoo clocks.'

Was it the Schnaps, Zulka wondered, or the Swiss education system? He had kept 37/38 to the last. Bill Jordan was seated, holding his face between his hands, without attempting to hide his distress. Too many things had happened to him in a very short space of time and this one was by far the worst. Filling in the doorway, Zulka introduced himself.

'Oberkommissar Zulka, Kriminalpolizei. Do you speak German?'

Gabor nodded.

'Do you know the identity of the dead man?'

Chapter 7 – Conspiracy in Vienna

'Yes, Herr Oberkommissar. Captain Nolan is a security officer at the British Legation in Budapest, on his way home on leave – was, I mean.'

He hesitated for a moment, then decided to say no more. Zulka had noticed it and wondered what the man was hiding. A British security officer! This, obviously, was not a simple murder. It required cautious handling and could not be dealt with by a brief interrogation here on the train.

'Your name?'

'Bill Jordan. I'm returning to England from a business trip.' He was using his new identity and his agreed cover story for the first time.

Another important business trip but definitely no cuckoo clocks, nor wooden horses. And the man's German did not sound like that of an Englishman. Zulka switched to English which was fluent but sounded very Austrian, not just Austrian but, specifically, very Viennese.

'You can tell me more about your trip, Mr. Jordan?'

Although he had already decided on holding this witness he made notes, listening to Bill Jordan's words, unable to fault his English. Jordan explained that he had taken part in negotiations for a business deal between Budapest and London, one approved and supported by the British Ministry of Trade. Then he remembered something.

'Captain Nolan told me that a man from the British Embassy would call to see him whilst the train is here in Vienna.'

Another unusual circumstance, Zulka thought, but not something this witness would invent.

'Your passport, please, Mr. Jordan.'

Jordan complied silently.

'And your travel papers.'

Jordan handed them over.

'I am keeping your passport and your travel papers for the moment, Mr. Jordan.'

Zulka turned to the French guard behind him, saying in German.

'Monsieur, I have finished my interviewing and do not require your presence any longer. Please leave your contact details with one of my officers. You may return to your duties.'

The guard, pleased to leave this scene of death, left hurriedly. He went to sign the duty book at the stationmaster's office and wire a

Chapter 7 – Conspiracy in Vienna

report to his superiors at H.Q. Zulka hooked his finger in the direction of one of his men.

'Armbruster, leave the door for a moment. I want you to take down the names and addresses of all the occupants of this carriage and other details as per protocol, except for this gentleman here – and the Rumanian priest's. I've got his already.'

At that moment, voices at the other door were heard, first the policeman's, then a woman's whose German was tinged with a slight but distinct English intonation.

'You cannot enter this carriage, madam.'

'I am a member of the British Embassy and have come in order to contact Captain Nolan, a member of the British Legation in Budapest, who is on his way to London. According to my information this is the carriage in which he is travelling.'

She had not raised her voice but its quality commanded attention and received it from Zulka.

'Bogner, let the lady in.'

She entered, stopped short and introduced herself, 'Mrs. Alexandra Heaven,' and held out her identity card.

Although not in uniform, Zulka gave a policeman's salute.

'Oberkommissar Alfons Zulka. I have been expecting you, *gnädige Frau*' (madam).

Strictly speaking, based upon Jordan's information, he had expected a man. This woman, however, made an immediate impact. She was dressed in a simple but smart, calf-length grey costume, with no jewellery except for a wedding ring on her finger. She wore no hat and her wavy light-brown hair framed an attractive face of fine features. Zulka assessed her to be about twenty-eight years old and her height at 1.65m. An English lady, as described in the books, he thought. He was slightly out. Alexandra Heaven was thirty-five.

'Oberkommissar? You've been expecting me? What has happened?'

'Mrs. Heaven, I regret I've bad news. I'm afraid your Captain Nolan has been murdered.'

She stood stock-still.

'Murdered?'

Her brows knitted as she scanned his face. He nodded and was surprised at her self-control and the speed with which she regained her composure. He proceeded to give her the bare facts of the situation. She listened attentively. She had met Nolan only once,

Chapter 7 – Conspiracy in Vienna

briefly, in Budapest. She made a quick decision, based on what little she knew about the happenings in Budapest.

'My dear Herr Oberkommissar, I imagine that under the circumstances you will not want Mr. Jordan to leave Vienna. I, myself, believe, it may not be wise for him to travel on. His business is conducted under the aegis of our Ministry of Trade. I propose to take him off this train until I get further instructions from London. Our Captain Nolan was going on leave and I intended to pass some papers to him. I cannot imagine why anyone should want to kill him. I can promise you that Mr. Jordan will be available for interrogation. Here is my card.' She smiled her most engaging smile. 'I assure you of our fullest co-operation, Herr Oberkommissar.'

Zulka was bowled over, but did not immediately submit. Her explanations were entirely plausible but Jordan was his major witness, in fact the only witness, and should really remain in police custody. On the other hand, Jordan was a British citizen and not a suspect. Mrs. Heaven, continuing to develop the most plausible spin to the situation, guessed his thoughts.

'Herr Oberkommissar, Mr. Jordan is involved in a business deal, which is considered of some significance. The shooting might even be connected. I'm sure you're aware that there is a lot of commercial espionage going on and there may be a lot of money involved here. In the world of business cut-throat competition there are some unscrupulous people about. Your government will want for the incident to get as little publicity as possible. Mine certainly will. If you take Mr. Jordan in custody the press is bound to find out that he was travelling with Captain Nolan. The shooting of one of our officers will give the media enough food for sensationalism. Keeping Mr. Jordan's name out of the headlines would be greatly appreciated and, I suggest, is also in the interest of your investigation. I'll have a word with Dr. Haberle at the Interior Ministry about it. Perhaps you will be so good and either send or bring with you the customary receipt for Mr. Jordan's passport and papers whilst they are in your possession?'

It was a smooth performance and Zulka was aware of that. At the same time what she said made sense and her reference to Herr Haberle melted Zulka's professional scruples.

'Of course, Mrs. Heaven. You can rely upon my discretion and that of my men. Perhaps you could do me a favour in return, or to be exact, Mr. Jordan could? I should like to use his ticket for one of my

Chapter 7 – Conspiracy in Vienna

men to continue our enquiries on the train. Mr. Jordan will be refunded, of course.'

Bill Jordan who had listened attentively, nodded his agreement. Then he added, 'I can give you some details, Herr Oberkommissar. The murderer was about five centimetres smaller than I, wore a thin yellow jacket and a plain gold ring on the middle finger of his right hand and a bright red scar across the back of his right hand, perhaps from a glancing bullet. His gun was a Luger, I believe and must have had a silencer.'

Mrs. Heaven and Zulka were staring. The latter felt renewed suspicions about Jordan's identity, who added in a matter-of-fact tone: 'I served in my regiment's security section as a trained observer.'

It made sense, sounded and was truthful, except that it did not reveal to which army it referred. Zulka was reassured but insisted that they left Nolan's suitcase in his care. Taking his own case, Jordan left speedily with Mrs. Alexandra Heaven.

Zulka finalised his dispositions.

'Armbruster. You travel as far as Munich in this compartment. I'll take you to your home to change into civvies and bring you back here. Try to find out more. Bogner, get the station police to move the body to our mortuary – in a covered postal buggy. I want no reference to the murder to get out before having handed in my official statement.'

The security guard re-appeared. How soon could the train continue its journey, the stationmaster wished to know.

'Right, monsieur. This is Detective Armbruster. He will leave now and return in about fifteen minutes. As soon as he is back here, the train may depart. He will travel as a civilian in this compartment, probably no further than Munich. He will interview passengers on the train, discreetly I assure you. Please inform the stationmaster that whatever explanation he will announce to the travellers, no word of the murder must leak out.'

Zulka felt he had done all that could be done, even though he did not believe there was the slightest chance of ever finding the killer. Perhaps, if the engine driver had stopped the train outside the station... But Zulka was a reasonable man and he acknowledged that the driver's action had also been rational.

'Let's hurry, Armbruster.'

Chapter 7 – Conspiracy in Vienna

* * *

Whilst Oberkommissar Alfons Zulka was rushing Armbruster to his home and back again to the station, MI6 agent, Alexandra Heaven and Bill Jordan, until recently Bela Gabor, were in a taxi on the way to the residence of the British Ambassador in Vienna's 3rd district. During the taxi ride, Jordan, still numbed by what had happened, sat silently beside Alexandra Heaven. She, too, did not speak, immersed in assessing the situation into which she had been thrown without any warning. Upon their arrival at the ambassador's residence, Alexandra Heaven asked the taxi driver to wait.

He had taken her to the Westbahnhof and waited for her there. Waiting was a large part of a taxi driver's life and in this case was even paid for. This particular driver worked regularly for the members of the British Embassy, simply by parking his taxi outside the ambassador's residence. An old admirer of the English, he considered himself privileged. His wife impressed on their friends and anyone else with whom she got into conversation that her husband was not just an ordinary taxi driver.

'He is special, believe you me. The members of the British Embassy always use his taxi. He reckons that, with tips, he earns as much, if not more, as he would if they employed him as an Embassy chauffeur. Of course, he keeps his taxi in beautiful condition, believe you me.'

Her little exaggerations about hubby had become solid facts in her mind, and were gradually growing. If she had a sympathetic audience she would sentimentally recall how her parents booked a ride on her eighteenth birthday to the Prater, Vienna's permanent fairground.

'His horses and cab were the best decorated, believe you me. It was love at first sight.'

'With the horses or the cab?' one of her listeners had asked on one occasion.

She had not taken notice.

'He lost several trips that day waiting there for our return, believe you me.'

Mrs. Heaven led Bill to a small waiting room on the ground floor from where she made a quick call on the internal telephone, before turning to him.

Chapter 7 – Conspiracy in Vienna

'Please take a pew, Mr. Jordan. I owe you an explanation. I was not prepared for this terrible occurrence, when I came to the station. I had to make things up as I went along.' She sighed, 'It was a shock. His poor parents. It must have been for you, too.'

Bill nodded.

'He was looking forward to seeing them.'

'I can imagine,' she said. 'You still seem to be on edge. You can relax—'

'Mrs. Heaven, Captain Nolan was murdered in my place. I heard the killer address him as Herr Gabor, my original name.'

She looked at him dismayed. After a short pause she collected herself.

'We've gained a little time for sorting things out, Mr. Jordan. I need you to fill me in. But I'm afraid I must postpone even that for a couple of days. A member of our government is due to visit Vienna and it requires a lot of security preparations. You'll have to stay with us for a while, anyway, I'm afraid. Not only in order to be available for questioning by the Oberkommissar, but also because London needs to send an officer to accompany you on the rest of your journey. In the meantime, a member of our staff will look after you. Ah, here is Shaver.'

A gentle knock on the door had announced the arrival of a portly man, who seemed possessed of a near-permanent smile.

'Mr. Jordan, this is Martin Shaver, our hospitality officer and expert on economic affairs,' she said. 'He will look after you. Do you know Vienna at all?'

Jordan nodded.

'Good. You are, of course, quite free to go out and about. I'm certain you're safe in Vienna. You have an entitlement to funds, did you know?'

'Thank you, Mrs. Heaven. I'll be all right, once I've changed some Hungarian currency.'

'Shaver will assist you.' She rose. 'He'll also satisfy any queries you may have about Vienna. I believe he has more answers than there are questions. I've to go to our Passport Office, my place of work, which is situated in the Inner City. I leave you in his care.'

Jordan followed Shaver out of the residence and out of the grounds. They entered the solid, though less impressive building next door. Jordan's accommodation was a small, well-furnished two-room flat. He was given the key to it, as well as somewhat

Chapter 7 – Conspiracy in Vienna

bulky key to the street door. As in most houses in Vienna, the street door was large and always locked. The building was basically an apartment house, run like a small hotel, except that the guests did not have to pay. His first action was to lie down on the bed, fully dressed. He fell asleep within seconds, sleeping the sleep of the exhausted.

Waking up the next morning, he had breakfast downstairs in what was signposted as Refectory, then went for a long stroll. He ended up on a bench in the attractively laid-out Belvedere Park, close-by. His situation was reminiscent of his last week in Budapest and, as then, he had plenty to think about. He suffered from a sense of guilt and generally felt restless and tense. But the sunshine had a thawing, relaxing effect. That first stroll laid down the pattern for the following days. By the kind permission of the staff, he took one of the daily papers, available at the refectory, with him. The *Neues Wiener Journal* (*New Vienna Daily*) of Tuesday, contained matters of interest:

'**Mysterious Orient Express killing – Police baffled.** An Englishman was found dead in the Orient Express on Sunday, when the train reached Vienna. Oberkommissar Alfons Zulka of the Margareten Crime Branch was called to the Westbahnhof to take charge. The Oberkommissar is one of Vienna's top crime-detectives. In an interview he pointed out that there were no witnesses, and the investigation was hampered by the fact that the international train, of necessity, was permitted to proceed in order to keep its time table. For those reasons, Zulka has doubts whether the murderer will ever be brought to justice. The dead man's name cannot be revealed as yet.'

Another item, on the same page, also caught Jordan's attention:

'**British Minister's visit to Vienna.** Mr. Clement Attlee, a minister in Britain's Labour Government, is due to arrive in Vienna on a state visit in the middle of next week. He will be guest of honour at a dinner arranged by the Chancellor, Dr. Johann Schober. Mr. Attlee, at forty-seven, is one of his government's youngest ministers. A lawyer by profession, he is the up-and-coming star of the British Labour Party. It should be

Chapter 7 – Conspiracy in Vienna

stressed that British Socialists are seen as less radical than their European counterparts. The visit is expected to last three days.'

Jordan's daily walks gradually increased in distance. He was struck by the huge number of political posters. Many advertised the Austrian National Socialist Party. Bill realised he knew little about that party and the Austrian political scene, in general. He confessed his ignorance to Shaver, whom he had come to join for his daily four-o'clock-tea at the residence. The smiling hospitality officer was happy to try and answer the questions of this taciturn Hungarian.

'The economic crisis is growing fast, Mr. Jordan. It was started by the Wall Street crash in America. A few large-scale bankruptcies there had a domino effect on the other American financial institutions and from there on those in Europe. Someone put it like this, "When America sneezes, the rest of the world catches the cold" and America well and truly has sneezed.'

'I don't get it,' Jordan admitted.

'Because of their financial problems the Americans have stopped buying goods from the European countries. They have also stopped lending money to European banks and businesses. Without these dollar incomes, Europeans cannot afford to buy goods from America and from the countries that accept American dollars in payment, which is all of them. When goods are not sold, people who make them and sell them lose their jobs. Austria, for instance, sells timber and leather goods. No country nowadays is self-sufficient, you see.'

Bill began to see, remembering some of the things his father had often preached.

'But where do these Nazis fit in, Mr. Shaver? We have several parties of them in Hungary and they're seen as a threat to our democratic government but that's just politics.'

Shaver shook his head.

'Just politics? Mr. Jordan, when people lose their jobs, they have difficulties surviving, even in buying enough food for their families. They want to blame someone and that Austrian demagogue in Germany, Herr Adolf Hitler, is offering them scapegoats galore, like democratic governments and Jews in equal measure. And he promises radical solutions.'

They were sipping their tea slowly. In Jordan's mind questions kept chasing each other.

Chapter 7 – Conspiracy in Vienna

'So what do you think is the answer to the problem, Mr. Shaver? In Hungary we even have people who want the Austrian emperor back.'

Shaver, screwing his eyes up, opened his hands in a gesture of comical despair.

'Is that all you want to know? Volumes of books have been written about these subjects. I studied Economics at the University of London. I'm the only one here who wasn't at Oxford or Cambridge. My views are strongly influenced by two Englishmen, Keynes and Beveridge. I don't suppose you've heard of them.'

Jordan shook his head in agreement.

'The truth is, Mr. Jordan, that I don't know the answer but I'm sure there isn't just one. I am however absolutely certain that a dictatorship is not the answer. In difficult times you do need a strong government which is OK as long as you can get rid of it at the next election. Hand unlimited power to a single individual and you've given away your basic rights. From what is known about these Nazis, they're ruthless and violent. The Italians have already got themselves a murderous dictator so it won't surprise me if the Germans do the same.'

The passion of his words although not in his voice but uttered without a single smile, surprised Jordan. His father had often talked about the capitalist system and about people's greed. When working for Six-Two, Jordan had come across a lot of views expressed by Nazis. He knew they were aiming to do away with democracy but he had been deaf and blind. Now his thoughts culminated in the image of Nolan lying dead on the carriage floor, the blood still fresh, spreading on his shirt and his eyes wide open with an expression of utter sadness. He knew he had brought this about when foiling a murder attempt by German Nazis for which they had tried to kill him and killed the wrong man. What kind of people took to killing so lightly?

During the war he had often grappled with thoughts about the wholesale killing going on. But it was a matter of survival then, of mass action, not influenced by individual consciences. This was different. He had heard the chief plotter express his anticipatory pleasure at killing the English lord for insulting the Führer and the German people. Clarity entered. This was clearly the real reason why Nolan was dead. Suddenly, Jordan experienced an emotion he had never before experienced, a huge anger that came close to

Chapter 7 – Conspiracy in Vienna

hatred, perhaps was hatred. These Nazis wished to deprive people of their rights to express their opinion. They used ruthless violence to prevent being criticised. Murderers were guilty of Nolan's death. Unsmilingly, Shaver had watched the changing expressions in Jordan's face, watched it slowly coming alive, watched the growing display of anger and determination and strong emotion. Jordan finally regained his calm.

'You've opened my eyes a lot, Mr. Shaver and reconnected me with my father's views. I suddenly know that I'm at war again. But this time I've chosen my enemies. It's personal.'

Jordan's daily walks suddenly had content. He had a lot to digest mentally and emotionally. German Nazis had plotted to kill an Englishman in Budapest. And Hungarians, presumably also Nazis, were ready to assist them. His enemies were not people belonging to a particular nation. He realised that he had never hated the British or the French. And whereas the murder of Nolan had an inflammatory effect on his emotions, their political aims were fast solidifying them. They wanted to eradicate the Jews using widely spread, senseless anti-Semitism in order to gain support. His best friend, now dying in England, came from a Jewish family.

Step by step, Jordan was adding a rational understanding towards a feeling of great and passionate loathing of the Nazis, of fascism and racial prejudice in general. Such people should not be permitted to use the freedom of democracy for spreading their poison. On Wednesday morning after breakfast, back in his room Jordan became aware of a lot of noise in the street. He stepped to the window and saw a steadily increasing number of people gathering on the pavements. They were chatting and looking expectantly down the street. Most of them were women, some with babies in prams, or small children by their sides. A large number of policemen kept them on the pavements and from coming too close to the Embassy's entrance. Their warm-weather clothes made it a colourful sun-bathed picture of cheerfulness.

Jordan realised that they were awaiting the English minister's arrival. A brief memory of the Budapest plot touched his mind, unconsciously sharpening his observation. As his eyes roamed over the crowd, he noticed a man on the opposite pavement who was holding binoculars to his eyes. Something about him knocked on Jordan's mind. He got his own binoculars from his case. The man had moved and stood on a stone step in the doorway of one of the

Chapter 7 – Conspiracy in Vienna

houses opposite. The next moment Jordan saw something that made him draw his breath in. Enlarging his focus, he thought he saw a distinct redness on the back of the man's right hand. Electrified, Jordan rushed out of his room and down the stairs and out into the street to the house. But the man had disappeared. A wild thought struck him. 'Here I am, having woken up in a hotel room and an important English visitor is due to arrive. Another plot?'

He got a hold on himself. The idea was ludicrous and the product of his imagination. 'I must calm down,' he told himself. 'It's this waiting about. Why don't I just pack and return to Hungary? They can't stop me.' Then he remembered Nolan, his promise to the dead man and György. 'I must stick to my agreements. But I must snap out of this,' he told himself. Not interested in watching the arrival of the British VIP, he went for his morning walk.

* * *

Zulka's man, Detective Armbruster, travelling on the Orient Express, had made more progress than could be expected. After the train had left the Westbahnhof, one of the attendants had opened the toilet in Carriage Six and discovered the murderer's rucksack and his Luger. The toilet window had jammed. One of the train attendants recalled a passenger, wearing a rucksack, who had told him that he was going to see a friend in Carriage Four, just after the train had left Budapest. The French security guard remembered almost bumping into a man exiting from that toilet, who had looked like an artist.

A passenger in Carriage Nine, a German woman, reported that she had nodded asleep in her seat and was woken up by a passenger taking the seat next to her, only minutes before the train was stopping at the Vienna station. Her ten-year-old son described him as wearing a 'cowboy hat' and carrying a folder like the one his older cousin had with his art drawings in school. The mother wondered why the man had bothered to come into the compartment and sit down when he was leaving the train a few minutes later and where he might have been all that time. The boy thought cowboys should be wearing wide dungarees. She thought the man's outfit was not suitable wear for an Orient Express traveller.

'He did not even wear a tie, can you believe that?' she told Armbruster, who could and did. But none of the witnesses had

Chapter 7 – Conspiracy in Vienna

noticed a scar on the man's hand. Zulka made the assumption that, as the murdered man had taken the train in Budapest, his murderer might have done the same. He sent Bogner to the Budapest main station and Bogner struck gold. The man in the ticket office remembered a fellow in a blue jacket and carrying a rucksack.

'He looked like a Swiss and spoke like a German and addressed me as if I was his servant. He was in a great hurry and purchased a ticket for Munich. Here, look. All my sales are registered with date and time and he bought his just exactly eight minutes before the train was due to depart. Here, you see: the ticket was for Carriage Nine. In a couple of weeks, I'll be able to tell you where he left the train, when we get the ticket stubs back.'

Zulka began to see a pattern. The assassin had not occupied his seat because he had proceeded to Carriage Four to do what he had come to do, i.e. shoot the English security officer. He had deliberately drawn attention to himself in his Bavarian outfit and carrying a rucksack so that, if at all, the search would be for someone dressed like that. Having changed in the toilet into his artist gear, he again drew attention to himself as obviously not being the man in the Tyrolean outfit. That suggested a further change of clothes. He was unlucky that the toilet window was jammed. His victim was travelling to London. The killer had booked as far as Munich to give himself plenty of time for the execution of his plan. But he got out of his compartment in Vienna and that suggested that he was an Austrian citizen and most likely a Viennese resident. His Bavarian outfit was normal wear in Austria and very popular in Vienna also.

If he had started in Vienna, it made sense that he used a local train to Budapest and, for that reason, needed to buy a ticket for the Orient Express when returning. It even suggested that he had not known in advance that his quarry would travel to London and on this train. If his theory was correct, it threw open a lot of other questions. But if it was correct, then might he not also have changed clothes when leaving Vienna? Zulka sent Bogner to the cloakroom at the Westbahnhof and, once again, Bogner struck gold. A man in a white jacket, wearing a wide-brimmed hat, had collected a small suitcase which, according to his ticket, he had deposited there only two days earlier.

The next question was obvious: did the man take a taxi, or use a tram, or walk? As he very likely had changed his appearance again it

Chapter 7 – Conspiracy in Vienna

was going to be difficult if not impossible to trace his next steps. The most puzzling aspect of the case was the motive. For what possible reason would an Austrian wish to kill an English security officer who worked in Budapest? Was there a personal connection? Was the killer what the Americans called a hit man? There were two Englishmen in that compartment. Mrs. Heaven's remarks implied that she, too, was not certain who the intended victim was. Zulka now was convinced that the key to the answers lay with the British and he was certain, he would never find out. He concluded that there was no point in interrogating Mr. Jordan.

* * *

Jordan's stroll had taken him to the *Stadtpark* (City Park), a strip of parkland running along a section of the Ringstrasse which bordered the Inner City. He was seated on a bench, trying to relax from his earlier, self-induced excitement. The bench was one of many on the path between the park and the narrow, deep, shallow bed of the River Wien. Jordan's lunch had been a pair of Frankfurters with mustard and a slice of dark bread, purchased from the kiosk near-by. Now he was leaning back, eyes closed, enjoying the sun on his face and even the occasional gusts of wind blowing along the river path. Just when he was blissfully drifting towards nodding off, he became aware of a man with a young boy sitting down on the neighbouring bench to his left, enjoying a similar meal. Without wanting to, his ears were witnesses to their conversation.

'These Frankfurters are tasty, Heinz, aren't they?'
'Yes, Father.'
'Did you like the school?'
'It's very big, Father.'
'It's one of the best *Gymnasien'* (grammar schools) 'in Vienna, Heinz. Mother will be pleased they've accepted you. Of course, there was no doubt about that. I know friends of the headmaster. You'll do well there.'
'Will any of my friends go there also, Father?'
'I doubt it. I'm sure you'll make new friends quickly. From good homes. But be careful. Unfortunately, many Jews also send their kids there. I told the headmaster what I think of that. And I don't want you to bring a dirty Jew-boy into our home again, Heinz.'

Chapter 7 – Conspiracy in Vienna

The last words jerked Jordan out of his semi-slumber. The man was an anti-Semite and was teaching his son to be one. Probably a Nazi, too. Jordan continued listening, now fully alert.

'I thought he was nice, Father, I didn't know he was a Jew,' the boy defended himself.

'Your mother and I, my son, we're true Aryans and so are you and we don't mix with Jewish scum. They're our enemies, an inferior race. Never forget that, do you hear me, Heinz?'

'Yes, Father.'

'We shall deal with them soon. They'll get what's coming to them. Our ranks are growing.' He was getting carried away. 'And I'm part of the elite, Heinz, your father's part of the elite. I know things only the most important men know.'

'Is this the meetings you go to on Thursday nights, Father?'

'Yes, it is.' He lowered his voice. 'Remember, you mustn't talk about that. You haven't –?'

'Oh no, Father. I'm ten, I'm not a little child anymore. Couldn't I come with you?'

'They wouldn't allow it, Heinz. Not yet, but in a year or two perhaps. I know you'll be a loyal follower to the Führer, Heinz. Maybe I will ask tomorrow at the meeting.'

'Will you really, Father? – Oh!'

A strong puff of the breeze had picked up the sheet of paper he had deposited on the bench whilst eating his sausages. It swirled high and disappeared.

'My enrolment, Father,' the boy was distraught, 'in my new school. Now I can't go there.'

His father had risen, looking around. He put his hand in a caressing gesture on the boy's head.

'Of course, you can, Heinz. We can get a copy.' He did not sit down. 'It's time to go, Heinz. Mother will come home from lunch with auntie and my patients will start arriving soon.'

A moment later they were walking past Jordan. He watched them through his eyelashes. The man sported a blond moustache. Both had straw-blond hair and both wore leather shorts and white knee-socks. A short while after they had gone, Bill rose, no longer desirous of relaxation. He turned to go when his eyes fell upon a spot of yellow caught up in the twigs of the bushes behind his bench. It was a piece of paper. Bill plucked it from the bush. He had guessed correctly. It was the boy's enrolment document, with a large

Chapter 7 – Conspiracy in Vienna

ragged piece torn away. He scanned it. The boy's name was missing, but his address was there in full: *Wien VI* (Vienna VI), *Gumpendorferstrasse 12/14*. The Roman VI meant 6th District. Jordan thought of the meetings, the boy had referred to. Of the 'elite'. They took place on Thursdays. Today was Wednesday.

Struggling with an idea that had popped into his head, he returned to his apartment where he found an envelope waiting for him. It contained a brief note from Mrs. Heaven, asking him to call on her on Friday at 10 a.m. at the British passport office. Was something happening at last? He was tensed up and needed action. At dinner, he shared a table in the refectory with an almost completely bald Englishman from Brighton, a courier who, having brought special post from London, was waiting for some to take back and whose favourite word was ruddy. The man looked as if he could take care of himself. Jordan was surprised at the courier's loquacity. A captive audience, he was privileged to listen to a detailed description of the courier's responsible job and of the many interesting trips to ruddy foreign capitals. He was shown the natty chain around the man's wrist, which would be attached to the small, securely locked briefcase and carried the most important letters and documents in the whole ruddy universe.

When he was on the move, international crime syndicates, as well as agents of foreign governments, would do any ruddy thing in order to obtain some of the papers he carried. But he was well prepared for these ruddy dangers and had always coped with them effectively, or would have done if they had arisen. He was too well known in that twilight world of danger and the ruddy crooks avoided to cross swords – figuratively – with him. Having ensured that Jordan was now aware of his superior skills and his superior reputation as one of the most successful couriers in the field, he switched to the morning's exciting ruddy events. He regaled Jordan with a detailed description of the great reception in the streets upon the arrival of Mr. Clement Attlee, the British minister. The Austrian crowd had cheered and applauded when the ambassadorial Rolls Royce drove up.

'We may have been their enemies in the war but the Austrians love us British, not like the ruddy Germans who want to be top dog in Europe – and in the world, believe you me. The Austrians call them Piefkes. It's not a compliment, I can tell you. They admire the way we do things, I tell you, the ruddy Austrians, that is. Yes, sir,

Chapter 7 – Conspiracy in Vienna

they do. Of course, Clem may be an up-and-coming in the ruddy Labour Party but this Labour government ain't goin' to stay in power for very long, don't you agree?'

He spoke the name as if he knew Mr. Attlee intimately and did not stop talking.

'We don't like ruddy lefties to run our country, do we? No, sir, we don't. Why change things, when we're doin' well. I tell you one thing, though, the Austrians, they'd like to have our brand of government. Though theirs won't last very long, mark my words. That ruddy fellow in Germany, Aydolf Hitler, you know, some of them are all for him, even want to be joined to Germany. He's an Austrian an' all. Did you know that the word, Nazi, is short for National Socialist party? It's the way they pronounce it. There's a lot o' them here in Austria and I say it's dangerous. Something oughta be done about it. Doesn't look as if the ruddy League of Nations is much cop. Yes, sir, something should be done.'

Jordan nodded in 'ruddy' agreement. The waiter brought their schnitzels and cucumber salad in vinegar. A happy silence descended over the room, except for the music provided by the genteel processes of chewing and swallowing and gulping and quaffing. Jordan was thinking over what the man had said. It did not prevent him from enjoying the meal. Despite being hammered by the courier's volubility, his remarks about the Nazis in Austria did find a space in Jordan's mind. He went to bed undecided and woke up, determined. By 7 p.m. on Thursday, Jordan stood in the shadows opposite the house No.12 in the Gumpendorferstrasse, one of the radial roads leading from the city centre towards Vienna's outskirts. There were few people about.

A quarter of an hour later he began to wonder. Had he misunderstood or misinterpreted what he had heard in the park, or had he come too late and the Nazi had already left for his meeting? Just then the man with the blond moustache came out of the house, carefully locking the heavy door behind him. He still wore his leather shorts. Jordan followed him. His quarry did not seem to suspect that he was being followed. A turning led them to a parallel radial road, where they both took the 58 tram, destination: *Unter Sankt Veit* (Lower Saint Vitus).

The blond moustache sat in the first carriage, Bill Jordan in the second. He felt the old adrenaline rising. It was a good feeling, like coming alive. His man left the tram one stop after *Hietzinger Brücke*

Chapter 7 – Conspiracy in Vienna

(Hietzing Bridge), a wide bridge crossing the River Wien. Bill followed the man as he entered a street called *Auhofstrasse*, where, not far into it, he stopped at a green garden gate, larger and higher than the ones they had passed, and rang the house bell. He was clearly visible under the light of a lantern. The gate was opened and the man went inside. When Bill passed it, walking slowly, he could not see the person who must have opened it.

There was no house number on the gate but a little metal sign said: D. Gastl, Diplom-Ingenieur. A long path ran from the gate towards the large villa. What now? Jordan was stumped. There was no point in waiting until the man came out again at the end of his meeting and following him back to his home. If only he could get into the property. But the high metal fence with three strands of barbed wire above it, discouraged the idea, as did his awareness that there had to be someone inside the grounds, who had opened the gate.

He began to stroll slowly to and fro, covering a stretch of about ten metres past each side of the gate. He saw other arrivals being let into the place, all men and almost all of them wearing leather shorts and open-necked white shirts. He was only a few metres from the gate, when two newcomers, both wearing suits, one grey, the other dark blue, were reaching it. The one in grey was small and wore a pince-nez. The one in dark blue, carrying an attaché case in his left hand, pressed the bell with his right. Jordan's eyes were drawn by the glitter of the light rays, reflecting from the ring on the man's middle finger and from the ring to the red scar across the back of the man's hand.

The next moment the gate opened. Losing his cool for a brief moment, Jordan shouted 'Stop!' and rushed towards the man who, remarkably self-possessed, moved his head to look at him. The next moment, two brawny fellows with open-necked shirts and wide, decorative braces holding up their greasy leather shorts, stepped from the open gate. Jordan heard one of them say to the man in blue:

'You go inside, Professor Kohlen, we'll handle this.'

'Good, Filz, I leave it to you and Möller,' the professor said. He and the little man in grey turned into the grounds. Seeing the two toughs, Jordan reined in. Both were blond and looked tough. The one whom the professor had addressed as Filz, was two centimetres taller than Jordan and six centimetres wider. He stepped close to Jordan, arms outstretched to bar his progress. The other one, a little

Chapter 7 – Conspiracy in Vienna

smaller, a stocky butcher-type, posted himself behind Jordan. It was obviously a practised drill by experienced heavies. Recognising it, Jordan excitement disappeared in a flash and his cool returned. The taller man, Filz, opened the dialogue.

'Going anywhere, man?'

'I'm just passing. Please let me walk on,' Bill spoke calmly.

'Yea, sure. Do you believe you're talking to idiots? Do you believe we haven't seen you passing our gate again and again the last ten minutes? Stopping in front of it? Peering in? Trying to get in perhaps, uninvited? This is private property, my dear friend.'

'But the pavement isn't and I'm neither your dear, nor your friend,' Bill replied. 'I'm asking you again, peacefully, to let me pass.'

'Peacefully, hah?' Filz bent forward, his face almost touching Jordan's face. 'Why don't you ask us differently – not peacefully?'

'Ja, why don't you?' came from the man behind him.

Jordan, realising how careless he had been, was still unsure about the best way of handling this situation. The big man's next remarks removed his doubts.

'We know why you're here. You're a damned snooper, in the pay of some shit-Jews, probably, and we're going to give you a lesson you won't forget for the rest of your life, my dear friend,' he sneered and straightened for action.

He was too slow. In that split-second, all the frustration and tension that had accumulated inside Jordan since the murder of Nolan, exploded into lightning action. His right knee jammed upwards into the heavy's crotch, exacting a loud cry of pain, whilst, simultaneously, his open hand hit his chin with the force of an uppercut. It pushed the big man's upper body backwards and he crashed to the ground. Using the momentum of his action to swirl around, the side of Jordan's clenched fist, made a hammer-like contact with the temple of the man behind him, knocking him sideways into the fence from which he slipped to the pavement, uttering a howl of pain, joining the moans coming from Filz, who was lying on the pavement, bent in agony, hands folded over his crotch. Looking at him gave Jordan immense satisfaction and he murmured, 'You did ask me to show you different. You should look for a different job, Herr Filz. You're not very good at this one.'

Jordan was trained in unarmed combat when joining Six-Two. His second movement was known as the matchbox blow because the

Chapter 7 – Conspiracy in Vienna

user was supposed to grip a matchbox or something similar. Its full force could kill a man. Without a matchbox and out of training, Bill's hand and wrist were hurting and the pain was growing. He knew well that the effects of his action on the two bruisers would wear off within minutes and wondered what to do next, when, out of the corner of his eye, he saw a fellow, all dressed in dark, sprinting towards him from the opposite pavement. The fellow stopped in front of Jordan, who had taken a defensive stance, holding his hands up in a gesture of peace. He addressed Jordan in a hasty whisper.

'Who're you? What are you doing, man?' Without waiting for a reply he continued, 'Leave, I urge you, before you'll make things worse. You've probably already caused plenty of damage. I've no time to explain. Just disappear, man. Hurry!'

The words were spoken in an authoritative manner, but without any hostility. They were good advice. Jordan turned to go, but the man touched his shoulder, 'The other side man and keep in the shadows.'

They rushed across the road, side by side, where the fellow, finger across his lips, exhorting Bill to silence, waved him good-bye. A quick glance across the road showed that the two Nazis were standing up, looking searchingly around, clearly still in pain, yet talking to each other excitedly. Jordan set off at speed, in the direction from where he had come. He found his way back to the tram stop and took the tram but only as far as the Hietzing Bridge, where he had noticed a taxi stand. He was back in his flat twenty minutes later. He gave his swollen wrist the hot and cold water treatment and, despite the pain, went to bed in an exhilarated mood. Whilst falling asleep, he gave a passing thought to the fellow in black, puzzling over his remark: 'You've probably already caused plenty of damage.' His thoughts did not linger on it. What occupied his mind well into his sleep was the growing conviction that the man the guard had addressed as Professor Kohlen, was very likely the murderer of Nolan. When he woke up the first thing coming into his mind was whether and how much to tell Mrs. Heaven of the incident. He had no difficulty finding the palace-like Passport Office. Despite her name, Mrs. Heaven's office was only on the first floor. She came to the point quickly.

'I've been in touch with Budapest, Mr. Jordan. As you can imagine they're all very upset and disturbed about Captain Nolan's murder. Major Pemmington has brought me up to date with your situation. He, too, believes that the assassin made a mistake. He is however quite clear that, except for the killer, no one can be blamed. His official report states that Captain Nolan died in the course of duty. He will get a military funeral with all honours in London.' She paused.

'I suppose it is unlikely that I can attend the funeral?' Jordan intercepted softly.

'I'm afraid so, Mr. Jordan. A security officer to accompany you to London should arrive within the next seven days. You'll probably be pleased to leave Vienna.'

'I shall be glad to get to England,' he replied, 'although – my life has been disorganised for some time and it is not getting better.'

Alexandra Heaven noticed the hesitation and then something else. 'Your wrist, Mr. Jordan, what happened?'

She nodded toward his right hand which he had kept resting on his lap. Her eyes were looking into his searchingly. Her question decided him. He gave her a report of the evening's events, without describing the details of his encounter with the Nazi guards. When he finished she thought for a moment, then she lifted the receiver of her phone, punching three digits.

'Alf, can you spare a few minutes? I've Mr. Jordan here. I think you should listen to what he has just told me.' – 'The same.' She put the phone down and said, 'Please tell Major Murdoch, our head of security, what you've told me. Meanwhile, would you like a cup of tea?'

He would but the next moment there was a knock on the door and Murdoch entered.

* * *

At this very same moment, in a sumptuously furnished room of the Hofburg, the old emperors' royal palace in the Inner City, another conversation was taking place. The man behind a massive oak table, impressively dressed in a red and blue uniform, with embroidered epaulettes and elegantly braided, was of broad build. His heavily-jowled, square face, dominated by a pair of narrow, deep-set blue eyes, wore an expression of unbreachable authority and of unbreachable equanimity, perhaps also seen as typical Austrian *Gemütlichkeit* (easy-going ways). Colonel Berthold Johann von Lebern was the head of the Austrian Geheimdienst, the Secret

Chapter 7 – Conspiracy in Vienna

Service, which, in its function, was comparable to Britain's MI5, although a much smaller outfit and even more underfunded. His hands on the edge of his table, Lebern was leaning forward.

'What do you mean, Körner, he knocked them out? A boxer? I used to do quite a bit.'

Agent Karl Körner, a slim sinewy man, tall, wearing casual clothes and an open-necked dark-blue shirt, smoothed his hair backwards. In line with a current fashion, it had no parting.

'To be precise, Herr Oberst, he kneed the big fellow into his vertex, pushed his head upwards which toppled him backwards and knocked the man behind him into the fence, all in one movement. I've not seen that done before.'

'Who was he? Tarzan? Hercules?'

'No taller than I, but obviously a professional. For my own sake I got him away from the scene as fast as possible, Herr Oberst.'

'The cuckoo, you did!' It was one of the Colonel's milder expletives. He thought for a moment. 'I'll get Heidi on it. If anyone, she'll find out who this miracle man is. Give her all the details. Have you anything new to report?'

'I'm afraid not, Herr Oberst. I've now photographed every man who entered the place during the last two meetings before yesterday's. I'm sure it's a secret Nazi group. If it's secret, they must be plotting. Why don't we just raid the place when they're all there?'

Lebern shook his head, unimpressed.

'I've got to be sure, Körner. Plotting's hard to prove. I have enemies who'd be only too pleased if I make a mistake. Now you've handed me a new problem. As if I haven't enough on my plate. Another unknown player. Most of your photos depict only the backs of men or, at best, bits of their profiles. I'm not after the small fry, damn it. If I could prove that someone like Hetzendorf is one of them, it would make me a happy man. If we could establish the identity of just one of these damned Nazis in Hietzing, so that I can put a little friendly pressure on him.'

'There's one thing, Herr Oberst. All these men going into the house and staying for almost two hours each time I observed them, I never saw any lights in the house coming on. They—'

The telephone rang. The colonel picked up the receiver.

'Von Lebern.' – 'Herr Major Murdoch?'

He looked at Körner who left the room.

Chapter 7 – Conspiracy in Vienna

* * *

Murdoch had listened to Jordan's story with mixed feelings of mostly disapproval.

'Mr. Jordan, Mrs. Heaven has been successful in not letting the media get wind of your connection with the murder, indeed of your existence. We're responsible for your safety. If, as we believe, you were the assassin's real goal, he now believes he has killed you. Are you attempting to ensure that whoever is behind all this, finds out you're still alive and has another go? You're not in Hungary and even there you were no longer a member of your security services.'

Jordan felt a trace of anger rising. He was not a little boy to be reprimanded, nor was this man his superior. But for the moment he said nothing.

'However,' Murdoch continued. 'No one at that place is likely to identify you.' He remembered something and added slowly. 'In fact, you just may…'

He picked up the phone and dialled a number.

'Ah, Herr Oberst.' – 'Indeed. Herr Oberst, early last year I passed on to you a name whom one of my men had heard refer to secret Nazi meetings.' – 'You recently mentioned your investigations of such meetings. Is one of them situated in Hietzing?' –'On Thursday nights?'

He covered the mouthpiece with his hand for a moment.

'The colonel's actually displaying excitement, Sandy.' – 'No, Herr Oberst, I assure you but, purely by accident, I may have some information for you. It appears that a British citizen, passing through Vienna, was involved in an incident there last night. You know?' – As he listened he grew serious. 'One of your men? That was his good luck. – 'I assure you, Oberst, I had nothing to do with it. The fellow came across the situation by coincidence…You know I cannot give you his name. It's our job to look after British citizens and, as I said, he is passing through. But he came here and reported the incident.' –' Indeed, Herr Oberst. Let me tell you what I have. This gentleman heard about a Nazi meeting in the evening at which some secret action was being plotted. By a fluke, he found a piece of paper left behind with the man's address.' – 'Herr Oberst, I was busy – the state visit. He's a bitter opponent of the Nazis and acted off his own bat. He went to the man's house in the evening and followed him to this villa in Hietzing. He was threatened by two

Chapter 7 – Conspiracy in Vienna

private guards. He got away with your fellow's help.' – 'A fight? He what?' – 'By himself?' Murdoch threw a searching glance at Bill. 'This he has not told me. He may have acquired such skills in the war, but I assure you, he's a civilian and he is not in my employ. The point is, Herr Oberst, that although I haven't the name of the man he followed, I have his exact address and the school into which his son has been enrolled.' – 'On the piece of paper, I mentioned. And our gentleman heard the name of another man who entered the villa to attend the meeting and the names of the two guards…' – 'Lunch, tomorrow? *Freilich*' (of course), 'Herr Oberst. At your usual?' –' Fine by me. *Auf Wiedersehn* then.'

He put the receiver down, saying, in a changed tone, 'It appears, Mr. Jordan, you've done some good. And you've been modest. Unfortunately, you've left footprints. I'm afraid there's little I can do about your suggestion that this Professor Kohlen could be the murderer. What about the man with him?'

Jordan shook his head. 'I only saw him for a split second. He was small.'

'Mr. Jordan, the scar may be a coincidence. Professor suggests university. He's not likely to be a sort of contract killer, or any sort of killer, even if he is a Nazi. I can tell you that the colonel is very impressed, indeed excited, at getting names. You have my regard but, please, no more heroics whilst you're in Vienna.'

Jordan nodded expressionlessly. Murdoch turned to Mrs. Heaven.

'Thanks for calling me in, Sandy. You might try and interest the Oberkommissar in checking out the man with the scar, the professor.'

Without waiting for a reply, he nodded to both of them and strode out. Jordan wondered about his calling Mrs. Heaven 'Sandy'. Its derivation from 'Alexandra' was not immediately obvious to him. Murdoch telephoned London, requesting they send the agreed escort for Jordan as soon as possible. He was worried, the Hungarian might come upon more china shops in Vienna.

* * *

On Monday, Bill's eyes fixed on a front page article in the *Neues Wiener Journal*:

Chapter 7 – Conspiracy in Vienna

'**Dentist arrested on suspicion of treason.** Secret anti-government plot? A widespread plot against the republic has been discovered by detectives, working under cover. Heinrich Trauner, a panel dentist, domiciled in the Gumpendorferstrasse, is to be charged with treason, together with five other men. So are Justin Möller and Manfred Filz, private security guards. Diplomingenieur Dominik Gastl, owner of the property in Hietzing where the secret meetings were held, states he did not know anything about the plotters.

Whilst he was away in Carinthia at the time, on an important engineering job for the government, his agent was in charge of hiring out the cellar rooms of his Hietzing villa for meetings by charitable societies. The organisers claimed that their meetings were strictly educational. However, a document has been found in the possession of Herr Trauner whose six signatories swear to work for the overthrow of the government under his leadership. The document is numbered Geheimaktion 7/10. It is, therefore, suspected that it is one of ten such documents which suggest that the secret organisation consists of ten active units over 60 members, all plotting for the overthrow of the Austrian republic. The six signatories in Herr Trauner's document will be tried for High Treason.'

Bill read no further. This was the second time he had been involved in a matter that was reported by the press. No word about Nazis but, instead, the suggestion that monarchists were involved. He shrugged his shoulders. The major was right. It was none of his business. He was leaving Vienna and would have nothing to do anymore with this particular episode.

The following day, he enjoyed a second meeting with this British security woman who bore the unusual surname of Heaven, whom the major had addressed as Sandy, an English word he knew as describing a beach or even a colour. She had invited him for afternoon tea at the Kursalon, a large concert and dance venue plus restaurant. It was situated at one end of the Stadtpark, the park where, just a week ago, he had heard a dentist injecting poison into his young son's mind. Entering through the more glamorous entrance into the park, which was highlighted by the gilded statues of Lanner & Strauss, Vienna's famous waltz musicians and

Chapter 7 – Conspiracy in Vienna

composers, he met Sandy Heaven at the bottom of the wide stairs to the restaurant's park side. They sat on the open air terrace, conducting a light-hearted conversation to the background of the light music by an elegant little orchestra in the pavilion bandstand down below. From time to time the music was joined by the shrill trumpeting cries of two resident peacocks taking their afternoon strut. Were they inspecting or parading? They seemed to be proud of their vocalising and, if they could talk, they would probably have blamed the orchestra for being out of tune with them. Light-hearted though the 'tea for two' seemed to be, it had a more serious facet. Sandy wanted to know a little more about this unusual Hungarian. Finding out things about people was an important part of her job. She was good at it.

'I can imagine that this revolutionary change in your life cannot be easy, Mr. Jordan.'

She stopped, whilst the waiter appeared with a trolley from which he served two trays with the ordered goodies. When he had gone, Sandy continued.

'I've heard how you dealt with the two guards in Hietzing, and Oberst von Lebern has been effusive with his thanks for the information Major Murdoch passed to him. I can tell you something else that'll please you, Mr. Jordan. Kommissar Zulka is, after all, going to look into your suggestion that Professor Kohlen was the man in the train who murdered Captain Nolan.'

'But how did this professor explain his presence at that meeting?'

'Satisfactorily, I have to tell you. He was invited to give a talk on the factors leading to the defeat of the Austrian and German armies. It might well be true.'

Gabor shook his head.

'He and that big guard knew each other well, Mrs. Heaven.' He shrugged his shoulders. 'What has changed the Kommissar's mind?'

'Zulka now knows that the killer left the train at the Westbahnhof. He has received more information about these meetings, which has roused his suspicion about the learned professor.' She laughed. 'One of Zulka's young detectives apparently has a way with female domestics at villas in Hietzing.' She added, 'I've given him an item in exchange.'

Jordan looked at her questioningly.

'I told him that while in Budapest you foiled a murder and we believe that you may have been the intended victim on the train. He

Chapter 7 – Conspiracy in Vienna

was happy about this information. The professor has given educational talks on the same subject abroad on several occasions. Zulka plans to investigate whether any political murders took place there on those occasions. He doubts, however, that he will be able to do anything at all without incontestable evidence. He has experienced obstacles from above before, when investigating Nazis.'

Jordan was digesting all that she was telling him.

'You have met with the Kommissar, Mrs. Heaven?'

She did not take it amiss.

'I had tea with him yesterday.'

He looked up.

'Here?'

She nodded.

'My favourite place. He no longer wants to question you. The statement you signed on the train is all he needs and he will return your passport by tomorrow.'

So this cosy meeting was just part of her job. She did it very well. He understood too much to be resentful. They were entitled to know about him. He had nothing to hide, so why not relax? He relaxed, really relaxed. During the next forty minutes, Mrs. Heaven learnt a lot about Bela Gabor, the wife he had lost and his lapse into self-pity. By the time she called the waiter, she had obtained a fairly precise personality sketch of him. He raised eyebrows and right hand to protest when she was paying, but did not argue.

'You are *still* our guest, Mr. Jordan.'

Her slightly accentuating the 'still' made him wonder for how much longer. He received the answer the next moment.

'You may leave Vienna by the end of the week, Mr. Jordan. The security officer who is to escort you to London, will arrive tomorrow. Shaver will introduce you. I'm on duty all this week, so I best say good-bye now. Give my regards to your travel companion. I'm sure you'll like him. And give my regards to England.'

She stood up, hanging her small, solid blue handbag around her shoulder. Jordan rose, too.

'Thank you for all your support, Mrs. Heaven. May I ask a personal question?'

She nodded, slightly astonished.

'Is Sandy your middle name?'

She laughed.

'It's an English short form of Alexandra.'

Chapter 7 – Conspiracy in Vienna

'Alexandra – Sandy – how stupid of me.'

They walked together to the bottom of the steps. The waiter clearing the table looked after them, then made for the staff telephone and dialled a number. The voice at the other end said: *'Braunes Buch Geheimintelligenz'* (Brown Book Secret Intelligence).

Jordan's information gave Oberst von Lebern sufficient information to take radical action. The villa's owner was warned off letting his hall for criminal activities and, in the end, nineteen men faced prosecution for treasonable action. One of them was Heinrich Trauner, who had led Jordan to the villa. Trauner, in the magistrate's court, announced that he was proud to be a Nazi and, therefore, the only true patriot in the court. He added dramatically that it was his greatest hope and a goal he would at all times pursue 'with heart and hand for the fatherland', a line from a patriotic song, that his beloved Führer should rule this German country. In this struggle he was prepared to die for his Führer. When he had finished, the magistrate judge pronounced his decision in dry and unemotional tones.

'You will appear in court on the charge of treasonable action, Herr Trauner, date and time to be determined. As this is a serious charge you will be kept in a police cell until your case is heard. It is unlikely that the criminal court will agree with your definition of patriotism so you best prepare yourself for free lodging in a prison cell over the next twelve years, or longer.'

He told his son that he was innocent of the charges but the Jewish judge had pronounced him guilty. The prosecuting judge was a Jewish lawyer, of course.

'I, too, was offered a lawyer, a Jew, Heinz, but I refused him, of course. I'd never do anything that would prevent you from being proud of me. Promise me, my son, that you will do well in school and go to university, where you will do equally well. Your mother and you will use your mother's maiden name from now on.'

Heinz manfully swallowed his tears and promised he would do all these things. That the judge had been a Jew, was a major inexactitude, one of several. But his father's lies in order to make himself out to be an innocent victim, were successful. The door closed behind him and Heinz began to cry. He was right to cry for he really was the victim.

Chapter 8 – The Lion's Cage

When Deuxième Bureau agent Vincent Georges Barbier returned to Paris from Nuremberg in September 1928, he submitted a detailed report on his observations of the Nazi rally. It did not mention the Nazi Stormtrooper's meeting with Count Winter's chauffeur. Nor did it include his niggling suspicion of another Deuxième Bureau man, Charles Bècher, who was sent to Germany in the same week. Initially, Bècher was going to Nuremberg and Barbier to Munich, where he had worked for a year at the end of the war. But Bècher had requested to be sent to Munich and the section head had agreed, largely because Bècher, a very ambitious agent, was down for promotion. To Barbier it made no sense. By itself it was merely slightly puzzling, but it added to a number of other observations that had built up suspicions of Bècher.

During the following months they had grown and he had involved Benoit Argentier, his only friend in the service, but who worked for a different section. Barbier's meeting with his wife had taken place in October and ended in an emotional reconciliation. As a result, he was waiting with a growing yearning for the end of July, when his current contract with the Bureau would end. He had informed his Section Head of his decision to leave who resented it and, driven by petty pique, arranged Barbier's tasks to be mostly night work. Thus when Barbier received a telephone call from Argentier, telling him that Bècher was talking to a man in a suspicious, clandestine manner at the Café Allaire, Barbier was free to grab a taxi and meet Argentier near the Allaire. Argentier, a stocky man with strong eyes and a small moustache gave him a hurried report:

'Bècher is inside the café's sidewalk section, sitting at a table with another man, although there are several unoccupied tables. I heard some of their conversation and am certain it was in German. Bècher called the man Vautant, or similar. That's all, Barbier. I've got to rush.'

Barbier made his way cautiously to the roadside of the Allaire's *terrasse* (pavement area). At first he could only see Bècher's face. When the other man's face came in view, he was stunned for a moment. It seemed to be that of Count Winter's chauffeur, the man

Chapter 8 – The Lion's Cage

whom he and Ronald Burnley had seen handing money to a Nazi SA man in Nuremberg. At that moment a *gendarme* (policeman), advised him to move off the road. Barbier had seen enough. By the time he reached his flat, he had made a decision. It was his duty to inform their section head of his suspicions. He did, but without explaining who he thought the German was.

His information was not received well. The section head's first reaction was to dismiss Barbier's suspicions altogether. However, upon checking Bècher's duty report of the day, he found no reference to his meeting at the Café Allaire. When questioned, Bècher stated that he had not considered it necessary to include his coffee break. He also claimed that his conversation was due to his sharing the table with the stranger and denied that they had spoken in German. The Bureau's rules regarding potentially suspicious behaviour were strict. A day later, both men received the order to attend a TCS, a *tribunal des chefs de section* (Tribunal of Section Heads).

It surprised both of them but, whereas Barbier received the news with equanimity, Bècher reacted furiously, uttering threats against Barbier. The TCS was the established fast method of the Deuxième Bureau to deal with disputes and accusations. It was manned by three section heads, two of whom were chosen in rotation. The third was almost always Colonel Yves Pascal Perroir, Head of the *Section des Petits Bouts,* (Section of Odds and Ends). The hearing of the case took place on a Wednesday in June. The first item on the agenda was the Tribunal's clerk reading out the details of the two men's identities:

'Barbier, Vincent Georges, born 1892 in Mulhouse, Alsace, moved to Belfort, France in 1910 and was called up in 1914. His war service file was not available at present. He joined the Bureau at the end of the war, following service in the Rhineland, Germany, with the occupation army.'

'Bècher, Charles, born 1895 in Strasbourg, Alsace, before the war, moved to Sacrebourgh in France, where he joined the French army at the outbreak of the war. He received a medal for outstanding bravery during the war. He joined the Bureau in 1918 and was in line for promotion due to successful operations in the course of his service.'

As the hearing progressed, two of the section heads tended to side with Bècher, after it emerged that Barbier had requested to be exempted from war service in order to look after his ailing mother, which was refused. Another factor was that soon after joining the Bureau he had left, in order to marry and, after a short time, had returned, to re-join the Bureau on a fixed-term contract. Colonel Perroir did not share their stand. He was a very experienced officer who had taken part in a number of tribunals. He trusted his judgement of men more than entries in official forms and had been watching the two adversaries carefully from the start.

Barbier was close on 179 cm (5ft10in) tall, of athletic build, square-faced, with dark-brown hair and brown eyes. Bècher was perhaps 2 cm smaller, had broad shoulders, a square, bony face, dark-blond hair and blue narrow eyes. Both reflected great physical strength and toughness. But Perroir saw more. He saw expressions of poison and hatred widening Bèchers eyes when listening to Barbier's testimony. Barbier's reactions to statements by Bècher ranged from surprise and disapproval to utter disdain but he remained open-eyed and sincere. The interrogation did not last long. Barbier stated that he had become aware that Bècher's report on one operation included incorrect data. Subsequently a number of incidents had raised a suspicion in him that Bècher was not who he claimed to be. He kept an eye on him as far as his own duties permitted this. After observing him at the Café Allaire, talking to a stranger in German, he had felt it his duty to report his suspicions.

Bècher did not deny having a glass of wine at the café and politely exchanging a few words with the man whose table he had joined. He denied that they spoke in German. He counter-claimed that he had seen Barbier several times talking to a blonde woman whilst on duty and correctly suggested that this had not appeared in Barbier's reports. He accused Barbier of acting out of jealousy because Bècher was due for promotion. Barbier's initial surprise turned to anger although his voice remained unperturbed. He responded that he was not, himself, seeking promotion, nor was he jealous of Bècher. He explained that the woman he had met was English. She had left Paris, it was a private matter and he refused to give her personal details but he stressed that there was a difference between his open meeting with an English national and Bècher's secretive encounter with a German. He had the impression that Bècher and the German knew each other.

When the section heads discussed the issue in camera, Perroir reminded the other two that Barbier had given notice to leave which

Chapter 8 – The Lion's Cage

proved that he was not seeking promotion. He agreed that Barbier's name with the same spelling and meaning could be German as well as French but pointed out that Bècher, without the accent, was also a German word, meaning beaker. He argued that, given that with Barbier's army records missing they were unable to draw a fair conclusion. Their recommendation had to be unanimous. They did agree that there was a significant degree of uncertainty, which forced them to agree on only one possible decision: Instant dismissal from active service. This effectively dealt with the security aspect but was not an absolute and final judgment. The two men remained on the reserve list and the case was passed to Colonel Perroir's *Section des Petits Bouts* for further detailed investigation. Perroir had expected no less. But he had not expected what happened subsequently.

It was a Tuesday morning, thirteen days after the hearing. Le Capitaine Marcel Duval, member of the Deuxième Bureau's Political Section was sitting at his desk, taking a coffee break. He looked lovingly at a leaflet with the details of his next musical delight:

Première à l'Olympia.

Fréhel chante comme un moineau   (Fréhel sings like a sparrow)

Où est-il donc? et d'autres chansons populaires   (So where is he? and other popular songs)

Vendredi, 20 Juin 8 p.m. (Friday, 20 June}

28, Blvd. Des Capucines, 9ieme arrondissement

Métro: Madeleine, Opéra.

At this point in his musings, Major Sarbonne, his section head, entered, a tall man with a near-triangular head, and stopped just inside the door.

'Afraid, have to let you go, Duval. Immediate transfer. Report to Colonel Perroir, Bloc 4, Room 5-7, today, fourteen hundred hours.' He drew his silver pocket watch from his outside breast pocket: '11.18. Excellent. You've time to clear your personal things. Leroux will take over. Good luck.'

He left before Duval could utter a word. Sarbonne's brevity of speech was normal, his speed of departure without explanation was

Chapter 8 – The Lion's Cage

not. Duval was not so much surprised, as flabbergasted. He threw one last look at the details of the concert, resentfully suspecting he was going to miss it.

* * *

Room 7 on the 5th floor of Bloc 4, was small. So was Colonel Yves Pascal Perroir. He sported a moustache and long sideburns, both revealing touches of grey, as did the full wavy hair on his head. Seated behind his desk, a red folder to the right in front of him, he was a picture of perpetual relaxation and friendliness. Duval had arrived punctually and stood opposite him. For a few seconds there was silence. Then Perroir spoke.

'Le Capitaine Marcel Duval. It pleases me that you agreed to be transferred to my section.'

Duval was feeling a touch rebellious.

'I was not given the choice, *mon Colonel*.'

'Ah.' Perroir's nod implied that he was not surprised, 'I needed an immediate replacement. Having read your dossier, Captain, I decided you're the best man for this task. However, I shall not use my authority to compel you. If you do not wish to work with me, decide now.'

It was unusual and, for one brief moment, Duval was tempted to take advantage of the offer. He looked at the man before him and met his probing, grey eyes. Was there a touch of anxiety in them? They seemed kind eyes, but they suggested strength and penetration – as if they could read his thoughts. Duval's father who had never said an unkind word to him used to have that effect on him. Perroir's next words went deep.

'Two valuable men have lost their lives due to my error of judgement. One of them, my second-in-command, necessitated quick replacement. Just so that you understand.'

Duval heard himself reply, 'I shall do my best, *mon Colonel*.'

Perroir nodded, picking up a tobacco pipe from his desk.

'Good.' He took a pouch and a document from the folder. 'You need to sign this. It's your transfer.' He smiled. 'You see, I felt certain you'd accept, from what I'd read in your files.'

He began to fill his pipe. Duval signed at the bottom of the sheet whilst staring at the heading: *Departement des Petit Bouts* (Department of Odds and Ends). He had heard of it and its nickname, *la pucelle* (the virgin), a pun on a previous nickname for the department, *Marché de puces* (flea market). Perroir smiled again. He was used to the reaction. Having attached the pipe stem to the bowl of his Meerschaum, he begun to ladle small piles of tobacco into the bowl, pressing them down with a small metal tool. His fingers were doing it automatically. His face was reflecting visibly what his lips were saying.

'Fourteen days ago I was one of three section heads attending a hearing of two agents, Charles Bècher and Georges Vincent Barbier, who accused each other of treasonable behaviour. There was sufficient uncertainty for both of them to be dismissed with immediate effect. Duval nodded.

'I read a reference to it in last week's Quarterly Reports.'

Perroir had finished putting things away in the pouch – including the lighter and said, 'The case was referred to my Department for further investigation. The other matter is the murder of two agents, Remeau and Argentier?'

Duval nodded, unconsciously staring at the metal plate attached to the pipe, displaying the initials GBD between two silver bands. Perroir noticed it.

'The pipe's a Cité de Luxe, one of the original GBD pipes,' he said. 'Ganneval, Bonnier and Donninger. I love this pipe. It helps to keep me calm when I am dealing with a painful subject, Captain, such as this one. Argentier was my second-in-command, a most experienced capable agent. I've been given the task of making further enquiries and of keeping Bècher and Barbier under observation for a maximum of one year. My department is the Deuxième Bureau's smallest. Its official regular strength is four men. That includes myself. I have no fixed agenda. Any job that does not fit under the headings of the other sections, may land on my desk. It does, however, empower me to draft agents from other sections.'

Duval was listening attentively. Perroir continued:

'When the two men were informed of the decision, Barbier showed no emotion. Bècher, however, raised his voice in raucous protest. As they walked out of the door, I heard him hiss: "You'll be sorry, Barbier, I guarantee it." I saw Barbier looking sideways at Bècher with a look of contempt, which left me puzzled. – Yes?'

'N-nothing really, sir, just a thought.'

'Go ahead.'

'It strikes me that Barbier was short of evidence for his suspicions of Bècher.'

'Indeed.' Perroir nodded.

'On the other hand, Colonel, a traitor would have had a well-prepared explanation – like Bècher.'

Perroir nodded slowly.

'Yes. My impression was and still is that Barbier lacks guile. However, my check of police records did not provide a single foreign visitor with the name of Vautant, or similar. As a first step I put both of them under supervision. Argentier found that Bècher was aware of it and succeeded in losing him. However, on the second day, Argentier, after losing him earlier on, found him again. He took a chance and made for the Café Allaire. Bècher was there, openly talking to a German. Argentier was hidden by the wooden lattice work around the café's open air sitting area. His German was not very good and he entered the bits he understood, in French.' Perroir picked up his note pad: '"Man addressed as Vautant – project abandoned – unlucky coincidence – new task – will pay for it." When Argentier reported this, he said he thought Bècher might have seen and recognised him.'

'Bècher knew him?'

'Indeed. That's when I learned that Argentier and Barbier were old friends, they had served in the army together and during the past two years Argentier had occasionally assisted Barbier in tracking Bècher. I was amazed but decided to deal with it after the job was over. We now kept observing three men, Bècher, the German and Barbier. Two days later, Argentier and Remeau, the young agent who had taken turns in following Bècher, were found dead, Remeau in the streets, stabbed from behind and Argentier slumped against his house door, late at night. A poignard was still stuck between his ribs, precise in reaching the heart. The weapon was a Bureau issue.'

Duval suppressed a sound of shock. He knew what was coming next. Perroir saw it in his face.

'You're right, Captain. The next day Bècher had disappeared. I've established that he boarded a Berlin train. The two men observing Barbier confirmed that he had not left his apartment except for lunch and supper at a neighbouring *bistrot*. I had them inform him of Argentier's death. He was cleared as far as my opinion goes. Nevertheless, a day later he, too, left. I had no authority to stop him. My report states that I believe Barbier's

Chapter 8 – The Lion's Cage

accusations against Bècher to be correct and that, in addition, Bècher is guilty of murdering two French agents. I consider it essential to discover for which German organisation Bècher was working when infiltrating the Deuxième Bureau.'

During his last sentences, Perroir, clearly unhappy, had twice stood up, picked up his pipe but not the lighter, and each time put it down again, then sat down again. He continued.

'We've found out that Bècher successfully duped the Bureau for a long time and I, personally, greatly underrated him. A grave mistake, Captain Duval, that has cost the lives of two valuable human beings. I had no warning that we were dealing with someone so dangerous. I still do not know why it has cost two lives. But we shall find out.'

Duval had begun to see the picture, as it was up-to-date. He voiced his thoughts.

'Bècher must have infiltrated the Bureau in the service of some outside body. This Vautant – an odd name for a German – may represent that body. Taking a Berlin train is no proof that Bècher was going to Berlin, or anywhere else in Germany. The obvious conclusion would be that Bècher is working for the German government. But that makes absolutely no sense. A more plausible explanation would be a German political organisation that is hostile to France. The most likely suspect would be the German National Socialist Party. Monsieur Adolf Hitler has recently declared he will abide by the rules of democracy. But he has also declared his aims of abolishing the parliamentary system and of tearing up the Versailles Treaty.'

'You're right, Duval. One of the best reports we have about that party, was written by agent Vincent Barbier almost two years ago. I've a reliable informer inside a tightly organised group of German Nazis residing in Paris.'

Duval nodded. He'd read reports on their activities. Perroir continued:

'He is certain, that this man Vautant has had no contact with the group.'

Perroir looked worriedly at Duval whose forehead wrinkled as he said slowly, 'If it's not the Nazis, can there be an unknown German organisation that exports spies and murderers? A secret criminal organisation?'

They looked at each other silently. It was not a credible conclusion but, at this moment, the only one that made sense.

Duval said, 'But why murder the two agents? Petty revenge?'

'That's my guess. Bècher's threat to Barbier suggests that kind of mindset. Revenge on the Bureau. It may reflect the true nature of the man. That brings me to a vital point. He was heard to say to Vautant: *er wird dafür zahlen*' (he will pay for it). This almost certainly relates to Vincent Barbier. Barbier does not know that he may be dealing with a powerful secret organisation and that a totally ruthless and revengeful man may be out to kill him, also. The overriding issue at present is to discover who is employing Bècher. It has become my major aim and you will understand better now why I requested you, Captain Duval.'

'But my section has been dealing with internal political issues, only.'

Perroir nodded.

'The nearest I could get. But if there is a secret German organisation that works on the level of infiltrating a national security institution like the Bureau then the possibility of links with some of our national political conspirators must be considered. I need you to obtain as much information as is available.'

It made sense. Duval started immediately, setting enquiries in motion. One of the first results was an extract from army security files, which reached him the next day:

'Vincent Georges Barbier, b. Strasbourg 1892, joined French Forces 1914, transferred to Military Intelligence under Maj. Armand de Courcy, *Deuxième Bureau de l'État-major général* (Second Bureau of the General Staff). Served with de Courcy in Munich in the *Bureau de forces d'occupation françaises* (Office of the French Occupation Forces), earned great praise. Barbier left the Deuxième Bureau in 1920 to marry an Englishwoman, Denise Merchant, and moved to England. *Signed:* H.G. April 1922: rejoined the Bureau. February 1924: compassionate leave to England for second child, girl, born 24/2/1924. Verified. H. G. Returned June 1924. Full service refused due to uncertainty about private problems, given five-year contract. *Signed:* H.G.'

Chapter 8 – The Lion's Cage

Duval knocked on Perroir's door and handed him the report. Perroir showed no surprise.

'He told the truth, Duval. Take a pew. I've got some things for you, also.'

He handed Duval a manila envelope, marked COL. PERROIR in hand-written bold capitals on the outside. It contained two sheets of paper, one ordinary white quarto-sized, the other a thin blue sheet of writing paper. Duval looked at the white one, addressed to Perroir, first:

'Paris, 14.VI.29. Colonel Perroir, I am not guilty of any of the accusations. The English woman whom I met is my wife. I have seen the man who met Bècher in Paris, in Nuremberg, where he was paying a lot of money to a Nazi Stormtrooper. The man was employed as chauffeur by a wealthy German aristocrat, a known supporter of Hitler. Bècher has killed my friend. I am off to Germany, to find the chauffeur. Afterwards I intend to deal with Bècher. When that is done I shall re-join my wife and my children – for good this time. Vincent G. Barbier.'

Duval withdrew the blue sheet, old, much handled. It was probably the second and certainly the last page of a private letter written in English, neat, forward leaning letters:

'...to see you again. You gave me hope that you will come back. You have two daughters who need you. I need you, Vincent. I have told you the whole truth. I have been suffering so long already for that one lapse, that one moment of weakness. All your other suspicions were wrong, my darling. You said you will come back.

Please come soon, Vincent.

Denise.'

Duval was touched.

'He sent you this, Colonel?'

He returned the letters.

Chapter 8 – The Lion's Cage

'No. The white envelope was found in his flat after Barbier's departure from Paris. It's been resting in someone's tray for days. Barbier could rely on my receiving what he left behind for me. The blue sheet was probably found in the flat by the searchers and put into the envelope. If only I knew where in Germany. It would make it easier to identify the Nazi aristocrat.'

The next morning brought more information in a formal envelope, sent by the Deuxième Bureau records files. Duval withdrew the two yellow report sheets. The first one was an army document, signed by Barbier's CO in the field: 'Sergeant Vincent Barbier, a tall and immensely strong man, is the coolest man in danger I have ever known. He displays no fear whatsoever. I am recommending him for a commission.' The second was of a later date, a Bureau report: 'At the end of the war, Barbier spent half a year in Munich, attached to Major De Courcy, who dealt with sensitive occupation matters. In September, '28, the Deuxième Bureau sent Barbier and Bècher to Germany to observe and assess the progress of the National Socialist Party. For obvious reasons Barbier was to go to Munich and Bècher to Nuremberg. At Bècher's request they were changed round and Barbier worked with a British agent on that occasion.'

Perroir also read both documents.

'That must have been the occasion when Barbier came across the German chauffeur. Any idea at all why Bècher would want to be sent to Munich?'

'No, Colonel, except – the Nazi H.Q. is there and Herr Hitler is still there. But he was not on that date. In '28, on the 14 September, Herr Hitler was also in Nuremberg, attending a special rally. I saw a report about it the other day when scanning a list of Nazi rallies.'

'A great opportunity to find out more about the German Nazis, wouldn't you say, Duval?'

'Perhaps he preferred working with the Brit?'

'Hotel Frankenhof, regular for our agents, which should make your search easier, Captain. The owner works with us.'

The information surprised Duval but he picked up on the clue.

'Perhaps history has repeated itself and Bècher is in Munich. There's one thing I mean to do right away.'

Perroir looked at him, his expression a question mark.

'I am going to have the accent removed from Bècher's name.'

Chapter 8 – The Lion's Cage

Perroir nodded, the trace of a smile on his lips. Then he turned serious.

'I've initiated the process of a legal warrant, Duval, for the arrest of Herr Karl Becher to be tried for treason and murder.'

Duval nodded.

'What exactly is Barbier's status at present, Colonel? Is he being re-instated?'

'As he has given notice of leaving that would be an unnecessary piece of *bureaucratie*. In his case it is irrelevant because his contract officially was that of a *reserviste*. He retains this status even when he has officially left. But I have taken steps to quash the tribunal's judgement. Meanwhile, Barbier is out there, doing what amounts to a job for us. He should have the Bureau's resources at his disposal, captain. We must try to find out where he is and offer him the Bureau's full support.'

Duval got up to leave.

'That's a task I shall pursue with all the means available, Colonel. I've promised it myself – and someone else.'

As he reached the door he quite suddenly was struck by an idea.

'Colonel, the Germans go a lot for their ancient gods and heroes. Vautant means nothing to me in French, but could it be Wotan, the Germanic head of the gods, I wonder?'

Perroir gave it some thought.

'Vautant? Wotan? I suppose it could. Worth bearing in mind.'

Duval had opened the door, when Perroir's voice made him turn around.

'To whom else have you made your promise, captain?'

Duval hesitated for a moment, then replied, 'To Madame Denise Barbier, although she didn't hear it, Colonel Perroir.'

He left hastily. The reply slipped through as the door closed.

'That's what I thought, Duval, upon my soul, that's what I thought. What are sentimental men like us doing in the Deuxième Bureau?'

* * *

Vincent Barbier had left Paris without a detailed plan of action and with very few facts to assist him. In September 1928 he had watched the chauffeur of Count Winter in a bar in Nuremberg, handing a sum of money to a Nazi Stormtrooper – surely in payment for something

Chapter 8 – The Lion's Cage

unsavoury. In Paris he had seen the same man in a café, talking with an agent of the Deuxième Bureau. The image placed Becher neatly into the role of the Nazi Stormtrooper, even without a payment being handed over. Barbier's intense loyalty to France made finding out for whom the chauffeur was working a first priority. The killing of his friend Argentier made it personal. Ahead, like a fair maiden's promised hand to her knight in shining armour, lay the reunion with his wife and his children.

Arrived in Nuremberg, he had taken a room at the Frankenhof, the same small hotel as on the previous occasion. Bureau agents had been reassured by their bosses that its owner and staff would never give information about their guests to anyone except the police. They did not, however, know that the manager of the Frankenhof had direct communication links with Paris. Like the last time Barbier registered his name as Georg Barbier, his profession as 'buyer of toys' and his place of residence as Koblenz, a German town he knew well from the occupation period. His first line of research was to locate the chauffeur car hire firm which had transported the Nazi speakers from the rally to Count Winter's castle.

It turned out to be a fruitful start, because there was really only one firm in Nuremberg which was large enough to qualify. He went there on several mornings, lingering around the cars, an admirer of them. Success came after only a few days when, claiming to have worked in the past as a chauffeur, himself, he got into conversation with one of the drivers, a little older than he, himself. He ended up inviting him for lunch, where they became chummy and agreed on lunching together the next day. On that occasion, between the soup and the main dish, they progressed to first names and to meeting again the following day. Konrad Leibl, a bachelor, aiming to impress his new friend, spoke freely about one of his most interesting jobs.

'There aren't many men in this town, Georg, who've been inside the grounds of Castle Wintereschen, I tell you. I've been there five times already.'

'Really?'

'Yes. Each, after a National Socialist party rally in town. I'm senior and always included. Among my passengers were Dr. Goebbels and Herr Röhm, what do you say to that, Georg?'

'You mean Herr Hitler's gang? You certainly meet interesting people in your job, Konrad. All I ever meet is boring toy

Chapter 8 – The Lion's Cage

manufacturers and traders. Did you take them back to their hotels? What kind of hotels do men like that use, I wonder?'

'None, because they always stay at Count Winter's castle overnight. I take them as far as the Great Hall inside the castle grounds. There's always a reception laid on for them. You can hear the music – one of those new gramophones. They've other guests there on those evenings, Georg, posh looking ladies with long faces, wearing long dresses with bare arms and bare shoulders and long décolletés. I know that, you see, because one night I carried some of my passengers' cases in. I've never seen such luxury before, I tell you, everything glittering in there, Georg. Tall mirrors and paintings with gold frames on the walls between the windows. The attendant, who was supposed to pick the cases up from my car, came running, just as I entered the hall. He was dead worried he might get punished. I reassured him that nobody'd seen me. I'd not gone further than the doorway. But we had an interesting little chat.'

'The owner of the castle must be wealthy,' Barbier said, 'but I've heard that Herr Hitler never goes anywhere without his personal guards. Do they also guard him during the reception?'

'Every single one of the twelve Stormtroopers. We take them to the next block, four in a car, you see. Mind you, they've got to carry their cases, themselves. You're right about the Count, Count Winter. They say, he's one of the richest men in Germany. Some even say in Europe. Aristocracy. More money than they know what to do with. I, too, asked about the guards and do you know what he told me, Georg?'

'No. What?'

'Herr Hitler never attends the reception. He always goes straight to his suite on the first floor where he has his dinner served. He's fussy about what he eats. I tell you. Only vegetarian stuff, apparently.'

'That's astonishing. Doesn't it offend Count Winter?'

'Now this will definitely surprise you, Georg, but the Count's never present either.'

Barbier knew the answer to this next question already. His reply nevertheless sounded hugely amazed.

'What? The host?'

'Yes. And that's not all, Georg. The Count's never seen by anybody, not even his own staff, I've been told. Something to do with a facial deformity, they say. What do you think of that?'

Chapter 8 – The Lion's Cage

'It's like something out of a scare novel. You know all this from the attendant, Konrad?'

'Ah, well, no. That bit I was told in strict confidence. But I can't see why I shouldn't tell you, Georg. You're going back to Koblenz in a few days, so there's no harm.'

'I find these things fascinating. Anything you tell me won't go further, I can promise you.'

'I'm sure, Georg. You see, from time to time I meet with an old mate, Alarich, a school friend. He's on his own, a widower like me. But his sister is married to a policeman and they've got two sons. A few years ago the older one got a job as a guard at the castle. But he didn't like it, Georg. It was too much like an army, he said. The contract he had to sign, included a statement that he would not tell anything about the Count and the castle to anybody. And when he left they warned him, he'd get into trouble if he didn't adhere to this part in the contract. He kept it, of course, and only told his parents. And his mother only told her brother in confidence and here am I only telling you in confidence.'

Barbier laughed.

'It sounds almost as if there were secret goings-on at the castle.'

'All the same,' Leibl said, 'the boy's parents would have preferred him to stick to the job.'

'Why's that?'

'The Count may demand a lot from his employees but he pays them real well, you see. When any of them are in difficulties, they receive help and support from him. And their families do. Single men get rooms in the castle's housing blocks. I've heard it said that there are folk living in the castle that have never set foot outside its walls. I can't really believe that. The married ones live in the village. And that's not all. The staff get good pensions when they retire. You can imagine he's got a loyal staff.'

'He sounds a good man, Konrad.'

'That's his reputation in the village, Georg, and beyond. He's paid for a lot of things for the community over the years. But he's also very powerful, so no one's likely ever to cross him.'

'One thing puzzles me. If the Count's not there to receive Herr Hitler's coterie, then who looks after them when they arrive and at this posh musical reception?'

'Oh, that's Kiele, Herr Manfred Kiele, the Count's chauffeur, you see. Well, he's not just his chauffeur, Georg. Alarich's told me the

Chapter 8 – The Lion's Cage

chauffeur's the Count's right-hand, his personal secretary and passes all the orders to the staff.'

'The chauffeur? Doesn't he have to transport some of the guests?'

'That he does not, Georg. I've seen Kiele, myself, every time we were on one of those jobs. He arrives at wherever the meeting takes place, just before it's over and supervises the transport arrangements. He checks our limousines. Checks? He inspects us like an officer inspects his troops. Next, he gives final instructions at the SA officer who's in charge. He, himself, always leaves before we do and by the time we arrive at the castle with the guests he's already there, dressed posh, doing the honours. As a matter of fact, Georg, I've never seen anyone ever carried in his car.'

Barbier did not mention that he had seen both, chauffeur and car.

'Really. A posh car, I bet, Konrad.'

'I'd say. A Grosser Mercedes! He could carry six people in it. But I don't blame him. The amount of cleaning I've to do after carrying passengers. People aren't careful, I tell you, Georg.'

'Still, such a big car and always empty?'

'Only of other people, Georg. Whenever I've seen it, the rear passenger seats were full of blankets. He must be carrying his lord and master sometimes; don't you think?'

Barbier laughed.

'Perhaps Herr Kiele sleeps in his car.'

Leibl's tone changed to serious, 'If he did he would still be better off than some folk who live rough in Nuremberg, Georg.'

Barbier was surprised. This was the only conversation in which they talked about the count and the castle at such length, although they continued to meet daily that week. At the end of that first week, Barbier felt frustrated. He had only added the slightest grain to his knowledge of the count and his driver. Finding out why Bècher had infiltrated the Deuxième Bureau was as remote from his knowledge as Einstein's theory of general relativity. Was Bècher employed by the chauffeur, Manfred Kiele, or his boss, Count Winter? Barbier tended to believe that Kiele was merely executing Count Winter's orders. Surely, only Winter had the wealth, the capacity and the power, that could undertake as huge and ambitious a project as that of planting a spy in the powerful Deuxième Bureau. But why? Barbier was determined to find out and Kiele was the stepping stone to the man at the top. Even if Barbier had known that in Paris his name had been cleared already it would not have stopped him from

Chapter 8 – The Lion's Cage

pursuing his quest. He came to the conclusion that his daily meetings with the talkative Leibl were not likely to be fruitful but that it was wise to maintain the relationship and the routine as a useful cover. But what would get him any further? As it happened, on Saturday Leibl told him that he had a Sunday job and was not able to meet him. It turned out to change the situation.

'If you want to enjoy a real *Nürnberger'* (Nuremberg) 'treat, Georg, I suggest the *Alte Küche* (Old Kitchen) in the Old Town. I'd planned to take you there, but Sunday jobs often go to those of us without family.'

Barbier not only followed Leibl's suggestion but expanded on it. He went for a stroll into the Old Town on Sunday morning. Mid-morning found him standing on the Fleischbrücke (Meat Bridge), a bridge with a roof-like structure above the arch. He was looking pensively down to the waters of the Pregnitz, the river running through the Old Town, when a male voice behind him commanded his attention.

'Ladies and gentlemen, some of you may notice the similarity of this bridge to that of the Rialto in Venice. Is it a coincidence? The city of Nuremberg has always had strong trading connections with Venice and some people believe that the design of our bridge was copied from the famous Rialto Bridge.'

Barbier turned around to see a small crowd assembled around the speaker who continued. 'Others argue that there are differences which make that unlikely. If you happen to have visited Venice, I leave it to you to decide. Ladies and gentlemen, this ends the tour for those of you who have only booked The Old Town, Part One. Part Two, the Castle Tour, starts at eleven, that is in exactly eight minutes. Tickets are still available from that little booth at the end of the bridge, over there.' He pointed to over there.

Castle Tour! The Town Castle, yes! The thought association revived an idea that had already made several brief forays into Barbier's mind. The problem was its total impracticability. Almost automatically he went and acquired a ticket. The tour started punctually and with it, the guide's well-rehearsed explanations: 'The castle was built in 1495... dominates the north-western corner of the Old Town... In the west it starts with the Luginsland Tower...'

Barbier was listening with one ear only and that one only on and off. His mind kept returning to its demand for action, without providing a single idea of making it feasible. Thus the sightseeing

Chapter 8 – The Lion's Cage

per se was not a total success. He only saw with his eyes and even so missed quite a bit. Luckily the mid-day meal made up for it. The *Alte Küche* was the genuine thing, an old cookhouse. Barbier sat at one of the few tables for single guests, in a large niche on one side of the massive chimney breast. He was enjoying the baked sausages, a speciality of the house. The large table inhabiting the rest of the niche was gradually filling with couples who seemed to be regulars. They gave the impression that they considered their conversation of absorbing interest to other guests. Barbier, as a matter of professional routine, submitted them to a brief scrutiny. One of the three women reminded him a little of an old friend. He was studying her features, when his attention was deflected to her partner, probably her husband. Addressing the man opposite him, the only one amongst them who wore a tie, he said, mockingly:

'*Mein so hoch geehrter*' (my so highly honoured) 'Achim Franck. I thought that after your promotion you'd be sure to be dining at Castle Wintereschen with His Grace, the Count.'

Disregarding a few giggles, Achim replied, 'It's not really a promotion, Lukas. I've just had another task added to my duties. You're your own boss, Lukas, I'm not.'

'But it is interesting, Achim,' Lukas's wife joined in, 'What exactly does the *Brandtstein Agentur*' (Brandtstein Agency) 'do? You've never told us.'

'We're the Count's estate agents, Lori. We deal with all matters relating to his estate: finance, maintenance of premises and woodland, taxes, complaints, non-personal correspondence. It's a massive job and the boss has now asked me to take over visits by individuals or groups. A lot of extra work, Lori, that's all.'

'Groups? Achim, do you mean these noisy National Socialists?' another man threw in.

'There are all sorts of groups, some even from schools. But you're right, Hugo, the National Socialists are included. They arrive from Munich and when they have one of their big meetings, they stay overnight at the castle. My job's only external administrative work, Hugo, thank God. I've nothing to do with things at the castle and to be honest, I'm glad about that.'

'They've had their annual rally in March, Achim, haven't they?' one of the wives asked. 'I found it a bit upsetting, I can tell you.'

'Yes, they did.'

'So you'll not have any of that extra work this year.'

Chapter 8 – The Lion's Cage

'I'm afraid, you're wrong, Heidi. They're having a day conference at the Luitpold Hall on Thursday and afterwards, as after rallies, will spend the night at Wintereschen. I've already booked their transport to the castle in the evening and to the station in the morning.'

'Friends,' Lukas broke in. 'I apologise for having offended against our rules, no talking shop or politics. I didn't mean to and I'll pay for one round. Lore has much more interesting news for the Alphabet Klub. She's found a couple with Q.'

The statement was welcomed by cheers and the conversation developed into a lively hubbub. Barbier was electrified by what he had heard. His stubborn determination and his patience had received a first little reward. The conference on Thursday would surely bring the chauffeur to town even if, according to Leibl, only briefly. By the time he fell asleep that night he had decided in principle on the action to take. But he needed more information and he would have to take a risk with Leibl. At lunch on Monday Leibl asked him.

'Did you go to the Alte Küchen yesterday, Georg?'

'I did. You were right. Good food, good service and atmosphere. I was sorry you weren't there, also.'

'Yes, I'm sorry, too, but, Georg, I had an uplifting day. I took a couple from Starnberg to Fürth, a Herr and Frau Schönfeld. Their son, Isidor, was playing the first violin in the town's symphony orchestra. Bruno Walter was conducting Beethoven's Sixth. I hadn't known. I've got to explain that Beethoven's my favourite composer, not original, I know. But the Andante near the beginning and the Shepherd's song at the end… You didn't know I was a sentimental old codger.'

'I didn't know you were so musical. A pity…'

'You haven't heard the rest, Georg. I told them of this passion of mine and, would you believe, when we got to Fürth they invited me not only to lunch with them but also got me a ticket for the concert. You see, Bruno Walter's now already one of the great conductors. I'd never have thought I'd be present at one of his concerts. And they said I must come and have dinner with them at Starnberg some time. It was a great day, Georg, a great day.'

'You hadn't known about the concert?'

'No, Georg. You see, it wasn't advertised here in Nuremberg. And do you know why?'

'Not the faintest.'

Chapter 8 – The Lion's Cage

'It's because of these men you call interesting people, Georg. Bruno Walter is a Jew and they're prejudiced against Jews, you see. Herr Hitler has mentioned Bruno Walter several times in speeches in very unpleasant terms. He knows nothing about good music, about any music, that man. So they don't advertise Bruno Walter here in Nuremberg, nor in Munich.' He was getting agitated. 'When I was fourteen, Georg, we lived in Munich and Bruno Walter was the Royal Bavarian music director there. A couple of friends and I, we did not miss a single concert of his, even throughout the war. We were students at the LMU then, you see, and always short of cash. Do you know, Georg, that one of Bruno Walter's friends was Cardinal Pacelli who as you know became Pope later. He was good enough for the Cardinal but not for Herr Hitler.'

He stopped quite suddenly, worried he had said too much. Barbier's astonishment was considerable.

'You went to university, Konrad? How did you end up as a chauffeur?'

Somewhat reassured by this question, Leibl shrugged his shoulders.

'Being a student had kept me out of the Emperor's war. But my father was called up and by the time the war ended, my parents were out of money. It happened to quite a few of us. One of my friends lived here in Nuremberg and his father started this taxi undertaking after the war and gave me a job. That's how I came here. His son now runs the firm. You've got my life story now, Georg. But I feel we're friends, aren't we?'

Leibl did not realise how pleased Barbier was, but if he expected Barbier to tell him all about himself now, he was disappointed.

'We are, Konrad. By the way, have you any idea what the Alphabet Klub is?'

Leibl was puzzled at this sudden change of subject.

'Alphabet Klub? Yes, I have, but – ah, the Alte Küche! They always eat there on Sundays. You heard of them there, no?'

'All the time, Konrad, loud and clearly. I sat next to them.'

Leibl laughed.

'A quaint idea. Members are married couples, one per letter of the alphabet, that's referring to the initial of their surnames. Quirky isn't it. It was started by Lukas and Lore Gessler.'

Chapter 8 – The Lion's Cage

'Yes, one of them was called Lukas and his wife Lori. You would have been interested in their conversation. One of them has just come to be in charge of visits to Castle Wintereschen.'

Leibl was not overly interested.

'I suppose he works in the castle's estate office.'

'You've hit it on the nail, Konrad. I heard him say that Herr Hitler and his lot are having a day conference at the Luitpold Halle this Thursday and he has already informed your firm. Haven't you been told?'

That increased Leibl's interest by a smidgen or two.

'I had the morning off and slept in.'

* * *

By the time Barbier went to bed that day he had worked out a rough plan for his action. The Thursday Nazi conference was his best chance of getting into the castle grounds. His first idea had been to get in somehow with Leibl's help but, successful or not, this might have got Leibl into trouble. There was only one way; the Mercedes of the Count's chauffeur. It required a large portion of luck, he knew that. But then everything did. If he succeeded in getting into the castle grounds, he might be able to find an explanation for Kiele's meeting with Bècher in Paris and whether the mysterious Count Winter or of one of the Nazi leaders, perhaps even Hitler, himself, was involved. Success was more than doubtful but doing nothing was not an alternative. At least, he now felt certain that Leibl was not a supporter of Hitler and he began his direct enquiries on Tuesday.

'You know, Konrad, I found what you told me about this man Kiele most intriguing.'

Leibl was astonished.

'In what way?'

'According to you, Herr Kiele, wearing a chauffeur's hat, will turn up at the Luitpold Hall on Thursday at some random time. He'll park his car somewhere and inspect your limousines wherever they happen to be parked. Then he returns to his Mercedes and drives back to the castle where he gets ready to welcome his visitors. It sounds a bit haphazard to me.'

Leibl shook his head.

Chapter 8 – The Lion's Cage

'It may sound so to you, Georg, but, you see, these people are good organisers, every detail is carefully planned and executed. Take this Thursday. It's an afternoon conference, set to end at 2100 hours and, believe me, it will end at 2100 hours. Our cars will be lined up on the road beside the hall by 2000 hours. At 20.15 hours prompt, Herr Kiele will arrive and park his car to the left of the water tower. He'll walk to where we're parked and stride along our row of cars, like a general inspecting his troops, checking that they are clean and in good order. Each of us will stand beside his car. Our front driver will receive a pass from him, without which we won't be admitted into the castle grounds. Next, Kiele gives the SA officer outside the Luitpold Hall his final instructions. These SA behave as if they were real soldiers. Kiele returns to his car and drives off, straight back to the castle, I assume, because, you see, I know he'll be there in the Great Hall when we arrive – unless he has a twin. I wouldn't put that beyond them either. The moment we stop outside the hall, attendants come rushing to the cars, pick up the guests' cases and take them inside. Next we transport the SA men to their quarters. As soon as that's done we drive back to Nuremberg where we keep the cars overnight. In the morning we drive to the castle and pick up our passengers at nine-thirty. We take them to the Neumarkt main station, a drive of thirteen-and-a-half minutes. When we arrive there, you can guess, Herr Kiele will be awaiting us and, after ensuring that everything is in order, will pay his bill to our front driver and leave. Now, you tell me what's haphazard in that, Georg. I always think that that's how it must have been in the army.'

Barbier could hear an element of suspicion in Leibl's voice. No matter. It amounted to as good a briefing as Barbier could have expected. He was even mentally allowing for the remote possibility that Leibl was one of them. He spent the next day on a careful reconnaissance. The village of Wintereschen was larger than he expected. A small, pretty lake and a number of small boarding houses and a few tennis courts made it quite popular as a minor holiday resort. The castle was separated from the village by a belt of woodland. Joining the folk promenading on the path around the castle moat, he studied every inch of the way. There were several spots where the wall might allow climbing over but crossing the wide moat, filled with mud and sludge, was a non-starter. Only the bridges to the three castle gates offered any possibility of entering or leaving.

Chapter 8 – The Lion's Cage

Of those, two bridges were large enough for vehicles to pass through and into the castle grounds, which were guarded by armed sentries, whose guardhouses could be seen just inside each gate. Observing each of the two gates at length hidden in the little crowds of gapers, Barbier noticed two men with a dog each, arrive and leave. The interval between each was exactly fifteen minutes. On his stroll along the outside of the wall he heard the dogs barking. They were obviously patrolling on the inside of the walls. Only the third entrance, connecting with a footbridge over the moat, offered a small chance for breaking through, not so much for getting in as, perhaps, for getting out. There was sparse traffic of men only through it and he observed that, leaving or entering, they showed a pass to a guard in front of a military type sentry box. Barbier reckoned that rushing this gate from the inside was a possibility.

On Thursday at the end of their lunch together, Barbier said, 'I hope your evening job will go smoothly, Konrad. *Auf Wiedersehn* tomorrow.'

Leibl's reply surprised him.

'I look forward to it, Georg, but perhaps this is the moment to say something that's been on my mind for some days. Frankly, I find it hard to believe you're a toy dealer. I don't know what a toy dealer looks like, but you don't look like one and you don't talk like one. And I can't help thinking that your interest in the Count's chauffeur and the castle is a bit more than just theoretical, Georg. Whatever it is, you have my blessing and well, yes, *auf Wiedersehn* tomorrow.'

Leibl walked away and Barbier made no attempt to reply. He now felt certain that Leibl was on his side.

Wearing a dark pullover, he arrived at the Luitpold Grove in good time. He settled on the only bench in the square, located a couple of metres from the water tower. There were few people about at this time. A couple of gas-lit lanterns, plus the moon and the stars, provided sufficient lighting for him to read the local daily paper, the *Münchner Neueste Nachrichten*, (*Munich Latest News*). He had never before read a newspaper so thoroughly and was imbibing news items he had never known before: 'the 60% car traffic increase between Mannheim & Heidelberg' – 'Herr Usinger urging the building of an Autobahn' – 'Josy Meidlinger's silhouettes for a wall projection of *Der Totentanz* (dance of the dead)' – 'the 80th birthday of Frau Irmgard Köhler-Hederlingwiesche' – the first colour television demonstrated in Berlin' – 'the *Galoppenwechsler* (speed

Chapter 8 – The Lion's Cage

changers)' – the latest gadgets with pipes holding different coins to be used by tram conductors' and '*Zwei Herzen im Dreivierteltakt,* (Two Hearts in Waltz Time), music by Robert Stolz, a sound film shown in Berlin' – until at last the time was close on eight o'clock. He looked around. There was nobody about.

Leaving the newspaper on the bench, he cautiously moved to the gap between bench and water tower and, in one quick movement, disappeared into the bushes. Leaning against the trunk of a tree, he waited. Much now depended on how correct Leibl's information had been. At 8.15 precisely, Herr Manfred Kiele, Count Winter's chauffeur, parked his Grosser Mercedes alongside the bushes close to the water tower. As if intending to assist Barbier, the door to the back seats of the car was opposite the gap in the bushes. Kiele, wearing his chauffeur's hat, got out of the car and made his way to the conference hall. As soon as he had disappeared, Barbier, bent low, emerged from his hiding. He carefully opened the door to the car's rear compartment. Exactly, as Leibl had described, there was a large stack of blankets on the floor. Barbier slipped inside and, closing the door, worked himself beneath the blankets. His size made it difficult to fit into the space.

After what seemed a very long time he heard Kiele arrive and utter a mild curse, perhaps because he had not locked the doors. Kiele settled in the driver's seat, switched on the engine. It started immediately and the car took off. To describe Barbier's situation as not very comfortable would be an understatement. Breathing was unpleasant, he was lying in a cramped position and the road was bumpy. However, there were two factors acting in Barbier's favour. One was Kiele's total conviction that no one would ever dare to tamper with his car. The other was that any attempt to enter the castle without permission had not the slightest chance of succeeding. There had been three known attempts by individuals, who had attempted to swim across the moat. None had returned from his venture. Police and local people had taken it for granted that they had perished in the moat.

After a journey of thirty-five minutes the car reached the castle gates where Kiele handed the details of the expected visitors to the guard. He then drove on the two-kilometre-long drive through the woodland to reach the castle buildings, and through a ten-metre-long archway into the inner yard, a square formed by blocks of housing. A half-dozen electrically-powered street lamps lit up the yard

Chapter 8 – The Lion's Cage

brightly. Kiele stopped the car in front of the one-storey building that contained his living quarters. The small, stocky man on duty in the tiny guardroom adjacent to the large main door emerged promptly in response to Kiele's call:

'Garage, guard!'

The guard activated the mechanism of the steel garage door, which simultaneously switched on the electric lighting inside. The door was sliding upwards with a stuttering rattle, sounding in Barbier's muffled ears like distant machine-gun fire. Kiele drove straight into the garage. Behind him the steel door rattled back into its locked position. Switching off the light, Kiele left the garage by a small, blue door of the garage. He stepped into the high-ceilinged passage that led from the front door on the right straight to the rear of the house, where the flats of the permanent house staff, guards and domestics, were situated. Kiele did not walk that far. About five metres down the passage, he opened a heavy, Gothic-style oak door on the right, to take the stairs to a square-shaped stone landing at the top which contained just one door, similar to the one at the bottom of the stairs. He opened it, thus automatically signalling his arrival to the caretaker and strode through a corridor past the caretaker's flat on the right. At its end on the left, was a third Gothic door that led to his living quarters. Kiele entered and locked it behind him. At one hour before midnight, the caretaker, Joseph Zinkel, would lock the other two doors, turning the upstairs area into a near impregnable fortress.

After hearing Kiele leave the car, Barbier forced himself to remain in his cramped condition for a long five minutes. Then he carefully worked himself out from the blankets. The top of the steel door contained three small rectangular windows through which a little light filtered through. He saw the little blue door and opened it carefully. The passage outside the door was brightly lit. He consulted his watch and calculated that the guests were due to arrive in another twenty to twenty-five minutes. His first objective was to find and search Kiele's rooms during his absence, in the hope of finding papers, letters or anything that would give him information about the man's activities. The problem was to find out where Kiele's rooms were. His second objective, was to find Kiele's boss, Count Winter. He heard footsteps coming from the left, the inside of the house, and closed the door soundlessly. The only weapon he carried in a sheath hanging from his belt was a hunting knife. In the

Chapter 8 – The Lion's Cage

security forces during the war, he had learned how to use a dagger effectively. The hunting knife was not quite as long as a dagger but it would do. The footsteps passed and stopped at the front door. A moment later he heard voices. He opened the door just wide enough to see two men standing in the doorway. The one with his back to him was saying, 'I'm taking over now, Raab. I've swapped with Ossi. He'll do eleven-fifteen.'

Raab was not amused.

'Listen, Schulze, I don't care, if the emperor of China takes over from you, but you're late taking over from me.'

'OK, Raab, I said, I'm sorry. You know I'm new here. It's only a few minutes. Ossi only just asked me to swap. You won't tell, will you? I'll make it up next time, Raab. Anything in the book?'

'Only Kiele. He arrived at 20.54 hours.'

'I heard him go up the stairs. He seemed in a hurry. Is he likely to go out again, do you think?'

'He's going to be busy with his NSDAP friends. They're due at the Great Hall in ten minutes, I guess. That needn't bother you, Schulze. Kiele always goes there direct from his rooms. He's got his own Bridge of Sighs going across to that block.'

'That means the lot that stays overnight?'

'Exactly, but luckily in a different block. Personally I don't like that lot. They think they're the lords of the universe. By the way, the Luger in the drawer is loaded. Me, I'm having an early night.'

Barbier closed the door silently. He'd give it another ten minutes before embarking on his venture. At least he knew now where to aim for.

* * *

Upstairs, Joseph and Maria Zinkel, caretaker and wife, were having a conversation, one Maria had started. Hearing Kiele's arrival gave Joseph an excuse to leave. He did not return until half an hour later.

'I've got tomorrow's orders, Maria. He's about to go across to the Hall now and won't need us anymore tonight. Our Rummy now? How about a hundred points tonight? I'll get the cards.'

'You're not getting out of it again, Joseph. Cards are our only entertainment, Joseph. I'd like a change, sometimes, like taking a stroll through the village. Not much to ask for, is it?'

'Sounds that way. What's the point in talking about it?'

Chapter 8 – The Lion's Cage

'I don't see why we're not able to leave the castle like the others, Joseph, at least once in a while.'

'You know quite well that that's what we agreed in our contract, Maria.'

'I never did, Josef. You agreed to it.'

'That's normal, isn't it? I'm your husband and it's husbands who make the decisions, that's for sure. You didn't complain about it then, Maria.'

'But why did you agree to such a thing, Joseph? Don't you ever want to go out to other places?'

'I owe my life to Kiele. Twice during the war, Maria. I was only a corporal. And when I got the French bullet in my leg he took me on as his batman. He—'

'I've heard this often enough. But why agree to not leaving the castle grounds? Does the count know, Joseph?'

'Of course. After the war, with all this unemployment in Germany – I've got the highest-paid job here, Maria. He has enemies and the only way he thinks he can be safe, if I've no contact with people on the outside. There were no jobs for love or money and—'

'Stop it, Joseph. I've heard that, too, too many times.'

'Then shut up, woman. You'll never get an answer if you keep interrupting me, that's for sure. I would have been stupid not to accept it.'

'You should've never agreed to never leaving the grounds.'

'That was the offer. Take it or leave it. Just think about it, woman. We can retire when I'm fifty and we'll get our own little house wherever we want to live in Germany. Not one other staff has such a deal.'

'Are you sure, Joseph? Why did he pick you?'

'He trusts me and I assured him, Maria, that he could rely on you also. Do you realise—'

Out of the blue the thin sound of the warning bell sounded. Someone had entered the corridor. Joseph shot up, concerned and rushed to the door, saying, 'It must be something serious for a staff to come upstairs without—'

As he stepped out into the corridor, Barbier was approaching. Zinkel had never seen the man before and barred his way.

'Who're you? What are you doing here? You're not permitted to come up here!'

Chapter 8 – The Lion's Cage

Barbier, recalled the conversation he had overheard downstairs.

'I'm new. I must see Herr Kiele.'

'You can't. Even if I let you pass. He's not in and his door is locked. You must have been informed that you're not allowed to use these stairs. You're in serious trouble, man, that's for sure.' He looked him over. 'You're not domestic and you've no security badge. But you've been admitted by the guards – you best come into my office and let me take your details. Follow me.'

He turned towards his door. Barbier, in a fast move, curled his left hand around Zinkel's head from behind, clasping jaw and lips. At the same time, the hunting knife in his right hand was touching Zinkel's throat. Barbier, younger, taller and fitter, was standing so close to Zinkel that the latter's arms were no danger to him. Zinkel did not try to use them. Barbier pushed him forward to the door and whispered into his ear:

'Open it.'

Zinkel did as he was told. They stepped inside and were confronted by Maria who had just reached the door, to see what was going on. For a brief moment she stood paralysed, then she opened her mouth to scream. There was nobody close enough to hear her but Barbier did not know that. He pushed Zinkel out of the way and, gripping Maria's jaw before her scream had escaped, stepped behind her and held his knife against her throat.

'A fair exchange, I think,' he said calmly. 'I've no intention to hurt either of you but if I'm forced to I shall. Is that understood?'

Maria did not dare to move her head. Zinkel, whose lips were bleeding from falling against the chair, nodded calmly.

'What do you want, man?' he asked. 'There's nothing worth stealing here. The door to Herr Kiele's rooms is locked securely and downstairs are the flats of our security men. They're armed. You haven't a chance.'

Barbier pushed his knife a little harder against Maria's skin, which caused a cry to escape from her lips, and a trickle of blood from her skin.

'I've my own ways of getting in and out. Your name?'

'Zinkel, Joseph Zinkel.'

'Right, Herr Zinkel. Sit down. I'm afraid the lady must remain standing. All I want is for you to answer a few questions. If I'm satisfied you've told me the truth, I shall leave without harming either of you.'

Chapter 8 – The Lion's Cage

Zinkel sat down.

'Go ahead.'

'I know where Kiele is. I want to know where the Count's quarters are, Zinkel.'

Barbier could not fail to see the strange expression appearing in Zinkel's glance at his wife, a mix of question, uncertainty and definitely fear. He also saw her response in her eyes and silent movement of lips, begging her husband to tell. But Zinkel's face had set. He was not going to answer. Barbier saw that, too, in his eyes. He increased his pressure and his knife was again nicking Maria's skin. She tried in vain to cry out and when Joseph saw her terror-filled eyes and blood running down her throat, his determination began to wilt.

'The Count also lives on this floor.'

Barbier's features did not betray his surprise.

'He does? In that case you have to tell me now how I can get to see him. And don't try to tell me there's no way. You're his caretaker so you can telephone him?'

Zinkel shook his head.

'I cannot, Mister. Even if I could, it would be of no use. He's not in and, as I've already told you, the door is solidly locked.'

For one moment, Barbier was puzzled. Zinkel seemed to be telling the truth but his answer did not fit in with what Barbier had heard about the Count. He gripped Maria's jaw harder, staring at Zinkel. Again he detected an expression of fear in the man's face. The door is solidly locked. Suddenly, from nowhere, the truth jumped into Barbier's mind. It seemed unbelievable, but nothing else fitted the facts. He gripped Maria's throat harder, causing her fear-filled eyes to screw up.

'Zinkel, my patience is wearing very thin. You've not told me the truth, at least not the whole truth. Time's running out.'

'I assure you, Mister, I've not told you a single lie.'

Barbier nodded grimly, slowly.

'I'll see. Think hard before you answer my next question, Zinkel. As soon as I've heard it, I'll leave. In what state of health I leave you two, depends on your answer.'

He paused to let his words sink in then said slowly, 'Is Kiele the count?'

His words had sunk in. They had done more than that. Joseph openly displayed fear mixed with utter astonishment. How did this stranger know? Of all the people in the castle Zinkel was the only one who knew. Even Maria had not known. Zinkel uttered a long sigh, a sigh of surrender.

'Yes, sir. Count Winter and Herr Kiele are the same person.' Zinkeltook a deep breath. 'Now keep your promise. I'm dead anyway. He's utterly ruthless. Let my wife go.'

Barbier did and Maria rushed across to Joseph, who got up and made her sit down. She was holding her throat and he stood beside her determined to do whatever he could to protect her from any further attacks. He had just betrayed the man who had saved his life twice and whom he feared more than anyone else in the world.

Barbier's thoughts were racing. He was in possession of facts he could not possibly have expected to obtain. Zinkel and wife were no danger to him now. He had no reason to linger. In fact, he would be foolish to do so. His original plan had been to hide in the grounds overnight and get over the wall during the day. Now he saw clearly that there was only one way. Knife at the ready in his hand, Barbier addressed Joseph and Maria.

'I'm keeping my promise and shall leave you now. But I offer you a deal, Herr Zinkel. If the count finds out you've given his secret away, you'll lose job and home, and probably your lives, too. But the Count can only find that out from me. If you say or do nothing that might endanger my life, I'll do the same for you.'

He saw their reaction in their eyes and did not wait for a reply. He knew that any idea reaching the count was beyond reality. He slipped the knife back into its sheath and left. He hurried quietly down the stairs and made it, unseen, to the little blue garage door. As unpleasant as it was, he resumed his cramped position beneath the blankets in the rear of the Mercedes. For a while he concentrated on the possible dangers ahead of him, thinking through a variety of possible scenarios. In the end he willed himself into falling asleep.

When he woke up he realised the car must be on the open road. He was perspiring due to the blankets that covered him. His joints protested against the cramped position in which he lay. But this was a short journey, he remembered, and he must be ready for action at the end of it. The thought had hardly reached his consciousness when he heard the gears being changed in succession. The car slowed down and stopped. They must have reached the Neumarkt railway station. He heard the driver's door being opened. But it was not being closed which suggested that Kiele might still be sitting

Chapter 8 – The Lion's Cage

inside. Barbier concluded that the limousines had not arrived as yet and decided to remain where he was until he heard them arrive. His conclusion was only partly correct.

Typically, there was a large open space in front of the station entrances. On each side, close to the front of the station building there were two oak trees. Kiele had parked on the right, close to one of them. But he had not remained in his seat. He had got out of the car to enjoy the tree's shade and actually stood close to the rear door behind which Barbier was sweltering. After a short wait the limousines arrived, six of them. They parked in an established order, three on the left and three on the right, leaving a broad approach way in the centre.

The movements of their SA passengers, filing from the cars into the station, were even more disciplined. Beneath his blankets Barbier could hear commands shouted, feet marching, a few individual 'Heil Hitlers!' plus brief bursts of applause, probably from bystanders, more marching steps and then relative silence. Kiele must surely now get out of the Mercedes to see the party off and to pay for the taxis. Barbier gave it another minute, then struggled free of the blankets and, without standing up, slowly opened the rear door. Keeping low, he twisted himself out. He ended up bent over between the station and the Mercedes. Luckily for him, Kiele had only just left his shady tree in order to stride across the square to the front car of the limousines parked opposite. If he turned his head at as little as forty-five degrees, he would see Barbier rising carefully behind the Mercedes.

The limousines parked along the left wall of the square had carried Herr Hitler and his top men. Those on the right had carried the S.A. guards. Their front car was parked a few metres from the Mercedes. Its driver was Konrad Leibl. He saw Kiele move away from the tree and, simultaneously, his friend Georg's head arise on the other side of the Mercedes. He could hardly believe his eyes, muttering under his breath, '*Heilige Eiernockerln*!' (Holy egg dumplings). The words had long ceased to be funny and they certainly weren't now. The next moment he hooted his horn as hard as he could. It had the desired effect. Kiele and everybody else briefly turned towards the sound and Barbier ducked back to the cover of the car. Leibl gestured his apologies to Kiele who walked on to the lead driver on the other side in order to pay the hire fee.

Chapter 8 – The Lion's Cage

The man signed a prepared receipt and passed it to Kiele. During that little transaction, Barbier, watching from his cover at the back of the Mercedes, saw Konrad, face tight, urgently eyeing him to get into his limousine. Involving Konrad was something Barbier had meant to avoid but it would have been crazy not to accept the invitation and he was not crazy. Within split seconds he had slipped into Konrad's limo. As soon as Kiele had paid his bill, he returned to his Mercedes and, without wasting a second, drove off.

The moment the Mercedes had left the station yard; the limousines sprang into action. The sound of their purring motors provided a triumphant background music as, one car after another, alternately from the left and the right, turned around elegantly, as if in a well-practised motor ballet into the drive and out of the station yard. Sitting behind Konrad, Barbier's ride back to Nuremberg was considerably more comfortable than the ones to and from Castle Wintereschen. Their conversation was short and at intervals, started by Barbier.

'Thanks, Konrad, I had not meant to get you involved in my affairs.'

'I'm not, Georg. I'm just giving you a lift to town.' After a pause, he added, 'Kauz Pillschneider, the driver behind me, must have seen you enter my car. I'll tell him we're friends. You're a traveller in toys, who spent the night in Neumarkt and I had offered you a lift to Nuremberg.' The words 'in toys' were laden with all the irony, Konrad could muster. In the same tone he added, 'It even contains a few grains of truth.'

'Which I was not able to tell you, Konrad, believe me.'

'I do. I'm glad I could help. I hate that lot. They're trying to destroy what little we've achieved since the end of the war. The French occupation's only just moved out from this region and now these fascists are moving in. It makes me feel bitter.'

A little way into the town, Barbier parted from Leibl.

'Konrad, thank you for everything. I'll not be able to meet you for lunch anymore. I'd not expected to make a real friend here.'

They shook hands, both certain, they would not meet again. It was eleven o'clock when Barbier reached his hotel. After a quick bath he enjoyed a snack to make up for the lost breakfast. He admitted to himself that his initial aim of dealing personally with Winter and Becher was beyond his capabilities but the Bureau had to be informed of what he had found out. Other than that he had only

Chapter 8 – The Lion's Cage

one aim: to re-join his family. He entered the telephone cell in the hotel. Ten minutes later he left it, utterly frustrated. He should have remembered that, following his and Bècher's dismissal, the Bureau's passwords would be changed, as a security procedure.

There were, of course, official numbers available to the general public, which required no password but, as long as he was not officially cleared, he could not entrust even the fact of his presence in Nuremberg to public operators. Equally he could not search out French agents in Germany. He might be on their list as a traitor. He could return to Paris but every particle of his being rejected the idea. He was determined to go on to England. Using the land mail for such sensitive material was not safe either. He would never know whether it had been received. Suddenly, Barbier felt cut off, isolated and lonely, very lonely. The temptation to just walk away was huge.

All he wanted at this moment, was to be back with his wife and children and try to make up for the mistakes of the past. The moment passed. He shook his head the way a dog returning from a swim would shake himself free of water. He must inform the Bureau! Then the answer came to him: Munich. When he had served there under Major de Courcy, they shared the offices with the British Liaison Officer, whose German interpreter was said to be a German coming from the Rhineland. Barbier knew better. They had been on good terms. The British personnel vacated before that of the French but the interpreter had remained under cover in Munich. If he was still there, he could help Barbier to make contact with Perroir. It was Saturday, the 6th July. He left the hotel early in the morning, walking on foot to the station where he took the next train to the Bavarian capital. Two hours later he stepped out into the streets of Munich. He had no problem in finding his way to the Hofbräuhaus. Only a handful of customers were sitting in the small ground floor day restaurant. He made his way upstairs to the large restaurant, which was similarly empty and addressed the waitress, who stood near the door.

'Excuse me, Fräulein, I am looking for Herr Michel Heller. Is he still working here?'

The waitress, nodding, was about to look around, when he hurried away, saying, 'Ah, I can see him.'

Heller was indeed just coming towards them from the bar. She watched the man, who carried a travel bag, walk up to Heller, saw them look at each other for a long minute and then clasp hands heartily. They turned to walk away in the direction of the bar, where Heller had a little room with a telephone.

At that moment, Hannes Bohlmann, whom she had been expecting, arrived. Standing beside her, he murmured, 'Incredible, Gerda. It can't be. I've not seen him for twelve years. What brings him here?'

Chapter 9 – A Murder is Planned

It was Sunday morning. In Nuremberg, Count Brandtstein codenamed Loki, was switching on his radio, calling Wotan in Schloss (Castle) Wintereschen.

'Loki calling Wotan!' He did not have to wait.

'Wotan responding. Over.'

'Special date today.' – 'Our Champagne Day, Wotan.' He referred to the Region, not the drink.

You on the Condé, Loki, I on the Châlons flank.' – 'But the Hills of Reims between us, Wotan.'

'Didn't stop us. Remember our first Sunday morning sked, Loki?'

'Twelve years ago.' – 'We've moved on a lot since, Loki.' – 'Yes, we have, Wotan.'

'Except for Budapest and Paris.' – 'You can't plan against accidents, Wotan.'

'The next execution will make up for them, Loki. It'll make the whole of Europe aware of our existence and our power.'

Loki did not express his view that this was unwise, but said: 'We've not discussed the next execution, Wotan.'

'We'll do so at our next schedule.' Wotan changed the subject. 'Anything new from the party?'

Loki hid his resentment.

'Hitler's bringing Röhm back.'

'Good. Röhm's by far the best of them. Anything else?' – 'No, Wotan.'

'Right. Close down. Wotan over and out.' – 'Loki out.'

This brief, celebratory schedule contributed to Brandtstein's growing resentment. He thought that Winter bore some responsibility for the Bècher debacle. The latter's killing of two Deuxième Bureau agents out of personal pique was an unnecessary provocation. But Winter held the purse strings and, at least for the time, Brandtstein would continue to be loyal Loki and obey Wotan. Winter had intended to visit Berlin in order to recruit replacements for the three agents who were enjoying the hospitality of a Budapest

Chapter 9 – A Murder is Planned

jail. The news of Röhm's return made him change his mind. Röhm would do this for him. He picked up the internal telephone.

'I've cancelled Berlin, Joseph. Get the blankets out of the car and have them cleaned.'

Zinkel obeyed, although he felt that this kind of task was below his standing. When collecting the blankets, he saw the clear signs of someone having lain between them. Now he knew how his visitor of last Thursday had got into the Castle and how he had got out of it. He should report it to the Count. He struggled with his sense of loyalty, a loyalty unbroken for a decade. In the end self-interest won the struggle, although he told himself it was for Maria's sake.

* * *

In Munich, Michel Heller had taken Barbier to Craig Jameson at the British Consulate, who billeted him in the flat that Ronald Burnley had occupied. The immediate effect of this was a flurry of telegrams, radio and telephone contacts: Heller, in an emergency schedule, informed Cormody of Vincent Barbier's arrival and need to make contact with Colonel Perroir of the Deuxième Bureau. Cormody forwarded the request to Perroir. Perroir wired the British Consul in Munich, whereupon Craig Jameson, MI5, the consulate's head of security, had the necessary equipment installed in Barbier's flat. Barbier reported to Perroir and learnt that he had been cleared and was officially on reserve. He sent a report of his foray into Castle Wintereschen to Perroir who instructed him to share the information with the British. Perroir also informed him of what little progress had been made so far in respect of the two agents murdered by Becher. The next day, Jameson, Heller and Barbier met in a room of the British Consulate. The conversation was carried on in English. Jameson opened the proceedings.

'Our respective bosses have decided that we should exchange full information on the issue that has brought you to Munich, Barbier, and any related ones.'

Barbier reported his activities after leaving Paris, in detail, going right back to his and Ronald Burnley's job in Nuremberg. The information was new to Jameson and Heller and startling. Heller's contribution was shorter. It was equally new and even more startling.

Chapter 9 – A Murder is Planned

'Three weeks ago a British agent, travelling on the Orient Express from Budapest to London, was murdered on the train, near Vienna. There are strong indications that the killer mistook him for a Hungarian whom he was escorting. The killing was connected with the foiled attempt by three Germans, in Budapest, to assassinate a member of the British House of Lords whilst there on a state visit. According to the plotters, who were overheard by the Hungarian I've mentioned, the reason for the attempt was his campaign against the threat to democracy in Europe by the growth of the Nazi Party of Germany. The plot failed due to the Hungarian's information. The circumstances surrounding the assassination attempt has led to the suspicion that a German secret organisation was behind the plot which, however theatrical this may sound, seems to be run by someone who calls himself Wotan. Your story, Barbier, has added materially to this suspicion.'

Barbier shot from his chair.

'Merde!' (Shit). 'This means that Count Winter is also Wotan. He is a multi-millionaire who funds Hitler and employs murderers.'

After what seemed a very long silence, Heller said slowly, 'It's worse, gentlemen. The head of the Hungarian Security force has found out that the victims of three unsolved murders which took place in Hungary during the last two years, were all leading politicians who had spoken out publicly against fascism.'

Another silence ensued until Jameson moved to the next topic on his agenda, addressing the Frenchman, 'Do I understand correctly, Monsieur Barbier, that your next step is to proceed to England?'

Barbier replied, 'That is correct, Captain Jameson. I have given notice of leaving the Bureau. My wife and children live in London.'

Jameson said, 'OK. The Consulate will make the travel arrangements for you and you're welcome to remain our guest, until your departure, Monsieur Barbier.'

The latter protested.

'I can pay for my travel and accommodation, Captain.'

'I've strict instructions to take responsibility for your personal safety,' Jameson replied, 'and the Deuxième Bureau has taken responsibility for your expenditure, Monsieur Barbier. Apparently you've been or are about to be…' He checked with his notes, '…reinstated into the Deuxième Bureau reserve.'

Heller took over.

Chapter 9 – A Murder is Planned

'My information from London is that MI6 and the Deuxième Bureau intend to develop total collaboration in this matter and my boss has requested that, whilst you are still here, you, Captain Jameson and I establish the basis of this collaboration. I understand that you may not be willing to do this but I suggest to you that there is at least one good reason for you to agree.'

Both Barbier and Jameson looked questioningly at Heller. He explained.

'The Hungarian, whom I mentioned, is at present still in Vienna, awaiting one of our agents to join him there and escort him to Britain where he, like you, will take up residence. You mentioned the agent in your report, Captain Ronald Burnley. Burnley will be part of the team to build up this collaboration, mainly because he became involved when he worked with you in Nuremberg.' He put his hand up, as Barbier seemed to want to say something. 'Colonel Perroir thinks it is possible that Karl Becher is here in Munich.'

Barbier allowed another interjection to slip out, this one quite tame.

'*Parbleu*! Of course! I should have thought of that. Mr. Heller, I'll stay here as long as it takes me to find the murderer.'

Jameson had been listening attentively but now decided that this came under his jurisdiction.

'Monsieur Barbier, you cannot go round Munich searching for Becher. If your boss is right, it opens up all kinds of problems. Let us be sensible. I have the necessary contacts to discover whether the man is here or not. As for your journey to London, we have fixed reservations on the train we use. Given this new development, the British consulate has an overriding responsibility here. I suggest you travel on the first available reservation. Until you depart we three can get started on developing the suggested collaboration. I suggest, we meet regularly. If you take your meals at the Hofbräuhaus it will facilitate things.'

A long silence followed his words. Heller broke it.

'Fair enough, Jameson. I take it you'll start by investigating whether Becher is in town.'

Barbier added, 'OK, Captain. I'll go by all of your suggestions, if it is all right with you, Heller.'

Heller agreed.

'As long as you remember, old friend, that at the Hofbräuhaus I'm just one of the head waiters.'

Chapter 9 – A Murder is Planned

Barbier rose.

'Fine, messieurs. Then I'll be off, now.'

He left, a little tired and with a lot to think about. Jameson's eyes followed him. He said, 'He got into that castle and out. That's some caper, Heller. I'm glad he's on our side.'

Heller nodded.

'Quite a feat. We worked in the same office, as I told you, and we got on well, but he was never a man of many words. Even so, I'd not have credited him with this level of daring. I see your point, Jameson, but having him daily at my place of work is not a desirable circumstance. When he arrived yesterday, Gerda saw him.'

Jameson apologised.

'It was the best I could think of. We have to keep close tabs on him. He's driven by anger as far as this guy Becher's concerned – Gerda? Burnley's Gerda?'

'The same. She could become suspicious. I don't think she'd ever give me away knowingly but all the same...'

Jameson rang the exchange of the Munich Police Directorate, speaking German.

'Jameson, British Consulate. *Kartei Zentrale, bitte.*' (Records Office, please.)

'Kartei Zentrale, Schmidt speaking.'

'Jameson here, Herr Sergeant. I've a personal question concerning the invitation from your son's English friends, Herr Sergeant.'

'Is tomorrow at eleven suitable, Mr. Jameson?'

'That'll be fine, Herr Sergeant.'

Polizei Sergeant Christian Schmidt understood that Jameson wanted to talk to him. He arrived on Tuesday, punctually at eleven o'clock. They spoke German.

'I'm hoping you can help me in a confidential matter, Herr Sergeant.'

'If I can, I shall certainly do it, Herr Jameson.'

'I'm concerned with a matter in which a German citizen is involved. The man may be guilty of serious crimes committed outside Germany. He is known to have visited Munich. He may even be here at this moment. I do not wish to cause you any difficulties—'

'My dear Herr Jameson, if this man is on our Residents Register or is or has been a visitor, it will be no problem. What is his name?'

'Karl Becher.'

Chapter 9 – A Murder is Planned

Schmidt used his Lamy fountain pen to write the name on the inside of his hand.

'Not difficult to remember. I'll have the results by Thursday morning.'

'How's your Reinhard, Herr Sergeant?'

'As you know, he's been in England twice now. It's serious. He hopes to become a member of the family. The latest is that he will start a two-year commercial course in London in September. He's very happy and so are my wife and I. We owe this to you, Herr Jameson.'

Jameson shook his head as they shook hands. He had done nothing but what was his job. When he entered his office, the internal phone rang its guttural tones. He lifted the receiver to hear His Master's Voice, the Consul General himself.

'Gaisford. Come and see me.'

'On my way, sir.'

* * *

Gaisford, not looking delighted, handed him a telegram. 'The FO. Do what you can.'

Jameson's eyes flew through the text.

'GAISFORD BRITCONSUL MUNICH

EXTEND FULL SUPPORT TO FRENCH AGENT VINCENT BARBIER REGARDING GERMAN SECRET ORGANISATION SUSPECTED OF MURDERS STOP IPKIRKPATRICK UNDERSEC FO.'

Jameson looked up.

'I've already—'

Gaisford interrupted him.

'We must, of course, oblige our French allies and give their diplomatic staff our full assistance. Their names need not be mentioned in internal reports. This kind of professional courtesy requires your full attention, you understand, Jameson.'

Jameson was full of understanding. Back in his office he contacted the lady serving the Consulate's service calls.

Chapter 9 – A Murder is Planned

'Mrs. Davies, find me the number of our Budapest Legation, please. I want to speak to Major Pemmington there.'

Next he rang the travel clerk.

'Douglas, what are our Orient Express allocations this month?'

'To London on Saturdays, from London on Tuesdays. Two dates each.'

'When are our earliest vacancies? I need one compartment to London.'

'That'll be Saturday, the 12th July, sir. One's already been taken up by Vienna.'

'Right, we better grab the other one quickly. Diplomatic staff, Douglas, name not available. Out of interest, find out who the Vienna travellers are, if you can and check whether they must not meet.'

'Standard procedure, sir. I'll get on to it right away.'

'Good man.'

* * *

Schmidt was as good as his word. He turned up in Jameson's office on Thursday morning, sounding a little excited.

'You've no idea, Captain Jameson, of the strange facts that I discovered when I looked up your Herr Becher. A Pandora's hornets' nest, I tell you!'

Jameson appreciated the combination. Schmidt consulted his pocket-size notebook.

'Karl Becher, registered citizen of Munich. Shares residence with wife, née Sabine von Steinfels, daughter of Count Adalbert von Steinfels. Date of wedding: 1st August, 1928.'

Jameson expressed his astonishment.

'That is an unexpected piece of information, Herr Sergeant.'

Schmidt continued.

'But listen to this, Herr Jameson. During the days following their wedding, reports came into the local station from people residing in the same street, about screams from a woman, heard on several occasions. After more complaints about screams, the local district police planned a spell of clandestine observation. The plan was not approved due to Herr Becher linked with powerful local patronage.' He looked up. 'Our police, as you probably know, Captain Jameson, does not interfere in domestic violence, unless one of the partners

Chapter 9 – A Murder is Planned

brings a charge. I found a few previous entries referring to Herr Becher's use of violence on women, even when hospitalisation is involved and no charges were brought. Then I came across a note from our *Moralpolizei'* (Ethics Police) 'to the effect that Sabine von Steinfels had had to leave her family home because of unacceptable sexual behaviour.'

'So they fit well together,' Jameson said.

Schmidt agreed.

'That is all I have for you, Herr Kapitän. You do understand that I could only give you this information verbally.'

'Certainly, Sergeant Schmidt. Could you possibly let me have the address?'

Schmidt thought for a moment, then scribbled it on a page of his notebook which he tore out and passed to Jameson.

'It is a single-story free-standing former farm house. Addresses of all residents are now available at the town hall. I have to rush. My respects, Herr Kapitän.' He rushed out.

Jameson looked at the address: Raunsteig 1, Hansastrasse. He picked up the phone.

'Hofbräuhaus, Herr Heller.' – 'Jameson. We need to talk.' – 'No, just you and I.' – 'Excellent.'

He put the receiver down. Heller arrived within the hour and Jameson passed the facts provided by Schmidt to him and added, 'You can inform Barbier that Becher's a local resident but that's all. I've no reliable means of knowing whether he is in Munich at present.'

Heller understood.

'Couldn't the sergeant?'

Jameson shook his head.

'You know he can't. I've no legal grounds to even suggest it.'

Heller was struggling with an idea. At last he said.

'We can't waste the information, Jameson. I might as well go the whole hog.'

'What are you talking about, Heller?'

Heller replied, 'I'll let you know. I better hurry back. Gerda is off in half an hour. I'll be in touch. He rushed out.

'Gerda again?' Jameson, puzzled, looked after him, then shrugged his shoulders.

* * *

Chapter 9 – A Murder is Planned

Back at the Hofbräuhaus, Heller did his usual pre-evening meals inspection tour of the first floor premises. Passing Gerda, he quietly said, 'Would you join me at the bar in ten minutes, please, Gerda.'

At the bar, meant his cubby hole at one end of the counter. She joined him promptly, curiosity at bursting level. The cubby hole was barely the size of two telephone booths.

'This is an unusual honour, Michel,' she said.

'It's an unusual matter,' he replied. 'It's also a very confidential matter and if I asked you not to mention it to anyone else, even your Steffel...?'

'Oh, I can promise you that.'

He had depended upon her agreement.

'It's to do with the friend who's in Munich at present, the one you saw when he arrived.'

'How can I help you, Michel?'

'He's here in a personal matter. I'm helping him as much as I can. He's after a Nazi, one of the worst sort, Gerda. You have one of your SAG meetings tonight, haven't you?'

The question surprised her. 'Yes?'

'Your group did a great job for Ronald Burnley. Do you think they might be willing to do an observation task on this Nazi?'

'I'd need details, Michel. None of them can afford the expenses, if there are any.'

'I can assure you about funds. The Nazi resides here in Munich with his wife. Essentially, what we want to know is whether he is in Munich at the moment. Straightforward observation of his address for three to five days should establish the answer. My friend cannot do it himself, Gerda, as the man knows him.'

'It sounds easy enough, Michel, almost boring.'

'The man's a criminal and utterly ruthless. If he believed he was being watched, the watchers could be in danger of life. If your lot will do this, they must remain invisible.'

Gerda crossed her arms in a superior way.

'Remember Steger and his friend? Steger was a murderer.'

'An innocent child, compared with this man, Gerda, please impress that on your friends.'

She nodded, convinced by his seriousness.

Chapter 9 – A Murder is Planned

'OK, Michel. Since my marriage I've become less active but I'm still a member. Steffel does not approve. The group's been energised by new blood, Noah Frey, a brilliant organiser.'

'Good. Please, don't give them my name, Gerda.' He looked around. 'We better get back to our posts otherwise people might talk.' He laughed.

He would never admit that the laugh contained more than a tinge of regret. Personal relationships had not come Heller's way for a long time.

* * *

Noah Frey, the man Gerda mentioned, had joined the Socialist Action Group a few months ago, recruited by one of his cousins, Hans Hollander. Hollander was the man who had organised Steger's and Lünecke's humiliation at their regular restaurant, the Au. Frey and Hollander met at a family gathering and got into conversation. Hollander became aware that Noah Frey, his remote cousin, also looked and sounded somewhat remote.

'Something troubling you, Noah? You're less cheerful than I've known you. I hear you've passed your doctors in Physics. With distinction!'

'I was lucky. How's your Socialist group going, Hans?'

'I've less time for it than I used to. I'm forty, you know. I suppose you'll join one of the big labs in town? They'll snap you up.'

Frey hesitated.

'I've had offers.'

'Die Qual der Wahl?' (The agony of choice)

Hollander smiled understandingly.

Frey shook his head.

'No. But I don't think I'll stay in Munich, if in Germany at all.'

Hollander looked at him questioningly.

'Do you want to tell?'

Noah Frey wanted to and did. A recent occurrence at the university. A Jewish student had brought his girlfriend to the New Term ball. When he went to the toilet he was attacked by three students and beaten up. Whilst he was lying hurt, his girlfriend was enticed out of the ballroom and, in a pitch-black store room, raped by three men. The three students, named by the Jewish student,

Chapter 9 – A Murder is Planned

provided solid alibis and his girl-friend had not seen the faces of the men who raped her.

'Raped? I can't believe it. That's awful.'

'I'm acquainted with him and his family. There's no doubt. It caused great distress and upheaval. Both families have left Munich. They are planning to emigrate.'

'But how does this affect your plans?'

'My dear cousin. We took the names of the three students to the *Rektor* and the university governors. They told us we were slandering the university. The people responsible were outsiders, gate crashers to the ball. They weren't. The three are bona fide members of the National Socialist Students Society and have been heard to brag about it. The whole matter was hushed up efficiently and there seems to be no way in which to bring these fellows to justice. I can't stomach it, I cannot live with it and that's why I don't want to stay and work in Munich. One of the Jewish students at the university, Barak Moses, a friend of mine, accused two of the guilty men to their faces. They threw themselves at him. Moses knocked one of them out with one blow and then gave the other one a good beating. It was witnessed by other students. But do you know what? They claimed that Moses had started the fight and he was excluded from continuing his post graduate added year. Your group may only make propaganda against the Nazis, but at least you're doing something. I wish, I could.'

He stopped, close to losing his cool.

Hollander lowered his voice.

'You want to do something about these students, Noah?'

'Every fibre inside me does.'

'Let's go for a stroll.'

They did and Frey's life changed radically in the most literal sense of the word. Members of the SAG participated in Frey's well-planned scheme of punishment. So did his friend, the pugilistic Barak Moses. Within a span of only two weeks a few unfortunate accidents befell three members of the university's National Socialist Students Society. One of them was hit by a collapsing builder's wooden scaffolding. He suffered a complexity of fractures which put him into hospital for almost a year and a wheelchair for much, much longer. Somehow his penis had got caught between two heavy joists. It left him qualified for the post of a eunuch. Unfortunately, no such jobs were available in Munich.

Chapter 9 – A Murder is Planned

The police investigation produced the existence of two notices warning pedestrians not to walk beneath the scaffolding. The builders were surprised but did not protest. The second student was found guilty of having stolen expensive drugs from one of the university laboratories. They were found in his locker. His claim, that he had lost the key and the stolen items must have been put into the locker by the thief, collapsed when the key was found in the pocket of one of his jackets at home. He was only given five months in prison but expelled from the university for good. The third disappeared one day whilst on his way home from a Nazi meeting. He was found two days later in a large well-secured freight container stored in one of the customs halls at Oslo Port, Norway, after the *Havn* (Port) Authority had received an anonymous report by someone claiming to have heard noises coming from the hall.

When freed the man was in a bad state, having been sea-sick amongst other things and without food throughout the voyage. The Norwegian Port Authorities, after allowing him to recover, held on to him for a few more days, trying to establish whether he had been involved in some nefarious scheme. Back home, an anonymous letter warned him not to return to the university unless he wished to go on another similar trip. He was sufficiently intimidated to obey the warning. No one seemed to relate their mishaps to their shared entertainment at the New Term student's ball. It remained unknown whether they, themselves, interpreted it as retribution but two of them ceased their membership of the Nazi party. The eunuch did not. He became a leading Stormtrooper in due course. Noah Frey was satisfied with the results, although they gave him no inner satisfaction when he met Hollander again.

'It should have been a public punishment. The Nazis are gaining more and more influence and support and no one seems to want to stop them.'

'You're a scientist, Noah. I don't need to tell you about reality. The Nazis are riding on a tidal wave. One of the factors that drives it, is hysteria, possibly an unstoppable force. My group's been active against individuals and gangs of Nazis from Day One. Why don't you join us, Noah? It might provide part of you with a degree of satisfaction, the bit that demands action. You're the planner we're short of. Think it over.'

Chapter 9 – A Murder is Planned

Noah Frey and Barak Moses thought it over and talked it over and became members of SAG, the Socialist Action Group, the next day.

'I'll postpone my personal career for one year,' Frey told the group.

As Hollander had foreseen, he made a difference, a huge difference. Heller's request for observing the movements of Becher was agreed unanimously and Frey took charge of the operation. The next day, in the afternoon, when Gerda had two hours off, he called on her for Becher's address. He also accepted her invitation for a cup of coffee. Gerda's husband was in Berlin on one of his sales trips. It was hot, clothing was light, and temptation was wafting in the air between them. But Gerda had to go to work. So, Noah Frey whose resistance to feminine electricity measured less than one Ohm, was relieved and went to a library, where he studied the Munich street map, instead. On Saturday he took a tram to the Hansa Strasse, a main street.

He got off at a terrace block of seven 3-storey houses, somewhat pretentiously named the Hansa Komplex. Raunsteig was a one-way street running from the Hansa Strasse at one end of the *Komplex*, along the back of its houses, and returning to the Hansa Strasse at the other end. Including the Hansa Strasse terrace of the houses, it formed a short rectangle. Opposite the backyards of Hansa Strasse houses stood a row of single-storey, free-standing former farmhouses, numbered 1 to 5, in the order in which the minuscule traffic flowed. With one exception, they were all in a great state of neglect. The exception was No.1, Becher's address. Frey, carrying a hard-backed folder and a large, official-looking pad with a sleeve for a pencil, had entered Raunsteig at the No. 5 end. He was strolling along slowly, appearing to inspect the back of the Hansa Strasse block and making notes. He was walking against the road traffic, which, on this occasion, consisted of one cyclist and a man pushing a wheelbarrow with a second-hand bedside cabinet in it. By the time Frey reached the last house which was almost exactly opposite No. 1, he had failed to find a suitable, accessible observation vantage point in the street.

He switched to Plan B and turned into the Hansa Strasse. He was pleasantly surprised to see that the corner shop was a café bar. A good omen, he thought. His plan, coinciding with a desire for a drink, propelled him inside. He sat down near the counter, put the

Chapter 9 – A Murder is Planned

folder on the table, and ordered a beer. He was the only guest, which, at this hour, was normal. Whilst the waiter was filling a glass from a barrel, Frey added an invitation to his order:

'Fill one for yourself, *Herr Ober'* (Mister headwaiter), 'it's a warm day.'

'You can say that again, sir,' the waiter replied, 'and I accept the kind offer.' He carried Frey's beer on a tray and his in the other hand, following his customer's nodded invitation. He sat down opposite him and raised his glass, '*Prost, mein Herr*!'

Frey responded, '*Prosit*!'

'Working?' the barman enquired, with a squint at the folder.

Frey nodded, opening the folder slightly, showing the heading:

Öffentlicher Straßenverkehr   (Public Road Traffic)
Seitenstraßen   (Side Streets)

He followed it up.

'You would not believe the things these bureaucrats at HQ think of. A study in depth of the town's Class Three streets, like the Raunsteig, behind your house. They want us to do 5 days of twelve hours' observation and my men have to note down every vehicle passing. I've just been through Raunsteig and the only vehicle I saw was a bicycle. It's crazy, I tell you.'

'Every…? What, horse and carts and all?'

Frey nodded, looking sorry for himself.

'Yes. But that's not the worst, I tell you. The bloke in charge wanted the work done al fresco, you know, in the open air, that means. I put my foot down. He may be a higher grade but I'm in charge of Class Three Traffic. I persisted and, I'm pleased to say, he's released the funds to pay for five days' under cover accommodation per street, so that my men can sit in a room, without getting wet, or molested, or worse. I always insist on basic standards for my men. And it brings results. So far, my teams have done the *Irarvorstadt'* (Irar suburb) 'and the Maxvorstadt Class Threes successfully. The gents in Statistics will have no complaints.' He took a sip, looking pleased with himself. Then his brow folded. 'But Raunsteig is a problem. Those ramshackle houses in the street don't look – well, a basic standard for what I'm able to pay, you know.' He took a long gulp. 'Ah, that tastes good. My chaps only need a window from which they can oversee the street. But they must have

Chapter 9 – A Murder is Planned

the use of a washroom! That's basic. I better finish my beer and get going. I'll have to knock on doors.'

Frey was banking on the waiter actually being the landlord. It seemed now he might be wrong and he was just getting up to leave, when the barman said, 'Be careful about these houses, Herr Inspektor. There's some queer folk occupying them.'

'You think so?'

'I know. But tell me, sir, what exactly do your chaps need?'

'Essentially I need a window which looks out on the street – why do you ask?'

'Well, sir. I'll come straight to the point. Your men could do their job perfectly well from the back of my house. The wife's away, visiting her sister in Sachsenhausen, she's been taken ill, poor thing. Her sister, I mean. Anyway, I haven't a tenant on the top floor, that's the second floor, not until I employ a man to assist me. The business isn't doing well enough yet, my first year, you see, but it's picking up. The flat's locked, of course, but the kitchenette at the back, it's got a good-size window looking out to the Raunsteig, it's got a table and two chairs, kitchen chairs only, mind you, but quite comfortable. Our front door's open all day, and there's a toilet next to the kitchenette, so, what do you think, sir? Assuming the payment's fair, of course. I'll show you right now, if you're interested.'

Frey took a deep breath. Plan B had succeeded at the first try. Plan C would have been risky, coming close to being unlawful. Half an hour later Frey left, having arranged the use of the kitchenette on the second floor for five days, from 8 in the morning until 7 in the evening, payment in cash. He had given the barman a deposit. The observation was set for Monday till Friday. He spent the rest of the day on the necessary details, a rota of two-hour duties for each man, overlapping hourly. He, himself, would start and end each day. He procured two pairs of binoculars and a hard-backed folder with a pad. He met his team for briefing and they agreed their timetables.

During the first two days, the watchers found the task boring. A woman left the house on Monday morning and returned with shopping. Otherwise there was no movement. Towards mid-day on Wednesday, a noisy motorcycle stopped outside Number 1. Its rider rang the bell. The door was opened by a man, remaining in the shadow of the doorway, who was handed an envelope by the rider. The pennant adorning the motorbike displayed the background colours black, red and gold with an inset of the German eagle and a

Chapter 9 – A Murder is Planned

small capital N in one corner. It was the emblem adopted by the Weimar Republic and the N identified the motorcyclist, or at least his bike, as coming from the city of Nuremberg.

When the messenger left, the man stepped out from the doorway to look carefully to the left and the right before returning into the house and closing the door. He had broad shoulders and blond hair. The two observers nodded to each other. They were looking out for a broad-shouldered man with blond hair and a woman for whom they had no description. One of them rang Noah Frey with the information. Frey, too, was satisfied that they had established the presence of Karl Becher in Munich. Had he known about Becher's boss, Wotan, he might have considered the messenger an omen, as he knew that the name Wednesday was derived from Wotan's Day. However, Frey did not feel they had achieved enough by simply establishing his presence. Gerda had told him, this Becher was a Nazi and a criminal. Of course, either the woman or the man might leave the house during the night. Even so, Becher was surely not likely to remain indoors every day. And if he did what then? But recalling the warning he had been given, tracking Becher might constitute a risk.

He changed the rota and joined the observers full-time on both remaining days, reducing their hours to one at a time. His reasoning turned out to be correct faster than expected. Half-way through Thursday morning, the door to Raunsteig No.1 opened and Becher stepped out. He walked briskly in the direction of the traffic. Not that there was any. Frey, who had left his bicycle outside the bar, rushed downstairs and, as the saying goes, got on his bike. He reached the other end of Raunsteig in time to see Becher emerge from it and turn left into the Hansastrasse, passing the Hansa Bar. Frey had no difficulty following his quarry unseen. Until Becher took the path through the *Theresienhöhe* (Theresien Height), the large meadow at which the Nazi Stormtroopers did their regular training. Following Becher here was too risky. He was either meeting someone here or took the shortcut to the main station. Frey took a small chance and cycled around the meadow, waiting at the other end. True enough, he saw Becher on the path still moving forward. Frey made his way to the station ahead of him and waited, well hidden inside the crowded, noisy hall.

When Becher entered, he followed him and joined the International Tickets queue a few places behind him. When he

Chapter 9 – A Murder is Planned

reached the window, he leaned forward. His hand was sliding a 5-Mark note very slowly forward on the counter as he spoke softly to the man behind it, whose eyes were following the hand as if hypnotised.

'The fair-haired man who bought a ticket. All details.'

The clerk said nothing. Tearing his eyes from the banknote, he tore a sheet of paper from the pad before him, which he normally used for entering the information requested by enquirers and did the same on this occasion. He moved the sheet forward towards Frey's hand and the two pieces of paper discreetly changed hands. It was obviously not an entirely new experience for the ticket clerk, nor was it unusual in post-war Germany.

Frey returned to Hansa Strasse where the next observer was just coming on duty. Frey asked him to inform the others immediately, that the task was ended. He wrote out a report together with a bill for expenses and took them to Gerda late in the evening when he knew she would be back from work.

Gerda offered him hot chicken soup and provided sufficient electricity to overcome his ohms. Tasty consumption was followed by pleasurable consummation. First thing on Friday, she handed Noah Frey's report to Heller who read it immediately. The handwriting was nothing to write home about, but the brief information was sensational. Michel noted the initials N.F. on the report. He telephoned Jameson.

'I've just received serious information about Becher, Jameson. It requires urgent consideration and passing on to our visitor.'

'OK, Heller. And I've got his travel details. This afternoon, say 2.30. Can you manage?'

'Have to. I'll let him know.'

* * *

Barbier arrived first. Jameson did not waste time and handed him the travel papers.

'Your travel arrangements, Monsieur Barbier. This Saturday, the 27th July. Here are your tickets. You travel as consular staff – no name and in style – on the Orient Express.'

Barbier's barely audible response was accompanied by a long sigh of relief.

'Enfin.' (At last.)

Chapter 9 – A Murder is Planned

Heller arrived, and he, too, wasted no time.

'I've had Becher's home watched.' He consulted a sheet of paper: 'Wednesday, 17th July: Messenger on motorcycle, displaying a Nuremberg pennant, handed an envelope to the man who opened the door. The man fits the description of Karl Becher. Thursday, 18th July: Becher purchased a ticket at the Munich Main Station paying with a voucher from the Brandtstein Agency. Travel details: Depart Munich Thursday 25 July, 22.10 hours.' He stopped for a moment, then added, 'Destination: Victoria, London. Orient Express. Carriage Three, Seats 33/34.'

A deathly silence followed. The other two looked at him aghast. Jameson pulled open a drawer and from it took out a sheet of printed paper, which he consulted, then broke the silence.

'Same train as yours, Barbier, but two days sooner. Becher will arrive in London on Friday, at 17.20 hours. But why?'

Heller nodded.

'Yes, why? We can reasonably assume that the letter he received was from his boss, Wotan, alias Count Winter, alias Kiele. If it contained the vouchers for his tickets then, presumably also his orders. But for what possible purpose is he being sent to London? Infiltrate one of our security services? Whatever it is, it's bound to be a nefarious one.'

Barbier, lips pressed together, said, 'Surely, you can stop him from travelling to Britain.'

Jameson shook his head.

'Germans no longer require special permission for visiting our country.'

Heller said.

'We could have him arrested by Special Branch – if he does not succeed in evading them.'

Barbier exclaimed, suppressed passion in his voice: 'You must give me his address, Captain Jameson. He has murdered a personal friend. I shall make sure he does not go anywhere.'

'Monsieur Barbier, you know, I cannot do that,' Jameson replied.

The struggle in Barbier's face was manifest. Suddenly he realised something.

'Perhaps there's no need to. The train travels through France, doesn't it?'

'Indeed,' Jameson replied, glancing at the sheet in his hand. 'It gets to Chalons at 08.20 and reaches Boulogne at 1300 hours.'

Chapter 9 – A Murder is Planned

Barbier relaxed.

'That will do. I shall inform Paris. Becher is wanted in France for treason and murder and will be arrested as soon as the train crosses the French borders.'

Heller said, 'We shall, of course, inform the Bureau. It's not impossible that he's after you, Barbier and assumes you've gone to Britain. Could he have your address in London?'

For one second Barbier was worried, them he shook his head.

'Nobody in France can possibly have details about my family's existence, even. And I'm confident that he'll be taken whilst travelling through France.'

Heller added the full stop.

'This killing organisation would not send Becher to England for a private revenge on the off chance that you've gone there. Our concern has to be that he's being sent there in order to fulfil some killing mission. Let's not forget what kind of man this. He cold-bloodedly killed two experienced agents of France's Deuxième Bureau in Paris. In England nobody knows him. And he is totally ruthless.'

There was nothing more to be said on the subject, indeed on anything else at the moment although the air remained filled with tension. Barbier shook hands and left. Heller handed Jameson a quarto sheet.

'Copy of the report. Tell the truth, I doubt the French will arrest Becher. Becher knows he's wanted by the Deuxième Bureau.'

'I agree, too. But why is Becher off to Britain, Heller? I need to warn my crowd. We've no way of finding out here. It's of concern.'

Heller shook his head.

'I normally trust in the MI5 and the MI6 to deal with any danger from foreign enemies but Becher is the exception. He is wily and totally without any inhibitions. I, too, must inform my lords and masters. I've got to go, Jameson.'

He left. Jameson picked up the internal phone and arranged to see the Consul. Then he dialled for one of the secretaries to come and take dictation. Heller who had the rest of the afternoon off, was seated on a bench at a corner of the Schönfeldwiese, a meadow in the English Garden, thinking over the situation. Was there any way of finding out why Becher was going to Britain? Probably not, but if an attempt had to be made on this occasion, there was no one else but himself to make it. It was not part of his duties but sometimes

Chapter 9 – A Murder is Planned

the perimeters set for action had to be transgressed and he decided that now was one of those 'sometimes'. He made his way to his flat and decided he required three loans – not of money. Then he rang a man, who was 'eternally grateful' for his continued silence in respect of an incident of the past. Next he rang the Hofbräuhaus requesting the Saturday off, reminding the manager that he was owed a day. Finally, he called on a locksmith whom he had helped out of an embarrassing situation at the Hofbräuhaus one night.

On Saturday, at about ten in the morning, a Post Office van pulled up outside Raunsteig, No.1. Heller, wearing a postman's cap and carrying a postman's bag around his shoulder, stepped out and knocked on the front door. There was no response. Heller knocked again, with the same result. The door lock was one of the new special security locks. Bending down to the keyhole, he shouted:

'Urgent telegram for Herr Karl Becher!'

As he straightened up he thought he did hear something. He put his ear to the keyhole opening and heard it again, more clearly, a woman's weak voice:

'Help! Help!'

The words sounded drawn out in pain. He straightened up and looked around. A cyclist had just passed. To one side of the house wild-growing bushes covered the space between Number 1 and No. 2. On the other side, a wide area had been cleared for the parking of vehicles. Heller cautiously made his way to the back of the house. There was no backdoor but there was a large window, reaching to the ground, the type that lifted upwards. Heller guessed that it opened to a cellar space for deliveries of goods. It was bolted on the inside. The ground in front of the bolt was hollowed out and he could see the bolt entering a brick, part of the sunken cellar wall. He took a Swiss all-purpose pocket knife from the post bag. Using the solid, pointed iron hoof-pick he began to hack at the brick and the soil in front of it. The brick was old and began to crumble the plaster away from the bolt. But the bolt continued into the brick below.

Heller hacked around it until he could get a grip on it. He started to move it to and fro, trying to lift it at the same time. After a few minutes, which felt like hours, he was able to clear the bolt. Even so the window frame, encrusted with dirt, took an effort to move substantially. At last he succeeded in sliding his large frame inside. Luckily, the cellar floor was only about one-and-a half metres below the outside ground level. Heller landed comfortably and let the

Chapter 9 – A Murder is Planned

window come down gently behind him at the same time. The cellar room had obviously not been in use for a long time. The floor was covered with dust. Swathes of spider webs were hanging about, some of whose skilful producers, large and small, were scuttling excitedly across walls and the floor. He thought it was lucky spiders were not able to bark. He stood still for several minutes, just listening and looking around. It seemed that, apart from the woman who had shouted for help, there was nobody else in the house.

He took the few wooden steps up that led to a door, but it was locked from the outside. There was no key in the keyhole. He drew the key ring with the set of three skeleton keys from his pocket, which his locksmith friend had lent him. Oddly enough it was the smallest hook that opened this large lock. Shaking the dust from his shoes as much as he could, he stepped out into a small passage and, using the same skeleton key, locked the cellar door behind him. He walked up the few stairs into the hall. He heard the woman's plaintive cry again, weaker, yet more distinctly and followed it to a door which opened to the staircase which led to the first floor. He opened it cautiously and went upstairs. He was appalled by what he saw and also by what he smelled. On a double bed lay a woman, wearing a pink nightshirt which was ripped in several places and covered very little of her very white body.

What seductive effect this might have produced was wiped out by the considerable stink that filled the air. Her wrists and ankles were tied to the four bedposts. Behind her long, red hair could be seen discoloured skin and swellings, evidence of violence. Her right cheek displayed the clear imprint of fingers and the left eye was swollen. Heller untied her knots. Her narrow green eyes watched him, as if she was an onlooker who was not involved. He helped her from the bed and to the bathroom. He had to turn on the water-heater and run the bath. He helped her into it and threw her dirtied and torn nightdress into the bin in the corner. She was able to soap and wash herself but needed his help to get out of the bath. He helped her to dry herself and with putting on a bathrobe. She was visibly recovering and, as they left the bathroom, said, as if talking to an old friend.

'Please go downstairs and wait for me in the lounge.'

He did and sat down on a divan, reminding himself of why he had come here. When she came downstairs, she was wearing a tailor-

Chapter 9 – A Murder is Planned

made two-piece, calf-length costume. She sank down on the divan beside him, attempting a smile.

'I don't know how to thank you, mister. Even when I heard you shout you had a telegram and shouted back for help, I didn't expect to get it because I did not think you'd be able to enter the house. I'm grateful to whoever has sent the telegram and to the Post Office for choosing you to deliver it. You can give me the telegram.'

'Where is Herr Becher?' he replied in a less than cordial tone.

'He went to Nuremberg early this morning. The telegram's probably from his boss. Perhaps it tells him not to come.'

'Why did he tie you up, Frau Becher?' Knowing what he knew, he did not ask about her having been beaten up.

'We had a difference of opinion. I'm really very grateful to you, Mister – I don't know your name and I look upon you as a friend. But I should like to have the telegram.'

He shook his head without expression. She suddenly became wary.

'Are you really a postman or one of my husband's secret friends?'

This was taking too long. He stood up and leaned over her.

'There's no telegram. Let me make something clear, Frau Becher. I'm not your friend and I'm certainly not your husband's friend. If you're really grateful, then answer my questions.'

She looked up and what she saw in his eyes convinced her that he spoke the truth. Suddenly she erupted.

'The rotten swine told me he was leaving me for good. He no longer finds me attractive and he's going to kick me out when he returns tomorrow. After all the sacrifices I've brought for him, breaking with my parents who're important people of high standing. He'll be back tomorrow morning because his train leaves from Munich. You're not the police, mister whoever you are.'

'What makes you so sure?'

'Because he's got the police in his pocket. His boss is very powerful around here. It's what he told me, when I threatened I'd go to the police.'

'That's why he tied you up?'

She pressed her lips together and did not reply. He looked at her, then leaned forward.

'Listen very carefully, Frau Becher. You're right. I'm not the police but I know all about your husband's boss, Count Winter and

Chapter 9 – A Murder is Planned

about your husband's murderous activities. I'm here for just one thing, information. I know why your parents disowned you, so don't try lying to me. I want all the information about your husband's journey. Don't waste my time.'

She had shrunk back when he mentioned Winter and her parents but replied in a stubborn, aggressive tone, 'I don't know anything about Karl's travels, Mister. The swine never told me what he was doing, so you can warn me as much as you like.'

The words sounded convincing, but he had noticed her eyes flickering mendaciously. He put his hands into his trouser pockets, shrugged his shoulders and said, 'Very well, Frau Becher. I know you're hiding something. Unless you tell me what it is, a letter to your husband will make him believe that you gave away secrets about him. I'm your husband's greatest enemy. It's in your interest to help me. And if you breathe a word about me to anybody, I shall send a message to Count Winter with some of the secret things I know about him and naming you as the informant.'

He paused. Her resistance was in tatters.

She said, pointing upwards, 'I'll tell you but it's not going to do you any good. In the bedroom, there's a cupboard beside his bed, the window side. In one of the drawers he keeps a lot of his papers. I've never found where he hides the key and without the key you can't open it, Mister. I wish you'd kill the rotten swine.'

Heller had no problem in unlocking cupboard and drawer, but found nothing of importance. On top of the papers in the drawer lay an envelope which contained an octavo sheet of headed note paper from the Brandtstein Agentur, Nürenberg. It was in German, of course. Heller read it.

'K.B. Obtain ticket to London immediately, as directed. Report here on Tuesday, July 9th, with your passport for full briefing. Bring passport photo. Usual accommodation. L.'

Heller memorised it, then put it back into the envelope and the envelope into the drawer. He re-locked drawer and cupboard and went downstairs. Frau Becher, née Sabine von Steinfels, was still sitting on the divan, looking like a collapsed rag doll. Her whole miserable life had fallen to pieces and she was at her wits end.

He stepped up to her and, in a moment of pity, said, 'Listen to me, Frau Becher. Your marriage is over, kaput. You're safe from me but not from your husband. Go home. Tell your parents, you've

Chapter 9 – A Murder is Planned

changed. Perhaps they'll take you back. Leave as quickly as you can. Have you enough money for the travel?'

His words were effective. She looked up at him and said, bitterly, 'That's one thing I still have. But couldn't you –? To the station?'

As sorry as he felt for this wretched specimen of womanhood, at the moment, he could not risk it. It would not do to let this red-haired woman to be seen beside him in the postal van.

'No. You must either walk or get a taxi.'

He, too, was close to feeling disheartened. With all their years of experience neither Jameson nor he had discovered for what purpose this ruthless murderer was travelling to London. Nor could he think of any further enquiries that might reveal that purpose. He had failed and that worried him deeply.

He turned to leave when, at the moment of closing the door behind him, he heard her voice.

'He's going to kill an English lord.'

Heller stopped dead and turned to stare at her. She was staring back at him.

'He made a telephone call, to whoever sent the letter, I think, and I heard him say, "I've never killed an English lord before. I'll enjoy it." And he will, mister, he will. He always does.'

Heller was stunned. But it made sense. The almighty Wotan did not accept the Budapest fiasco. So this time he was sending someone to do the job who he believed would not fail. Heller rushed out of the house. He drove the van to its postal residence, dropped the keys into the letterbox and hastened home. He picked up his phone and was connected.

'Jameson.'

'Heller. I must see you at once.'

Heller's tone of voice required no interpretation.

'I'm here.'

Fifteen minutes later Michel Heller sat opposite Jameson. He came straight out with it.

'Becher's going to London in order to kill Lord Davidson.'

Jameson's eyes widened into an expression of total disbelief. It made immediate sense to him and he asked no questions. Indeed, he said nothing for an eternity and neither did Heller. Then Jameson broke the silence only just with a whispered.

'Jesus Christ! I should have…' He took a deep breath. 'I've to inform London. Top speed.'

Chapter 9 – A Murder is Planned

Heller nodded, 'Me, too.'

Jameson said, in a voice filled with doubt, 'Perhaps the French will take him off the train.'

Heller's looks refused to share the hope. Something that had been knocking on his memory walls, broke through. He shook his head.

'Heller's gone to Nuremberg with passport photos.'

'Passport...' Jameson nodded slowly. 'Of course, he will travel under a different name.'

Heller, also nodding, joined his last four words in unison, 'Under a different name.'

Jameson added, 'We must warn the French but I doubt it will make any difference.'

'I can't imagine that Becher is attempting this on his own in London,' Heller said, getting up to go.

'You mean British Nazis may collaborate with him? In murder?' Jameson replied. 'Hard to believe. But surely London is equipped to foil the plan.'

Heller stared at him.

'How do you find a clever and ruthless killer in a world city like London, hiding amongst eight million people?'

Heller had never felt so hopeless and helpless before. Looking at all the facts as he knew them, he found Becher to have every advantage. When he closed the door behind him, Jameson sat down to draft and encrypt. He stared at the paper for a long time before getting started. The truth was, that Heller's words had taken full effect and yet, drafting, encrypting and sending, it was the sum total of efforts he could make.

A message was still all Jameson could do about it. He did and despatched it and having done so, sat down and indulged in staring at the ceiling.

And Heller, entering his flat, also settled down to drafting, encrypting and sending a priority text to Cormody, MI6 and, having done so, sat back, staring helplessly at the ceiling. There were times when this job was close to unbearable and made him feel like giving up.

This was one of those times.

Acknowledgements

The action of "Mazes" takes place in Europe in the years following World War One. A lot of research went into making the background as accurate as possible. But the stories and non-historical characters are my own.

Below are the names of the people and organisations that provided me with helpful information. I express my sincere thanks to them all. Every contribution I received was equally important to me, but I give extra mention where I felt that the correspondent spent extra time and made a particular effort in providing me with the information or advice. I hope I have not forgotten anyone, but if so, it is entirely unintended.

Bob & Barbara Applin, Basingstoke Archaeology & History Society went to so much trouble in their assistance that we became friends in the course of our correspondence.

Sabine Elisabeth Barthelmeß, on behalf of the famous Royal Court Brewery in Munich, too, was especially helpful with information. I was pleased to forward a small contribution to her favourite charity. As can be seen below, she was not the only member of the famous Munich Royal Court Brewery to contribute.

Dunbar History Society & Dunbar Library.

Members of the Security Service Enquiries Team added to the considerable information I was able to gather from the books by Christopher Andrew (MI5) and Keith Jeffery (MI6). I also happened to attend a lecture by the latter on a cruise. Having said all that I must add that for the sake of the story line I took considerable freedom with the information I had received.

Dr. Natalie Evans' medical information was absolutely essential to me.

Ingo Gegner and Herr Hopfes, Munich Town Hall.

Herdina Bianca, Austrian Passport Office,

Peter James, writer of crime fiction.

Kate O'Brien, Military Archivist, Liddell Hart Centre, University of London,

Communal Service, Town Surveying Service, Munich

Kontaktformular, Formular Generator, Vienna.

Löderer K. James, British Embassy, Vienna.

Dr. Ina Müller, Munich Tourism. As a lot of the action takes place in Munich, Dr. Ina Müller's information was especially helpful.

Sven Müller, Munich Police Headquarters.

Susan Opie, editor

Peter Pirker, Vienna University and friend, whose assistance and advice also boosted my writing skills, such as they are.

Virginia Pringle, Basingstoke Archaeology & History Society.

Rosalind Pulvermacher, Historian, Foreign & Commonwealth Office.

Sebastian Rau, Munich Royal Court Brewery.

Juriaan Simonis, Researcher, Criminal Law, Netherlands Public Prosecution Service.

Surrey History Centre.

Steffen Taube, Trees Care Office, City of Leipzig.

Mike Thomas, Orient Express history. His specialist knowledge provided me with important information.

Simona Tobia, researcher.

Chris Trueman, History Learning.

Graham Waite, Netherlands Public Information Service.

Harriet Wells, British Embassy Berlin.

Mary Whirdy, Irish Ferries.

Wikipedia, a major source of information.

Nathan Williams, Reading University Library.

I enjoyed writing "Mazes" but must express my special thanks to the members of my family, whose contributions were most valuable and helpful. My son, Richard, in particular, edited a lot of my work as it progressed and without his computer skills I might probably not have managed it at all.